STACK
Keep
K.f

That Summer

That Summer

JANET APPLETON

VIKING

VIKING
Published by the Penguin Group
Viking Penguin Inc., 40 West 23rd Street,
New York, New York 10010, U.S.A.
Penguin Books Ltd, 27 Wrights Lane,
London W8 5TZ, England
Penguin Books Australia Ltd, Ringwood,
Victoria, Australia
Penguin Books Canada Ltd, 2801 John Street,
Markham, Ontario, Canada L3R 1B4
Penguin Books (N.Z.) Ltd, 182–190 Wairau Road,
Auckland 10, New Zealand

Penguin Books Ltd, Registered Offices:
Harmondsworth, Middlesex, England

First published in 1989 by Viking Penguin Inc.
Published simultaneously in Canada

1 3 5 7 9 10 8 6 4 2

Library of Congress Cataloging in Publication Data
Appleton, Janet.
That summer.
I. Title.
PS3551.P64T4   1989   813'.54   88-40298
ISBN 0-670-82026-1

Printed in the United States of America by
Arcata Graphics, Fairfield, Pennsylvania
Set in Garamond No. 3

For Bill

ACKNOWLEDGMENTS

First of all, I want to thank my husband, Bill, the love of my life, who stood patiently and lovingly by through twenty-nine sometimes harrowing years of my trying to "find" myself, and without whose encouragement and steadying hand I would still be searching. I am grateful, too, to my children, Bill, Jane, David, and Katharine, for their endless enthusiasm about my work and for never doubting that I could do it.

I owe many thanks to Linda Lee, writer, agent, and teacher, whose workshops inspired me to discipline myself, work like the devil, and shoot for the stars.

My dear friend, fellow writer Elizabeth Dalton, knew I was writing a novel before I did, and from that point on, offered her experience, strength, and hope whenever I faltered. She was counselor, sounding board, and cheerleader all in one, and I am more grateful than I can say.

I must also thank my agent, Andrea Cirillo of the Jane Rotrosen Agency, who encouraged me, calmed my nerves, and made my introduction into the business end of writing absolutely painless, and my editor at Viking Penguin, Pamela Dorman, who bravely took on my voluminous meanderings and showed me how to control them and shape them and, yes, cut them, too.

Acknowledgments

Finally, every fledgling writer must at some time or another dream of the big break, that letter of acceptance from a top-notch house or some other miracle of good fortune that suddenly catapults one from anonymity into "the Big Time." Most of us realize that the odds of that happening are infinitesimally small and go on writing anyway, hopeful that if we work long enough and hard enough we shall be rewarded. I was one such writer.

Then, out of the blue, bestselling author John Saul "discovered" me and my forty-page-long unfinished novel at the Pacific Northwest Writers' Conference (1986) and offered an introduction to his friends at the Jane Rotrosen Agency. Not only did John's generous spirit result in the publication of this book; it also changed my life completely and, needless to say, made all my dreams come true. There is no way I can ever repay his kindness. My hope, however, is that somewhere along the line I will have an opportunity to help someone else the way he helped me and thus pass on the gift. I know John would like that.

That Summer

ONE

ROOM FOR RENT, INQUIRE WITHIN demanded a neatly lettered sign attached to a wrought-iron railing in front of a vintage brick house on Walnut Street. I hurried toward it: this might be the place I was looking for.

I had been in Boston two days, ensconced in venerable Barclay Hall, a residence for young women. Mother's idea. I was about to defy her for the first time in my life and relocate without her permission. The year was 1957; I was eighteen and perfectly capable of living on my own for the summer. I had combed Beacon Hill practically since dawn in search of a room, a cubicle, a closet to rent.

I stood on the sidewalk for a moment admiring the four-storey house before me. It had shiny black shutters, an ornate wrought-iron widow's walk outlining its roof, and a bay window on the second floor that opened out to a tiny curved balcony of delicate wrought iron that resembled lace. This looked very promising indeed. I climbed the steps to the black-lacquered front door and, pulling a metal ring that sounded the bell, waited.

Presently the door opened, and there stood a sweet-faced man in odd, soft trousers and a sweater of heather blue.

"Good afternoon," he said. His eyes regarded me blandly enough, but his eyebrows leaped across his forehead in anticipation.

"Good afternoon," I said confidently. "Your sign—is the room still available?"

"Indeed it is," he said, opening the door wider. "Would you like to see it?"

"Yes, I would," I said, as he ushered me into the hallway, a cool, dark tunnel.

"Give me a moment to get the key," he said, and disappeared through French doors on the right, leaving them slightly ajar. I could see a triangle of hooked rug, the corner of a plump, flowered chintz sofa, and, in full view, on a Bombé chest, an enormous, Oriental porcelain vase of celadon green. It was filled with porcelain flowers that did not appear in any way to be real, thick-petaled peonies and glossy chrysanthemums among them.

"Here we are," he said breezily, returning, a door key dangling from his pinkie. "I suppose introductions are in order. I'm Malcolm Balch, the owner. And you are?"

"Ann Merrill," I replied, extending my hand. "I'm in Boston just for the summer. I'll be a freshman at Wellesley in the fall. I have a job at Colchester's Used Book Store starting tomorrow."

"Ah, yes," he said, nodding. "Colchester's. A pleasant enough walk from the Hill. Shall we?" He led the way up the open staircase. "And your family? Where are they?" His voice had a hollow, muffled quality, as if he were speaking from a closet. He was obviously interviewing me.

"They're in Beverly," I said. "I could have commuted, I suppose, but I thought living in town would be much more convenient." I decided not to divulge prematurely that on Friday my overprotective mother had deposited me, bag and baggage, at Barclay Hall, in the Back Bay. In fact, my agreeing to stay there had been a prerequisite for my living in town. "Under no circumstances will a daughter of mine take a room in a common boardinghouse," Mother had said. "You'll stay at Barclay Hall, where you'll be safe and protected, among people of your own kind, or you'll stay at home and take the train every day instead."

"I thought I'd like to try a summer on my own," I continued, the memory of my mother's ultimatum giving a slight tremor to my voice.

"Very admirable," Mr. Balch said. "And the trains are utterly filthy." He hesitated for an instant on the stairs and ran a finger over the lower rung on the banister, then examined it for dust. Mr. Balch smelled of furniture polish.

Although to all outward appearances I was my mother's daughter through and through, traditional, almost staid, I had a drop or two of bohemian blood in me as well, which I hoped to nurture over the summer. Obviously such a task would be impossible within the darkly stodgy walls of dear old Barclay. But Beacon Hill was to Boston what the Village was to New York—that is, the perfect environment for my metamorphosis.

At the third-floor landing, Mr. Balch opened the door to a bathroom. There was a sudden blast of warm air accompanied by a blazing glow of sunlight which entered the room through a many-paned window above a claw-footed tub. Growing accustomed to the strong light, I saw that the walls were painted lavender, and lavender towels stocked the shelves of an open cabinet and hung neatly from towel bars. "I dyed them myself," he said, beaming, as I absentmindedly fingered one. The exterior of the tub was decorated in oils with a seaside scene: a little cove, three gulls with arched wings, and, in the foreground, lavender daisies that swayed with dune grass.

"Did you . . . ?" I asked.

"Oh my, no," he said. "I should say not. My friend Claude's the artist. Fourth-floor studio. At the Cape for a few days. He comes and goes."

"How wonderful to have such talent," I said politely, squinting at the tub. "Excellent perspective."

I absolutely loved this place. All of it. The sink was spotless.

"Now, you'll be sharing this with a young woman named Georgia Mitchell," he said, gesturing toward a closed door across the hall. I didn't relish the thought of sharing a bathroom with anyone, which must have shown on my face. "A lovely young lady," he continued, somewhat overenthusiastically, I thought. "A sensitive girl," he added, eyeing me. At this moment I realized that a pair of sneakers the size of loaves of French bread, poised on the floor beneath the tub on a lavender mat, must belong to this sensitive girl.

Mr. Balch had drifted out into the hallway and soon opened a door with a flourish. "As bright as . . . a yellow dress," he said triumphantly. Without a single dark corner in it, the room was huge and square. The sun colored it a shade warmer than yellow, and there seemed to be a kind of motion in the sunlight. I could imagine the room swelling, bursting, pouring itself like melted butter through the lip of a ladle. I loved it.

Mr. Balch discussed the various amenities. The walls were freshly painted white. Muslin curtains trimmed with ball fringe were new. An ornate iron bed was covered with a spread my mother would have called an "India print," in indigo and green, with peacocks. A handsome little secretary with tooled leather writing surface and numerous drawers delighted me. I would write letters there and begin a journal. Without Mother around to go through my things, I could write what I wished.

I smiled at Mr. Balch, who continued to flutter. The mahogany desk chair had a seat he had caned himself, he explained. A lamp shade decorated with cut-out songbirds was also his creation; and, crouched in a corner like a crab, a curvy mandarin-red table was set with an old black teapot and a saucerless cup he had planted with African violets.

"We provide everything you need," he said, which I could see was absolutely true.

Then he went on with details about clean sheets, the Yardley's Lavender Soap with which he kept the bathroom stocked, and the contents of the utility closet on the landing between Georgia's room and the stairwell. As I watched him, I couldn't help being impressed with the sweetness of his smile and with his girlish, upturned nose. It looked as if it had been buffed to a waxed shine, and sat primly above his thin, almost lipless mouth. But his eyebrows interested me most. They lay still as basking snakes as he spoke, only to leap up fitfully as he paused for breath and dance a wild fandango across his brow. They had a life of their own. Suddenly I knew that Malcolm Balch was as queer as the day was long—a bona fide fairy. How wonderful! I had never met one before. Things were going better than I had ever expected they would.

While he stood at the open door of the walk-in closet and pointed out its wide shelves and various drawers, something drew me to the window. I pulled back the curtains. Three storeys below lay a brick-paved courtyard that stretched between the ivy-covered rear walls of surrounding buildings. Reaching up from a cut-out in the bricks, a flowering tree gave shade to two white kitchen chairs arranged conversationally, at angles to one another. I wondered who had been seated there. The courtyard was empty except for these and drifts of brown-edged petals that tumbled and scattered in the faint breeze.

"I'm afraid the courtyard doesn't belong to this building," Mr. Balch said, joining me at the window. "In case of an emergency one may lower the fire escape, of course. Otherwise, I'm afraid it's not allowed. There's the fire escape itself for a breath of fresh air, if you like. A young tenant some years ago got herself quite a tan just sitting on the fire escape all summer." He opened the window for me to illustrate the ease with which one might climb out to a wide landing, spacious enough for sitting.

Just then, a door on the first floor of a building across the way opened. Out walked a fat, white-haired old woman attired in, of all things, a royal-blue sailor dress with a middy collar and red tie. She seemed to be in conversation with someone—herself, it appeared. She wore boxy summer sandals—the cheap kind that disintegrate into layers of soggy cardboard when wet—and ankle socks.

"Frances Fellows," Mr. Balch said quietly, with a hint of sadness in his tone. His beautiful brows remained fixed in a plaintive arch.

"Our little seafarer?" I said, hoping that I didn't sound rude.

"The mind of a child, really. Pretty much a recluse. Speaks to no one but her cat. Feeds it raw chicken livers she buys at the kosher market. Quite extraordinary . . . the cat, I mean. Twice the size of a normal cat. Vicious, too, so they say. Diet can do that, you know—have an adverse effect on the personality. Organ meats particularly."

5

"I love it here, I really do," I said, unable to contain myself any longer. "I'll take it. If I may, that is." I had never been anywhere else as intriguing as this. I smiled warmly at Mr. Balch, again, knowing that he could not possibly appreciate what finding this house and this room and even what dear, queer Malcolm himself meant to me. He smiled back.

"No gentlemen visitors, of course," he said.

"Of course," I murmured, rather elegantly, as if the thought would never cross my mind. I didn't know anyone in Boston, anyway, gentleman or otherwise, and this rule made everything even more perfect. Mother, when I finally told her I had left Barclay, as I now saw I must, couldn't help approving. I imagined introducing her to Malcolm Balch, cautious landlord, gracious host, and chaperon nonpareil, if ever there was one. He certainly seemed to be "our kind of people," and I couldn't imagine a safer environment. Never mind that he was a homosexual; Mother was hopeless as far as such things were concerned. There was a whole host of issues, ideas, and practices that Mother, having no firsthand knowledge of them herself, denied the existence of. Mother would see Malcolm Balch simply as a refined man with a fine old house and a fine old name. It would be unthinkable to her that anyone thrice gifted in these ways might have even a teeny-tiny skeleton in his closet, much less be a fairy.

"May I move in this afternoon?" I wanted to ask what the rent was, but I was terrified. I had only enough money to last until my first payday. Mr. Balch had gone back to the walk-in closet and was giving a rundown of its particulars once more.

I wondered about Georgia, this girl with feet the size of badminton racquets.

"But if that's too soon," I said, "we could make it tomorrow evening after work. I've been staying at Barclay Hall. Mother insisted upon it—uh . . . temporarily, of course—until I found something more to my liking. I'm sure I could stand it there for one more night if I had to."

"This afternoon would be perfect," he said. I breathed a sigh of relief. The girls at Barclay ran to the horsey, overbred type whose idea of a high old time was to make a run to Peck & Peck for cashmere sweaters. They were too much like my friends at home—insincere and boring. Whoever Georgia was, I was sure she would be at least a little more exciting.

"About the rent, Mr. Balch . . ."

"Will twelve dollars a week be agreeable with you?" he asked gently.

"Oh, yes," I said. "That will be just fine."

"Delighted to have you, Miss Merrill—Ann, if I may call you that. We don't stand on ceremony here, I'm afraid. My tenants usually call me Malcolm. Feel free."

"Why, thank you," I said. "I shall."

"Two weeks due in advance, of course. You can pay me now or wait until you return with your things—although I don't expect to be home this afternoon. A friend has invited me to a little party for his mother. She's eighty-nine years young today."

"I'll pay you now," I said, following him out of the room and down the stairs.

"Miss Mitchell should be home by and by." On the second-floor landing he turned to me, his index finger held to his lips. "I like to pass quietly here," he said in a whisper. "Law students on this floor—Mr. Perlman and Mr. Knowles. Very quiet gentlemen. Do nothing but study day and night, all year round. I try to impress upon all my tenants the importance of a peaceful household. For everyone's sake, you know."

"Oh, of course," I whispered back. It was too perfect. Mother's only reservation about Barclay was that I would get little sleep what with all-night canasta games and hen parties.

Down on the first floor again, Malcolm went into his apartment for a receipt book as I counted out my money. I began to think about how to break the news of my escape from Barclay to Mother, when something caused me to turn around abruptly, as if someone had come up behind me. No one—nothing was there. I found myself staring at an arrangement of tall, dried branches set in a pewter vase on the long library table where piles of sorted mail lay. Moving closer, I saw that the branches had flat, round, leathery leaves, and an odor emanated from them that had been apparent from the moment Malcolm Balch had opened the door for me.

In fact, the house was filled with the strangely soothing smell. I imagined it everywhere: in the cubbyholes of my little writing desk, between the blankets and the peacock spread of my iron bed, within the looped fibers of the lavender towels. I walked toward the table, reached out, and gently pressed my fingernail into one leaf, scoring it lightly. Instantly a fresh pungency burst forth. I knew: it was eucalyptus.

It made me think of the Middle East, of Greece, of Turkey; certainly such a smell could not have originated anywhere but there. I closed my eyes as if suddenly drugged and began to see ancient, intricate tapestries, heavily fringed, swaying to the rhythm of music from another land, played on instruments whose names I had never known. I heard brass bells. My hair was coal black, my skin burnished bronze. I wondered what opium smelled like. I took a deep breath, confident that this heady muskiness would ooze through the delicate inner membranes of my lungs and insinuate itself through the walls of capillaries and alter me, irrevocably.

"I really must dispose of it one of these days," Malcolm said, offering me my receipt.

"The eucalyptus?"

"Oh, no—I meant the pheasant." He pointed to the far end of the table, where a dust-laden, taxidermied bird perched on a chunk of fake prairie. I hadn't noticed it until now.

With a feeling of annoyed impatience, I allowed the dusty, dead bird with the clouded eyes to wing its unfortunate way far back into the darkest canyons of my mind, where it belonged.

After leaving Malcolm I went straight back to Barclay and put in an emergency call to my great aunt Chloe, who lived in Windsor Marsh, a town not far from Beverly. Since my second birthday— the age when, according to Aunt Chloe, I became capable of carrying on an intelligent conversation—she had been my mentor, my "fairy godmother," my constant ally. She understood everything.

"You'll never grow up at all if you don't get out from under that mother of yours," she had told me countless times. I had decided to live in the city for the summer at her urging. Now, clearly, I had taken liberation one step farther; only Aunt Chloe would understand. Besides, she had often suggested that I try to meet interesting people as a means of expanding my horizons, and I couldn't wait to tell her about Malcolm Balch.

I was trembling as I dialed the operator, then waited for Aunt Chloe to answer.

"Chloe Langley speaking—who's there?" she said. She hated to have to guess who the caller was, even for a second.

"Aunt Chloe, it's me, Ann."

"Well, young lady, I thought you were in Boston by now."

"I am. I'm calling from Boston. I've done something awful, Aunt Chloe, absolutely awful—but wonderful, too."

She chuckled. "You haven't slept with a black man, have you?" she said drily.

"Aunt Chloe! Seriously, I need your help. I want you to tell me I haven't done the wrong thing."

"Go on," she said.

"I've moved from Barclay—or I'm about to, I should say."

"Well, good for you," she said. "Find yourself a garret somewhere, did you? I remember the first little place I had in the Village—above a tea room, don't you know, and we could smell whatever they were baking that day."

"But Mother's doing to die!"

"Be good for her. I never thought very much of your staying there, I must say. Too institutional. Why, it looks more like City Hall than a place to live. All that granite and those ridiculous marble women guarding the front door. I think they're wearing helmets of some kind, like a couple of Brünnhildes escaped from Valhalla."

"It's awful," I said. "Everything in the place is painted beige and the rooms are ugly and the girls are boring and the food—Aunt Chloe, it's sickening. Creamed codfish on Friday night." She laughed again. "So I couldn't stand it. I mean, the whole point of my being here—"

"Was to be independent," she interjected, "and surround yourself with interesting people and new ideas and—"

9

"Exactly! So that's what I'm doing. I walked all over Beacon Hill today and finally found the most wonderful place to stay and the most wonderful little man owns it."

"Well, I'll be," she said. "What street are you on?"

"On Walnut Street, in a beautiful old house just dripping with wrought iron."

"Ah yes, Walnut Street. All that iron originally came from Spain, brought it over as ballast in ships."

"And the room I have is lovely and the rent's cheap enough and the man who owns it and lives on the first floor is Malcolm Balch and—"

"A fine old name, Balch."

"—and I think he's queer!"

"Well, hallelujah! How do you know?"

"Oh, it's pretty obvious. He dyes towels and grows violets and is very domestic. He also held my door key on his pinkie finger like it was a cup of tea and was going to a birthday party for his *friend's* mother and he really looks it."

"That can fool you sometimes—you'll just have to wait and see. But I would say it looks quite promising. What are you going to tell your mother?"

"I'm not sure. I'm not going to tell her about Malcolm, though— not *all* about him."

"Just tell her the truth, like you've told me. You're old enough to stand up for yourself when you're right. Make your own decisions and follow your own intuition. Your mother's behind the times. Why, at your age I went to Europe to dance. Of course we were chaperoned . . . but if you leave it up to your mother, she'll hang on to you till you're thirty. It's not healthy. I've told you that."

"I always feel better when I talk to you. Obviously, I miss you already."

"I'll be coming into town in a couple of weeks for a meeting at the church. Perhaps I'll drop by and see you." Aunt Chloe was a Christian Scientist and often came in to Boston for services and lectures at the mother church.

"Would you?"

"I'll stay for a minute or two anyway, just long enough to inspect your digs and your Mr. Balch if he's about. Miriam Peabody is driving me in, and you know her—she never drives over thirty, and if we dawdle, it's midnight before we get home. And she's blind as a bat at night to boot. But I'll stay a minute or two. And if worse comes to worst I'll have a word with your mother." That final comment was music to my ears.

I hung up the phone and went to one of the TV rooms to drum up some help for my move. I probably had enough money for a cab, but if I could hitch a ride with someone at Barclay who had a car, that was my first choice. I had begun to feel better, more confident, less frightened. Talking to Aunt Chloe had reminded me of my courage and spirit of adventure. I had almost forgotten I had it, those few drops of bohemian blood I had inherited from her.

By four o'clock I had packed and, after a chummy chat with Gillian Crocker, horsey blond girl number one, had accepted her offer of a ride down to Walnut Street in her old MG, top down. As we pulled into a parking space right in front of the house, I looked up in the direction of a long trilly "Yoohoo" and immediately recognized Georgia—a dust mop of hair and two lanky arms dangling out the third-storey window.

"You need help?" she yelled, waving her arms back and forth. As she spoke, a long string of spittle had drooled from her mouth, and it now lay in the middle of the top step like an aerial view of Lake Winnipesaukee afroth with whitecaps. "Oops," she grinned, holding one palm cupped beneath her chin to prevent another such display, "you need help?" She gestured with her free hand toward Gillian's car. For a split second I imagined that she had the power to wrest my suitcases out of the backseat and levitate them up within her reach.

"It's okay," I called back, seeking to keep Georgia and Gillian as far apart as possible, but she had ducked inside. In a flash, she burst through the front door and bounded to the sidewalk.

"What can I take?" Georgia bellowed as she grabbed a suitcase and ripped a hangerful of clothes from my hand.

"Thank you," I smiled—at least I think I smiled. I gathered the rest of my things and bid an embarrassingly hasty goodbye to Gillian, who sat grimly at the wheel of her little car, staring straight ahead. "My cousin Georgia," I gushed with a sort of helpless shrug. Not wanting to divulge the real reason for having left Barclay, I had explained to Gillian earlier that I was being forced by Mother, whose anguished phone call had come during the night, to move to Walnut Street posthaste to keep tabs on Cousin Georgia from Maine, who had arrived in Boston the previous day with some mad plan up her sleeve to present herself at the door of the Colonial Theater and thence begin her career as a great actress. I had pointed out how terribly unstable people with theatrical yearnings were and how everybody had always counted on me to keep Cousin Georgia on the straight-and-narrow.

"I thought she was a lot younger than you," poor Gillian said, a decidedly dazed expression on her face.

"I might have given that impression," I said, rolling my eyes a little for emphasis. "She's just so terribly young for her age, if you know what I mean."

"Do I ever," Gillian said. We waved to one another as I went into the house mulling over Georgia's real age. She looked about twenty-five; she acted thirteen. She was in my room when I got there.

"Hi, I'm Georgia Mitchell," she said, lunging toward me, thrusting her hand at my midsection. I took it. Her grip was crushing.

"How do you do," I said. "I'm Ann Merrill."

"Annie, how wonderful to have you here!" she said, taking the liberty of reducing my name to its folksy diminutive. "I have a floor-mate at last. It's been so lonely here without you—honest to God." She sat down on my bed. I immediately wished she hadn't. Who did she think she was, anyway? I was totally disarmed by this girl. She was an unattractive study in beige: no-color hair and skin to match. At Barclay Hall, that bastion of boring beige, she would have been invisible. All arms and legs, she was what Aunt Chloe would call "a gallop of a girl." I watched her cross her long legs—and there, beneath a faded, brownish-grey print skirt, were those feet. She wore no shoes. She had the longest toes I had ever seen.

"Excuse me," I said, as I pulled the hanger full of my best dresses out from under her.

"Oh, Annie, forgive me," she said. "I hope I didn't spoil anything." She reached out and touched my shoulder with her fingertips as I brushed past her, heading for the closet. I had caught a brief glimpse of her eyes and as I hung my clothes, I was aware of them fixed on me, the most unbelievable color. I wondered if perhaps it was a strange play of light that made them look luminous, as if the irises were underlaid with mother-of-pearl—they were grey-blue, like the eyes of a weimaraner. It had to be my imagination, my training in art; I sometimes saw things differently than they actually were. *No one* had eyes like that.

"Do you work?" I asked. I wondered what on earth she did. A zoo keeper, maybe? A token seller for the MTA?

"Yeah," she said. "I'm a proofreader."

"How interesting," I said. "I start working at a bookstore tomorrow." I had no idea what a proofreader was, but it sounded respectable, even responsible. "Where are you from?" I asked. She had a trace of an accent I couldn't place. She laughed—a booming, yo-ho-you're-never-going-to-believe-this kind of laugh. I turned and looked at her.

"Well, kid, most recently I'm from the loony bin. Before that— way before that—I was from Rhode Island. A place called Morning Hill. I grew up in a Catholic orphanage there." She giggled— inappropriately, I thought, as if she were making a little joke to herself. She then took a cigarette from a foreign-looking blue box in the pocket of her skirt. "Try one of these?"

"No, thank you," I said, wondering exactly what she meant by "loony bin."

"French," she said, looking at her cigarette before taking a drag. Her fingernails were bitten to the quick. "You see," she continued, "I just kinda have this habit of going loony and they have to put me away in the loony bin for a while."

"Well," I said, "that's probably a good place to be in if you need to be there." My voice sounded quite normal and not at all alarmed.

I was becoming frightened, however. I closed the closet door behind me and strolled over to the window. The courtyard was empty except for a large yellow cat that crouched near a small mound of blowing petals, ready to pounce.

"Oh, Annie," she crooned, "we are going to have the most wonderful, wonderful time together." She was grinning at me again, jouncing up and down on my bed as she spoke. "It's been so godawful lonely here. I'm not good at being lonely." I said nothing. She looked from me to the floor and wiggled her toes, then shrugged her shoulders and raised her arms, her hands palms up. "Don't you love the smell of this place?"

"Eucalyptus," I said, balanced gingerly against the windowsill. I had caught a glimpse of something that disturbed me. There were white welts, at least they seemed to be welts, on each of her wrists. Several of them.

"That's what it is, all right," she said. "Eucalyptus. I think they used to use that to embalm people in ancient Egypt. Oil of eucalyptus or something." They weren't welts, they were scars, as if something or someone had torn or hacked at her flesh. "And the courtyard!" she moaned delightedly. "Isn't it wonderful? It's like a stage. Like the Globe Theatre and you have a front-row seat and maidens and Moors and witches come out every night."

She continued talking a mile a minute, telling about how she had come to find a room in this house, how she had begun to feed the pigeons on the ledge by her window every night and how she had given each of her favorites a name. She made vague references to her psychiatrist, her employer, a friend who lived not far away in Louisburg Square. Now and then she spoke, for several minutes at a time, as if she were completely unaware of my presence.

Then, abruptly, she stopped talking. Once again I found myself drawn to the scars on her wrists. She had cut herself; I just knew it. She jumped from the bed. "I just remembered something. Something I must show you. Seeds. I've had them forever. I'm saving them. Do you want to see them? I have dried flowers to go with each packet, so you know in advance what they'll grow up to be. I'll be right back with them."

She bolted from the room, setting furniture and knickknacks

a-toddle. But she stopped somehow, as if in midair, to close my door soundlessly behind her as she went.

"Seeds," I thought out loud. What a strange person she was! Yet there was something about her that I liked. She really didn't seem to care one whit what she said or how she looked or behaved, that was for sure. Interesting. And different. Different from me, anyhow.

TWO

I waited for Georgia to return, but she didn't. I sat there expecting her to burst through the door any second. Feeling awkward after the first minute or two, I practiced smiling toward the door, then staring nonchalantly out the window, so that when she finally made her entrance it would seem I had scarcely noticed the passing moments. But she did not return. How very odd. How inconsiderate.

I began to tiptoe about the room. Then I strolled for a while in exaggerated, long strides. Next, I opened one of my suitcases and made a stab at arranging my comb and brush and mirror on the top of my dresser. It was useless. I could not seem to engage in even the smallest task, lest Georgia barge in, rattling her seed packets, and stop me in the middle of whatever it was I was trying to do. I couldn't even lie down on my bed: I would feel embarrassed if she returned to find me sprawled there. But that was what I really wanted to do—lie down and take a little nap. The past few days had been tiring. But there was no point at all in trying to rest. No sooner would I drift off than Georgia would barge in and wake me up.

Besides, I always felt just a little guilty sleeping during the day. There was something slovenly about it, as Mother had pointed out more than once. In fact, sleep at any time in our household was an activity that received only minimal sanction. Father often spoke glowingly of the ancient philosophers who barely slept at all; and, after a fitful night of insomnia, Mother would leap from bed at the crack of dawn amazingly refreshed, ready to whip through the house vacuuming and dusting and washing windows simultaneously. Lack of sufficient sleep was apparently a trademark of the virtuous.

So here I was, like a door left ajar, a telephone off the hook, in a foolish kind of limbo.

My irritation increasing, I sat down at the writing desk and, although I had no intention of actually using it for a bona fide letter, removed three sheets of Crane's stationery from its box. I took my best fountain pen and arranged it at a carefully estimated angle across the upper-right-hand corner of a blank page. I sat motionless, ready to spring into a fit of writing the moment I heard footsteps. It would then appear that Georgia could not have left at a more opportune moment, that I had been composing an important letter in my head as she had rambled on about her background, and was relieved to be able to jot it down, at last, the instant she sped from the room. But I heard no sound whatever. Not a peep. Not from the landing, not from her room, not from the bathroom. The house was perfectly still.

Hurriedly, I took pen in hand and wrote, "Dear Mother," in my usual rhythmic forehand, making an effort to produce as casual an effect as possible. But it didn't look right—too squiggly and weak and babyish. I crumpled up that page and made a fresh start. "My dear Senator," I penned in a large, rounded backhand. The "S" in "Senator" was a figure of great beauty, with a flamboyant final stroke in the shape of a coiled spring. That suited me better, from the point of view of both technique and of content. I squinted at what I had written. My distinctive penmanship marked me, I was sure, as an original—no Palmer Method copycat. I had used this script in a particularly insightful letter I had once written to Eleanor Roosevelt, expressing my admiration for the way she had succeeded in life despite the handicap of an unfortunate lack of physical beauty. I always suspected that Father "forgot" to mail it, as I never received a reply. He did that sometimes—took it upon himself to censor things I meant to be mailed by simply throwing them away. It was enraging. It was just this restrictive parental attitude I had come to Boston to escape.

Yet here I sat, like an idiot, immobilized. So much for my new freedom! How could I let a complete stranger do this to me? She came crashing into my life, raved on wildly about nothing at all, smelled up my room with her French cigarettes, dangled her exquisite feet in front of my face, and then, *poof,* disappeared from the face of the earth.

I would remember the color of her eyes until the day I died.

Forty-five minutes had passed.

Finally, I lay down on my bed and thought calmly about the importance of punctuality as a social grace. Naturally, I had never been late for anything. It was obvious to me that punctuality was the responsibility of every civilized person.

Still, I thought, there was something about her. Poor thing. Perhaps she had rushed to her room to fetch the seeds only to become involved in some meandering hallucination, some mad dialogue with imagined voices. I deduced that under such circumstances one might naturally lose all track of time. I would have to make allowances for her, that was all. She was very unusual. Fascinating. Aunt Chloe would be thrilled for me. First Malcolm Balch, now Georgia Mitchell, all in one day.

Aunt Chloe's opinion meant more to me than anyone else's, as she was considered to be the most creative, intelligent, and witty person in the family. If I looked at it objectively, that probably wasn't saying too much, since practically everyone else in the family was pretty unremarkable. The men tended to be bankers and lawyers; the women, although college educated, spent their time pouring at teas and accumulating hours as grey ladies. "Your aunt Chloe is uniquely gifted," my father would intone solemnly, as if from the pulpit, as if the utterance of these words weighed heavily upon his soul. I suppose they might have; he would have much preferred to confer this honor on a member of his own sex, I am sure.

First of all, Aunt Chloe had her doctorate in history, which all the world knew was primarily a man's subject. She was an expert on the Civil War. She even had a collection of old guns from that period, a fifty-eight-caliber Springfield rifle used at the Battle of Shiloh among them. Strangely enough, she and I never talked about history unless it was the history of our family. She was the official keeper of the family tree and knew details of the comings and goings of our clan since it had arrived in Norwalk, Connecticut, in 1632.

In addition, before marrying my uncle Harry and settling down to get her Ph.D., she had trained in physical culture (which I assumed was a refined form of gym) and the dance. She had traveled all over the world, performed before the crowned heads of Europe. Somewhere along the line she had taken up mountaineering and after scaling Mount Rainier had, in a moment of lighthearted exaltation, placed a bit of lace from her underwear around the marker that commemorated the ascent.

Then, of course, there was her painting, something she had done since childhood. In later years she exhibited and sold her watercolors. I was terribly proud of her and grateful for her attention to me. I loved it when people pointed out that my talent in art came from her and when I discovered something about myself that was even slightly similar to something in her personality and character. Deep inside, I harbored the hope that someday I would begin to "bloom" and would wake up to find that, magically, I had turned out just like Aunt Chloe, after all.

Over the years, I spent many happy times with her in Windsor Marsh, population 506, home of the renowned Pickfield Stables and site of three-mile-long Palace Dunes Beach, a strip of platinum sand that was a mecca for hordes of serious sunbathers and ocean swimmers who flocked there each summer.

Uncle Harry died the year I turned eleven, and Aunt Chloe now lived alone in the big house they had named Marsh Cliff. It was actually an old barn that had been renovated, and it stood on a low bluff overlooking marsh land, about a mile and a half from the beach.

I liked my summer visits best, those bright mornings when I woke up to the whine of locusts in what I called the "high bedroom," under the eaves; or the endless steamy afternoons spent reading in the alcove under the stairs, the stone floor of the living room like a great slab of ice at my feet.

Marsh Cliff was often a busy place. Aunt Chloe encouraged friends to stop by: people from her dancing days, students of history looking for a special book or just an afternoon chat, political friends who had worked with her on Adlai Stevenson's campaign. Neighbors might drop in to share sweet corn from their gardens and discuss nothing more sophisticated than Japanese beetles. She even cultivated the friendship of the little old man who tended the local cemetery, mowing the grass and watering. From time to time he would come in for tea and bring her up to date on recent deaths and burials, how well attended they were and how many floral pieces had been sent. The man's wife was bedridden, and Aunt Chloe offered a sympathetic ear for all his troubles.

She loved people and rarely passed judgment. Although I loved my mother dearly and always would, there were things I could never tell her. It was unthinkable that I tell her about my suspicions concerning Malcolm, and by the same token I could never tell her that Georgia had grown up in an orphanage—a Catholic one to boot. Mother would want to hear that I had met a young woman named Georgia Mitchell, of the Newport Mitchells, who had attended an Episcopal school in Switzerland—and that was exactly what I would tell her.

No longer concerned that Georgia would come back at all, I found myself lying beneath the peacock spread, remembering my visit to Aunt Chloe's last August. I had arrived at Marsh Cliff in time for lunch, which we took on the veranda, and afterwards we retired to rocking chairs to talk. It had been cloudy for several days, and close to the sea there was a fine mist in the air. The trees in the orchard behind the house were gauzy, grey-green ghosts, not so much rooted in mist as suspended in it, as diaphanous and transient as images on a scrim. Aunt Chloe and I were the sole spots of color on this monochromatic day. Even the remnants of our lunch—

her orange peel, my sliver of uneaten alligator pear with two pink shrimp curled at its side—seemed wildly vibrant.

Aunt Chloe loved to talk about her life, and I loved hearing about it. We had just settled into our chairs, and Aunt Chloe had just begun to uncoil her beautiful silver hair—something she often did as she reminisced—when a little boy, no more than five, appeared at the bottom of the steps leading up to the veranda. He was dark skinned, with large brown eyes. Seeing him, Aunt Chloe smiled.

"Well, come up, come up, you've come this far, you might as well come all the way." Slowly, shyly, the boy climbed the steps. Aunt Chloe held out her hand to him and shook his. "Ann, this is Tony Scanzotti. He likes to come visit me, don't you, Tony? He's a fine young man. One of these days he'll be old enough to scramble up those apple trees and get the ones at the very top. Then I'm going to pay him a dollar to help me. What are you up to today, young man?" Tony looked at the floor for a moment, then leaned close to Aunt Chloe's ear and whispered. She listened intently, then said, "Aha! She's got some, has she? And she's going to cook them right now?" Tony nodded and smiled. "Good boy! Then you run and tell her to do absolutely nothing until we get there. You understand? All right. Now you go and get yourself a Fig Newton in the kitchen, then off with you." Aunt Chloe chuckled as the boy raced through the house to the kitchen for his treat. By the time he returned and headed home, she had pinned up her hair again. She stood up, rerolled her nylons just above her knees, and smoothed her skirt.

"We are about to be served a second lunch! Well, are you coming with me?" she asked. "Old Mrs. Scanzotti down the way has offered to cook us up some squash blossoms. Fetch a jar of jam from the cupboard, will you? I don't want to go empty-handed. She's such a dear woman, don't you know—no bigger than a minute and old as the hills, eighty-six or eighty-seven at least." Aunt Chloe was seventy-six herself.

"Shall we take the car?" I asked, returning with a jar of home-made strawberry preserves. Aunt Chloe occasionally had sciatica.

"I should say not! We shall walk gingerly. It's cool enough."

We started through the front gate. "You said she was cooking squash *blossoms?*" I inquired.

"Supposed to be delicious. Sophia raises plants just for the blossoms. I stopped at their vegetable stand one day for string beans and there she was in the garden, creeping up on squash blossoms. I had no idea what she was up to. She'd sneak up on a blossom like it was a rabbit, then reach out and clamp it shut with her fingers just in case there was a bee inside. Then she'd pluck it and hold it to her ear. If she heard a buzz, she'd hold the blossom out at arm's length and let it open for the bee to fly out. She said the next time she fixed a mess of blossoms she'd give me a cooking lesson. Actually she said nothing of the sort. Speaks no English whatsoever. The children translated. Tony says she's making a salad, too. A remarkable woman."

"I never knew you could eat them."

"Well, that's not the only thing you've never heard of. She once sent me over a bowl of spaghetti and fresh sauce she'd made— the time my sciatic nerve kicked up and I was in bed a week. Most delicious. I had Eduardo, little Tony's brother, ask her what was in that sauce. It had a rather peculiar texture."

"What was it?"

"Chicken lungs."

"Oh, no!"

"Hearts and livers and lungs. Eating the lungs was like eating little balls of sponge rubber."

"Aunt Chloe," I moaned, "how could you?" She chuckled. An older boy leading a goat was coming toward us down the road.

"Eduardo, is that you?" Aunt Chloe yelled. "My, how you've grown since I saw you last! Hurry up and come walk with us. Does your grandma know we're coming?" Eduardo waved and nodded and yanked the rope so that his goat would walk faster.

"Did you know what was in it before you tasted it?"

"No, that was after the fact."

"Didn't you nearly die when you knew?"

"No, no. Once you have partaken of lamb's balls, my dear, a few chicken lungs seem awfully ordinary, don't you know." I stopped in my tracks and stared at her, mouth agape. When she saw my expression, she threw her head back and howled with laughter.

"You don't mean . . . ?"

"I most certainly do," she said, walking on. "Quite a delicacy. They used to serve them at the Northpoint Grille, a favorite haunt of your uncle Harry's." Eduardo reached us, and when Aunt Chloe held out her hand, he gave her the goat's rope and ran back toward home. The Scanzotti children, of whom there seemed to be at least a dozen, had lined up in the yard to receive us.

"You're teasing me," I said as we turned into the yard.

"They serve 'em fried. It's about time you developed a sophisticated palate. The world doesn't live on pot roast and mashed potatoes, you know." She then dropped the goat's rope onto the ground, and as the animal walked off to browse in some low bushes at the side of the house, she made a point of squinting in an exaggerated fashion in the direction of its rump.

"Aunt Chloe!"

Just then a raspy voice called out, and I looked up to see a tiny old woman with skin like polished leather standing in the doorway, grinning at us toothlessly and welcoming us in Italian.

"Sophia!" Aunt Chloe said, leading the way up onto the porch. The children, who had stood silently staring at us, dispersed and ran hither and yon, giggling. Aunt Chloe shook Sophia's hand. Sophia held Aunt Chloe's hand to her lips for an instant, then ushered us into the house through a small, messy living room to a tiny, cluttered kitchen. "How love-ly to see you, So-phee-ah," Aunt Chloe chanted in careful syllables, as if speaking slowly and loudly would make Sophia understand.

Sophia replied in a lengthy Italian diatribe delivered with enthusiastic gestures, after which she sat us down at the kitchen table.

"So-phee-ah, may I pre-sent my grand-niece, Ann—Anna. Give her the jam, dear. Anna doesn't know quite what to think of our squash blossoms, but she's game." I bowed from the waist and smiled. Sophia held the jam jar to her breast for a moment, then put it in a cupboard, from which she also took water glasses for the three of us. She filled each one-third full of red wine from a plain bottle, then poured in ginger ale.

23

"Ah, how elegant!" Aunt Chloe crooned. "Some of your own wine? Sophia, did Antonio make this?"

"*Sì,* Antonio." We raised our glasses and sipped. I was actually a little horrified. The only thing I had ever drunk was eggnog with a little rum in it my father had allowed me to taste one Christmas Eve.

"Good for you, my dear," Aunt Chloe encouraged, watching me tentatively savoring, then swallowing, the wine. Sophia brought lettuce and tomatoes to the table, a salad bowl, and a smaller dish piled with rinsed squash blossoms. She chopped several cloves of garlic, rubbed them in the bowl, and then began assembling the salad. The squash blossoms went in at the end. Finally, she poured a generous amount of olive oil and vinegar over it, then set it aside. She worked deliberately, making sure Aunt Chloe made note of every move she made.

Before beginning to cook the remaining blossoms, she offered Aunt Chloe a little more wine. "You wanta?" she said.

"Oh, yes—*sì,*" Aunt Chloe said, holding her glass up to be filled. "How lovely! I like it this way—don't you, Ann? It puts me in mind of the times I visited my cousin Rosemary in Providence some years back, and she and I would have a claret lemonade at the Biltmore Hotel before dinner, don't you know."

After pouring olive oil into a frying pan and putting it on the stove to heat, Sophia filled a teacup with flour and spread it out on the table with the palm of her right hand. Then she dredged the wet blossoms in it. We joined her at the stove as she fried them.

She brought out plates and forks and a loaf of Italian bread. She served Aunt Chloe and me before serving herself.

"Wonderful, Sophia—this is all just wonderful! I can't tell you how much I appreciate what you've done." Aunt Chloe took a forkful of salad, then closed her eyes and shook her head back and forth ecstatically. "You will never taste anything quite this good, Ann—dig in." She shoveled another forkful into her mouth.

Tentatively, I sampled my salad. "Delicious," I said.

Sophia, a delighted smile on her lips, tore off a chunk of bread for herself, then passed the loaf. I watched carefully as she mopped up the excess oil on her plate with the bread, popped it into her mouth, and began the arduous task of gumming it into a form suitable for swallowing. Aunt Chloe and I followed suit and mopped, too.

When we were finished eating and complimenting Sophia and thanking her the best we could, Aunt Chloe rose to leave, but Sophia beckoned to her and led her out the back door into the barnyard instead. I went to the front of the house to talk with the children, but they were gone. Looking out into the fields, I saw them all running with the goat in the distance.

After a few minutes Aunt Chloe and Sophia came strolling around the side yard. Aunt Chloe was holding four eggs.

"Sophia was showing me her chickens, some very fine birds. Now we have fresh eggs for breakfast." Aunt Chloe then took Sophia's hand. "You must come by my place one day soon," she said. Sophia nodded vaguely and flashed her Gerber-baby smile. "I'll cook something for *you,* and then we can hear my Caruso records again. I know how you love Caruso."

"Ai-yai-yai, Caruso! *Sì,* Caruso!" Sophia clasped her hands and rolled her eyes.

As Aunt Chloe and I walked back to Marsh Cliff, I said that while I had enjoyed our visit with Sophia, I felt awkward, to say the least, because of the language barrier. Aunt Chloe obviously hadn't felt awkward at all. "But how can you talk with someone who doesn't understand a word you say?" I persisted.

She looked at me, puzzled, and said simply: "Why, I think Sophia and I understand one another completely."

Later that evening, as we sat on the veranda, Aunt Chloe talked about some of the more interesting people she had met through the years. As I listened to her, I couldn't help noting that while some of the people she remembered were indeed unusual—artists and dancers, for example, who would be considered unique by anyone—quite a number of them were ordinary until Aunt Chloe discovered something about them that made them unforgettable, if only to her. Like Sophia.

Months later Aunt Chloe heard that I had been offered the job at Colchester's in Boston by a friend of a family friend. She had already made it clear to me that I was more likely to discover interesting people in the city than in the country. "Your more complex people flock to the cities," she said matter-of-factly. "More freedom of expression there, don't you know. Why, in one summer in the city you'll meet more unusual people than you ever thought possible! You'll come home a different girl, knowing more about yourself than ever before. And that's the point, my dear. I've always considered it the only achievement worth spending a lifetime on—self-knowledge. I would even go so far as to suggest, in the near future, a little traveling. Very broadening!"

A sound on the stairs brought me back to the present. I listened intently as light footsteps, not possibly Georgia's, passed my door and started up the stairs. It must be the artist who lives on the fourth floor, I thought, the one who had decorated the bathtub. Wherever Georgia was, she had obviously forgotten about me.

It was now late afternoon, and the sun had left my window; my room was darker and cooler. Chilled, I pulled back my blanket and top sheet and stretched out beneath them, feeling quite drowsy. I thought once more of what Aunt Chloe had said about knowing oneself. Sometimes it seemed to me that I knew myself too well. Unless I were suddenly to undergo the metamorphosis I secretly hoped for, at which point all bets would be off, I was rather easy to figure out.

I was an attractive, occasionally charming, intelligent young woman with a pleasant personality, a paragon of good taste who happened to have a small talent for painting.

I was from a good, solid family. My manners were impeccable. One day not too far from now I would meet and marry a handsome, intelligent, well-educated young man from a similarly fine family. We would have a huge wedding with photographs by Bradford Bachrach and gowns by Priscilla of Boston. We would honeymoon in Bermuda. There would be two children: a boy and girl, both blond of course, the girl in pinafores and dotted swiss, the boy in a grey-flannel Eton suit. We would live in a stately white colonial with dark-green shutters on a lovely street in a good town—Hamilton, Wenham, Lincoln, Concord, Marblehead. I would join the

Historical Society and the DAR. I had my papers, thanks to Aunt Chloe. I would go to teas in beige linen dresses with pearls and spectator pumps and white gloves. I would entertain at small dinners with canapés on silver trays and jellied consommé garnished with sliced lemon for the first course. I would drive a station wagon.

I had been born for this and groomed for it. I already had two place settings of my china, Wedgwood's Columbia. I had chosen Gorham's old pattern, Fairfax, for my sterling. I could spot a cashmere sweater at fifty yards, ditto Capezio shoes, and knew beyond a shadow of a doubt that no other piece of jewelry was as indispensable as a string of cultured pearls and no other item of clothing as useful and as tasteful and as classic as a good camel's hair coat, providing it was top-stitched around the collar and equipped with genuine mother-of-pearl buttons.

I knew exactly how to use a finger bowl. I knew the proper form for monograms. I had my own engraved calling cards. I knew how to tell whether an invitation was engraved or simply printed. I knew the proper form for answering such invitations: "Miss Ann Merrill regrets that, etc. etc." or "Miss Ann Merrill accepts with pleasure. . . ." I knew what length of gloves to wear at what time of day and with what sort of costume. I knew that a lady never accepts gifts of a personal nature from a young man and that no young lady anticipating a life as other than a streetwalker would ever wear an ankle bracelet. I knew to wear a hat in church, to remove one glove for eating and shaking hands, and to refrain from discussing details of illnesses, deaths, funerals, animal behavior, bodily functions, and childbirth at table.

It was in poor taste even to hold hands with a young man in public. It was in poor taste to open a napkin more than halfway before placing it in one's lap. Gum chewing was never allowed. Toothpicks were decidedly déclassé. Satin was an inappropriate fabric for any purpose. Orchids were "common," and last choice for a tasteful corsage. Corsages, in fact, were to be discouraged, except in rare cases, when the length of said corsage should be no more than four inches and floral components were to be chosen carefully with an eye for originality and muted coloration—for example, the corsage Mother had ordered for me for a certain dance to which I was to wear a blue dress: an arrangement of blue bachelor's buttons and stephanotis with a small silver ribbon.

The lists went on and on. While others might be fated to roam aimlessly through life wondering what to do with themselves, I, by virtue of my family background, intensive training, and natural proclivities, would travel an easy, comfortably predictable course, arm in arm with the man with whom I would meet my destiny. My fate was sealed. How fortunate I was! Why did I ever yearn for more?

I looked toward the window, where a breeze was moving my curtains and the sound of voices rose up from the courtyard. My bed was soft, the pillow sweet smelling; a pattern of faint shadows on the ceiling faded in and out, in and out; and in and out of my consciousness moved bits of conversation and fragments of familiar faces, and I dreamed I was falling.

When I awoke it was dark. For a moment I didn't know where I was. Sitting up, however, I soon remembered and fumbled for the lamp on the little chest by my bed and turned it on. My watch said nearly ten. I hadn't eaten and was suddenly famished. I remembered some fruit and banana bread my mother had packed for me and retrieved them from my suitcase. It was then that I heard music playing in the courtyard. I got up and looked out.

I saw a man sitting on one of the kitchen chairs under the tree. A dim light illuminated him just enough for me to see that he was dark, with a long, thin frame. His shoulders were hunched forward, his head bowed, and a shock of curly dark hair fell forward, obscuring his eyes. He held a guitar close to the curve of his torso as if it were a rescued child. The music was flamenco. Suddenly he stopped playing and took a long drink from a glass at his feet. He puffed on a cigarette and stared off into a corner of the courtyard. Then he resumed playing. I watched and listened for a long time, seeing his head bob as he reached an intricate part of the melody, watching the smoke from his cigarette drift up through the limbs and leaves of the tree. I thought of taking my pillow and sitting on the fire escape, but I needed a bath for work the following day. I gathered my nightgown, bath powder, and slippers and crept from my room to the bathroom. The last thing I wanted was to meet Georgia again at this late hour. I ran hot water into the decorated tub. I took a fresh bar of Yardley's soap from the shelf, unwrapped it, and was tossing the wrapper into the waste-basket beside the toilet when I saw a note taped to the lid. Written on lined paper, it read:

> Annie, when I saw your face,
> I thought of organdy and lace.
> I thought of blossoms drenched with dews,
> The moment that I looked at youse.
>
> Love,
Georgia

P.S. As I am sitting on the pot, it occurs to me that someday this bathtub will hang in the Louvre and be worth a million dollars. That'll bring a smile to Mona Lisa, all right. Claude, the artiste in question, fourth floor apartment, is supposed to return tonight. You must meet him. He is, in a word, divine. See you after work. Good luck on your first day—

G.

I smiled in spite of myself. A poet, no less—a little rough around the edges, but a poet all the same. There was something about her, that was for sure. And I loved the sound of Claude. I allowed myself a quick fantasy: a torrid summer romance with an artist, a passionate, brooding man much older than me who would first become interested in me as a student, hovering over my shoulder as I put brush to canvas under his critical stare, and then would be swept off his feet by my cheery girlishness and would take to instructing me in the ways of love. Just the sort of thing I had hoped for this summer. Let the metamorphosis begin!

Suddenly flushed all over, I undressed and stepped into the tub. For a moment the guitar music seemed louder; but as I sank into the water, it faded somewhat, its sound mingling with that of lapping wavelets. I lay back and breathed deeply of lavender and eucalyptus. I raised one pink leg, rested its heel on the rim of the tub, and knew that life as it had been was drawing to a timely close. I inched down even lower into the water until my pink-nippled breasts floated on its sudsy surface like wet blossoms.

Where was the freckled and innocent girl of just hours ago? Who was the fetching creature rising from the mist and foam before me now? This rosy nymph, this brazen Eve, this Venus without half-shell, this waxen, wet water lily, this masterpiece by Monet!

Or was it Manet? I could never get those two straight.

THREE

I wish I could say that my first day at Colchester's Used Book Store in any way lived up to my rather modest expectations. Whereas I had been led to believe that my primary responsibility would be cheerfully serving the store's sophisticated clientele in locating and selecting books, what I actually did was dust. There were tables, shelves, boxes, nooks, crannies, rooms and more rooms filled with books. They were arranged informally, I was told. "Irrationally" might be more to the point. Interspersed between wastelands of books seemingly cast about willy-nilly were little pockets of Dewey decimal systematism. But everything varied from shelf to shelf, from room to room. It really wasn't my concern. My job was to dust.

As the intermittent stream (hardly the droves I had imagined) of undistinguished customers browsed, wandered, made nuisances of themselves, and occasionally purchased books, I was sent forth with a feather duster to the back of the store to the Old and Rare section, which occupied a room of its own. I headed straight for a wall of shelves upon which a cardboard sign marked OLD was tacked.

It became instantly apparent to me that except for a fine layer of recent deposit that could safely be removed, dust was an integral part of the bindings and pages of these books, as necessary to them as plasma was to me. It occurred to me that a professional duster of the caliber of my mother could wipe out the "Old" without a trace, in a morning. I approached, therefore, gingerly, whisking away that topmost patina with a gentle flick of my feathers, and stood stoically by as each minute particle frolicked wildly in the air for one hovering second, then arranged itself exactly in its former position. Occasionally, in a moment of creative self-expression, a single fleck of dust would find its way to a new spot. I watched with restrained glee as morsels of the decayed binding of *Miss Dunbar's Guide for Refined Young Ladies,* circa 1847, sifted down to caress the illustrated, lithographed pages of a tome rashly named *The Volume of the World,* which depicted "savage Esquimaux" and assorted naked natives of the Sandwich Islands among its plethora of engraved plates. And I was paid for this!

In mid-morning, as I worked through European Authors (including, inexplicably, ten volumes of Mark Twain and an entire shelf of Zane Grey), I was interrupted by Ruth Carmichael, my middle-aged employer. She took me out through the back door, which led to an alleyway, where we would take our break.

"Quite a madhouse, isn't it?" she said, apparently taking my breathlessness due to dust exposure as a symptom of hurry and stress. She had soft, wavy blue hair. Her face was shell pink. Her eyes were as blue as a postcard sky, and her mouth was made for kissing babies. She was dressed in powder blue, with pearls. Her fingernails were carefully manicured and glossy from buffing. I suspected she wore Charles of the Ritz cosmetics. Surprisingly, she offered me a cigarette from an engraved case. I took one.

"I don't think I dusted at all well," I said. I blew a long tube of smoke in the direction of a ray of sunlight that cut diagonally through the dank darkness of the alley. She smiled. We sat down on the cement steps.

"Sometimes I think this entire city is made of dust," she said, removing the little white gloves she wore to protect her hands. "When it piled high enough they sculpted buildings out of it— even people, for all I know." She laughed and with a delicate gesture removed a curled shred of tobacco from her tongue. "Did you have a chance to look through any of the old books?"

"A little," I said. "Fascinating."

"That's the fun of working here," she said. "Do take some time when you have a few spare moments to become familiar with the Old and Rare."

"That will be okay, then? I don't want to neglect my work."

"But that is part of your work, dear, and you'll be glad you did. One of these days someone will come in looking for something special and you'll be glad you know your way around."

I thanked her. She took a gold pocket watch from her snakeskin purse. Its lid flipped open silently, and a bright, round reflection wavered at her throat for an instant before it leapt to her cheek— a little spotlight of gold. I thought of the Blue Fairy in Pinocchio. We sat there a few moments more without speaking while she took a fresh pair of gloves from her purse and worked them carefully over her hands and fingers. Then she stood, stamped out her cigarette, bent to pick it up, and held it in the palm of one glove to be discarded inside. I followed suit.

"I guess we'd best be going in," she said. "Give Oscar a chance to have a little rest." Oscar was my co-worker. He was tall, homely, and very nervous—the kind of boy who picked his nose when no one was looking, but someone always was. He had an Adam's apple that jutted out right behind his collar button, so that when he spoke, his tie moved. Ruth said that he was a full-blown genius and went to MIT. I thought he was a jerk. I watched him as he sauntered out to the alley, wiping his horn-rimmed glasses on the bottom of his sport coat, thinking to myself what a total waste it was that an idiot like Oscar had a body that moved with the ease and grace I usually associated with much handsomer, more self-assured men. Just then he turned to say something to Ruth in his annoying deep voice. He seemed always to be forcing himself to speak in a timbre lower than what was natural for him, as if someone had told him he sounded sophisticated that way, or (and it made me sick to even think it) sexier. The only hope for him would be a girl who was either blind or horribly desperate. No normal person on the face of the earth would ever have him—

unless, of course, one had an unfortunate weakness for purely physical, below-the-neck attributes: broad yet graceful shoulders; a good, solid chest tapering to a narrow waist and hips. Such inconsistency could make one weep!

As he went through the door to the alley and gave a fleeting, furtive glance in my direction, his caramel-brown eyes locked onto mine for a split second and my heart sank. I began to tremble with revulsion. Oscar Benson had noticed me—in "that way." It was going to be a long, sickening summer.

I turned my attention to Zane Grey, liberating the russet-orange volumes and placing them in Westerns, where they belonged. I found myself wondering whether their fabric bindings had been chosen in just that color to evoke visions of rocky buttes and canyons seen in places like Wyoming and Nevada—places that might as well have been on the moon as far as I was concerned. New Englanders were not likely travelers, most of them believing, as my father did, that everything west of New York City (with the possible exception of Chicago) was a vast wasteland void of anything even approximating culture and populated by monosyllabic, banished misfits. Had they been able to make it in the East, they would have—why else would they have left? Still, for years I had secretly dreamed of travel. I took full responsibility for this blemish on my otherwise admirable character. And it *was* considered a blemish: just because Aunt Chloe, remarkable and unique as she was, had traveled extensively did not make it acceptable for me. Aunt Chloe had proven herself many times over and was not subject to the expectations and criticism of others. But I was young, unproven; and my desire to travel marked me, I knew, as ungrateful at the very least. According to my father, harboring longings for the Painted Desert or the Grand Canyon when good and glorious Cape Cod was there for the taking probably indicated a considerable propensity for mediocrity, which I should do my best to control.

Nevertheless, travel had often occurred to me, even before Aunt Chloe suggested it. I had dreamed myself paddle-wheeling down the broad, brown Mississippi River on a sultry afternoon. I had imagined myself dancing beneath palm trees on a terrace in tawdry Los Ang-uh-lees, as Father called it. And one afternoon, after reading a particularly moving passage in the *Encyclopaedia Britannica* about the majesty of the Rockies, I stood on a wide and windy plain, knee deep in wheat, and gazed in stunned reverence at the snow-capped peaks, which in my mind's eye ran in a thin, neat line from the Canadian border to the Gulf of Mexico and could be viewed in their entirety from one vantage point somewhere in Montana. No one in my family except Aunt Chloe had ever left New England.

Shortly after noon, Ruth asked me to join her for lunch at a tiny restaurant named Giles, which seemed to be patronized solely by women. The specialty of the house was a simple dish consisting of sliced mushrooms sautéed in butter, served on toast points. It was delicious.

Ruth told me all about herself: her childhood on the Cape, her "flaming youth" as a flapper, and the young man she was to have married had he not been killed in an accident.

Ruth laughed easily and often, spoke in a lilting voice that made me wonder if she had ever been a singer, and seemed possessed of such natural good humor and charm that I was quite taken with her before our meal was half over. I was thinking what a lovely woman she was and how fortunate I was to have her for my supervisor and friend, even to the point of admiring her shimmer of blue hair, when her manner suddenly changed; her brow became furrowed, and she began to tell me about her dear mother, with whom she shared a house in Jamaica Plain.

For the next half-hour I heard more about the bowel habits of the aged than I was sure I would ever need to know. It was soon to occur to me that charming, refined Ruth was somewhat fixated in this area. As she delicately nibbled a mushroom cap and accompanied it with a tiny wedge of butterlogged toast, she regaled me with such details of human evacuation as I had thought, until now, were the domain of registered nurses and physicians and an occasional pharmacist on a slow day.

She became, before my very eyes, a living pharmacopoeia of cathartics of every description and subtlety of action. Her voice rose alarmingly as she swung into a discussion of enema bags and alternative solutions one might brew to be used in a variety of symptomatic situations. She touched on the wonders of suppositories. I was sure that everyone in the place could hear her. But other than embarrassment, my reactions were twofold—horror and hysteria: horror that she had broken the rule of deportment that specified that bodily functions were rarely discussed, and never at table; hysteria at the irony in the situation. Dear Ruth, white gloves and all, the very quintessence of propriety, burdened with an interest in the banal that boggled the mind. It was all so terribly funny, made more so by the animated vivacity with which she accompanied each new detail. I had all I could do to keep from laughing. I drank sips of water and tea, alternately, in an attempt to control myself. I poured salt onto the table and drew little designs in it to keep myself preoccupied, if only for fragments of seconds at a time. I waited for any excuse to smile, even slightly, even smiling pseudosympathetically now and then, to relieve the pressure building within me. I imagined myself suddenly unable to stem the flow and erupting in saliva-spewing laughter, pounding the table with my fists, my face in my plate. By the grace of God it didn't happen, and I remained, to outward appearances, controlled.

Finally, as she checked her gold pocket watch to see if we were spending too much time at lunch, she told a rambling tale of her tiny, feeble mother, driven mad with constipation ("The humours back up into the brain, you know"), who managed to wedge herself between her bed and the wall one night. Ruth could neither pry her loose nor move the bed for fear Mother would flop to the floor once she became unpinned and thereby break every bone in her porous little body.

While the poor old woman screamed and raved, Ruth positioned herself on the bed with her, kept her warm, spoon-fed her mouthfuls of egg custard to keep her nourishment up, and said the Rosary for her all night long. The cleaning woman freed them both when she arrived at seven the next morning.

The afternoon hours passed quickly. First, Oscar Benson was assigned to teach me how to use the cash register. Then Ruth had
me sit at her desk and watch her do a little bookkeeping. Then I
dusted books in the children's section. Finally, after helping a few
customers and rearranging some stacks that had been disturbed
during the morning by browsers, I was sent into the back again
to familiarize myself once more with the Old and Rare.

I was sitting at an oak table poring over an ancient geography
book filled with outrageously inaccurate lithographed renderings
of, among others, "The Pyramids at Giza," when Oscar came back
to inform me that it was just about closing time.

"Oh, sorry," I said. "I guess I lost track of time. I'll be right
there."

"No, it's all right, really," he said. "Everything's all done. Ruth
said she'll show you closing procedures tomorrow. Tuesday's usually a slow day." He pulled the chair beside me away from the
table, turned it around so that the seat was between his legs, and
sat on it, his arms folded across its curved back. He stared at me
without expression, but a small mound of muscle at his left jawline
pulsated as if it were infused with blood. Disgusting. "Where do
you go to school?" he said in that ridiculous low voice.

"I just graduated from high school. I'll be going to Wellesley
in the fall."

"Ah, yes, Wellesley. Grand school. Grand school." He was an
idiot. He removed his glasses and chewed on one earpiece; the
area around his eyes looked pallid and damp, his naked eyelids as
translucent and huge as a baby bird's. Too bad his eyes were that
warm, delicious caramel color. Sometimes God didn't plan at all
well.

"I'm looking forward to it," I said, realizing for the first time
in ages that I really was. I had visited the Wellesley campus with
my cousin Charlotte several times, even before I had made up my
mind to go there, although there had never been any real question
of it. I would be the eighth girl in my family to attend Wellesley.
It was a tradition.

"You seem to be quite bright," he said, raising one eyebrow and regarding me critically. He was sweating. His neck was wet. His parents were rich. I could tell by the way he spoke.

"How do you know?" I said, fingering a few pages of my book, tipping my head to one side and scrutinizing him coldly out of the corners of my eyes. "I wasn't aware that we had had that much to say to one another. Learning how to operate a cash register may not be the equivalent of an IQ test." I could be mean if I wanted to.

"Well—uh," he stuttered, obviously affected by my tone, "—it seems fairly obvious to me. And you must be, if you've been admitted to Wellesley."

"Perhaps," I said. Actually, I was flattered. I was not accustomed to being complimented on my brains by boys. Mother had always said that the reason I hadn't had millions of dates in high school was my superior intellect. I posed such a threat to the adolescents I encountered. She had said that older, more secure "men" would find me an exciting challenge.

"I go to MIT myself," he offered, his head wobbling a little as he spoke. Obviously thought he was a big cheese.

"An engineer, huh?"

"Well, eventually I'd like to become an architect," he said.

"Then you'll appreciate this," I said, as I passed him the old geography book with the strange illustration of the Pyramids.

"Wow!" he said, putting on his glasses and scratching his head. Then he laughed again, a really affected stage laugh. I hated him. I had never met such a phony baloney in my life. Suddenly he looked at me solemnly. "You wouldn't by any chance be free this evening?"

"No."

"No?"

"No." His face sort of twitched. I softened. "You see, I've just moved into this new apartment, and there are boxes absolutely everywhere, if you know what I mean," I lied. He smiled, obviously relieved that I actually did have other plans. He then jumped up with great scrapes of his chair, stood upright for a second, and abruptly keeled over to his right, simultaneously reaching out with an extended arm and the flat of one hand to catch himself against the wall; he swung one leg out to cross the other at the ankle—all of this an awkward and thoroughly comical, not to mention frightening, attempt at a casual, offhand pose. He removed his glasses once more and leered at me through half-closed eyes.

"I just thought I might show you around MIT. I assume you haven't seen it. It's a grand place, really. 'Course the place is deserted in the summer. I usually grab a bite to eat at Bickford's after work, then take a walk by the Charles. I'm assuming you like jazz . . ."

"What?" I hadn't understood him. He pronounced it "jahzz." Now I was sure that his parents were rich.

"Jazz," he repeated. "Dizzy Gillespie, Ella Fitzgerald?"

"Oh, of course. Why, yes—I love them," I lied again, not knowing why I bothered. He was a goon.

"Oh, grand," he said, beaming, "just grand! I was thinking that we could go on up to my room and listen to music. But if you're busy . . ."

"Yes, I am." He was so pitiful. I couldn't believe that this had happened to me—that I had just met this jerk and he had the gall to ask me up to his room. Mother had told me about guys like this. They wanted only one thing. I just hadn't imagined that they could be ugly and unsuave, if that was a word.

"I understand. Completely," he said. I got up and began to walk out of the room, and as I did he lunged after me, fell in step no more than a foot behind me, and placed a clammy hand on each of my shoulders. Chills ran up and down my spine. His large thumbs grazed my neck. He pushed me ahead of himself as if I were a piece of furniture on wheels.

"I found her," he practically screamed at Ruth, who looked up, startled, from her books. She said we could go. I grabbed my purse and sweater and walked out the door with Oscar the Obnoxious at my heels.

"Hey, maybe I'll call you later. That is, if you have a phone yet." I felt his hand grip my shoulder as if to hold me back.

That was the last straw. I whirled around. I positioned the left inner sole of my Capezio slipper against the outer right sole of his Florsheim oxfords and glared up into his face—or, rather, into the lenses of his glasses. He was extremely tall (something I hadn't really noticed before); and this close up, there was a certain indescribable odor to his clothes or his body, an odor it pained me to admit I liked, a smell almost as evocative as the scent a dog has when it comes in from the rain—not necessarily overwhelmingly pleasant but natural and unforgettable.

"Do not touch me," I sneered, getting a hold of myself. "Evah!" I turned on my heel, as they say, and started up the street. Immediately, for reasons that I will never understand, I swung into what I called my "dancer's stride"—a graceful lope I had invented the summer of my fourteenth year when it occurred to me that walking pigeon-toed was a bit too cute for a young woman of my not-so-latent possibilities. I held my head high and moved my shoulders in an easy, sashaying rhythm. I thrust my legs out from the hip, then the knee. My hips swayed, but almost innocently. The message conveyed, I hoped, was subtle, tasteful, bordering on subliminal—perhaps a little too subliminal for anyone as idiotic as Oscar Benson. But I could feel his caramel eyes devouring me, savoring every infinitesimal wiggle, sway, and bump I made. I loved it. He was, after all, a captive, and deep down inside I knew that all the genius he could muster (and I judged that to be considerable) could not save him.

Yes, he was a captive, as all the other young men I had ever known were, of hormonal imbalance, a condition that dulls all attempts at intellectual thought or rational action. Of all the things Oscar Benson might *think* he wanted—an A in advanced physics, the brain of Einstein (or in his case, of Frank Lloyd Wright), a chair at Harvard, every flavor of Howard Johnson's ice cream— there was only one thing that he *really* wanted, and that something was sex. Sex, sex, and more sex. Sex now. Sex immediately. Sex continuously. Sex forever. Sex eternally. Sex until death. Sex after death. Sex in the morning and sex in the evening and sex in the rain and the snow and in cars and on bicycles, world without end, Amen. He sickened me, but all the same, I loved making his life miserable. I stopped walking. Slowly, I turned around, prepared to see his tortured face, the look of rejection and of unrequited lust. He was gone. "Damn!" I turned onto Beacon Street and walked faster. The hell with the dancer's stride. No appreciation anywhere, anyway.

By the time I had reached the point where Beacon ran along one side of the Common, I was summing up all I knew about Oscar Benson. In the first place, the name Oscar was awful, just awful. I tried to imagine the mentality of a mother who would name her baby Oscar. But if I looked at it another way, it could be said to have a certain ring of power to it, strength of character— even virility, I thought, grimacing. He was very tall. There was power in that, too. He had that unique, almost gamy smell I couldn't get out of my mind. And he was slender, not the least bit skinny, and tall, as I mentioned before, so that you could say that he was rangy, taut. I liked the sound of that.

Still, he was more or less ugly. Well, not truly ugly—just ordinary. It wasn't as if he had a beak of a nose or bad skin or no chin. He wasn't a pinhead. At thirty he might be quite handsome; that happened sometimes. He might be very handsome. As a matter of fact, certain people, under certain conditions, might describe Oscar, under the right lights and dressed in just the right clothes, as exuding a certain strength of character, which although not particularly attractive in a young man looked awfully good on an older one.

Let's face it, he had none of the wantonly adorable greasiness of a Tony Curtis, my favorite star. But I had always been a sucker for a good mind, and Oscar Benson was a genius—Ruth would vouch for that. It stirred me. Imagine a man with a mind like that—a great, glorious, crackerjack of a mind. All of this genius trapped in a tall, rangy, taut, and handsome body. And he had stood beside me at the cash register and had said such patient things to me, things like "Don't let the drawer hit you in the ribcage as it pops out." How clever of him. How thoughtful.

And kissing—I had read that educated men kissed better. What would kissing Oscar be like? My heart sank. The word "repulsive" drifted through my mind. Oscar Benson was the kind of boy who thought saliva was sexy. To make matters worse, he had fat lips.

They'd feel mushy, all covered with spit. He might drool, like a puppy dog. I could say, "Oscar, darling, stop lapping me for just a moment, will you, and wipe your mouth dry." And he'd pant and dangle his tongue out of the side of his mouth and wipe his lips dry in my hair.

And then his mouth would feel all warm. It would cover mine completely, like those red wax lips that you wear over your own by biting down on a little tab on the back. And when his lips parted, I could touch the sharp cutting edge of his brilliant white teeth with my tongue, and I would feel them press into my flesh to bite me gently, sometimes a bit harder.

I had just passed under the blue awning of a chic private club and was continuing my way down Beacon Street when a sudden blast of cool air, probably off the river, blew straight at me, lifting my hair and my skirt. I jumped into a doorway for a moment.

Where was I? Kissing Oscar.

Oh, yes . . . And when we made love, Oscar would, of course, be wild and noisy and out of his head with passion, completely insatiable.

I headed down the street again.

But there would be brief moments in between for going to museums, drinking espresso in coffeehouses, taking romantic, city walks in the rain, and reading *The New York Times* on summer Sunday afternoons by the Fens.

As I turned at last onto Walnut Street, I knew beyond the shadow of a doubt that Oscar Benson was, as a matter of absolute fact, husband material, the first bona fide case of husband material I had ever met—excepting, of course, Saul Rivkin, the brain of my class in high school, who was, additionally, unfortunately for me, Jewish. He made it very plain one day in Mr. Lester's class in family dynamics, a required course for all seniors, that his family expected him to marry within the faith, that his mother would have a nervous breakdown if he didn't and his father would disinherit him from his share of the family jewelry business. He was so adamant and snotty about it, I began to feel like a second-class citizen just because I wasn't Jewish. That same night, I went to bed early with a thick book my father had ordered from somewhere and never read, entitled *Great Religions of the World*. I wanted to ascertain exactly how much of an adjustment would be necessary to transform me from an Episcopalian to a Jew. Saul Rivkin was gorgeous. I was willing to change. But it didn't take long for me to realize that becoming a Jew involved more than going to temple now and then. I had too many extracurricular activities as it was without taking on something else.

In fact, a whole lot about Judaism was confusing to me. Circumcision, for instance. Even now, months later, I was still confused about it. I couldn't remember: did Jewish boys get circumcised while gentile boys didn't, or was it the other way around? My brother, Evan, *had* been circumcised, I knew that, on the kitchen table at the age of two, for reasons to which I was not made privy. Since Evan *wasn't* Jewish, that settled the question. Gentile boys were circumcised, Jewish boys were not. That probably explained a number of things—a certain attitude of superiority I had noticed in Jewish men, for one. It had never occurred to me until now that of course they would feel superior. They *were* superior. They were whole!

What was it that made me think that Oscar was at least part Jewish? The dark hair? The warm brown eyes? The shape of those lips of his, sort of Victor Mature–ish? His ample nose? The impression I had that he thought he was several cuts above everyone else, a man to be reckoned with? Yes, all of the above. Oscar *was* Jewish. Oscar was *un*circumcised. And grateful. And wondrously, monumentally whole.

In fact, as I approached the black, enameled door of my new home on Walnut Street, I saw clearly, excitingly so, that Oscar was a magnificent specimen of young, turgid manhood—something along the lines of the anatomical equivalent of the Colossus at Rhodes. I had known this somewhere deep in my being from the second I set eyes on him. I hesitated on the top step for a moment, flushed and breathless, feeling guilty for even toying with this idea in plain view of passing motorists on Beacon Street. I couldn't recall ever being so blatant about anything in my life. What had happened to me? It must be my new environment. It was doing things to my thoughts. To my libido.

I was suddenly worldly. In just one day I had passed from a green little eighteen-year-old with only three boyfriends in her past, three practically innocent liaisons, to a real woman with a vital interest in comparative male anatomy. I suddenly recalled a passage I had read in a sex manual I had found in my father's library. I had never questioned this passage until now. It stated positively that the size of the male organ was not as important as the skill with which it was used.

Ha! I wasn't born yesterday.

Oscar—oh, Oscar. I couldn't wait to see him again!

"Hi there." A bellowing voice startled me. A bolus of saliva landed on the step at my feet. I looked up. Georgia was astraddle the windowsill three stories above me, one long leg dangling precariously.

"What are you doing?" I said, my voice tinged with annoyance. How long had she been there? Had she watched me walk up the street talking to myself? Had she read my lips?

"It's feeding time," she said, leaning forward toward the side of the building and scattering bread crusts on a narrow, decorative ledge that ran along its perimeter. She cooed. Instantly, two ratty-looking pigeons flew in from parts unknown and rose and fell in an excited hover over her head.

"I'll be right up," I called as I put my door key into the lock. Once I was inside the front hallway, Malcolm Balch appeared through the French doors, a welcoming smile on his lips.

"Your first day?" he said, his eyebrows arched high on his forehead.

"Just wonderful," I said, pleased at his interest.

"I couldn't be more thrilled," he said. "Oh, I've been thinking of you, keeping my fingers crossed."

"That's awfully sweet of you," I said. The smell of eucalyptus was overpowering yet soothing.

"Well, I won't keep you," he said, backing into his apartment again. "I was just curious to know how things had gone. Oh, and I nearly forgot . . ." He hesitated, a look of concern on his pleasant face. "You'll find that I've taken the liberty of hanging two nice pomander balls in your closet. Keeps clothes smelling fresh in all this humidity."

"Why, thank you," I said. "I have an aunt who always uses pomander balls." His eyebrows jumped twice.

"It's an old-fashioned idea but a good one," he said. Just then Georgia yelled my name from upstairs. Malcolm and I winced simultaneously.

"I'd better get up there," I whispered.

"I think you must," he whispered back, wiggling his fingers at me in a little wave as he backed into his apartment again.

FOUR

When I reached the third-floor landing, Georgia was waiting for me, bouncing up and down like a two-year-old. She immediately clasped me in an enthusiastic hug—at least that's what I think she intended it to be. She encircled my head with her long arms, then squeezed the circle shut. My face, a grimace of pain, was at her armpit.

"Did you have a good day?" she breathed, pushing me out at arm's length, glaring at me with bulging eyes.

"Yes. Very good. Very good," I said, countering her exuberance with stoicism. I attempted to extricate myself from her grasp by simply turning slightly in the direction of my door. Hugging was not something my family encouraged as a spur-of-the-moment activity, certainly not with strangers. Apparently sensing my hesitancy, she gave me a hurt look; and before I knew what I was doing, I hugged her back and allowed her to more or less haul me along by one arm into her room.

"You must come and visit. I even brought you a Coke from work. It's still cold. Sit down right here," she said, clearing a place for me on her unmade bed. She pulled a Coke bottle out of her faded red terry-cloth beach bag, opened it, and handed it to me. I thanked her and took a long swallow. "You must be boiling," she said. "It's as hot as Hades out there, honest to God. You're just in time to meet my little flock."

She then turned to the window. She had lifted the rose draperies up and out of the way by looping them over the curtain rod. No birds were there at the moment so she raised the sash, leaned her head out and began to imitate a dove, as I had heard her do before, although in all honesty the sound she made was more like a gurgle than a coo. Yet in seconds several tin-eared pigeons flew in for bread, which she replenished from a brown paper sack at her feet.

"They all have red eyes, Annie," she said, annoying me again, calling me by that name. I felt like a farm girl. "The most beautiful red eyes. A wonderful red it is, so deep and . . . sweet." She shrugged her shoulders helplessly. "The color of sweet wine," she continued, "or berries, or currants. Look! Do you see them?" Her voice rose giddily, her eyes wide, darting from me to the birds and back. Her eyes now reminded me of mineral pools I had seen in a photo somewhere: marine blue or sea green underlaid with transparent silver.

"Yes, I do see them," I said, as enthusiastically as I could. Their eyes, in fact, were not entirely red at all, but the irises were outlined in a thin band of red. I was more interested in *her* eyes.

"Wonderful eyes," she said. "Honest to God, they're really beautiful! And this one—do you see this little one? I call her Eve because she was the very first to come to my little oasis. Come see her, Annie—she's lovely, aren't you, Evie? As graceful as a dancer and with a fine swan's neck." I approached the window to have a closer look at Eve, an ordinary, iridescent grey pigeon. "Look. Red eyes," Georgia repeated. "Isn't it incredible? You are so beautiful, Eve, aren't you?" With this, she put her face close to the bird's and cooed. Eve flew off. Georgia leaned dangerously out the window, arching her long torso to see where Eve had flown. "Oh, she's up at Claude's window," she said with a delighted smile. "She'll be back. She always comes right back. I guess I scared her. She'll forgive me, I'm sure of it."

In seconds, another bird flew in with a flutter of its papery wings and strutted along the sill to eat out of Georgia's hand. She greeted this one like a long-lost friend, even reached out to pet him—a very brave gesture, I decided, since this particular bird had the ugliest patch of naked bird skin on his neck. Wasn't she afraid of catching something—a bird virus or lice?

"Look at *his* eyes, Annie. A deeper red than Eve's. I wonder how the world looks through those eyes. Pretty rosy, I suppose!" She laughed at her small joke. Two more birds flew in, grabbed crusts and flew away. "I wonder what I will do for them in winter," she said. "Something more nourishing than just bread, I think."

She sat down on a rocking chair she had moved closer to the window, stretched her long legs out in front of herself, and rested her heels on the sill. She was wearing brown oxfords with laces, the sort referred to as "gunboats," which accentuated the length and narrowness of her feet. She couldn't have made a worse choice. Ditto her dress, which was black cotton with an attractive waist-cincher belt in bright stripes. But the dress was badly faded and shaded to brown in places, and the flat bow that was to have adorned the neckline had fallen off, and all that remained were a few dangling threads. The bow itself was on her bedside table, apparently discarded.

Suddenly she pointed out a framed print above her bureau. It was familiar. I had seen it many times: a small girl of about eight in an old-fashioned dress against a vague background, the hint of a tree branch angling in with a few leaves, and a goldfinch perched on her finger. I smiled at Georgia and nodded.

"How I would have loved the olden days!" she said, looking at the picture with squinted eyes. When she opened them wider, I thought they were teary. "You could just walk out anytime and catch one. They were unafraid then, completely unafraid. Honest to God, that must have been something! Think of it—to hold a sweet, warm-winged thing in your hands, and when it was ready to fly, there would be one small moment, the tiniest moment, when you felt a sudden puff of warm air from beneath its wings." She smiled at me crookedly. "Wing breath, you could say it was. Wing breath." For an instant her eyes rolled back in her head, her lids fluttering; then she looked at me quizzically. If I was supposed to say something at this point, God only knew what it was. I pretended there was still a drop of Coke left in the bottle and tipped it up to drink. Looking back at her, I saw that she was dreamily watching her flock once again, oblivious to me.

Georgia's room, I noticed, was very different from mine. It was more elegant, with its furnishings of matched mahogany and a subdued color scheme. In fact, it seemed more suited to me than to her, although I loved my room and would not have wanted to exchange it.

Matching the dull rose draperies, the walls were papered, tone on tone, in a traditional colonial print—scenes in a park. Long-skirted ladies with parasols strolled along the banks of a mean-dering stream among weeping willow trees, while little boys in nautical outfits sailed their boats. Carrying out the rose color scheme further, a large hooked rug in a floral pattern covered the floor and a rosy beige spread covered her bed, which was a fine old specimen with a massive, soaring headboard.

It was then that I noticed the one piece of furniture that did not match. It was a bright-blue painted chest with a bowed front and fat, clawed feet. It occupied a corner. A crucifix hung above it. On its top were a large domed basket with a set of coral-colored rosary beads draped over it and a votive candle in a ruby glass holder.

Was this some sort of shrine? Some little corner reserved for prayer? I was uneasy at the thought.

"Look, Annie—Eve's back," Georgia said, without turning to look at me. She was standing at the window once more.

I believed that religion belonged in churches, and that if one absolutely insisted on having religious displays of any kind outside of church, these should be kept hidden from sight. I was always grateful to have been raised an Episcopalian and not a Roman Catholic, with their penchant for statuettes, pictures of Mary and Jesus done in lurid, tinted foil, and bad reproductions of *The Last Supper* on every dining-room wall.

Georgia's little prayer corner worried me. She was probably a religious fanatic and would attempt to turn the entire third floor at Walnut Street into some quasi-Catholic retreat. I would get the nod for the job of altar boy.

I was just about to stand and excuse myself when Georgia turned to me as if to speak, smiled, and turned back to her birds once again. Once more she had left me dangling. Like a fool, I continued to sit there, waiting for her permission to leave. Here we go again, I thought, as motionless as if shackled by ball and chain.

Then a vase of red blossoms caught my eye. On closer examination they were no less than fifteen ugly paper poppies, the kind you bought from veterans around Memorial Day. How very quaint to save them and make an arrangement of them. Georgia certainly was frugal.

Still not a word from her. I noticed a handsome umbrella stand of what looked like Italian pottery, highly glazed and painted with hummingbirds and trumpet-shaped flowers, standing in the corner. It contained one black, man's umbrella, probably Georgia's (she wasn't exactly a slave to fashion), and one rather disheveled monkey on a stick. I couldn't help smiling. Mother had never allowed me to have one; she said they were cheap and disgusting looking— which, of course, they were. I had all I could do to keep myself from going over to it, taking it out of the umbrella stand, and marching around the room with it over my shoulder. I had a tacky streak in me, that was for sure. Someday it might control me. It would begin innocently enough, with the monkey; but from then on anything could happen. I might take to ankle bracelets, Franco-American spaghetti, Elvis Presley, rhinestones, see-through blouses. At that point, the bottom of the barrel, I might find myself compelled to purchase great quantities of wax fruit. That would be my final downfall.

"Well, I guess I should be going," I finally said.

"No, no, no! You must stay!" she pleaded, spinning around to face me at last and sitting down in her chair. "Tell me about your day. I'm so inconsiderate, babbling on about these silly birds when you've had this grand adventure."

"Well, there's not much to tell, really," I said. "It went quite well, I guess. I think I like it there." I almost mentioned Oscar Benson to her but knew instantly that would be ridiculous of me. I had been such an idiot to get carried away like that about him on the walk home. How embarrassing. I would see him the next day and just die, remembering.

"I'm so glad that you like it, Annie. Honest to God, I had this terrible fear all day long that you wouldn't like it and you'd quit and go home and I'd be here all by my lonesome again."

"Oh, you don't have to worry about that," I said. "Even if I absolutely hated it, I'd stay. I don't really care much about the job at all, about whether I like it or not. I came here to learn about things, you know?" Good grief, what was I saying? I wasn't going to tell this oddball my whole life's story, was I? "What I mean is, city life is so much more interesting than living where I live, and I couldn't wait to get out on my own. Mother, of course, hated the idea of my moving in town for the summer, but thank heavens I have this aunt, Aunt Chloe, and she's very progressive. I mean, at my age she was traveling all over Europe. And she just insisted that I move to Boston for the summer if I possibly could. Says it'll be very broadening." Actually, I felt quite sophisticated, by association at least. Not everyone had an aunt as cosmopolitan as mine. Georgia, however, didn't seem at all impressed.

"That's a riot of a name, Chloe." I could have hit her.

"I suppose it is," I said archly. "I never gave it much thought. I must be accustomed to it, I guess. It's a very old name, you know." In fact, I had always loved the name Chloe. It was a perfectly straightforward name, though of course there had been that unfortunate song. It certainly was more substantial than Georgia. "And you," I countered, looking directly into her dull grey eyes, "are you from the deep South or something?"

"No. Didn't I tell you? Rhode Island. Poor little Rhode Island."

"Oh, yes," I said, staring at the floor.

"Tell me, what do you think of our landlord, Mr. Malcolm Balch?" she said, sliding one uneaten bread crust off the windowsill and popping it into her mouth.

"Malcolm?" I said. "Why, I love his eyebrows, I guess."

"Me too. Aren't they wild? The rest of his face is so sweet and so placid, like some lovely bucolic meadow with a lazy little hill where his nose is, and then those blackbird brows fly over it, dipping and bobbing along." She made an attempt at moving her brows the way Malcolm moved his, but ended up looking more like Groucho Marx. I laughed. "Am I doing it?" she said.

"More or less," I said. "I don't know, I kind of wonder about him, don't you?"

"Ha! Who wouldn't? Yeah, he's queer all right, if you know what I mean."

"I'm afraid I do," I said.

"Queer as a three-dollar bill," she said. "Yeah, I'm sure he is. Must be. Honest to God, his apartment looks as if it was furnished by a woman. Have you seen it yet?"

"Just a little of it through the door."

"I've been inside," she said. "Twice. And in the hallway that goes from the living room back to the kitchen, he has all these huge photographs hung up of this young, kind of too-pretty guy in a tight suit and ice skates. A professional. And he's doing all these poses—you know, one with his leg lifted way up in the air behind him like he's God's gift or something."

"Really?" I tried to sound restrained. I didn't want her thinking I had prurient interests, even if I did.

"Honest to God," she said for the one hundredth time—my least favorite expression in the whole wide world. "And his bathroom is all done in pink, with sea shells and a china bowl filled with sponges and one filled with fancy wrapped soaps, and the place smells like an expensive whore's underpants."

I gasped. What a vulgar thing to say! And it had rolled right off her tongue. I would ignore it; I wouldn't want her to carry what might have been just one isolated lapse in decorum any farther. It was pretty clear to me now that she *wasn't* a religious fanatic.

"That is rather suspicious, isn't it?" I said. "Who do you think the ice skater is?"

"His boyfriend, I presume," she said, shaking the paper bag, which now held only crumbs, onto the windowsill.

"That's really strange, isn't it?"

"I guess they just love one another," she said, with a shrug.

"*Love* one another? Do they do that?"

"Hmm. I'm not sure all do, but some do. I suppose love is love. If you and I could love a man, why couldn't a man love a man? That's the way I see it."

"Well, it's not exactly normal, is it?" I said.

"I don't know why not," she said.

"Well, it's hardly natural, is it?"

"What else could it be, dear heart," she said, leaning forward in her chair, her hands clasped between her spread knees, looking at me thoughtfully. "I mean, whatever they do, they do it with the same basic parts everyone else has, at least to my knowledge, so it has to be natural, strictly speaking. You know, like some people couldn't go a day without anchovies, even though I could."

"I just can't imagine it," I said.

"You just can't imagine them *doing* it? Is that what you mean? Well, who *can* you imagine doing it? Anybody? Think about that. I have. I've tried to imagine all sorts of people doing it, and every single time, no matter how wonderful the people are that I sort of put to the test this way, the picture I see in my mind's eye is always just a little bit funny. Everybody but me, that is, and certain gorgeous hunks who shall remain unidentified, for tax purposes. . . ." She burst out laughing, rocking back and forth in the chair. "When it's you doing it, everything changes," she finally continued. "I can picture fairies doing it just as well as I can picture anybody else doing it—which is to say, not very well."

"I can't," I murmured, feeling uncomfortable. Things had become much too graphic. Also, I was beginning to wonder about Georgia. Was she a fruit too?

"Didn't you ever have a friend when you were young, a girl-friend, and you loved her more than anyone else in the world and you wanted to hug her and hold hands with her and even kiss her?"

"Of course not," I said, but that was a lie. I *had* had a friend just like that, Mary Armitage. I thought she was the prettiest, funniest girl on the the face of the earth and I wanted to be with her forever. She had cornflower-blue eyes and dimples. She wore a hand-knitted blue angora sweater one winter, and every time I saw her in it, I wanted to rush up and hug her to death. I adored her. In the fifth grade she fell in love with Dick Burlingame and I wanted to kill her. I wanted to kill myself. I cried every night for weeks. I even called out her name in the darkness and begged her to come back to me. That summer I was alone, friendless and miserable. But in the fall I met Teddy Jenks, and even though he was Catholic, Mother said that it was all right for him to be my boyfriend as long as I remembered that Episcopalians and Roman Catholics could never marry. I said I understood completely. Later, Mother told me she would never have given her consent if she hadn't been so desperate. Although we went through junior high and high school together, Mary and I never spoke again. Every time we passed in the halls or ran into one another at a football game, we each would look away, as if we had never known one another at all. "I guess all kids have an attachment like that," I said, before I realized that I was contradicting myself.

"I know I did," Georgia said. "Her name was Justine Murphy. Justine Magdalene Murphy. But when I met her—we were really young and she had just arrived at the home—I thought her name was Just Deen. So I called her Deenie. Anyway, she would come up to my room and we'd stay up half the night together with a flashlight under the covers and we'd read to one another and tell stories and talk about what we were going to do when we grew up. Deenie was going to be a nun and go to Africa and save all the poor heathen children. I was going to go with her as her assistant and I would write a book about all her adventures in the jungle and so on, things like *Sister Justine and the Man-Eating Tigers of the Amazon,* about how she said the rosary for them in an outdoor church she built in the jungle and they came there while she was praying and they all sat around in a circle and let her walk among them without biting her and all the natives thought she was a saint.

"Then sometimes we would play Love Story and we made up all these settings like the Sahara Desert or a castle in Merrie Olde England—that's what Deenie called it. One time I'd be the prince and she would be the princess and the next time we'd switch. We'd lie together on my bed and put our arms around one another and sometimes kiss on the mouth, but it was pretend. And when I was the princess and Deenie was the prince, she would kiss me and then use this really funny low voice and say, 'You are the most bee-oo-tee-ful creature in the world. I shall take you away to my kingdom and make you mistress of *all* you survey.' That was Deenie's favorite expression, '*all* you survey.' " She paused and looked off into space, shaking her head.

"And that's where you lived when you were small, the home? Justine too?"

"Saint Theresa's Catholic Home. The convent was right next door. Some of the nuns took care of us. I thought I told you."

"I guess you did," I said. "I guess I imagined an awful dungeon sort of place, with everyone sleeping together in one room, and nothing like really close friends."

"It was beautiful there," she said. "All orchards out in back, and the convent surrounded by gardens. . . ."

"It sounds lovely." Georgia was looking at me with the most peculiar smile on her face, with a redness suddenly appearing around her eyes as if she were about to cry.

"Oh, Annie, I feel like I've known you forever. Forever! Do you feel it too?" I was stunned and embarrassed, but I managed what I hoped was an enthusiastic smile.

"I'm so glad we met, Georgia," I replied in a formal tone. She turned her face away from me and stared at her hands, obviously disappointed. I couldn't help it. I wasn't comfortable with her. She was absolutely unlike anyone else I had ever met.

"Looks like your pigeons have flown away," I said, changing the subject.

"They'll be back tomorrow," she said, pulling the drapes down from over the rod, brushing off the sill and lowering the window halfway. "You like them, then?"

"Very much. And it's very kind of you to feed them."

"And you're not afraid I'll catch some fatal disease from them? I bet you are. I bet you were thinking that, back there when I asked you to come closer to see Eve. I saw it on your face, you know. You were thinking that any day now I'd come down with some awful fever."

"To be honest, I was. Perhaps you should—"

"I knew it! And I must tell you, Annie, dear heart, sweet innocent, that I love them with all my heart, and love is always a little dangerous. Always. I read that once and it's true. You have to weigh the benefits against the risk. Just think, I have heard the sound of their wings. I have seen the color of their eyes. Do you know that when they walk they squeak? It's something about their feathers sliding on one another. Who else would know that?" She sat down on the rocker once more and rested her head against the leaves and acorns carved on its back. The dark finish on the wood where her head lay had worn thin, and the grain and color of the oak beneath it glowed in an irregular circle, a halo. Something about her voice had changed, or maybe it was just the oppressive humidity of the evening; I was mesmerized by her. "I have even dreamed of them," she said, mysteriously. I was hooked.

"You have?" I said.

"You want to hear it? You won't think I'm crazy?"

"Of course not," I lied. She cleared her throat and swallowed hard, then grinned and shrugged her shoulders.

"Okay, here goes," she said, fixing her gaze at a spot near the ceiling. "I'm gonna tell you this like you're my psychiatrist. He makes me start at the beginning and tell every single detail, just like I'm narrating a story or something." She cleared her throat again, and when she started talking, it was in a low, calm voice, as if she were reading from a script.

"It began with an evening sky of flat dull grey. No color of any kind. It was still as the air is still before a summer storm. You could almost smell it. Then, from out of nowhere, the sun appeared. The horizon was flat and black, unmarked by treetops or hills, just a band of black and the sun above it, deep red like hot coals. But it didn't glow at all and was as one-dimensional as a disk. It didn't alter the color of the grey sky around it. I'll tell you what it was the color of—the blood spot in the yolk of an egg. But somehow sweeter. How can I tell you what I mean? It was so red and sweet that when you looked at it, saliva would pool in your mouth. You'd want to taste it. Can you see it?"

"Yes. I think so."

"Good." She stood up and walked to the window and peered through its upper panes. "Then suddenly it wasn't the sun at all, but a thin lid closed over it, a milky, grey lid, and the red color behind it turned the shade of a bruise. And I knew right then that it was the eye of an enormous grey dove. Then the eye opened and began to glow and the grey sky became streaked with bands of coral and mauve like the oily sheen on the head of a dove. I walked toward it. I was borne on these beams of soft color closer and closer to the sun. I could see myself getting smaller and smaller. But then I took on the color of the light—coral and mauve and pink and maroon and rust and red—and then hotter and hotter and closer and closer until I glided right into that eye, and just when I thought I would burst into flames, I felt my body become all smooth and wet and I knew that I was gold and was melting!" She stood before me, her hands at her chest, her fingers spread wide, her wide mouth forming the silent letter "O."

"And I melted. I was part of the sky and part of the dove and a part of all this color all around me and, honest to God, Annie, it felt so good. Peace at last. And when I woke up, it was as if I had experienced God. I felt all new."

She smiled down at me with that sweet, wise smile of hers. I couldn't speak. I couldn't move. I searched her face for something, not sure what.

"You think I'm crazy, don't you?" she whispered, settling down beside me on the bed. Yes, I did. But I was willing to believe that she wasn't, that she was unique and wonderful and the most remarkable person I had ever met.

"No, I don't," I said. "You just have an extraordinary way of expressing yourself." She couldn't be crazy. It sounded like a dream about death to me; but I had had those too, or almost— dreams in which I was about to be killed by some vague yet malevolent creature, dreams of falling from windows.

"I'm glad you don't," she said, her thin, damp hand on mine. "Everyone thinks I'm as nutty as a fruitcake. Ida says I shouldn't have these dreams. She says I wouldn't if I gave myself to Christ to be healed." She withdrew her hand and began fingering the scars on her wrists. I didn't have the courage to ask her about them yet.

"Ida?"

"Ida Printaine. She's this friend of mine who lives up in Louisburg Square."

"Oh, yes," I said.

"She looks after me, I guess you could say. There's something about her. Once she starts on something, she never gives up. She buys me clothes that I never wear. She has awful taste, but she keeps buying them for me anyway. She calls me all the time, like I'm a kid or something. She should be calling me any minute to see if I want to have dinner with her tonight or breakfast with her tomorrow. She's been doing this for years."

"What a pain," I said.

"Yeah. She means well, I guess. I don't know, I was thinking that maybe you and I could have dinner tonight together. I mean, unless you have other plans. If you do, I'll understand completely, I—"

"No, I'd love to," I said. "I was hoping you'd know a place nearby."

"We could go to the Riverview," she said. "Everyone does. It's not right by the river or anything, but the food is good and it's cheap."

"I think I saw it the other day," I said. "Is it on Charles Street?" She nodded. "I'll need to change first. I'm all sticky."

"Me too," she said, smoothing the front of her wrinkled dress. "And Annie . . . ?" She looked at me expectantly, her mouth compressed into a thin line which turned up like a Kewpie doll's at either end. "Did you get my poem?"

"Yes, I loved it. It was funny. I . . ."

"No, you don't have to say anything. I'm a poet. It's something that I have to do, so I don't need compliments on it. But, you know, I got so involved in composing the poem that I forgot why I wrote you a note in the first place. I wanted to say that I didn't mean to skip out on you yesterday. When I got to my room I remembered that Ida had called sometime earlier, before I got home, and when I went down to call her back she had already stopped by for me, so I just went with her. I hope you weren't mad."

"No, of course not," I said. "I figured something you hadn't counted on had come up."

"Then when I got back your room was so quiet and I didn't want to disturb you."

"I fell asleep."

"I tried to make the poem funny, but it was true, too. That's what I thought of when I first saw you—organdy and lace." For a second I thought she was going to hug me again, and I stepped back toward the door.

"That's really sweet of you," I said.

"I'll knock for you when I'm done," she said, as I opened her door and walked out into the hallway toward my room.

For the next half-hour as I changed my clothes and got ready for dinner, all I thought about was Georgia—her eyes, her voice, her mannerisms, the things she said, her scars. I was intrigued, but not without misgivings.

As a matter of fact, as I sat on my bed ready to go, waiting for her knock, it shamed me to admit to myself that I had quite a few misgivings about going out with her in public. I winced just thinking about it. How would she look and behave? I imagined her traipsing into the Riverview, cutting a wide swath, throwing herself into a chair and bellowing her order to some poor waitress, who would then rush to our table only to trip over Georgia's enormous feet, which she had inconsiderately left sticking out into the aisle. I hated scenes.

Then again, I told myself, this was the city of Boston, not the town of Beverly. In the city everyone fit in, regardless of individual oddities. What was I so concerned about? Why, Aunt Chloe had told me about being in New York once, shopping on Fifth Avenue, and coming across a drunk sprawled across the sidewalk, sleeping it off, while elegant ladies stepped over him in their I. Miller shoes and Bonwit Teller dresses and simply went about their business without so much as a second glance or a sniff of disdain. Not that Georgia was anything like a derelict. Probably no one would even notice her.

I was in the midst of castigating myself for being so shallow and stupid when Georgia charged through my door without bothering to knock. I should have known.

"I'm ready—you?" she said as the door hit the wall behind it, bounced back, and hit her in the shoulder. "How do I look?" she preened, smiling at me wetly, tucking one last bobby pin into the perky bunch of poppies she wore in her hair. She was a colorful sight, all right—lime green toreador pants and a yellow blouse. "You don't think these look silly?" she asked, primping in my hand mirror.

"Of course not. Their centers match your outfit perfectly." I couldn't keep from smiling at her. I thought of a picture of myself at about five in the backyard under the grape arbor. I wore organdy curtains for a ball gown, and over it, trailing romantically behind me in the grass, a magnificent cape of maroon velveteen with gold fringe that had once hung in a doorway at Christ Episcopal Church. I beamed into the camera as only those who are well aware of their haunting beauty have the self-possession to do.

"I had them in this little vase in my room," she said, continuing to adjust the poppies, "but I just *had* to wear flowers tonight, so I just whipped them out, yanked those little tags off them, twisted their stems together, and *voilà,* as my darling Claude would say."

Voilà? This Claude fellow sounded more interesting every time I heard about him. *Très intéressant,* if I did say so myself.

FIVE

"Hey, beautiful blondie, whachoogonnaeat?" a chubby young man behind the glass-fronted counter shouted in my direction. I was now, I suddenly realized, at the head of the long line at the Riverview Cafeteria. I had been so engrossed in people watching that I had not noticed myself inching forward.

"Me? Uh—excuse me?" I stammered, not yet absolutely sure that he was speaking to me, not at all sure of *what* he said, given the noise of the prospective diners around me. He placed his hands on his hips, tilted his head, and flashed a smile at me: two rows of large, vanilla-colored teeth; two rows of waxy, liver-colored gums; a glint of gold from a molar. Clearly, he fancied himself a lady killer.

"Your pleasure, miss? What may I serve you tonight?" he said indulgently, with some kind of accent, probably Greek. He squinted at me, ran his tongue over his lower lip, and looked me over as I had never been looked over before. I had heard that foreign men could be like this.

"A BLT and tea, please," I said, coolly. I lifted my chin haughtily. I would put a stop to this. Incorrigible, he winked at me, never took his eyes from me, and yelled at the older, balding man behind him who was making sandwiches to order.

"Hey, Nick, you got a BLT and tea?"

"Sure, sure. One BLT and tea coming up. Whachoogonnado, missy, blow us all up? Ka-boom!" He burst into insane laughter while reaching for a knife and a fat tomato. Everyone within earshot laughed. It took me a second to get the joke, then I laughed, too. It was apparently the thing to do here at the Riverview, where everyone seemed to know everyone else and where something as offhand as ordering food could be a hilarious group activity. A place with an atmosphere like this would absolutely kill Mother. I stepped aside and let Georgia order.

"How ya doin', kid? Hot enough for ya?" my admirer behind the counter asked Georgia, hardly taking his eyes off me.

"Hi, Guggie. This place is like an oven, as usual." She fanned herself with one hand and blew air toward her forehead, where it lifted a damp lock of her hair. She then ordered—inappropriately enough, I thought—a bowl of hot soup and something called a cold plate. So far, no one seemed to take undue notice of the poppies in her hair.

"Yeah, it's always hot in here, ain't it? I stink." Guggie pointed his oily nose in the direction of his armpit, where a huge halfmoon of perspiration gave a translucent greyness to his white, recently food-soiled shirt. "Whew," he whistled with a grimace, ladling soup into a heavy bowl. "Gonna rain tomorrow, though," he said, placing the bowl of soup on Georgia's tray, then waving his arms as if they were wings in an attempt to dry off. He winked at me again. Mother's heart would have stopped right here. I, however, was spellbound. I liked the way Guggie looked at me, as if I were a morsel of baklava dripping with honey. I loved the way he smelled his own armpits. In my family, armpits were referred to in word and gesture about as regularly as syphilis. Yes, he was Greek. For an instant I imagined him leaning against a Doric column, a wreath of leaves twining through his black ringlets.

"It's going to rain tomorrow, is it?" I said, getting myself under control but wanting to keep him talking.

"Yeah," he said, squinting at me once more, turning the word

over in his mouth, manipulating it with his tongue so that it slithered out between his lips like a sigh. I looked away.

"Gonna rain tamarra? Don' tell me." The moaning voice came
from a frail, toothless man who was spooning something with
macaroni and tomato sauce into a deep container in the steam
table. "You kiddin' me, Guggie? You serioos? Naw, please don'
rain on my ball game. Not again." He crossed himself and gestured
emotionally toward heaven.

"I dunno, old man, you some kinda jinx," Guggie said. "Every
time you gonna go, it rains. Or they lose. Whachoogonnado, eh?"

"You got no right to talk, Guggie," Nick, the sandwich maker,
interjected. "Every day a you life a jinx to me." He wound up,
kaiser roll in hand, and pitched toward the back of Guggie's head.
The crowd went wild. Guggie took the blow with a slow smile.

"Low and outside," he drawled. "Ball four. You're through, old
man. I'm callin' up the relief pitcher. Wash up the grill, will ya?"

"That was over the plate," Nick cried, egged on by his toothless
cohort, who was doubled over laughing, his mouth the yawning
red maw of a fledgling bird.

"Hey! Go to work, you guys!" Guggie warned good-naturedly,
handing Georgia and me our filled trays and ringing up our orders.

"Aren't they a riot?" Georgia said as we made our way to a table
she had reserved for us earlier by tipping two chairs up against it.

"Honest to God," I said for the first time in my life, "this is
the most wonderful place I've ever been in." I smoothed my palm
along the pink Formica tabletop. The walls of the Riverview were
painted pea green. The chairs we sat on were of blond wood with
red Leatherette seats. The floor was brown asphalt tile. So this is
what a city restaurant is really like, I thought. Not the kind of
place one might visit before the theater or after a long day of
shopping, the Riverview was designed for city dwellers to take
their meals in while mingling with neighbors. A functional place.
Plain food. If you lived in a nearby apartment or room and didn't
want to cook, or couldn't, you went down to the Riverview for a
little nourishment. Simple as that.

"It's not fancy, but I love it here," Georgia said. "They're all
Greek, you know."

"I wondered," I said.

"Everyone comes here—just everyone." Georgia took a forkful of potato salad from her cold plate and looked around. She pointed out a table of student nurses from nearby Massachusetts General Hospital. Their dormitory was an old brownstone on Charles Street. The girls, about my age, were not dressed in white but decked out in black-and-white checked dresses with starched white collars and cuffs, black stockings, and black shoes. They looked more like prison matrons than nurses.

At another table sat an animated group Georgia said were students in "drah-mah" at nearby Emerson College, in town for summer classes or jobs. She pointed out a particularly short, blond fellow named Freddie and said that he planned to become a comedian someday and was "a riot." He looked kind of like a comedian to me—something about his smile, as if his cheeks were made of rubber. His best friend, Ron, was beside him. Ron planned to become a serious actor. He and Freddie had plans to go to New York after graduation and become big stars. How exciting! And someday I'd see them on *Ed Sullivan* or *Studio One* and I'd tell my children that I met them here at the Riverview, a thousand years ago.

"I hope they make it," I said, smiling at Georgia. How incredible to be a part of all this, to be so close to fame and fortune, to sense the hope—yes, that was it: the city, the Hill, the Riverview itself were a throbbing cauldron of hope! And now I was one of them, these young hopefuls. What would become of me? Wouldn't it be something if I too found fame and fortune, and someday they would see my picture and say, "Oh, yes, she was one of the crowd at the Riverview in the fifties," or "Ann Merrill? Sure, I remember her. How could you forget a face like that?"

Then Georgia pointed out a rather mousy-looking elderly couple, whom I imagined living in some dingy apartment somewhere, the kind of place that always smells of cabbage or fish. Instead, they were none other than a well-known artist and his wife, who lived on Pinckney Street in a lovely old house, the third storey of which they had converted to a studio, with huge slanting windows to let in the northern light. And he looked so ordinary. Fascinating.

I couldn't help noticing that although Georgia seemed to know a great deal about many of the patrons of the cafeteria, no one except Guggie had spoken to her; no one smiled or nodded in her direction. And as she continued glancing about the room, pointing out this and that person to me, it seemed that anyone who caught her looking at them immediately looked away. Perhaps it was my imagination.

It wasn't. At that moment one of the student nurses gestured in our direction for the benefit of the friend beside her with her back to us, and in a second or two that girl turned in her chair and stared, looking Georgia and me up and down, a cruel smile on her lips; then she turned abruptly away. She and her friends lowered their heads and giggled. I didn't take my eyes from them. Mother had always said that only hard, unintelligent, cheap girls became nurses. I now believed her. Their manners were disgusting; their capacity for human compassion, negligible.

Just then the front door to the Riverview opened, and in walked a thin, undistinguished sort of man with a slight limp. He appeared to be in his early thirties—maybe a bank clerk, by the look of his pinched face and pasty complexion. I could see him locked up in a vault somewhere poring over books and reconciling his heart out for the next forty years. He was, however, expensively dressed— in grey, which surprised me, as I always expected lower-echelon workers to be dressed in brown, poorly tailored brown at that. He carried a handsome briefcase engraved in gold with his initials, STC. As he inched closer through the crowd, he held his head extremely high and scanned those around him through half-lowered lids. One corner of his mouth was clamped between his teeth. He was annoyed—perhaps with the crowd; perhaps he had hoped for a quick meal, then home to his account books and stamp collection.

He was the sort who would eat sensibly, I thought. A little meat, no potatoes, thank you, a slotted spoon full of grey-green string beans, whole-wheat bread with a little butter, a glass of milk, and stewed prunes. Before bed he would let out all the stoppers, have a half glass of beer and three Ritz crackers smeared with Kraft Pineapple Neufchatel Cheese. He would always save the tumbler.

As he approached our table, trying to find a space for himself in the food line, he looked at me very briefly, and I saw that his eyes were as densely black and gleaming as two camera lenses. So cold. I had heard the expression "He undressed her with his eyes." He had just done that to me, and as he turned away, a faint smile crossed his lips—a horribly attractive smile. Georgia finally saw him and lunged across the table, grasping my hand painfully in hers.

"You will never, *never,* not in a million years guess who that is," she whispered.

"Who?"

"Stanley Crosshill!"

"You're kidding!"

"I swear to God," she said, holding up her hand.

"The famous Stanley Crosshill? The political cartoonist? You're kidding!" He had been in the papers ever since I could remember. My father thought he was one of the funniest and most perceptive men alive. I hadn't even known he lived in Boston; I would have thought New York or Los Angeles. I would have thought he was much older.

"It's him," Georgia said gravely. "And, Annie, you had better watch out. You better, really."

"For what?"

"He adores blondes and redheads. He kind of collects them. Girls with really innocent looks are his preference. Like you. And when he sees you and decides he wants you, he tells someone to tell you. In fact, it's usually this older friend of his. Then he sends his car for you and you have dinner with him at Charles Court. It's down by the river. Very ritzy—all sorts of famous people live there—you know, the kind who have a place in the country and a place at Palm Beach and an apartment in town. Well, if he likes you he keeps you."

"How terribly sweet of him," I said. "Suppose you don't want to keep *him?*" Georgia gave me a look, an exasperated look, as if I had said something really stupid.

"Ann-ie," she groaned. "I mean he *keeps* you. You know—you become a kept woman."

"Oh!" I said, feeling terribly embarrassed at my own naiveté. "Oh, yes, of course! I didn't think you meant that kind of 'kept.' He does have a rather devilish smile. My God, if Mother could see me now!" I said, realizing that this was no lighthearted matter. "What if you don't want to be kept?"

"You know, I'm not sure you have that much to say about it. I mean, he gives you your own room there and pays all your expenses and buys all your clothes, and I guess you sort of belong to him, at least for a while."

"You're kidding," I said, not sure that this was at all plausible but afraid to sound like I was still wet behind the ears. Funny; he didn't seem to be the type, except for the eyes and the smile. There was something tired-looking about Stanley Crosshill, a used-up quality that I was sure nothing could ever erase. I remembered an old horsehair love seat my grandmother once had. Long after it had been reupholstered in velvet, it still smelled old and musty and still made you itch after you had sat on it for a while. Old horsehair was in its blood.

"Why would he have to keep anyone?" I asked Georgia. "Why wouldn't he just get a girlfriend and get married like anyone else?" He wasn't ugly. He was famous. He no doubt had lots of money.

"He's probably kind of strange where women are concerned," she said provocatively. "Some men are, you know. They can be perfectly logical human beings in every other way, but when it comes to women and sex . . ." I cringed that she had said this word so loudly in public; I was sure everyone had heard her. "Well," she continued, "they have strange appetites." I knew it; I had seen it in his eyes. "And they have to pay for it—at least they think they do." Georgia salted and peppered her soup. "So I'm telling you, you better watch out. You're his type. I know he saw you. He's looking at you right now. He's sitting behind us, you know."

As if by reflex I turned around and looked at him. He wasn't looking at me at all but at the black-stockinged legs of a student nurse who had come up to get in line for something else to eat. I was astonished to feel an intense pang of jealousy, as if I wanted those cold beady eyes devouring only me.

Georgia had slumped way down in her chair. "He's looking again," she hissed, lowering herself even farther.

"Don't be an idiot, Georgia. He's not going to leap over here and grab me." I took a bite of my BLT. "It's just that I'm new here. He's looking at me because I'm a new face, that's all." Appeased, she sat upright once more and began slurping her soup. No one seemed to hear her. I didn't really care. Although I continued to eat, my mind and body were occupied elsewhere. Stanley Crosshill's eyes criss-crossed my back, slithered about the nape of my neck, and glided down the lateral surface of my bare arms. Simultaneously, I felt them like cool hands measuring my waist and the heft of my calves, then like icy pointed tongues tickling my ankles. It was thrilling in a frightening sort of way—the pressure of his eyeballs sliding over my body like steel ball bearings on a slick floor.

"Strange appetites," Georgia had said. What did that mean? It wasn't that I was totally unschooled. I had read all of Frank Yerby. I had read *Forever Amber*. I had read a whole host of such books, thanks to my friendship with Sybil West, whose mother belonged to the Book-of-the-Month Club. For more literary fare, I had the library of Peter and Monique Perkins, for whom I baby-sat. My favorites there were *Anthony Adverse* and *Green Mansions*.

In one book, quite frank in its handling of sexual matters, there had been a male character who loved to have women dress up in costumes for nightly forays in the bedroom. If memory served me, by day he carried on a dignified vocation as the headmaster of a fancy boy's school, some place like Andover or Choate, except in England. One night he'd be in the mood for something pastoral. He'd want a saucy milkmaid in a dirndl over petticoats and starched pantaloons; he'd want her in fat blond braids beneath a ruffled cap and an off-the-shoulder peasant blouse. The next night, in a classic mood, he would call for his goddess and she'd appear from behind a marble column, her body wound round with yards and yards of white crêpe, her arms wrapped in snake bracelets, her feet encased in leather sandals, the kind with long thongs that circle the calves and fasten beneath the knee and drive men out of their minds.

The stubbing of Georgia's chair on the floor tile brought me out of my reverie. She went to the counter for iced tea. I felt awkward when she was gone, not only sure, now, that Stanley Crosshill was having a visual field day with me but painfully aware that I was being stared at by the nurses as well. Boldly, I stared back with what I hoped was a look of pure hatred. It worked. In a moment their smirks vanished and they gathered themselves together and left.

Being kept—what an intriguing possibility! Not that I would ever do it, of course. I mean, I didn't *think* I would, unless there was some kind of future in it. Maybe that was an angle that deserved consideration.

Suppose Stanley Crosshill was my destiny and he had been looking for me all his life. Within a matter of hours I would be invited to dinner at Charles Court. I would find him strange and somehow haunting and sensitive behind those steely eyes. I would find him lonely, brooding, unfulfilled though famous, and oddly idealistic, even innocent. I would put up no resistance. I would simply smile, enigmatically. I would move in. And from the first night it would be devastatingly clear that Ann Merrill would be kept by no man. Quite the contrary: she would keep *him* instead.

I had certain qualities—call it breeding, call it substance—certain fascinating qualities other women just didn't have. I knew how to please a man. All through history there had been women like me—the Helens, the Cleopatras, the Marilyns—who had the power to drive men wild with desire and love. Some had been courtesans, some queens. I was more the queen type myself, at least to the outside world. In private, I would be twenty-four-carat courtesan. Just the tiniest, teensiest bit vulgar. I would say dirty words at just the right moment with perfectly enunciated diction. I would drive him wild. I would have him in the palm of my hand, so to speak.

He would be my slave. He would do anything to please me. There would be trips to the Riviera and sandwiches at the Ritz. I would travel west whenever I wished. I might even sail down the west coast of South America and see the Andes falling into the sea, just like an old friend of Aunt Chloe's did. I had always known that something like this would happen to me. I had, however, planned on being just a bit older. No matter; I was ready for it. In a minute I would turn in my chair and face him. I allowed all the air to expire from my lungs in preparation for this moment.

"And so," Georgia said, interrupting me with the slam of her iced-tea glass on the tabletop, "he just keeps you until he tires of you and moves on to somebody else." She removed the rind from a thick slice of baloney on her cold plate, nibbled the meat off it, and placed it in a broken circle on her still unopened napkin.

"I guess he just hasn't found the right one," I mused. "I hope he never does—it would serve him right."

"I wonder what he's looking for," she said.

"Perfection, probably."

"Well, that leaves me out," she said, giggling.

"Me too," I said with a magnanimous shrug. If that was what he was looking for, he had found it—in spades. The next time Georgia and I came here, I would wear my lavender dress with my merry widow push-up bra underneath and my hair in a high French twist, which I knew made me a dead ringer for Grace Kelly.

"Would you do something like that if he asked you?" Georgia said.

"Georgia! How could you ask that? What do you think I am?"

"Shhh! Take it easy, will you? I'm sorry. I didn't mean anything. Just something about your mood ever since he walked in. . . ."

"Don't be an idiot, Georgia. Would *you*? Live like a pet? Not if he was the last man on earth."

"Yeah, me too, I guess," she said, folding a paper-thin slice of tomato around a black olive and tucking this neat package daintily into her mouth. She chewed. "He must think he's hot stuff."

"I'm sure he does. God's gift to women. . . . I don't understand men at all. They think they're so indispensable."

"He has a sports car. A Mercedes. Gunmetal grey."

"Oh, I love those!" I said.

"Yeah?"

"When I get rich someday, I'm going to buy one," I said. I poured the last drops of tea from the green pot into my cup.

"He has a penthouse," she said.

"A penthouse?"

"Honest to God, that's what they say." She watched me for a moment without saying anything more, then began to laugh. "Oh, Annie, I can just see it—you sweeping out the front door, Malcolm fainting dead away inside." I was not amused. But her reaction served, as far as I was concerned, both to change the subject and to show off to adorable advantage the gooey globs of potato salad festooned between her front teeth. I nearly gagged and put down the final small crust of my sandwich. She immediately snapped it off my plate and wrapped it in her napkin along with the remainder of her Parker House roll and the baloney rind. For the birds, I deduced. She tucked the little bundle into her purse. "You want to take a walk by the river when we're done?" she said, offering me one of her French cigarettes.

"Let's save it for when we get down there," I said, not wanting to inflict the smell of burning fur on the diners who lingered over their meals.

When we finally got up to leave, I nonchalantly whirled in the direction of Stanley Crosshill. He looked up. I glared at him almost defiantly. He gazed down at his plate and fidgeted with his fork for an instant before I turned and followed Georgia out of the Riverview and onto Charles Street.

Evening. This was what the French called "l'heure bleue." The air was cool and soft. Charles Street was quiet. As we stood outside the Riverview for a few moments as if to reorient ourselves, I felt happier than I had ever felt and somehow freer, as if I was beginning to sense my own true identity for the first time.

In one day I had received reinforcement of my desirability as a woman. Dear Oscar, dear Guggie, even dear Stanley (and God only knew how many others) had given me their stamp of approval. Until today I had been a sleeping beauty waiting for a prince to come along and breathe life into me. But look what had happened—a whole squadron of princes. My heart pumped pure adrenaline.

Unmindful of public opinion for the first time in memory, I raised my arms and pirouetted down the sidewalk, a stunned but slaphappy Georgia giggling wildly at my heels, adding a certain element of unbridled hysteria to our little procession. I didn't care.

SIX

A church bell tolled the half-hour as Georgia and I strolled down Charles Street, turned into Pinckney Street, and headed toward the river and the park that ran along its banks called the Esplanade. Between the Esplanade and the bottom of Pinckney Street we stood at the curb on Storrow Drive and waited for an opening in the steady stream of traffic, to cross.

Looking at Georgia, I was amazed to see that she apparently considered this a rather exciting small adventure. Her hand was on my arm, tentatively, as if we were about to begin a race. She looked this way and that at the cars speeding past, eyes intent, lips drawn back in a tense smile. Any second now she would spring forward, giving me no warning. I prepared to bolt, stepping forward on my right foot. Suddenly she jerked my forearm, shouted, "Go! Go!," and grabbed my hand and dragged me after her across the highway. The interruption in the flow of traffic through which we threaded ourselves was barely adequate, and at the other side my heart pounded, not just from running but from this unnecessary brush with danger. Georgia, however, was elated and laughing. She galloped ahead of me across the Esplanade toward the river, finally throwing herself down on a low bank beside the water.

"Is this okay? Right here?" she yelled, as I slowly headed in her direction. The Esplanade was a favorite meeting place for people living in the vicinity, and they were out in full force to-night—couples strolling hand in hand, groups of friends sprawled on the grass, talking.

Reaching Georgia, I sat down and dangled my legs over the river bank as she was doing. She took out her cigarettes again, and we just sat quietly for a while, smoking and taking in the scene around us.

Nearby stood the music shell where, in good weather, the Boston Pops Orchestra played under the direction of Arthur Fiedler. On the river, a number of small sailboats skimmed along.

"Pretty, isn't it?" Georgia said, looking up at the sky. The swish of traffic had become faint background noise, barely noticeable. Instead, there was the staccato lap of water at our feet.

Across the river stood the almost futuristic buildings of MIT. The one with the dome on it interested me particularly. I began to think of Oscar. I imagined the dome was some kind of observatory and that he was somewhere beneath it, slide rule in hand, preparing for nightfall, when the sky would blacken and relinquish its secret cache of stars. He would then do whatever it was that scientists did in the dark, calculating or calibrating. There was something thrilling to me about a person who loved science.

Could it be that Oscar and I, not Stanley Crosshill at all, were meant for each other? I believed that people who were meant for one another could communicate telepathically. I concentrated on trying to remember Oscar's face, not altogether successfully, and sent him a message acorss the river, beaming it in to the domed centerpiece of the MIT campus.

"Think of *me*, Oscar," I willed silently. "Not Andromeda, not Cassiopeia, but *me*, Ann." I closed my eyes. "Come to me, Oscar, with your wise, mathematical mind. Come to me, Oscar, come . . ."

"What?" Georgia was staring at me.

"What?" I said.

"I thought you said something," she said.

"You're hearing things," I said.

"I know when I'm hearing things, Annie," she said, laughing. "You said something. I heard you."

"I guess I was just thinking out loud," I said. "I met this guy today at work. I guess I was thinking about him."

"Oh, I get it," she said. "Was he cute?"

"Not exactly what you would call a hunk—don't I wish. He is a genius, though. He goes to MIT. What a jerk. He asked me to go up to his room with him. Tonight. I only just met him today. He must think I was born an hour and a half ago. I just can't get over it."

"It comes with the territory, honest to God. The smarter they are, the more stuck on themselves they are. He must think he's something. God's gift."

"He must," I said. "Actually, the funny thing is that there *is* something almost sweet about him, in a disgusting kind of way, if you know what I mean."

"Hmm," Georgia said, sounding almost melancholy. What had I said? Oh, God, why hadn't I thought of it? Here I was discussing men again with a person who probably hadn't had a single date in her life. It was undoubtedly a very sore subject with her. She had been terribly generous and nice about Stanley Crosshill, but everyone had her limit. I noticed she was fingering the scars on her wrists again.

"Georgia," I began, "I keep meaning to ask you about those marks on your wrists . . . if I'm not being too personal, that is." She looked at me, startled. Her mouth opened as if to answer; then she turned away and stared at the river; then she looked at me again and frowned. The next breath I took was uneven, audibly so. I knew what her answer would be, now. There was no innocent explanation for the scars. I shouldn't have asked. One of Mother's axioms was that personal remarks were always in bad taste. I groped for a phrase to say I was sorry, that I knew it was none of my business; but nothing would come to me.

Georgia raised the back of one hand limply to her forehead in an outmoded little gesture of despair, rather like a bit of stage business. "Oh, darlin'," she said in an exaggerated drawl, "are you shoo-ah y'all want me to speak of it? Ah'm certain y'all don't wanna know the trouble Ah've seen. What a burden to bay-uh, honey-chile."

"I'm sorry, I . . ."

"No, no, darlin', you may most assuredly ask me anything that you so desire and Ah shall be honored to respond. It's just that Ah hate to cast a pall on this here party."

"It's all right," I said, "you don't have to answer, I . . ."

"I tried to kill myself," she said, matter-of-factly, dropping the fake accent.

"I thought so . . . I wasn't sure," I said, my voice tremulous.

"Yup, that's what I did all right, kiddo. A little judicious blood-letting never hurt anyone."

I stopped staring at my knees and looked out across the river without seeing it, wishing I could take back my question as well as her answer. Seconds later I realized I had this inappropriate little smile on my face—an awkward, shaky, cover-up smile that I couldn't seem to stop. My mother always smiled this way at funerals as she passed by the casket and at Christmas when she deposited money in the Salvation Army kettle. I covered my mouth with my hand.

Georgia sighed.

"Why?" I heard myself say.

"Who knows? I hated everything. Me. My life. Every day. Every interminable night. You see, I can't even talk about it and make it sound real. Every time I talk about it I find myself using these phrases I've read in books or heard in movies. 'The interminable night.' God, I make myself sick! I don't know. I can't tell you why. I just hated everything. Everything was ugly. I wanted to sleep. Just sleep." Her voice had grown soft with these last words. She looked at me, to see if I understood, then turned away, disappointed. "Look, Annie," she said, her voice with a determined edge to it, "I hated everything so much that, looking in the mirror, I would want to tear my face to ribbons."

"God . . ."

"So I tried to end it. I cut myself up. Twice. Two separate occasions. It didn't work. Obviously. Either time." She laughed, a brief, fragile flutter of air that caught in her throat.

"I'm glad," I said.

"Someone found me every time. Someone who wasn't supposed

to be there was there." She paused as if thinking this over with
regret. "And they rescued me. Isn't that wonderful? And they
took me to the good old loony bin and they sewed me up and
drugged me up and finally, much, much later, when they thought
I could take it, they woke me up, and do you know what the first
words were that someone said to me?" She paused again, smiling
at me out of one corner of her mouth, her eyebrows raised. " 'How
could you *do* this to me?' The 'do' had about fourteen *o*'s in it.
Enter guilt! Enter self-recrimination! Enter Ida, dear Ida, with her
chocolates and her French pastries and new robes and slippers and
a copy of the life of Saint Thérèse of Lisieux, the holy little sim-
pleton. Ida suggested that I pattern my life after hers. Then Ida
would pray for me and lecture me for hours regarding my lack of
gratitude and love. She has the most uncanny ability to make me
feel miserable."

Ida again. Who on earth was she? "Why didn't you just ignore
her or tell her to leave you alone? Couldn't you tell her not to
visit you again?"

"Not really. You see, among other things, she was paying my
bills. And I've known her forever. As she sees it, God showed his
grace to me after my mother died and placed me at the home and
brought the two of us together, she and I. She has this idea that
we are . . . inseparable, I guess you could say. That's why I live
here, near her."

"Oh, I see," I said, but I didn't really. "Then you met her at
the home when you were small?"

"Yes."

"She was a friend of yours then?" This probably explained it.
This Ida person had known Georgia since they were both small
at the home. Naturally she would want to remain in touch with
Georgia, both of them being orphans, having no one else. And
Georgia, being as unstable as she was, must have been quite a
worry to her friend.

Suddenly I noticed Georgia looking at me strangely. She hadn't
answered me. She looked away when our eyes met.

"Oh, well. That's all in the past," she said. "All in my deep,
dark past. I go to my shrink now and it helps a lot. He really is a

wonderful man. He says that one of these days I'll be fine, just fine." She broke into a broad smile. "He says it's boring as hell to work with people who never get better, and he just won't allow that to happen to me."

"I'm glad to hear it. I really am. I still feel guilty that I asked you. It mustn't be easy to talk about." She shrugged her shoulders. "I'm glad it didn't work. I'm glad you're still here," I said, wanting to pat her arm yet not quite daring to. "I've never known anyone quite like you." It was true. I had never known anyone even remotely like Georgia. "I mean it," I added in the awkward silence. "I've never known anyone even a little bit like you." She grinned and lowered her head as if embarrassed at the compliment.

"And Ah have never seen a real live magnolia blossom, darlin'—have y'all?"

"Nor have Ah," I said, giggling at myself, fanning myself with an imaginary fan, relieved to be on less serious ground.

"Ah believe that they are as white and fragrant as gardenias, with just the slightest smidgeon of cerise at their itty bitty throats."

"And they grow in absolute masses on trees," I drawled.

"And Ah fairly swoon away," Georgia said, letting herself fall backward onto the grass with her arms stretched out over her head. "That's what you'd be good at, Annie—being a southern belle."

"I most certainly would not," I said. "Southern belles are stupid."

I joined her on the grass, which smelled freshly mowed.

"Georgia?" I said. She had gotten strangely quiet, and I was afraid she might be crying.

"Don't look at me, Annie."

"What's wrong?"

"Nothing," she said, unconvincingly. She sat up and pointed at my feet. "Just your tiny little feet and your impossibly tiny little hands, that's all. Everything I'm supposed to be and am not, you are."

"Georgia, don't be silly!"

"For pouring tea and dancing the minuet. Even your skin is perfect—just look at it. Look at the skin on your arm. Pink. Look at mine beside yours." She laughed raucously. Luckily, no one was within earshot of that laugh; no one was close enough to see her face. She looked like she was screaming. "Bilious, isn't it," she said. "Almost jaundiced looking. Actually, a nice bright jaundice would be better than this. And see? All my blood vessels show through. They're not blue like yours, though—oh no, mine are this elegant khaki green. They match my eyes!"

"You have beautiful eyes," I said, not wanting to correct her regarding their color. "We're just different types, that's all. I'm fair; you're olive-skinned. Look at all my freckles."

"Your humility again. That's *not* all, either. Someone will want to marry you and take care of you forever. He'll adore you and call you 'baby' and you'll just flit around in the adorable house he buys you, being adorable and helpless and terribly, terribly cute."

"Thanks a lot," I said, realizing that she meant all of this in a decidedly uncomplimentary way. She was jealous. And rude.

"Can't you just imagine someone calling *me* 'baby'?"

"I don't think I'd want that. My mother used to call me that. And I'm not all that great. I'm certainly not perfect. You . . . you see me differently than others do. I know I'm not ugly, but I'm not exactly some great beauty, either."

"Men *love* little girls."

"No they don't. They love grown women."

"How many guys have you had?" she said, almost taunting me.

"Thousands," I said.

"How old did you say you were?"

"Eighteen," I said.

"How many times have you done it?"

"I'm not going to do it until the right person comes along." Georgia giggled and rolled on the ground like a two-year-old. "Until I'm in love, really in love."

"Well, you haven't missed much," she said, regaining her composure. Her comment puzzled me. I had heard it before but didn't believe its implications. It was the kind of comment I would have expected from my mother, who, in the only conversation we had ever had about sex, confided to me pridefully that she was a "passive" sexual partner. I wasn't sure of what that meant exactly, but it seemed a far cry from some of the fantasies I had had.

Not that I felt guilty about my own feelings and thoughts; I really didn't. I considered myself almost completely normal most of the time.

"I've *almost* done it," I said.

"Who was he?"

"Oh, just a boy I went with for a while last year."

"And this all transpired in the back of his father's Buick, right?"

"On the beach, as a matter of fact."

"Not bad," she said, "although I've done it in stranger places than that."

I just stared at her. I didn't know whether she was lying or not. Her attitude was far from what I had expected. She looked like the kind of girl who had never been near a boy in her life.

"Like where?" I asked.

"Oh . . . " she said, taking her time, "on a picnic table once at a park, and in a vacant house another time. But the weirdest was the time I did it in a tunnel."

"The Sumner tunnel?"

"God, no—a tunnel under one of the hospitals where I was a patient. The whole place was connected by underground tunnels— you know, all the separate buildings. And this guy and I were sent to Brain Wave to have a test, and on the way back he just shoves me into this little alcove, behind some laundry carts, and there's this old, crummy, overstuffed chair in there and he sits on it then pulls me over on top of him. Actually, that was the very first time for me. He told me to sit on him so it wouldn't hurt so much going in. That was about it. I mean, I loved it, poor slut that I am, I really did; but you know, I was so drugged up at the time I wasn't even sure who he was."

"Oh," I said. "Other than hurting, how did it feel? I've always wanted to ask someone."

"Ecstasy, my child—pure, unadulterated ecstasy." She groaned, then moaned, and both of us burst out laughing.

"I thought you said I hadn't missed much."

"I didn't want you to feel bad."

"Actually, the boy I almost did it with was trying to decide whether to become a priest or not. If he could resist me, he was determined to head straight for the seminary after graduating." Dennis Hagen—I'd never forget him and the torture he put both of us through. He had it in his head that if he and I were alone together and he could keep himself numb through an afternoon of necking, he was a perfect candidate for a life of celibacy. His mother wanted him to become a priest more than anything else in the world.

"So what happened? I guess he made it, huh, if you didn't do anything?"

"No—he flunked his own test. It was me who didn't want to do anything. He was all for it. I guess I kind of tricked him by suggesting we go to the beach and then wearing my white bathing suit."

"Annie, you little tart—a future man of the cloth!"

"I couldn't help myself. I mean, the way he put it to me, it was me against Rome. Anyway, I've always thought celibacy unnatural, even harmful."

"Well! I see a side of you I never dreamed existed."

"You don't think I'm really awful, do you?"

"You're a cock tease, that's what you are," she said, standing up and brushing bits of grass off her toreador pants. "Big, bad Annie. He could have become pope, you know. I suppose you never thought of that." I got up too, and we stood silently, facing the water for a minute. It was almost dark. A neon sign on the Cambridge side of the river was reflected in bright wavy lines on the water. "You have robbed the world of another great prelate. For shame." I knew she was kidding now.

"He and Marie Johnston got married on June tenth. They say his mother cried through the whole thing." We both laughed a little, and Georgia took a deep breath.

"I can't wait to do it with Claude," she whispered.

"How long have you been going out?"

"Well, we haven't exactly gone out yet. I'm in love with him. Wait till you meet him, you'll see what I mean. He's so wonderful. Oh, on the outside he pretends to be cold and distant, but inside he's the most sensitive person I've ever known. He brings me bread for the birds. A friend of his waits on tables, and Claude has him save the leftover bread for me."

"How sweet of him," I said.

"You know, Annie, sometimes your life is going along like it always has and you begin to think there's no hope at all, then someone comes along just at the right time and changes things, forever, and all of a sudden there are possibilities you never thought existed. That's the way it is with Claude and me."

"I'm really happy for you."

"Yup, the old days will be gone forever, all the crazy things I did, hacking away at myself and . . ." Her voice trailed off. Then she looked at me and hugged herself. "Annie, this is the most glorious night, and I am so happy to be alive."

"Me too," I said.

"Then let's celebrate!" she cried. "Come on, I'll race ya!" She bolted off across the Esplanade, me after her.

"I can't keep up with you—my legs are too short," I hollered, doing my level best to sprint along. I watched with embarrassed amusement as she added a few off-balance jumps and twirls. Her long arms flailed the air as she traveled along through the darkness. "Oh, no," I said aloud to myself as she burst into song in the most awful, tone-deaf chorus of something or other, her voice wavering madly with every bounce. She was almost at the highway.

She would stop there and wait for me. I slowed to a lope. I waited for her to reach the curb, then turn and watch me approaching. But she didn't. I stopped running. I stood stock still and watched in horror as she ran headlong into the path of on-coming headlights.

"Georgia!" I screamed, my cry mingling with the sound of squealing brakes and men's voices yelling and swearing out their open windows. She had been hit. I began to run toward her, terrified of what I would see. I had not heard a scream, and after the initial shouting I heard no other voices. I couldn't see her. Suddenly the automobiles that had stopped accelerated and raced away and there, through a break in the traffic, I saw a figure standing beneath a street lamp on the other side—Georgia, alive and well, her index finger in her mouth. As I reached the curb opposite her, she mouthed, "I'm sorry."

"You're out of your mind," I yelled, waiting for a break in the traffic to cross. She shrugged.

"I didn't mean to do that—honest to God, I didn't," she yelled back. I shook my head. When it was finally safe to run to her, she started talking before I got there. "I thought I had plenty of time," she said.

"Well, obviously you didn't. I saw you. You didn't even look."

"The cars just seemed to come out of nowhere," she argued. "I felt so good and so happy. Didn't you ever feel that way? And lose track of what you were doing?"

"No!"

"I just felt so incredibly young and alive and in love and I was singing at the top of my lungs and it felt so wonderful, Annie. Haven't you ever felt that way?"

"You almost got yourself killed!"

"But I didn't!" she said impatiently. "I *had* to do what I did. I couldn't stop. That's the way it is when you feel like that—you have to go with it." She looked at me pleadingly. "Haven't you ever noticed that everything is so dead around here? All these dead brick buildings and people with tired faces and streets that don't go much of anywhere. Even the river there is dead and black—even the sky tonight is barely lit with stars. But you and I, Annie, are alive. Annie, feel this." She took my hand and placed it in the center of her chest.

"Georgia! Someone will see. . . ." I wrenched my hand from hers. She could be so corny.

"It was my heart."

"Yes, I know." I started walking up Pinckney Street, but I could still see her face as it had looked in the pale light from the street lamp.

"Don't be mad at me," Georgia said, coming up alongside me.

"I'm not," I said, purposely not meeting her eyes. Then she walked ahead of me and turned the corner at Charles Street, a faint wash of yellow and green that disappeared into the night.

Back at the house, I had just started up the stairs when Malcolm called to me from the French doors. "Everything all right?" he asked.

"I think so," I said. "Did Georgia just come in?"

"Not two minutes ago," he said cheerily.

"That girl walks faster than anyone I have ever known."

"And more noisily," he whispered, shaking his head in disapproval. "Or perhaps I should say 'energetically,'" he added with a smile. "She certainly has spirit, doesn't she?"

I laughed, not terribly enthusiastically. From upstairs I heard a toilet flush and a door slam. I hoped it was the door to Georgia's room. I was still unnerved by what she had done. "Well, good night, Malcolm," I said, starting up the stairs again.

"Sleep well, Ann—another busy day tomorrow."

Stopping on the third-floor landing to find my room key in my purse, I heard Georgia's door open. She peeked out.

"Good night, Annie. It really was fun. I hope I didn't ruin it for you."

"No, of course not," I said. "I had fun too. Really."

"I'll see you tomorrow," she said, slowly shutting her door as I opened mine.

SEVEN

Although I got up earlier than necessary the next morning, Georgia was already gone when I went to the bathroom and found another of her effusive poems with an appended note on the toilet seat. She had really outdone her earlier effort at capturing me in verse.

In the note, she said that she had left early to have breakfast with her friend Ida in Louisburg Square. She mentioned that the night before—long after I was asleep, apparently—Claude had come down and invited her up to his place for a glass of wine. Six exclamation points followed this confession; six more followed the statement that she had traipsed up there in her nightgown. Finally, she asked if I'd go to the Riverview with her again tonight if she promised to behave and somehow refrain from throwing herself into the path of oncoming vehicles. She was flippant about it; yet even hours later I still shuddered, recalling the squeal of brakes and the horns.

I also wasn't exactly thrilled by her having signed the note "your soul mate." I didn't believe that she and I were sisters under the skin. Although before meeting Georgia, I confess, there were times when I thought of myself as a little bit bohemian, compared to her I was a complete square. This was hard to take. I had so hoped to find out otherwise. But regardless of what Aunt Chloe had said about my courage and spirit of adventure, it was beginning to be plain as day to me that at heart I was a conservative, inhibited Merrill, and that it would take more than a gentle summer metamorphosis to make me anything else.

My first task after dressing for work was to write to my mother and break the news of what I had done since seeing her last. I was about to sit down at the secretary and begin when I suddenly remembered that I dreamed of Georgia sometime during the night, and in that dream, very much like the real-life episode, Georgia ran into the street, except in the dream I somehow threw myself between her and the speeding cars and saved her from certain death. I had to admit to myself, recalling the dream, that a disturbing thought had been going through my mind since I first met Georgia: that I had been "sent" to Boston and Walnut Street to save her. I was such an egotist—as if God, in his infinite wisdom, would send a recent high-school graduate, a girl at that, on a life-saving mission of this magnitude! There were doctors for jobs like this. Or just a man—Claude. A love interest. Love could cure anything.

But maybe friendship would help.

I was getting too melodramatic. It was highly likely that Georgia was already saved. She had as much as said so. Yet a rather sinister part of me wanted desperately to be instrumental in her recovery, just for the self-centered satisfaction of it.

I wouldn't think of that again.

I sat down at the secretary and began to write the straightforward, truthful letter Aunt Chloe had urged me to write. But it was idiotic to tell Mother that I had come to Walnut Street to, for lack of a better phrase, find myself. Mother believed that no woman ever found herself until she found a man. She might even prefer an imaginative lie to the hard truth that I had willfully disobeyed her in leaving Barclay. In fact, if I was very careful, I might be able to construct a scenario of events so horrible that Mother herself would have left Barclay had she been in my place.

Suddenly, two seemingly unrelated words ran through my mind like banners trailing across the sky behind a small airplane: "mayonnaise" and "communism." I stopped writing to think this over.

A little background info here. Mother had always been an absolute fanatic about mayonnaise and had lectured me since birth, around Memorial Day, Independence Day, and Labor Day particularly, on the care to be taken when using mayonnaise in or on anything, especially during the hot months of the year. Suppose the dining room at Barclay were found to be remiss regarding mayonnaise? Suppose I had noticed that a pot of mayonnaise used at lunch was used again at dinner, after spending the afternoon nestled next to the steam tables. What if the same pot were seen the following day, its contents wearing a stale, mustard-colored skin?

Upon hearing of this, Mother would greet the news of my departure to Walnut Street—or even to Albania—with relief. She would congratulate herself for instilling in me proper mayonnaise techniques, thereby saving me from death by food poisoning.

But, if I knew Mother, she would go farther than that. She was the sort who could be swayed from the most firm convictions by something minuscule—the fly in the ointment, so to speak. Upon finding that Barclay was inept in mayo management, Mother would infer that much else was wrong with that grand old establishment which had held such a warm place in her heart.

An example: Once, after spending a winter researching camps I might attend that summer, after finding Camp Fair Harbor on Martha's Vineyard and deciding that it offered all the facilities and opportunities she demanded in a camp, she withdrew my application upon reading under "Sunday Worship Options" in the camp brochure, "Congregational Church services, if desired." Now, Mother was no one's fool. Everyone knew that the Congregationalists were radicals. She was not in the least concerned that I would be corrupted by taking in such a church service; after all, I was a staunch Episcopalian and, as such, affiliated with considerable antiquity, authenticity, old family money, and intellectual status—a class act. I was not likely to be wooed astray by an outfit as devoid of charisma as the Congregational Church. What *was* clear to Mother was that any camp that aligned itself so blatantly with radicalism was admitting to some grave malignancy deep in its administrative bowels.

Like communism.

Whenever Mother felt negative about anything, you could bet money that her fears about communism were at the bottom of it. "Better safe than sorry," she mused, solemnly setting fire to the camp beanie that had arrived with the receipt for her deposit. As the flames rose, I knew that Mother envisioned leaky tents and leakier boats, an inadequate infirmary supply of tetanus antitoxin, and horsemeat on the camp's dinner menu. Fair Harbor had obviously been chosen by the Red Menace to spearhead its drive to undermine the health and welfare of American youth. Tucked between the flapjacks each morning would be messages from the Kremlin, quotes from Karl Marx. I went to Camp Winona instead and thanked my lucky stars for people like Mother and Joseph McCarthy.

The same thing would happen with Mother and Barclay. The tainted mayonnaise would signify that an infinitely more evil plan was in the works, that Barclay was a clever front for a communist cell. Once the residents were in a sufficiently weakened condition, the brainwashing could begin in earnest.

Thus, I began my letter:

Dear Mother,

No doubt the news of the recent health department raid and salmonella scare at Barclay Hall has reached you. The *Record-American* ran a full-length photo of poor Gillian on its first page.

That was as far as I got. Mother would worry. If you couldn't trust Barclay Hall, whom in this wide world could you? Mother would be nervous. Hysterical. I wouldn't have a minute's peace all summer. I thought better of it.

I would have to invent a cleverer lie—one calculated not only to thrill Mother to the core by its implication that nothing but uncommon good fortune had come my way but also to force her to agree totally with my decision to leave Barclay for a far more attractive destination, Walnut Street. If I was very careful, Mother might even think that moving to Walnut Street had been her idea.

Not so deep down, Mother was convinced that astonishing things could and would happen to any child she had conceived and reared. Nothing in the way of good fortune would seem farfetched to her. Mother would find it altogether plausible if my brother, Evan, after word got out concerning his performance on Student Government Day, was called to Washington to advise President Eisenhower. Neither would she be surprised if I were "discovered" while ordering a clam roll at Howard Johnson's and crowned Miss America on the spot. Clearly, for children of such a gifted mother, the sky was the limit.

I began another letter with new guidelines, and after only a few words I knew I had hit pay dirt. I could not write fast enough.

Dear Mother,

I shall not waste a word. The most extraordinary thing has happened. You will never guess the astonishing good luck I have had in the few short days since you left me at dear old Barclay. I shall start at the very beginning. This is too wonderful to leave out even the smallest detail. How such things happen to me I shall never know! The Merrill good fortune, I suppose.

There I was my first day at the book store when an elegant little lady dressed in cashmere from head to foot approached me as I toiled away in the Old and Rare section where I was arranging some priceless volumes attested to be the original printings of *Great Expectations* and *David Copperfield*. I thought of you and how you love Dickens. "You haven't perchance come upon a copy of Thomas Widdington's classic work on Elizabethan England, *Archangels and Queens,* have you?" this dear lady said. "I saw it once here," she continued. "I suppose it's gone. No matter." But of course, it wasn't gone at all. I had been reading it myself in preparation for my course in Shakespeare, second semester. You of course recall my love for Elizabethan England. It was a great pleasure to place this book in the charming old woman's hands. She stood there smiling, thumbing through the pages. For some reason I mentioned that I would be attending Wellesley in the fall and that my love was English literature. While I spoke she gave me the most interesting look and as I paused, not wanting to interrupt her further, she told me that she had taught at Wellesley for years, was now retired and writing her memoirs and that she needed this book, *Archangels etc.*, to check a point of reference. I nearly died! Naturally I went on to say that all the women in my family had gone to Wellesley and wouldn't you know that she remembered both Cousin Trish and Cousin Candace, only recalling Trish's name, however, but having vivid recollections of Candace, even to a description of her poor posture and her propensity for gathering lint on everything she wore. She did recall Candace's fine mind, however, and seemed to think that intellect ran in the family because I could tell from that point on that she knew how intelligent I was. She just treated me that way, I couldn't begin to describe how, exactly, except to say that there was a certain reverence in her voice, and often as she spoke she reached for and took my hand.

Well, to make a long story short we had lunch together at Locke Ober's. Her name is Marion Balch. Perhaps you recall hearing of her, although she came after you graduated. She informed me that she now lives with her husband on Walnut Street on Beacon Hill, just down from Mt. Vernon Street, and that her husband fancies himself some sort of quaint innkeeper and that they rent out several rooms, to the most carefully screened people, of course. She then said that her niece Hilary had just left for summer at the Sorbonne and that her room was now free. One thing led to another and by the end of our luncheon, Marion had asked me if I would like to take Hilary's room and join the household at Walnut Street.

I begged for a little time to make my decision, as I had already grown to love Barclay and adored all the girls. But after work I felt that I owed her the courtesy of at least looking at the room, which I did and fell in love!

Mother, you won't believe this, but it's practically an exact replica of my room at home—pink flowered wallpaper, ruffled curtains, Gibson Girl prints on the walls. Best of all, right next door to me on the third floor lives a lovely girl named Fabiana. A ballerina. Fabiana is her stage name. She won't even tell me what her real name is, says that if I knew who she really was I'd treat her as if she were special. I have never known a more aristocratic person. She has taken me under her wing (yes, Mother, I *had* to move in here) and last night took me to dinner at an English restaurant down on Charles Street owned and operated by the most adorable pair of English ladies, sisters they are, who remind me of tiny sparrows, plump and grey.

The food there is wonderful, nourishing and cheap—pot pies, Yorkshire pudding, crumpets, tea cakes, lamb with mint jelly, etc. We had a veal pot pie with mushrooms and trifle for dessert. Yummy. So, you see, even though I now have to purchase my food separately, I can do so economically and with such divine company.

Mother, dear, everything is so

I stopped writing. I couldn't do it. Couldn't send it. Oh, Mother would believe it, all right. It just seemed so immature of me. And where would it all end? I thought of the future and how I would have to, if I sent this letter, keep the lies going forever and ever. I imagined myself at fifty carrying on about the summer I had spent with Marion and Malcolm and divine Fabiana the ballerina. At least until my mother died. And there was always the chance that cousins Candace and Trish might surface one of these days at a family gathering and be asked about Marion Balch, their old English professor.

But more than that, I felt that I owed it to myself to tell the truth. If Mother gave me any trouble, I could always fall back on a little lie, and justifiably so—maybe even work in a little something about communism or food poisoning, if necessary. But for now, I would tell her the truth; let the chips fall where they may. Directly after work I would write her a matter-of-fact note, more in the form of a memo, really, detailing my activities since I had arrived. Mother could take it or leave it.

I finished my makeup and started off for work. I hesitated for just an instant outside Malcolm's French doors to smell the eucalyptus. But my mind was still on the defunct letter, and I half-expected the nonexistent Marion Balch to emerge from her apartment, clad in an elegant robe of china silk. She would raise the bone-china teacup she held in her hand in greeting and ask if I had time for café au lait before I left. "So terribly sorry, I have to run," I would say, smiling graciously as I rushed breathlessly to my second day on the job, my white-linen pleated skirt swinging out as I stopped abruptly to close the door behind me. Just before it shut completely, there would be the sight of Marion's face, her blue eyes sparkling wetly between wrinkled white lids of such thin skin they made me think of folds of tissue paper in a gift box. Old people always loved effervescent young women like me. They always claimed to have once been just like me, probably more a case of wishful thinking than anything else.

I ran down the steps and into Walnut Street, which was still cool, dark, and smelling of night. Ahead of me shone Beacon and the trees of the Common awash in a nearly palpable overlay of sunlight—as if sunlight could occur as a fine mist, blown in like puffs of pollen across a field.

When I grow old, I thought, thinking of Marion again, I shall look just like her, carefully turned out, with a bright and lively outlook.

I had just turned the corner and started up Beacon Street when I saw an older couple approaching and realized it was none other than Malcolm Balch and a small, attractive blond woman. As they came nearer, I heard the woman say, in a distinctly fervent tone, ". . . But then I found *you*, Malcolm, and all my worries were over." Well! Malcolm and I exchanged hellos as they passed, and when I looked back a few minutes later, they had just turned into Walnut Street. Malcolm wasn't a fruit after all. He had a girlfriend and was taking her back to the empty house with him! Aunt Chloe was right in cautioning me not to draw conclusions too early.

This thought remained with me as I continued toward work. It was too early to tell much of anything for sure, whether Malcolm was queer or not, whether Georgia was cured or crazy, whether

Stanley Crosshill was meant for me or Oscar Benson or Sabu the Elephant Boy for that matter. In all likelihood the man I would marry was home for the summer in Sheboygan, Wisconsin, or standing duty on a destroyer in the Pacific or wandering in a moor in Scotland, wondering if we would ever meet. I could just see him: a mass of dark curls framing a craggy face; a sort of flowing shirt and a pair of suede breeches. He would be young, gorgeous, with passionate eyes and a deep, husky voice.

I walked through the door of the bookstore. Oscar Benson sat at Ruth's desk beside the cash register; he jumped up and grinned at me adoringly. He couldn't possibly be Jewish, I thought, or any of the other exotic things I had made up about him the day before. He was about as exciting as vanilla pudding, as capable of true passion as a three-year-old. "Ruth's in the john combing her hair," he said in that stupid low register that made me want to scream.

I pretended to glance at the title of a book on a nearby table, gathered my composure, then walked steadily toward him.

EIGHT

"Good morning, Oscar," I said, skirting the desk and placing my sweater and purse in a cubbyhole reserved for it behind the counter.

"And *how* are you this morning?" he said, his voice an intimate whisper.

"Just fine, thank you," I said. "I guess I'll comb my hair, too." I hauled my purse back out of the cubbyhole and by mistake dislodged my sweater and sent it falling to the floor. Oscar, the cavalier, lunged to retrieve it. His eyes met mine disconcertingly as he stood holding my sweater in a little heap in his hands, waiting for me to take it from him.

"Why, thank you," I said, sounding more awkward than I would have liked. His teeth were very white, and there was that something about how his bottom lip curved (or was it the top?) that stayed in my mind as I inched past him. "My hair," I stuttered, stupidly.

"It looks great to me," he called.

"It's a mess," I yelled back, my voice much too loud and shaky to sound natural. I had lost my composure. Damn! The bathroom door opened and Ruth appeared. "Good morning," I said, my voice hysterically enthusiastic. Ruth was taken aback. One of her eyes blinked, birdlike. With her blue hair, and dressed in blue again today, she reminded me of a parakeet.

"Well, good morning to you! Lovely morning," she said. "And it couldn't come soon enough for me. Long night with mother last night. I finally tucked her away around four, then I crawled into bed myself. All blocked up again she was, and you know she couldn't be. She only picks at her food. I just don't know, dear. I don't know."

"What a shame," I said, as sympathetically as I could. I went into the bathroom and closed the door, almost not hearing her say: "It's a cross to bear, dear." Then, her mouth against the door: "Tell you later." I could hardly wait.

I drew the comb through my hair, then made a final check of my appearance in the mirror. I looked tired and pale. Probably a blessing in disguise. Not looking my best might keep Oscar at bay. If I hadn't been so vain, I would have blotted off all my lipstick and looked even worse. I just couldn't do it. I closed my purse and strolled into the store as nonchalantly as I could.

"Well, *here* she is," Oscar announced, as I approached Ruth's desk. I ignored him. Several cartons of books had arrived, Ruth said, many of them by French authors, some printed in French. I was to go through them and place them on the appropriate shelves. Oscar had already carried the boxes to a small room in the back that was reserved, at least more or less, for foreign-language texts and books by European authors.

"Oscar dear, go back there with her, would you, and make sure she knows what she's doing—then you get busy in the storeroom. All that trash must be taken care of this morning." I led the way to the back of the store near the Old and Rare, not altogether comfortable with the fact that Oscar was practically breathing down my neck. I stopped beside the cartons of books on the floor in the Foreign room. Oscar pointed out the empty shelves I would fill and lifted the flaps on one carton, removed several books, checked their titles, and placed them on their sides on a shelf. He was wasting time. He was trying to prolong this wildly intimate moment for as long as he could. He was so transparent.

"Ah, good, good, I've been looking for this one," he said, peering at the jacket of one book, then handing it to me with a finger on its title. "Sartre," he said, his eyes meeting mine again. His voice was softly unsteady, as if he were ever so slightly out of breath. I glanced at the title. *No Exit.* Neither the author's name nor the title meant a thing to me. Probably some tawdry little novel by some perverted Frenchman. "Existentialism," Oscar said, as if to jog my memory. "Sartre?" He had this stupid, expectant look on his face, his mouth dangling open. His tongue protruded, its tip resting against his lower lip like a fat marzipan strawberry.

"Ah! Of course," I said, foolishly opening the book and flipping a few pages. Thank goodness it was written in English; otherwise I would have been mortified. I knew some French but hardly enough to read a book written in it.

"You're familiar with this, then?"

"Actually, I'm afraid not," I said, confessing. "I *have* heard the term, but I'm afraid I don't know what it means." What an idiot I was! I should have said I couldn't *remember* what it meant. The subtle difference could have saved me from seeming to have lived in literary squalor all my life.

"I see," he said. "Well, if you haven't been exposed to it, there could be no way that you would know what it meant. In that case, this is a perfect opportunity for me to deliver my short course in Existentialism 101—if you're interested, that is."

"By all means, go to it," I said sweetly, with a slight trace of a southern accent. I just loved being lectured by boys. It made me feel so wonderfully stupid and helpless. I batted my eyelashes at him. Twice. I leaned against the wall, tilted my head to the side ever so demurely. He looked at his feet and cleared his throat.

"Well . . . now . . . it's really all quite elementary. How can I best explain it? . . . Ah! Of course. See this bookshelf? It's a book-shelf—no more, no less. It has no other options. To be a bookshelf is its destiny." Except in the instance of fire or urban redevelopment, I thought.

"But what of man?" His eyes had glazed over. "What is he? What is his destiny? The existentialist holds that man determines his own destiny. 'Essence,' they call it. Man chooses what his essence will be." There was something oddly sensuous about this.

"It's a philosophical idea, you see," he said. "Of course there's much more to it than that. Oh, they go on from there and conclude that there seems to be no good reason why anything exists at all and that all life is futile, that there is no God, that God is an invention of man, invented out of fear. That there is no soul. That man is born an empty page which he must fill in, alone." Oscar had quite a noble look on his face for one who had just said something so depressing.

"Hmm," I said, raising my eyebrows in an attitude, I hoped, of deep interest. "And this Sartre writes of this?"

"Yes, yes! He's one of them. An existentialist."

"Did he invent it or something, this philosophy?"

"No, not really. Kierkegaard and Nietzsche were the ones who started the ball rolling, then Sartre and Camus and de Beauvoir and—"

"All of them French?" I said. Oscar broke into a delighted laugh, the same one my father used once when my mother tried to explain the theory of relativity to us.

"Except for Nietzsche and Kierkegaard, yes. Most of them French." He was gentle, correcting me.

"Very interesting," I said, turning to a bookshelf, standing up the several books that Oscar had placed on their sides, bending over to take three more volumes out of the carton. I didn't look at him; I wished he would go. He didn't. He moved a bit closer to me, in fact, sort of sidestepped toward me, and before I knew it he was off again, expounding on existentialism in a voice much louder than was necessary for normal conversation. He *was* lecturing, after all.

"You see, Ann," he shouted, "the existentialist isn't interested in trying to grasp the ultimate meaning of life. I find that quite fascinating. And they say that what we must do is grasp the fact that there is no meaning to anything and go bravely on anyway. I like the sound of that—'go bravely on.'" He had hit that low register again. He had inched closer to me as he talked and now stood so near that I thought I could feel the warmth of his body. And there was that intriguing odor to him—a pleasant one, wool and starched white cotton mingled together with a clean smell and a trace of that undefinable other scent, that "essence of animal." I was overcome with a nearly irresistible urge to press my face against his chest and inhale him.

I looked into his face and saw again those warm, caramel eyes. Not deep and intense as I would have expected them to be, they were calm and friendly and bordered with a fringe of long, curly lashes any girl would have been delighted to have for her own.

But it was his mouth, specifically his lips, that really held my attention; and I allowed myself, for the merest fraction of a second, to imagine what it would be like to run the tip of my tongue along the raised outer margin of his upper lip. Then, unable to stop myself, I pictured the two of us lying naked in a bed somewhere, me on top of him, just kind of licking him all over, particularly down the side of his neck, for my eyes had now rested on that part of his anatomy, and it just seemed to me that my mouth belonged there in that cozy, fuzzy nook. In fact, something strange had happened, and I now thought of Oscar as being all warm and hairy and infinitely touchable from head to foot.

"What are you smiling at?" he said.

"I didn't know I was," I said.

"I'll bet," he said. "You were thinking that I was making one helluva jackass out of myself getting carried away like this. I guess I sound pretty pompous. I just do sometimes. I don't mean to, I just do."

"I wasn't thinking that at all," I said. "I was thinking about how embarrassed I felt not knowing about ex-is-tentialism. See? I can't even say it. You're not going to believe this, but this is the first word in my whole life that I've stumbled over. I guess I feel kind of dumb. I never heard of Sartre, either. I'm pretty unschooled."

"And I had to go and ram it down your throat. I don't even understand it fully myself, all the ramifications of it anyway."

"You certainly seem to. I suppose you've become an exis-ten-tial-ist yourself."

"Not me," he said, "I'm a Methodist." He laughed. I laughed too—a bit too energetically, perhaps. What I was thinking was that Mother approved of Methodists and said that they were almost like Episcopalians, except that their churches were plainer and their services less interesting.

"You have an incredible laugh," he said. "Wow." Then there was an awkward silence while each of us seemed to draw back from the other.

"I guess I'd better get to that storeroom," he mumbled, not moving an inch.

"I guess so," I said, sighing inadvertently. He still didn't move. He couldn't seem to drag himself away from me. It was as if there were a magnetic field between us, drawing us to one another. What a cliché! But I swear, I felt the hairs on my arm straighten. I rubbed them. "I'll see you later," I added.

"Okay. I guess I better get on with it."

Finally, he was gone.

The remainder of the morning passed uneventfully enough, except that I felt increasingly uncomfortable whenever I was near Oscar. I didn't know how to behave. My first mistake was in trying not to react to him at all. The harder I tried, the more out of hand things got. When he observed me just glancing at him a couple of times, my head jerked away so violently, one would have thought I had been ogling him for hours. And once, after observing this little piece of frenetic business, Oscar smiled to himself in a decidedly self-satisfied way. I hated it and yet was powerless to do anything about it.

My second mistake was in allowing him to come within ten feet of me. Right before Ruth and I left for lunch, I was ringing up a sale on the cash register when I hit the wrong key and the drawer wouldn't open. Oscar to the rescue! He leaned over me to correct whatever mistake I had made, whereupon I recoiled from the possibility of any part of his person touching me, with such exaggerated flailing about that I scared the wits out of him. He jumped out of the way, nearly colliding with Ruth, who had just come out from behind her desk. He asked what he had done, wondering for a second if he might have stepped on my foot. Thinking quickly, I replied that he had given me a shock. Hadn't he felt it? The customer waiting for his purchase looked puzzled. Another queer, gloating smile lingered on Oscar's lips.

I was discovered. Oscar knew what I was thinking and feeling, or at least he thought he did. It was maddening. I didn't know myself what I was thinking or feeling. All I was absolutely positive of was that his mouth reminded me of the mouth on the statue of David. The rest of him, with the possible exception of his warm brown eyes and a certain place on his neck I felt myself drawn to, was ordinary—perhaps not as goofy as I thought yesterday, but ordinary.

It was a relief to leave the bookstore for lunch. It was restful to half-listen to Ruth's account of the night before with her mother. I just sat there and ate and drank and smiled now and then at what seemed to be appropriate times. Mother, it turned out, was not the invalid I had envisioned the day before, but got about quite well most of the time—until about sundown, it seemed. She was a diabetic, something Ruth had neglected to tell me. She gave herself insulin each morning. On the afternoon of her eightieth birthday (the whole family had congregated for a celebration) Mother had consumed a large quantity of cake, then retired to her room for a nap. After the guests left, Ruth went to her room to sleep, too. Mother, upon waking up at dusk, thought it was morning, gave herself a shot of insulin, cooked herself a bacon-and-egg breakfast, and called the paper boy to complain that her morning paper had not been delivered. Luckily, the paper boy's mother was able to convince her that it was still Sunday night, not Monday morning at all, at which point Mother panicked: she had now given herself two shots of insulin in one day. She flew into Ruth's room, screamed at her to wake up, and insisted that an ambulance be called, as she was now overdosed with insulin and near death, not to mention feeling as if she had just made acquaintance with that bugaboo senility.

Ruth called the doctor, who after hearing about the amount of birthday cake Mother had devoured that afternoon, as well as the hearty breakfast she had consumed, pronounced her out of imminent danger.

Ruth told me this story without cracking a smile, between

mouthfuls of chocolate pudding and whipped cream. When the tale was finished, a narrow wreath of cream outlined her lips, and little trillium-shaped chocolate wrinkles nestled in their corners.

She then filled me in on the latest details of the upcoming marriage of Grace Kelly and Prince Rainier of Monaco, and on this note we returned to the store. I felt refreshed and anticipated yet another period of relaxation, as Oscar would now take *his* lunch hour. I hid out in the bathroom until he was gone. Then Ruth and I sat at her desk while she put me through a dry run on the books to see if I was getting the hang of things. A few customers trailed in, browsed, exchanged chitchat, and drifted out.

Finally, Ruth leaned back in her chair and, to my surprise, told me how happy she was that I had come to work at the store and how much I reminded her of her niece Kathleen, who, she said, "won't be with me for long." Ruth's eyes filled with tears, and she took out a fresh handkerchief to wipe them. I wondered if the girl had some fatal disease.

"Is she very ill?" I said.

"Oh, my, no, dear—hasn't had a sick day in her life. She's leaving for the West Coast in September, for heaven only knows how long. We've been so close, and now the baby . . ."

"Oh," I said, "she's going there to live."

"Yes. She and her husband and the new baby are going to Seattle. He'll enter medical school there. Kathleen will work to help put him through. I so hoped he would go to Harvard, or even Columbia, but they want to travel. . . ."

"I guess I don't blame them, really."

"Yes, yes, a nice change," Ruth said vaguely, looking at me as if I had just said something strange. "I was so concerned about the baby," she continued, "Maureen Ruth, after me, but they've contracted with a British firm that sends over English nannies, and they've corresponded with a lovely woman who'll make the trip to Seattle with them, by train, then stay on for at least a year."

"But you'll miss them, won't you?"

She nodded, then reached over and briskly patted my hand. "They say that there are Indians walking the city streets in Seattle," she said after a moment, wide-eyed.

"You're kidding."

"Oh, yes," Ruth said. "It's quite a wild place all right. And Kathleen's such a quiet, refined girl."

Just then Oscar, or someone closely resembling Oscar, returned from lunch. Actually, he looked a lot like Oscar—same height, same weight, same tantalizing lips, same thrilling, deep voice. But there the resemblance more or less ended. He had changed. The minute I saw him swagger through the front door, I knew something was different, a certain *je ne sais quoi*.

His jacket was slung rakishly over one shoulder. His tie was loose, his collar open, his warm, damp neck exposed. His usually neatly parted and combed hair was charmingly askew, a lock of it falling devilishly onto his brow. He walked straight toward me, his eyes locked onto mine, without even acknowledging Ruth's presence.

He removed the pipe from his mouth, smiled, then replaced it between his sensuous lips. That was it—Oscar was smoking a pipe. Standing directly in front of me, he squinted his eyes as if they were seared by smoke and said, in that phony bass voice of his, "Hi."

"Hi," I said, unable to say more.

"I'm back," he said. Rim shot!

"So you are, dear," Ruth chirped, but I could hear laughter in her tone. "Have a good lunch, did you?"

"Remarkably fine," he said. "The Blue Ship Tearoom. Whale." He was still looking at me, swaying back and forth as he stood before me, one hand on his hip. A tearoom, no less. I would have given anything to have been a fly on the wall.

"All that way? I shouldn't have thought you'd have time," Ruth said.

"I hailed a cab."

"Good for you, dear, good for you."

"It's a grand place. You've got to hand it to the chap who owns it, an amazingly agreeable fellow. We spoke at some length. A real prince of a guy."

"What kind of whale was it?" I asked. "I didn't know you could eat whale. Isn't it against the law?"

"I believe he said it was humpback. Or was it sperm?" His left eyebrow lifted momentarily, then relaxed. "A fine flavor to it, not unlike swordfish. And served in quite the same way, lightly grilled, with parsley butter."

"It must have been enormous," I said drily, imagining a cross-section of whale the size of an amphitheater. He ignored my feeble attempt at levity.

"It would be good if we could all have lunch someday down there. Maybe at the end of the summer. It's just a grand place. One helluvan outstanding establishment. Outstanding!" Oh, shut up, I thought—you're an idiot. You are behaving like a complete fool. Gregory Peck always smoked a pipe in movies.

"Many people would agree with you, dear," Ruth said. "The food is positively delish! . . . You haven't forgotten about the windows, have you, Oscar?"

"Never fear, Benson's here," he said. "I'll get right to it. I'll just light myself a pipe first. Meerschaum," he said, holding the pipe out at arm's length, scrutinizing it. "Finest smoke in town. As is. No seasoning required."

"Thank you, dear," Ruth said. "You know where the bucket is in the storeroom, and the squeegee, and the ammonia's right up there on the shelf above the sink, and the long apron. . . ." What an interesting counterpoint this was: Oscar the dandy, debonair, urbane young scholar, vs. Oscar the janitor, the sultan of squeegee. He carried on, however, undaunted.

"Say no more, madam. Everything is under complete control." He ambled toward the storeroom crooning "Shoobie-doobee-doo" to a slightly familiar tune.

Ruth finally exploded in giggles. "Isn't he the cutest thing? And I believe he's quite smitten with a certain young lady."

"Shh, Ruth! He'll hear you!"

"Mind you, you could do worse than Oscar Benson, dear," she said. "A lot worse. He's a lovely boy—a young man of quality if ever I saw one, and with such a bright future. They think the world of him over across the river. He came to me well recommended. Has he told you he's on the fencing team?"

"The *fencing* team?" I didn't even know that fencing was considered a sport.

"Oh, yes! Sword fighting, just like in the movies. I'm confessing, dear, that if I were a few years younger, I'd have my cap set for Oscar Benson myself. Fencing! Can you imagine? Now that's what I call romantic, don't you?"

"Possibly," I said, feeling forced to say something. Truthfully, it sounded asinine to me. All I knew about fencing was that every now and then in a movie magazine there would be mention of some vacuous movie starlet taking up fencing to help prepare her for some stupid role in a B movie. I gave a little accidental groan.

If anyone was going to be smitten with me, why on earth couldn't it be an ordinary hunk of a football player? I'd even sacrifice something in the way of intellect if I could just find a gorgeous hunk of physical animal whose vocabulary ran to words like "hike," "punt," and "gouge." Apparently, that would be asking too much.

There was no point in denying it: I adored the look of a man smoking a pipe. I had more than ample opportunity to indulge that infatuation to its fullest in the next few hours. I don't know how he did it, but he also managed to fit in some window washing as well; mostly, though, Oscar smoked his pipe and did pipe-related chores. Every time I looked at him, he stood scanning his work area, rocking back and forth on his heels, pipe between teeth, thumb and forefinger at his chin, in a pensive attitude, as if he were making calculations of some sort—the square footage of the front windows, perhaps, or the square root of Ruth's age.

When he wasn't deep in thought like this, there were practical matters to attend to: filling the pipe, tamping tobacco down, drumming on the tobacco with his index finger, refolding the pouch of Madeira Gold, inserting it into his breast pocket, striking match after match, lighting the tobacco again and again and again, puffing. He gestured with the pipe, rubbed its bowl, smiled crookedly around the pipe stem, unscrewed the stem from the bowl, inserted pipe cleaners, and scooped out the bowl with the spoon at the end of the tamper. It was hypnotizing.

I was just coming out to the front from one of the back rooms to see if Ruth was ready to take a break when I caught sight of Oscar as he knelt in front of the glass panes in the front door, squeegee-ing. He looked up at me, grinned around his pipe, and winked.

"Oscar!" I shouted, unable to contain myself another second. He was making complete asses out of both of us.

"Just who I was thinking of," Ruth said from behind me. "Time for you and Oscar to take a nice long break." Oscar dropped his squeegee and stumbled to his feet.

I turned abruptly and walked, sober-faced, toward the door to the alley, grabbing my purse from its cubbyhole as I went by.

"I'll be right there—soon as I get out of this apron," Oscar called. "Don't hurry on my account," I wanted to say.

In the alley I plunked myself down on one of the steps and lit a cigarette. I didn't normally smoke around boys, but this time I just didn't care. I took a long drag and tried to calm myself. I closed my eyes, and within seconds I felt as if my whole being had been infused with novocaine. What bliss! My pulse was normal, my respirations slow.

In this condition I would wait the day out, then reorganize and regroup overnight. Come dawn, I would have devised a new strategy for dealing with Oscar. Then, I promised myself, I would put an end to this awful nonsense. Even if I had to be cruel about it, I would make Oscar leave me alone.

"Hi," he said, coming out the door.

"Hell-o," I said solemnly, not looking at him. Like the slow-witted dolt he was, he crowded onto the step beside me and smiled. "Alone at last," I could hear him say to himself. He whistled a few bars of some tune, looked up at the sky, then drew back from me in an exaggerated fashion and held his hands up, thumbs at right angles to his fingers, as if framing my face for a scene he was about to shoot. He had the strangest expression on his face. He was probably nauseated from smoking so much. Lucky for me, he had left his pipe inside.

"Well, I've made my decision," he said, letting his hands fall to the steps beside him.

"And what, pray tell, might that be?" I said, feeling almost serene enough to drop off to sleep.

"About you," he said. Here it comes, I thought, my heart starting to pound. I dropped my cigarette, stamped it out, and glared at him as unflinchingly as I was able. So much for stoicism. Meanwhile, he was intently examining my face, then my arms, hands, and hair. His eyes had gone all soft.

"Well?" I said, not being able to stand another second of this. I *knew* what he was about to say. Maybe not the exact words, but something adoring and compliment—

"You're not beautiful," he said.

"I know," I said. I'm gorgeous, that's what you want to say, isn't it, Oscar? I looked away, bored.

"I wouldn't even call you pretty, exactly." My forehead knit momentarily in a reflexive frown. *Touché,* I thought. This was all pretty original—surprisingly so. I had to hand it to him.

"But you're too good-looking to be called cute. Cute girls sound like mice when they talk. And on the whole they're a lot shorter and a good deal fatter than you. They often have these really round, vacant eyes . . ."

"Really," I said. "You seem to have made quite a study. . . ." I said, allowing my voice to trail off. He didn't appear to be listening. He was looking at the sky, which had begun to cloud over. I wrinkled up my nose and scrunched up the rest of my face in an effort to look as ugly as possible. He looked down at me again. I noticed how tall he was. Even just sitting beside me he towered over me. Seeing my expression, he laughed and looked off into space, shaking his head in good-humored bewilderment. Then he lifted the arm closer to me and in a flash it was behind me, his hand on the step on the other side of me. His arm was around me!

"What you've got is a certain look about you, that's for sure," he said calmly. I nodded as if I had heard it all before. "One heck of a lot of a certain look," he said. "I like it. I really do. I like it like crazy." His tone was so sincere, his voice so soft and soothing, I made the mistake of looking right into his beautiful eyes, and for a split second I couldn't seem to look away. "You look like you *are* someone," he continued. "Someone of value." A shiver went through me.

"Thank you," I said.

"And your hair is incredible," he said. I laughed nervously. "What are you laughing about?" he whispered, leaning his head close to mine.

"I don't know," I said. I sounded helpless.

"Your laugh is incredible, too. I guess I already told you that."

"Thank you," I managed again. A lock of his straight, dark hair was down on his forehead again. It was silky and shiny clean. He pushed his glasses up on his nose with his index finger. It was a somewhat Roman nose, a classic nose.

"Are you free Saturday night by any chance?" he said.

"Yes," I said.

"Would you like to go to a movie with me?"

"Yes."

"There's a good foreign flick at the Brattle. Do you like foreign flicks?"

"Yes." I had never seen one.

"This one's from Sweden. It's gotten really fine reviews."

"Oh, that sounds good," I said.

"And afterward maybe we could go up to my room."

"I don't think so," I said.

"Or we could get something to eat or something. I think I can get my buddy's car."

"There's a coffeehouse near my place," I said. "We could go there for a while."

"Fine—fine. That sounds really fine." He smiled at me again and heaved an enormous sigh, apparently glad that this was settled. He removed his glasses and pretended to look through them for smudges, then folded their earpieces in and tucked them into his pocket. He watched his feet for a moment, then me, with an earnest, concerned look that made me wonder if perhaps he had a sudden headache. Then he touched my chin with his hand and turned my face to his and kissed me so softly that had I not had my eyes open I might not have known. I took a quick breath as his lips left mine, before they touched mine again—not gently this time but with such pressure and circular motion that my mouth opened. Our teeth met, then his tongue went between them, startling me so that I tried to draw back, but I didn't get far. He stopped kissing me but only barely moved away. With my eyes closed I felt his mouth on my forehead, then my cheeks, then my neck.

"You're so incredible," he moaned. "I have to do this. I hope you don't mind."

"What are you doing?" I said. My question was answered by his mouth following the curve of my neck. He reached up and pulled the fabric of my blouse aside, ditto my right bra strap, and his mouth was planted on my shoulder. His eyes were closed. I could see him quite well if I looked out of the very corners of my eyes. My nose was in his ear, an astonishingly perfect fit. They were made for one another. Actually, I was rather embarrassed— my breath must have sounded like the fury of the Colorado River rapids to him. When I smelled the odor I had smelled earlier, the odor of wool and starched, ironed cotton, as well as the exciting smell of his clean hair, like newly mown hay, I was suddenly possessed with a need to press my body close against his so forceful, it frightened me. We could not go on like this. I tried to move away.

"Stay for a minute," he said, searching for my mouth again with his.

"Oscar, no. I really need to—"

"I *need* you to stay here with me for a while. Another minute." One of his hands was now at the back of my head, his fingers grappling with my hair. His breathing was completely out of control. I had heard that they could get like this, boys, but I hadn't experienced quite this frenzy before. I had also heard that, well, things could happen, precipitously. I just didn't think I could handle the responsibility.

"Oscar dear," I said, sounding like his mother, "this is hardly the time or the place for . . ."

"I know . . . but all I can think of is you and being with you, alone with you. That's all I've thought about since the first minute I saw you." He rubbed my arm with his fingers, and I found myself thinking that I would like his fingers to touch me in other places.

"But that was only yesterday," I said.

"But I feel like I've known you forever and there's no need for any . . . uh . . . formalities. I just want to touch you. All I want to do is touch you." And he did the most extraordinary thing. He turned me toward him on the step and angled his body so that it was directly opposite mine. He raised his hands, palms facing me as if we were about to play patty-cake. Instead, he placed one open hand on each of my breasts and squeezed lightly and stared directly into my eyes.

"Ahhh," I sighed. It just came out of me. I couldn't have stifled it if I'd tried. I closed my eyes and felt his warm hands touching me.

"I think you like it when I touch you," he whispered. "Do you? Tell me if you do." I grasped his wrists with each of my hands but made no effort to move them. "Tell me if you do, will you?"

"I don't know. I really just don't know, right now," I said. I opened my eyes, moved his hands, and stood up. He didn't try to stop me. He just sat there, took his glasses out of his pocket, and put them on. I went up the steps past him and into the building, heading straight for the john.

Standing in front of the mirror, I looked as if I had been shot out of a cannon. Needless to say, my hair and lipstick were in dire need of repair, and my blouse was askew. The zipper of my skirt, normally a side zipper, was at my midsection. I adjusted it and my blouse, drew my comb through my hair, and redid my lipstick. I stood back, hoping to see a more usual me, but that stunned expression was still in my eyes. Something altogether wonderful or absolutely horrible had happened to me. It was written all over my face. In fact, it was *still* happening, for as I looked in the mirror and adjusted my gaze, then the position of my mouth, then my blouse once again, all that was actually on my mind was his voice, his words, the word "touch." It sent shivers up and down my spine.

I felt as if I were losing my mind. For a few minutes out there, just before my nose settled into his ear, I had seen that wonderful place on the side of his neck and was overcome by an insane, grinding desire to bite him there again and again until he was senseless. At that point I would tear off all his clothes and play with him. For hours. For days. Until I couldn't stand it anymore. Then I'd beg him to wake up and we'd—

"Ann? Are you all right?" My God, Ruth was outside the door! I made a quick exit, mumbling something about having had to put a pin in my slip strap. I raced to the Old and Rare, where an assortment of odd pages were stacked, waiting to be returned to their proper places in various volumes. Two things were now painfully clear to me: I was a slave to olfactory sensations, an absolute slave, and I had the morals of an alley cat. How could I have let him do what he did? In broad daylight? I had known him only two days. Two days! What was happening to me?

About an hour before closing time the rain began to fall, and although it appeared at first that it was just a summer cloudburst, it lingered. Ruth asked me to stay for a few minutes past closing so that I could watch her lock up and put the money away in the little safe hidden behind a cupboard in the storeroom. If she and Oscar happened to be sick one day, I would be left alone with the store and would need to know about it.

Although I expected Oscar to hang around and wait for me, he left at five o'clock sharp, waving to me casually as he passed the front window on his way to the subway. I was almost relieved to see the last of him.

As Ruth and I closed up and headed for home, the rain was still falling hard. Ruth walked with me for a short distance, then turned down in the direction of the banking district, where she had arranged to meet a friend for dinner. Kathleen was caring for Mother tonight.

I hadn't gone far when Oscar jumped out from a doorway, brandishing a bright smile and, just as importantly, a large black umbrella which he unfurled with a great pop and swoosh as he approached me.

"I might as well walk with you a ways," he said, gathering me toward him underneath the umbrella and putting his arm around me. "I'll take the subway from Park Street," he said, and off we marched.

In the matter of a few short minutes we discussed his future plans to be an architect, my plans to become an English teacher, the fact that he was not from a well-to-do family at all and went to MIT on a combination of his money, his parents', and whatever he could land in the way of scholarships. Somehow or other we ended up discussing poetry we had been forced to read in high school, and when we passed the corner of Beacon Street, where I normally turned, he was in the midst of reciting a few lines from *The Rime of the Ancient Mariner,* so I walked on with him. I could cross the Common from the Park Street station and get home that way.

"How far do you live from here?" he said, some minutes later as we stood at the subway entrance.

"Just over there," I said, pointing across the Common through the trees, "just down from the State House."

"Maybe I'll walk you the rest of the way," he said.

"You really don't have to," I said. "The rain seems to be letting up."

"Well, the truth is," he said, shrugging his shoulders, "I don't have much of anything else to do. Besides, this way I'll know where you live for Saturday night."

We started out, hand in hand. But before going far, Oscar stopped walking and looked down at me.

"What?" I said, puzzled by his expression.

"I just wanted to look at you," he said, leaning toward me, zeroing in on my mouth. He was going to kiss me again. "You're incredible," he sighed, as I pulled him along with me toward home. I would say goodbye to him on the front steps. If Oscar got into the front hallway, I might never get him out.

NINE

Just as we started up the front steps, Malcolm came out, followed by a gorgeous, tanned young man whose incredible physique was shown off by white tennis pants and a tight cotton shirt. Malcolm stopped and held the door open for us, and before I knew what was happening, what with greeting Malcolm and sizing up Charles Atlas, Oscar had followed me into the front hallway, closed the door, and stood his umbrella in the corner behind it. The hall was as black as a cave. I absentmindedly checked the long table where the mail was stacked and tried to plan my escape. The rain had completely revived me; I could easily wait until Saturday for more of Oscar Benson.

"I live on the third floor," I announced coldly, turning to face him. "We're not allowed to have men in our rooms."

"Oh," Oscar said, crestfallen. "That's a good idea. I guess."

"Yes, it is," I said. He smiled at me. I was still standing at the table. He was a foot or two from the front door. "I'm not sure we're even allowed to have men in this hallway."

"Hmm," he said, looking around. He took a step toward me, glancing toward the French doors. "Who lives in there?"

"Malcolm. The older man we met as we came in." My heart pounded in my ears.

"Oh, the fag?" he said.

I nodded. Obviously, he was right. He took two more steps and then grasped my hands in his and pulled me along with him as he walked backwards toward the door again. He stood against it and placed my hands at his waist. I was a weak woman.

"What are you doing?" I said to the floor. He was going to kiss me. I didn't want him to.

"Just this," he said, "just this." He lifted my chin and lowered his face toward mine. The last thing I saw was the lazy curve of his upper lip and above it, as he removed his glasses and awkwardly stuffed them into his pocket, his eyes, sleepy slits veiled with long lashes.

The second that his mouth touched mine, I felt him tremble. I tried to hold myself very still, but it was useless. My mouth trembled, too. My hands dropped to my side. I couldn't let him know that I loved kissing him. I took a step back, but he pulled me toward him again, hard. His hands were at my ribcage, moving down. Oh, God, I thought, but that was my only thought; my mind was empty.

His mouth on mine I felt as a stirring within me—everywhere. His hands, moving down to my hips, kneading the soft layer of flesh above the bone, sent ripples of nearly painful feeling to my throat, to my breasts, to a place deep in my pelvis, a place I identified instinctively as the very core of me.

His hand played at the buttons of my blouse, then slipped beneath its fabric and arrived, warm and lush, at my breast. I drew back, pulling his hand from me. "No," I said.

"I'm sorry," he said.

"It's okay," I said, but it wasn't.

"Then I take it back," he said. "I'm not sorry at all."

"Then why did you say it?"

"Because you expected me to."

"I think it was appropriate," I said. I looked up at his face, hoping to see some sign of remorse there. Nothing, just that gentle smile of his, relaxed and indulgent.

"Why?" he said. "Because I touched you, or almost touched you, there? Underneath your blouse?" I said nothing. What an arrogant SOB! "Then where may I touch you, Miss Merrill?" I wanted to tell him to go straight to hell. I wanted to hit him and run upstairs and never see him again. But I couldn't do that. I wouldn't let myself. I just glared at him. "Hmm, no answer," he said to himself. "How about the hand? May I touch your hand?" I glared at him. He took my hand and moved closer to me. I could have spit into his face. "And your arm?" He rubbed my arm with an index finger. "How about your . . . your neck . . . your hair?" He ran his fingers up and down my neck, then reached underneath my hair. He was playing with me. I jerked my head away, and his hand fell free. "And I know that you'll let me kiss you, because you have now, several times." I noticed for the first time that his voice had dropped down into that phony low register. He was nervous. "You've even kissed me back," he said. "And you'll let me touch your waist and your hip, but—"

"There is something disgustingly perverted about you, Oscar," I said, finally composing myself, looking up into the stairwell, my head held high.

"There's something incredibly normal about me, you mean," he said. I faced him.

"You are obviously deluded," I said.

"Nor-mal," he insisted. "At least when I'm with you. I mean, I'm not like this with just anyone. Not just for the hell of it."

"Well, pin a rose on you!"

"I mean," he said, "I mean, I wouldn't exactly refuse if I was seduced by some wild woman. . . ."

"Spare me the sordid details." He looked at me self-consciously, looked behind him at his umbrella standing in the corner, then sighed.

"All you seem to be interested in is making out," I said, hating to use that expression but realizing that it was useful for a time like this when one wanted to avoid being too explicit.

"You don't understand," he said.

"What don't I understand?"

"That it's normal for me to want you, to want to touch you. I can't help it. That's the way I feel about you. I just took one look at you and I knew that all I wanted to do was touch you and kiss you and—"

"You're out of your mind," I said.

"It's true, Annie. And it's *good*. Don't you see that? It's meant to *be*. And more is going to happen, Annie, just as a matter of course, just like that, the way everything that is good happens."

"Just as a matter of course?"

"Because each of us wants it to happen."

"Suppose one of us *never* wants it to happen?"

"That's impossible, Annie—you know it as well as I do."

"Nothing's impossible," I said, unimaginatively. I wondered if he told every girl he met the same thing.

"Look," he said. "You like it when I kiss you. You even like it when I touch you. You're afraid, but you like it. I can tell. I can feel you liking it, then being afraid."

"I'm not afraid of much of anything, Oscar—certainly not you!"

"I'm afraid too," he said, his expression solemn. The instant I heard those words, something happened to me, a sensation of something giving way. I thought of wind uprooting a tree, casting it across a plain as if it were weightless. "We'll just go along being scared together," he said, "okay?"

"Okay," I said, not really aware of what I was agreeing to, not really caring. Oscar put his arms around me as if to comfort me, then said he'd better go.

"Not yet," I said, drawing him closer to me.

"What?" he said, looking down at me quizzically, with an amused smile.

"Just be close to me like this," I said, "and put your face close to mine, and—I know this sounds silly, but I want you to breathe on me, just breathe into my mouth." He did. His breath was heavenly: a hint of a layer of pipe tobacco and, beneath it, the odor of something young and vital and sweet. I closed my eyes and smelled organs and bone marrow and cells. I smelled blood and muscle tissue and saliva and cartilage—the scent of human life, a scent so basic, so intrinsic, as to be, under most circumstances, indistinguishable from the smell of air.

I stepped closer to him and, meaning to say that he smelled so good, I said that he tasted so good, and he kissed me again. But this time I didn't close my eyes or try to regulate my breathing or try to stop my lips from trembling. I put my arms around him and pressed my breasts against his chest. When his hands were on my hipbones once more and he was pulling that part of me against him, I simply let go of all that had held me back before and looked into his eyes and allowed myself for the very first time in my life to feel a male body with my own. All of it. I moved back and forward against him, to feel him again and again.

"Annie, Annie."

"I love your breath, Oscar."

"You're a hedonist, Annie, I knew it."

"Your body is so warm, your skin is so warm. . . ."

"I'm a mammal," he said. I giggled. "Your place or mine?" he added. "I can't wait. You don't want to wait, either."

"Oscar . . ." I began, extricating myself from his arms. "Don't tell me anymore how I feel. Don't act as if you can read my mind. And I've already told you I won't go up to your room and you can't come up to mine."

"Okay," he said.

"And no one can tell the future, even though they think they can. You don't really *know* what's going to happen between us."

"Yes I do."

"No."

"Whatever you say," he finally agreed, throwing up his hands in mock despair.

"Now you probably should be going," I said, feeling once again that I was in control of things.

"I have to ask you something first," he said.

"What?"

"Has anyone at any time ever told you you look like the Campbell Soup Kid?" He began to laugh. My mouth hung open. He laughed louder. I turned away from him and took my sweater and purse from the table where I had left them.

"I do not understand you," I said slowly. "First you tell me that I'm not beautiful, not pretty, not even cute, then you're all over me with your hands like you can't get enough of me, then you say I look like the Campbell Soup Kid!"

"I was only joking," he said, obviously concerned. "And you *are* beautiful. I love the way you look. I love the way you talk and laugh and kiss me, and, Annie, I love the way you *feel* and the way you *taste*. It's just that with the color of your hair, and your face is kind of round, *beautifully* round, and—"

"It's too late, Oscar. I'm going." I headed for the stairs.

"No—wait a minute—"

"I'm going, Oscar. I never should have—"

"Wait—don't be mad at me!"

"I'll see you tomorrow. Don't forget your umbrella."

"Are we still going out on Saturday?"

"How could I possibly resist?" I said, pausing on the second step. "It's not often that a girl has an opportunity to go to a movie with someone who's a dead ringer for Jerry Lewis!" He tried not to smile. "Oh, I beg your pardon," I said. "I should have said a dead ringer for Cyrano de Bergerac! I hear that you engage in a little swordplay when things get dull over at that bastion of higher learning. . . ."

"We were made for each other, Annie."

"Don't be too sure," I said.

"I'll call you tonight," he said, walking over to the telephone and taking his fountain pen out of his jacket pocket.

"Don't bother. I won't be here," I said. "A friend and I are going out to dinner." I then continued up the stairs to the second-floor landing, out of sight. In a moment I heard the front door open and close behind him. I imagined him rushing along down Beacon Street and Charles Street for the subway, wondering who on earth this friend of mine was, male or female. He deserved it.

I leaned against the wall for a few minutes. I thought I heard Georgia running water upstairs in our bathroom and I hoped I wouldn't have to see her right away. All I wanted to do was to think of Oscar. He was wonderful. Men were wonderful.

I closed my eyes and with my own hand tried to approximate the feeling I'd had as his fingers had undone the buttons of my blouse and then gently squeezed my breast. I should have let him do more, I thought. What if I had? What if he had reached behind me and undone my bra and then reached under it, in front, with both hands, large, warm hands, and cradled my breasts in his palms, then fingered my nipples? I felt them grow hard at the thought of it. Nature was so amazing.

Up in my room, I took off my clothes, put on my robe, and glanced at myself in the mirror, suddenly embarrassed by my own conduct. Oscar wasn't the perverted one; I was. Whatever would become of me? Nymphomania?

Yes. It was all too clear. Nymphomania began just like this. On a Tuesday in June. Shortly after a summer shower. One would find oneself kissing a boy of one's acquaintance and smelling his breath and wanting to plaster one's body against his; and then, within seconds, one would find oneself *needing* to touch him, underneath his clothes. *Needing* to!

Where would it all end? Suppose I went mad with it and wanted every man I looked at, had to have every man I set eyes on? Guggie . . . Stanley Crosshill . . . Malcolm Balch . . .

Nymphomania! I would have to guard against it or accept my own ruin.

TEN

Despite my fear of nymphomania, as the week wore on, my date with Oscar on Saturday night was ever on my mind. What would happen? What would he do? What would I do? Judging by his behavior at work, taking every opportunity to kiss me and touch me and whisper sweet nothings in my ear, he had every intention of trying to go all the way with me on Saturday. As far as he was concerned it was practically a fait accompli.

Every afternoon when he walked me home to Walnut Street, there would be that same scene in the front hall outside Malcolm's door—except that with each passing day Oscar grew bolder and bolder. Neither the sound of footsteps from inside Malcolm's apartment nor one of the law students strolling through the front door could diminish Oscar's ardor. He had lost the shreds of decorum he once might have had.

In a way it was charming, certainly complimentary, even amusing. In another way it was almost frightening—not to mention stimulating. To be honest about it, I had begun to look forward to these moments at least as much as Oscar did.

Which brings me to a subject that I found it necessary to give considerable thought to in the remaining days before our big date: penises. Inevitable. Obligatory. Not that I hadn't thought of penises before. I had—but only for split seconds at a time, envisioning them as great white monolithic structures of more or less the same consistency as marble.

One evening after work—Georgia had a dental appointment way out in Roslindale and wouldn't be home for dinner until late— I lay on my bed in my underwear, intending to take a short nap, and found myself thinking about penises instead.

Of course, to be honest about it, I had already come in contact with Oscar's penis. I had felt it a number of times—not just a faint bulge, as I had experienced with others, but the entire length of it, arching up and out against me, feeling so hard that I wondered that it was not made of some superhuman stuff. How could it be made of just skin and muscle and blood? How could it be soft and completely unnoticeable one minute and the next be hard as a rock and upright, reaching almost to his belt line? I had even caught a glimpse of a hooded prominence to the left of his fly, although I tried not to be obvious about it. It had made a pup tent out of his pants, so enormous that it took my breath away. I was briefly overcome with a terrible urge to touch it, just to get the feel of it in my hands, to squeeze the tip of it—not entirely for sensuous pleasure on my part but as a kind of scientific experiment, an anatomy lesson, if you will.

I tried to imagine what it would be like if Oscar or someone like him, someone who volunteered for the experiment, lay in a hospital bed, blindfolded for his own comfort, while women like me milled around him, touching it, rubbing it, lifting it up, and turning it over, just to see at first hand how the thing worked, just examining the daylights out of it. I, for one, would be quite interested in watching it swell and rise and even come. It was hard for me to envision the mechanics of it.

I thought of my poor mother. Once, after drinking a considerable amount of sherry at Cousin Candace's wedding, Mother confessed to me, nearly hysterically, that for years during her adolescence she thought that all the young swains she danced with at the Starlight Ballroom in Centerville packed revolvers. A hands-on course such as the one I advocated could have done wonders for a person like her.

It wasn't that I had never seen one naked. I had—my brother's—but only when we were both little and it was little and white and wrinkled and was referred to as his "kee-kee," an odd word my family used for genitalia of both sexes. For some reason, my kee-kee was mentioned a whole lot less than Evan's. In fact, at times I was downright amazed that Evan's kee-kee seemed to be more or less constantly on everyone's mind. Countless times I heard him warned not to touch or rub or play with his kee-kee. Every time he zipped his trousers someone would scream, "Watch out for your kee-kee!" Whereas mine was to be kept clean, Evan's was to be *preserved* from all possible harm.

I would always remember an incident that occurred when Evan was about five and I was seven. Mother was having afternoon tea in the living room with her friend Lucy Peckham and my grandmother, when a teary-eyed Evan wandered in to stand before Mother, his short flannel pants grasped by his fist at the crotch. "My kee-kee hurts," he whined. There was an audible gasp from all three women, and I could see terror in their eyes. Evan was immediately spirited away to the bathroom, leaving me to nibble petit fours from the tea cart alone.

It was an unwritten law that although I was allowed to bathe with Evan every evening, I was not permitted to observe his kee-kee at any other time.

Well, there I sat, nibbling, when it dawned on me that Mother, Grandmother, and Aunt Lucy were speaking in whispers as they administered treatment to my brother and that they were taking quite a long time. Suddenly Mother raced out past me to the kitchen, where she rummaged around in a drawer for a special ointment she had mislaid, then tore into the living room, where she took sharp scissors and cotton batting from her sewing basket.

I heard her close the bathroom door tight and slide the bolt. I imagined all of them huddling around Evan as he sat on the toilet, half-naked, all of them whispering and applying cotton and ointment and yards and yards of tape. Evan was bleeding to death, I was sure.

I popped another finger sandwich into my mouth and remembered some Sundays when Mother and Aunt Lucy served on the

Altar Guild at our church. They allowed me to come with them
if I agreed to sit on a red velvet chair and be quiet. I would watch
them both work in the tiny room where the vestments, altar cloths,
and communion vessels were kept. They would huddle together
and whisper as they went about their work with a queer sort of
slow motion, handling the linens and silver pieces oddly, not as
they would handle things at home. The tiny room they worked in
was about the size of our bathroom and graced by a stained-glass
depiction of Moses in the wilderness, a pale figure dressed in white
standing in an overgrowth of branches and green leaves. On a
sunny morning the room would be bathed in green light from that
window, just like our bathroom would in the afternoon, sun
streaming through the green dotted-swiss bathroom curtains my
mother had made.

I was thinking of this when Evan trooped gamely back into the
living room as part of a processional led by Grandmother. She
looked the way she did when she came down from the communion
rail, hands folded limply at her waist, eyes focused on something
approximately thirty feet above us. Evan was ashen-faced and walked
with his legs spread wide apart to accommodate the hefty wad of
cotton batting between his legs—definitely a case of overkill, a
huge bandage for what I had myself seen was a minute body part.
He was placed gingerly on the sofa with Daddy's prized copy of
Quentin Durward to look at. Cocoa was administered, as were tiny
peanut-butter sandwiches from which the crusts had been removed. There seemed to be no end to the number of frosted petit
fours it took to stem the flow of blood and bring the roses back
into the plucky little fellow's cheeks. I was livid with envy. To
make matters worse, my father doted on Evan for days and ordered
me to allow him the use of my bicycle until he felt better.

I couldn't help feeling somehow less significant after that. It
had been made perfectly clear to me that while I, being a girl,
would need to cultivate table manners, a pleasant speaking voice,
and a respectable IQ if I were to be successful in life, Evan would
never have to concern himself with anything weightier than the
care and preservation of his almighty kee-kee.

I remembered thinking what a lucky duck Evan was while at

the same time thanking my lucky stars that, whatever its mystique, I did not have such an organ. First of all, they were ugly. They seemed to have been attached to the human body as an after-thought. They just dangled there, white and wiggly. There was something unhealthy looking about an organ that at times, around its tip, appeared to be a most frightening shade of ice blue. Finally, the penis seemed uncontrollable. It had the capability of swelling up and arching out of its own free will. Evan would be sitting across the tub from me when all of a sudden he would giggle and point down at the venerable kee-kee. There it would be, raising its shiny blue head through the suds like a tiny beluga whale. When Mother left the room for a moment, I'd act out *Moby Dick,* using my barrette as a harpoon.

It suddenly occurred to me that the apartments across the court-yard had a perfect view of me, lying there, so I got up and pulled the shade but left the window open, hoping for a breeze. The drizzle had stopped, but clouds still blanketed the city, and the air was muggy. Rather than a restful serenade by Cesare, the guitarist, a cacophony of other sounds filled the courtyard, sounds of evening: the clatter of dishes, a door slamming, windows being raised, the distinctive voice of Curt Gowdy calling a baseball game.

I removed my underwear and lay down again naked on the bed. With the room in semidarkness and the deep shades of green and blue of my peacock spread, my skin looked less pink, more ivory. I felt fragile and light, as if I were weightless as an eggshell. I closed my eyes. I touched my own forearms with trailing fingers. My skin was so smooth and soft that as I lay there, I pretended that my fingers belonged to someone else, a man, who touched me in the darkness.

Then my fingers, his fingers, traced little circles on my perfect breasts and the space between them, then his hands spread wide apart, and each found a breast of its own to feel and squeeze against a palm.

His hands moved to my waist and hips, at first trailing as light feathers, then grasping my flesh just for the feel of it, the sensation of something soft and spongy between his fingers.

Oscar would do that to me, I thought, touch me like that. He had said it. Suddenly the fantasy changed. The man *was* Oscar.

His finger slipped between my legs. Then his entire hand, inching my legs apart little by little until they were opened wide.

I saw him kneeling beside me, his body as white and smooth as mine, glowing like a marble statue in the moonlight. He was beautiful, lithe, strong, his skin warm and faintly damp. I could smell his breath of live cells and blood and marrow and something else totally male—semen. I could smell it in him. I could taste it in his mouth, like salt, the taste of a man. And a woman tastes of bread, I thought, not knowing why or how.

I looked at him again, the length of him, his long, taut body; long arms; long, swollen lengths of oval muscle. Long legs, hard bones, hard strips of tight muscle. Still kneeling, he spread his legs apart as if to straddle me, and in the moment that he hesitated and all I heard was his breath in gasps, I saw his penis arched away from his body in the most elegant, aesthetic angle, hard and white and long as a tusk. I reached for him. He swung his leg over me and came to me, all mouth and hands and legs and penis punching against me again and again until I opened to him completely and he entered my body as deeply as he could go, as deep as I was; yet I lifted myself to him to bring him deeper still. It was too much to bear without bursting, as I was filled with him, filled again and again. . . .

As I lay there, myself again, Oscar had vanished. My hand was still between my legs, and I felt the wetness there, even more now than when Oscar kissed me. I dipped my finger deep inside me and carried the wetness away from the opening and smeared it between the little folds of skin, the odd soft places which were a part of my anatomy, so familiar yet so puzzling. Before another moment had passed, Oscar was with me again, moving in and out of me, inserting himself, then drawing back slowly, with an easy, maddening rhythm; then faster and faster and faster until I saw nothing and heard nothing and all I thought of was that I was this core, once more about to burst, and when I came at last, I could not help crying out with the intense, excruciating pleasure of it pounding over me in great waves that slowly subsided and I lay smiling, drifting, numb, suspended like a one-celled animal in an ebbing sea.

For once I would not allow myself to feel guilty for what I had done. I was beginning to discover the very life within me. The journey had begun.

Once again I thought of my mother, whom I loved so much in spite of everything. There was a quality about her that I had never understood—a quality of having never allowed herself to bloom completely. Fear was at the center of this, I was sure. Somewhere along the line she had lost herself. Aunt Chloe once said Mother had lost herself in me. Without Evan and me, she didn't know what to do. I worried about that sometimes, felt guilty for wanting to be apart from her, to have my own life. What would become of her then?

Once, in my senior year, I was going to a football game in another town with a group of girlfriends. We were planning to stay overnight there after the game and dance, at the home of a friend's grandmother. Mother was almost as excited as I was and had helped with the preparations. She could be such fun at times like this, helping me choose the clothes I would take, making treats for us to take along for snacking. My friends envied me. When they arrived to pick me up, I ran out to the car with all my things. I turned to see Mother standing in the living-room window, a sad, empty look on her face. I waved to her. She waved back, then just stood there. I half-wanted to run back into the house and tell her she could come, too. Even as we reached the end of our street and I looked back, she was still there, a dark shadow on the glass.

I wondered if that was what would happen in the end—if I would always leave her sad and empty behind me, farther and farther back, until she was nothing more than a black stick figure on the horizon.

It was well after eight when I heard Georgia come loping up the stairs. I jumped into my robe and met her at my door when she pounded, half-hysterical that I might have gone on to the River-view without her.

We dressed and met at the top of the stairs and started off at a lively clip, Georgia stating, hurriedly, that she hoped we would be in time to see Stanley Crosshill.

"Tonight should do it," she said. "This time's the charm. And when he asks you to dinner I hope you'll remember your old friends and ask him if he has a similarly rich friend who has the hots for tall girls with the hots—me, in case you didn't know."

"You're more excited at the prospect than I am," I said, as we walked toward the Riverview.

"Ain't it the truth, kid," she said softly, not throwing her arms around me but taking my hand in hers and we walked a few steps together like that, as if we were girls walking to school, like Mary Armitage and I used to do before we became rivals for the world's population of men. And if I had been less inhibited and more secure in my own perception of myself, I would have told Georgia then that I really liked her, I liked her very much. But I took my hand from hers. No matter how innocently she meant it, the last thing I wanted was to be seen walking through the streets hand in hand with another girl.

We turned the corner at Charles Street. The Riverview was straight ahead. And although I was now convinced that Oscar Benson held the keys to my future, like the little tart Georgia had said I was I began to think of Stanley Crosshill, too.

"Okay, this is it," Georgia announced, holding the door of the Riverview open for me. "Give it all you've got, kid. Let's see those dimples, that all-American Ipana smile. . . . Oh, shit, I knew it! We missed him."

She was right. The Riverview dinner crowd had dissipated. No mad hubbub, no wild melee, no more jokes from the Greeks behind the counter. No Stanley Crosshill. No one of any interest, actually. A quiet dinner tonight.

The lull before the storm: in approximately forty-eight hours I could be making mad, passionate love to Oscar Benson.

ELEVEN

It was, I suppose, a cruel irony that after spending so much time preparing for my Saturday-night date with Oscar, on Saturday morning I came down with the intestinal flu and spent the entire weekend in bed. Actually, Ruth had been concerned about my color as early as Friday afternoon, and by the time she called on Saturday to check on me, I was unable to come to the phone. Georgia spoke with her instead, and so it didn't surprise me that by three o'clock Ruth had made an appearance at Walnut Street. I awoke from a fevered sleep to see her pink face floating above me like a disembodied cherub's, with Malcolm, eyebrows awiggle, beside her.

"Ruth," I began, another wave of nausea sweeping over me, "I'm all right, really—just the flu." I leapt up from the bed and raced to the bathroom. When I returned, Ruth had sent Malcolm for a hot plate and was instructing Georgia to feed me spoonfuls of heated broth, one at a time, as soon as I could keep anything down. She brought the jar of broth to my bedside for inspection.

"It's an old family recipe," she said, "passed down through the generations. Chicken and celery, rosemary and garlic, two leeks, a handful of barley, *and*—this is the part that does it, dear—baby beef livers cooked and pressed through a sieve. It'll bring your strength back." It made me woozy just thinking of it. "I used to make it for Kathleen when she was small. Excellent for colic. As soon as you can hold a bit down, dear." At that point Malcolm wandered in with the hot plate and set it on my bureau. "Ah, thank you, Mr. Balch," Ruth said effusively, her tone girlish and a little breathless. "Just warm this up and feed it to her slowly, as soon as she can tolerate it," she repeated for his benefit.

She returned to my bedside and arranged the bedclothes, folding the top sheet neatly down over the blankets and tucking me in. She then strode to the window and opened it wide. "Fresh air in the sick room," she said cheerfully, "nothing more healing than that." She came over and placed her cool hand on my forehead. "About a hundred and one, I should think," she said, her brow furrowed. "Just rest, dear, just rest. You'll need Monday and Tuesday off to recuperate. We'll manage just fine." She leaned toward me and whispered in my ear, "You may find yourself constipated by the end of the week. I'll leave these for you." She placed a small box of pills under my pillow. "Two at night before you retire." "Now, Mr. Balch," she said, standing up, "I shouldn't trouble you again, I know, but I wonder if you have a fresh lemon on hand."

"I believe I do," he said. Ruth's eyes were blinking rapidly, her rosebud lips drawn up at the corners. Was she flirting? "I try to keep a few on hand," he added. "Wonderful for the skin, they say. I use them in my bath." Behind him, Georgia stifled a giggle.

"Do you really?" Ruth said, following Malcolm toward the door. "Just the juice? I'll show you how to make lemon tea for her. First broth, then lemon tea. Do you just pour the juice in when the tub is full?"

"Well, you could," Malcolm said, holding the door for Ruth. She turned and blew a kiss at me. "I slice them right into the water."

Ruth laughed in little high notes tripping down the scale. "Rather like a punch bowl, Mr. Balch?" They were gone. Georgia burst out laughing.

"What a pair," she said. "Old Ruthie's got the hots for him, that's for sure." I was too weak to laugh.

"I'm not sure about him at all," I said. "I saw him with a woman the other day."

"Oh, yeah, the blond?"

"She *was* blond. They were walking together and—"

"Yeah, that's Mrs. Cousins. Pinkie Cousins. She's one of those society ladies he does work for."

"What do you mean?"

"Malcolm makes models," she said, "of historical places. Scale models of houses or little villages. Like, he was working on this model of the old Salem waterfront. Every little detail had to be just right. He made the cutest little trees out of bits of natural sponge and painted them green. Honest to God, they looked real. . . . Sorry."

"What?" I said, another wave of nausea beginning. I sat up on the side of my bed.

"He really is queer, you know. He's had someone staying with him down there, at least part-time."

I couldn't wait a minute longer. I got up from the bed and dashed to the bathroom again.

On Sunday night, Georgia, who had been in touch with Oscar by phone all weekend, relayed that he too had come down with the flu that afternoon and probably wouldn't be back at work until midweek. Our date was tentatively postponed until the following Saturday, pending our recovery. I was just feeling well enough to experience a pang of disappointment. Saturday seemed like a million light years away. That evening Ruth called and told me not to worry about her being alone at work. Kathleen would fill in part-time for both Oscar and me. With Kathleen's departure for the West looming so close at hand, I knew they would enjoy this unplanned time together.

Since Saturday, Georgia had made a habit of leaving both our doors open so that each of us could walk freely from one room to the other during the day, as if the third floor at Walnut Street were one sprawling apartment. I liked it. Claude, whom I still had not met, was rarely at home, and then only late at night or very early in the morning, so Georgia and I were not interrupted by anyone other than Malcolm using the stairs. He came up now and then to deliver mail or brew another cup of hot lemon tea for me or inquire about my health; but Malcolm had become so familiar as to be hardly considered an interruption at all. Although I no longer doubted that he was a homosexual, whatever disapproval I might have once felt had been replaced by genuine fondness. In some ways he was like a perfect parent: doting, yet keeping an appropriate distance. I felt secure and safe with him in the house, watching over us all.

Georgia was in high spirits. I had begun to think that my concerns about her mental health were ill founded. She appeared happy. Whatever had influenced her in the past, she now seemed no more likely to harm herself than I was.

I had even gotten a kick out of being sick away from home and Mother. There was something undeniably adult about leaning over the john in the throes of the dry heaves without parental supervision—the steadying hand on the back of the neck, the cold cloth applied to the forehead. If this was some kind of test, I had passed it with flying colors.

Speaking of Mother . . . at long last I heard from her, on Tuesday, in a letter so pleasant, for the most part, that it actually shocked me. She seemed to have taken my move from Barclay in stride. Either that or Aunt Chloe had spoken with her and smoothed her feathers, for the majority of the letter was taken up with plans she and Father had to spend the last two weeks of August on Chebeague Island in Maine, where they had taken a cottage. Evan would be at camp then, she said, working as a junior counselor, and if anything went wrong I was to contact Aunt Chloe, as no one would be at home in Beverly. She went on and on about who would mow the lawn in their absence, who would take care of the cat, the dinner dress she had bought for evenings at the Freeport Cove Hotel.

At the very end of the letter, however, she did mention Georgia, whom I had briefly described. In typical Merrill fashion she urged me to look around for friends with whom I would be "more compatible." She went on to say that "pity for someone else's lot in life is a poor basis upon which to build a friendship" and finished with another typical statement: "I have always found it much more rewarding to confine myself to associations with those of my own kind, people from similar backgrounds, with similar high standards." So much for my yet unspoken plans to invite Georgia home to Beverly for a weekend.

By the time Oscar returned to work on Wednesday, we had practically become strangers. Whatever small bits of conversation we were brave enough to engage in came off sounding ridiculously stilted, as if translated from a foreign language.

"Gravely c-concerned over your . . . uh . . . h-health and welfare . . . uh . . . I have been," Oscar stuttered during a lull his first day back.

"I too . . . uh . . . greatly . . . I mean, *really* . . . I worried about you," I said, my lips trembling as if I were about to cry.

"I trust that you are . . . uh . . . completely . . . uh . . . are you better?"

"I am feeling well," I said. "Yes, quite well indeed. And you?"

"Ah, yes, of course—grand. I feel quite grand. Quite well. Too. Me too."

"Oh, good," I replied, offering an encouraging smile. He smiled back and chuckled softly.

"Okay?" he said, nodding, sighing.

"Yes," I giggled. "Everything's okay." We turned from one another and drifted off in opposite directions.

By Thursday afternoon, though, Oscar and I were back to normal and during our break carried on as if we had never been apart. He began kissing me and touching me and prophesying all sorts of semilurid events in the near future. He even walked me home for the first time since I had taken sick, and we took up where we had left off in the downstairs hallway. It was, therefore, wrapped about one another that Georgia found us the moment she crashed through the front door and she and Oscar met, in person, at last.

I knew it was Georgia and not Malcolm or one of the law students from the sound of her footsteps. I must have been too involved to think clearly, because I made the mistake of assuming that, like any decent person, she would have the good sense to whisk past us as if we were invisible. In fact, I even took the time to wave a little to her behind Oscar's back, a friendly little wave of dismissal. It said, "Hello there and goodbye there. As I am obviously enjoying pure ecstasy, I must thank you for not interrupting."

I waited to hear her footsteps scurry past and hurry up the stairs. But she stood there, and I hated her for this, waiting for us to "finish." I broke away from Oscar and glared at her. "What do you want?" I said.

"Oh, sorry," she murmured demurely, lowering her opal eyes. "I just had to tell you something."

"Shoot. What is it?"

"Oh, never mind—it's nothing," she said shakily, her eyes darting back and forth between Oscar and me. She gave a helpless shrug. I clenched my teeth.

"Georgia, this is Oscar Benson. Oscar, this is my friend Georgia Mitchell."

"Hi," Oscar said.

Georgia shuffled forward and offered a limp hand. "Well," she drawled, "Ah've certainly heard a thing or two about you. How lovely to meet you at long last." She looked him over as if he were a plate of grits and red-eye gravy.

I cleared my throat and turned toward the stairwell, hoping to give her the idea. "I'll be up in a minute," I said.

"Maybe we could double-date sometime," she said to Oscar. As she walked between us to the hall table, where she slowly went through three little stacks of mail, none of which was hers, I had an opportunity to take note of Oscar's expression: a half-hearted smile, raised brows. He put his glasses back on. "Not tonight, though," she continued. "Annie and I have plans tonight. . . . Oh, I'm sorry, maybe you hadn't told him that yet."

"I'll be up in a minute, okay?" I said.

"I'm *going*," she said, walking to the stairs at last. "I just thought you'd want to introduce me, that's all."

"Of course I did." The phone rang at that moment and rescued me. I answered it. A low, woman's voice asked for Georgia. I handed her the phone. It was a short conversation.

"Ida wants me to come for dinner—isn't that perfect? Now the two young lovers can be alone like they want to be, and Georgia gets to go and help Ida eat her capon. How wonderful!"

"Georgia, really—Oscar and I have no plans, we were just saying goodbye. I thought we were going to the Riverview."

She patted my arm condescendingly. "Well, maybe we could go for a little walk afterward. I won't be long." She slung her purse strap over her shoulder, glared briefly at Oscar, and swept past us out the front door.

"Why do I get the feeling she doesn't like me?" Oscar said, taking my hand and pulling me gently toward him.

"I should have warned you. Frankly, right now I would gladly murder her. She's awfully unpredictable."

"So am I," Oscar said, yanking me toward him, and before I knew it his tongue was working its way between my teeth, his body was ground against mine. I fell into the kind of mindless, impassioned semiswoon I was learning to love.

"You're such a hedonist, Annie," Oscar cried, as I tried to insert my hands between the buttons of his shirt and accidently popped one, like a tiddlywink.

"I know, I know," I said, pulling up his undershirt. I had looked up the word; it suited the new me to a tee.

On Friday after work, Oscar and I said goodbye to one another at the Park Street station. He was to spend the evening with a close friend in Cambridge who would be lending us his car for our date on Saturday evening.

Feeling a little guilty about leaving Georgia alone on Saturday, I had promised her that she and I would spend Friday night together. We had plans to go to a movie and out for pizza afterwards at this "really crummy little dive" she knew about in the Italian section of town, where an old man in back made the greatest pizzas this side of Sicily. We'd live on popcorn and Jujy Fruits until then.

Making the final turn at the corner of Walnut Street and heading toward the house, I noticed that Georgia's pigeons were bobbing along the ledge outside her window but that Georgia was nowhere in sight, nor was her window raised. Another impromptu summons from Ida Printaine, perhaps? For they seemed less like invitations to me with each passing day.

Perhaps she was late from work. Perhaps she was only changing her clothes.

It was hot and humid; but, as always, the front hallway welcomed me like an oasis. I stood silently for a moment outside Malcolm's door and let the still, cool air revive me. The usual smell of eucalyptus hung on the air like a fragrant petal above a still, dark pond. The house was quiet. From the far end of the hall table the eyes of the dead, stuffed bird shone through the darkness like two scattered jet beads on an old dress.

I started up the stairs, my high heels echoing as they struck each riser.

"Georgia," I called out before reaching the second-floor landing; I had forgotten about the law students. No answer. I almost turned at the top of the stairs and went straight to her room, but the bathroom door was open and I glanced in.

Georgia stood there facing me, in front of the wash basin. The sun, low in the sky at this hour, shone round and orange as a chunk of burning coal behind her, so bright that her body appeared in half-silhouette, like an apparition bathed in the sepia tone of a color negative. "Hi," I said, reflexively, but before the word was completely out of my mouth I knew that something was wrong.

I squinted to see her better and blinked, hastening my eyes' accommodation to the intense topaz light. "Hi," she said, her voice a thin rattle. She stood rigidly still, backlit, her thin body outlined beneath the batiste of her nightgown.

Then I saw the blood. It was on her face, her neck, thin streams of it, streaks and rivulets of blood. A knife was in her hand, or some kind of pick. All I saw was a fleeting glint of metal. I thought of mirrors flashed from distant mountaintops, of signals of distress sent across the open sea. Then I walked right by into my room and closed the door behind me.

I stepped from my shoes and felt the cool hardwood against the hot soles of my feet, although the room was stifling. By rote,

I removed the hairpins from my hair, but without moving, just standing there beside my empty shoes.

For in my mind I was still on the landing. The amber rectangle of the sun-struck bathroom was before me still: the ghostly figure of Georgia, those wide, white eyes set in a horrible stare, and all the blood, which in my mind was not quite red but tinged with rust or brick or the shade of sweet vermouth, and gleaming wet.

What had she done to herself? I hadn't been close enough to gauge the severity of the cuts. Had she cut her own throat? My God, she could be bleeding to death this very instant! My heartbeat bobbed up into my neck like a cork in a whistle.

I had to do something—call for help or race back into the hall and call Malcolm. I could climb through my window to the fire escape and scream until someone heard me.

But I didn't move. A queer, heavy feeling came over me, and before long I was painstakingly searching my memory for rules of etiquette that might govern an event such as this. What exactly did a proper young woman do when she returned home from work one day and found her admittedly insane but recently high-spirited friend slashing herself to ribbons?

Startling me with their clatter, three hairpins fell from my hand to the floor. How long had I been standing like this—an hour or ten seconds? I turned and looked at my door. Georgia was still out there, doing God only knew what to herself. I was in here, alone, my door unlocked, vulnerable to attack. In a terrifying flash, I saw Georgia hurl herself through my door, her eyes bulging from their sockets, her hair flying, and in one hand a curved, poised knife. Yes, she would attack me too. Why had I not instantly known it?

After all, what did I know of madness? If it could turn her against herself, could it not turn her against me?

I crept back toward my door, carefully, so as not to make a sound on the old floor. I scarcely breathed. I looked at the black key protruding from its lock beneath the doorknob, but something had happened to my vision. The key had become the handle of a long, thin knife that was plunged to its hilt into a gaping white wound. Then there was blood and torn flesh, and somehow, as if the door had become transparent, I saw Georgia's face and those wild, white eyes of hers.

I reached for the key. It would take only a simple, nearly noise-less half-turn to secure it. I would lock the door, then make my escape to the courtyard. No one would blame me for running.

"Annie?" The brass doorknob above my hand appeared to re-volve in its neat little orbit. She was coming in. My heart pounded in my ears.

"What?" I clipped the word, the roof of my mouth so dry I couldn't enunciate the *t*. I grasped the knob tightly in my fist to prevent it being turned all the way. I heard her breathing.

"Could you help me, Annie?" It was a trick. I didn't move.

"What happened, Georgia?"

"I don't know . . ." she said, her voice shaky, her lips so close to the door I was sure they had brushed against the wood and I thought of an incessant moth's wings against a screen. "Annie? Please?"

I opened the door.

The sound of her voice had done it, had torn through my fear as easily, as neatly, as swiftly as a sheet of new paper against an unsuspecting, tender thumb.

She stood in the doorway, the fork still in her hand—not a knife or a pick but a fork. I now saw clearly that she had drawn its tines down her face from forehead to jawline, mercifully lifting it to spare her eyes and their sockets.

"Come in," I said, standing aside. "Let me see you." I led her toward the window and drew back the curtains. Had I ever really believed that a time like this would not come? Part of me wanted to grab her and shake her and scream into her face; and part of me, as she stood quietly by the window lifting her face to the light, part of me would have held her and kissed her torn, gouged face and wept with her, for there were tears in her eyes.

I had no idea what to say or do. Fragments of old ideas came to me, about happy endings and good things happening to good people and brighter tomorrows, and I saw them for what they were, then let them go, unsaid.

I examined her face.

"God, Georgia—how could you do this?" I said, not meaning for my tone to sound as harsh as it did. She began to sob, her tears and her blood running together and washing down her cheeks.

Instinctively I moved closer to her and held out my arms, but I couldn't hold her. My hands barely brushed her arms, then remained in midair near her.

My mind raced, thought upon thought rushing past, vision after vision: Georgia feeding birds, Georgia lying on her back in the grass by the river, Georgia standing up and going to the counter at the Riverview while the student nurses mocked her with their cruel smiles. Suddenly I hated everyone in the world. I could have screamed.

"We're going to have to call your doctor," I said finally.

"No," she said.

"Then this friend of yours, this Ida."

"No!" she said vehemently. "I have an appointment with my doctor tomorrow morning. It can wait till then. He'll see for himself then, anyway. And don't tell Malcolm. He worries about me too much as it is."

"But I'm too worried about you not to. I'm afraid you'll do something else. You said this was all in the past, that you'd never do anything to yourself again, but you did. I won't sleep tonight."

"Everything's all right now," she said in a slightly exasperated tone, as if I were overreacting. "Honest to God, it is. I always feel so much better when I've done whatever it is I feel I have to do." She smiled at me. Thin threads of saliva draped between her upper and lower teeth reminded me of cat's cradles you made between your fingers with yarn. That was what I had heard the nuts did at the state asylum—just sat making cat's cradles all day long.

"You'd better sit down," I said. "Here, on my bed. I'll go and get something to clean you up with. Just stay here. I'll be right back." I started out of the room to the bathroom, then remembered the fork, still in her hand. I went back to her and snatched it from her and flung it across the room. It ricocheted off the wall and skittered under my desk. I was angry. She was out-of-her-mind crazy, and I hated her for it.

In the bathroom I took two clean washcloths from the cabinet

and wet them with cold water. I almost waited for warm, thinking
that might be more soothing, but I didn't want to leave her alone
any longer than I had to. I glanced at my face in the mirror,
momentarily startled to see it there. I should be at home, I thought,
where all my needs are met, where no one expects me to manage
much of anything. Maybe that would be best for me—to go home,
tomorrow on the morning train. Leave Georgia and Oscar and
every other crazy person I had met in the past two weeks and go
home to the country, where life is indeed simple and easy.

"Annie?"

I rushed back.

She was all right, just sitting still at the end of my bed. "This
may hurt a little," I warned, gently daubing at the blood. She lifted
her chin and shut her eyes like a dutiful child.

Aside from the long abrasions on her skin, the force of the
metal had raised welts. Each irregular, bloody scrape was neatly
edged with rows of white, swollen ridges. Just looking at them
caused me to shudder.

However, most of the cuts were shallow, I judged, and there
would be minimal scarring, perhaps just thread-thin lines, which
would be barely noticeable except under bright lights. Tiny strings
of flesh still dangled from the very edges of some of the more
severe cuts, but now that her face was clean the effect was less
frightening.

"You gonna make me all beautiful, little Annie?" Georgia finally
said in a high, child's voice. I had taken my hairbrush from my
dresser and begun to brush her colorless hair.

"I'm doing my damnedest," I said. "But I have to tell you it's
an uphill battle." I hadn't meant to be so honest. It just came out
of me. "Actually," I added, more softly, "my grandmother always
brushed my hair when I was upset."

"It's soothing," she said. "I feel sort of—well, *fancy*, having my
hair brushed. You know?"

"It doesn't feel as good when you do it yourself," I said. I had
turned her so that she faced away from me. Her eyes were still
closed, her chin tilted. She balanced herself on the bed with the

very tips of her long fingers spread out like roots of a banyan tree among the blue peacocks and green leaves.

But when she turned back to me, I was shocked once more by her bruised and battered face. I took the washcloth again and dabbed at some smears of dried blood at her hairline.

"I don't understand how you could do this," I said, wondering if she knew. Probably not. Probably something had come over her, something she was compelled to act upon.

"I suppose I should explain," she said. She took the washcloth from me and absentmindedly swabbed at the blood that remained on her arms and hands.

"Do you know why you did it?" I said.

"Really quite simple," she said. "Nothing to it at all. I saw Claude and a woman walking up the street together. Right out here, outside the building. I hadn't heard them come down the stairs. I'd been in the bathroom taking a shower. I got home early. I didn't know he was up there with anybody, although I had heard, shall we say, noises. I thought he was alone."

"How do you know she was up there? Maybe they met in the street." I pulled the chair away from my writing desk and sat down on it near the bed.

"Because, dear heart, the noises I heard were those of rampant humping. That was what I heard. I didn't realize it until I saw them. Honest to God, I thought it was a friggin' rocking chair." She threw the washcloth across the room. Her expression was a cruel sneer. "Anyway," she continued brightly, "I came out of the shower and wrapped myself in my robe. I didn't stop to get dry. I was just going to sit by the window and open the robe and let the air dry me, I was so hot. So I walked over to the window and there they were, the dear young lovers strolling up the street, and she had her arm around his waist and he had his hand on one of her cheeks, for Christ's sake, feeling it like it was a muskmelon. Then I realize that I know the bitch, that she works at this French restaurant on Newbury Street and she's from Alsace-Lorraine or someplace and Claude told me he was interested in her only because of her wonderful complexion—as a painter, you know—and I guess I didn't figure that the complexion he was talking about was the skin on her ass." She sighed and looked at me impassively.

"Is that it?" I said. "I mean, is that why you did this?"

"I told you I love him."

"So you cut yourself up like this?"

She sighed again. "I told you that I thought he was beginning to care for me. I thought I saw it in his eyes, honest to God, the way he looked at me. You know how you can tell someone likes you—by the look in his eyes?"

"Yes, I remember you said that," I said. "I just don't get it. He does something you don't like and so you cut yourself up. Why didn't you cut *him* up?"

"I'm just not the violent type," she said to my astonished ears.

"Then what do you call this?" I said, gesturing toward her face.

"I could never do anything to hurt *him*. Anyway, Annie, don't you see? I don't think you do."

"See what?"

"That it's my own fault. All of this is. The fact that he doesn't love me." She looked at me helplessly. "If I was only more than I am. If I was only more, in so many ways. But I'm not."

"We are what we are," I said lamely. "And if you're not enough for Claude what's-his-name, then you'll be enough for someone else. The heck with him. You'll be just exactly what someone else is looking for."

"Oh, Annie, you are so optimistic! What you don't know is that I hate myself." She grinned at me, wrinkling up her nose. "I despise myself. Despise! I look in the mirror and I want to vomit. I'm ugly. Ugly! Imagine it—*if* you can! Can you? Think about it. What would you do, Annie?"

I became terribly uncomfortable. What could I say to her? Then something she had just said jumped out at me. "Georgia, you said you'd do this, didn't you? You said that there were times when you looked in the mirror and you hated yourself so much you wanted to tear yourself to ribbons. I heard you. That's what you said, that first night down by the river."

"Yes, I did, didn't I. It happened just as I said it would. You don't understand, Annie, what a prison this is, what a prison this body and face is. Sometimes I see myself and I want so much to scream, as if if I screamed loud enough I would turn inside out." She laughed. "Because all of this that I am on the outside is not me, not really me. Inside, Annie, on the inside, I—I bloom."

She looked at me, a hesitant, vulnerable smile on her lips, then looked up at the ceiling, then out the window. "Didn't you have two face cloths?" she said.

"The other's on the bed beside you," I said.

She picked it up, fingered the wet spot it had made for a few seconds, then pressed the cloth to her face.

"This feels so good and cold. I suppose I look even uglier now, don't I?"

"Not ugly," I replied. "I don't know what to say to you. It kills me to see you like this."

"I'm sorry," she whispered. "I really am. What a shame that you have to be here and see me like this. I didn't think. I'm sorry to have done this to you."

"To *me*? What have you done to *me*?" But I knew what she meant, and I realized that I felt resentful toward her for spoiling everything. I had been so hopeful about my summer in Boston, even as short a time ago as this afternoon. Now she had done this and everything had changed.

I watched her rub the face cloth on a spot of blood on her nightgown. "Do you have a clean one?" I asked.

"No," she said. "This one was clean just a little while ago. No great tragedy—it's not too bad." I went to my closet and took a clean gown out of the drawer. As I approached her, she lifted her arms like a child and let me replace the dirty gown with the clean one, threading her arms through the sleeves.

As I sat back down in my chair, it was impossible not to notice once again Georgia's pathetic appearance. She sat on the very edge of my bed with her legs dangling, her ankles tightly crossed. Her long, tubular arms were crossed in front of herself as if she were shielding her body from my view, shoulders hunched forward, the clingy nylon gown pulled across her breasts. I thought of the body of an old woman, breasts swinging down from the bones of her ribcage like loose ropes of dough.

"Well, now, that's better," I said. Actually, my mind was on something else, on letting someone know what Georgia had done, maybe Malcolm, no matter what Georgia said. I realized how impractical it was to think that I could spend every living minute with her until her doctor's appointment in the morning.

"Do you like flowers, Annie?" She interrupted my train of thought.

"Of course," I said absently.

"Someday I'll show you all the pressed flowers I have. I told you about them, didn't I? They're in little cellophane packets. Each variety wrapped separately. Each with its own seeds. I've had them for years. They were Mother's. They say she gathered them on a trip she took one year out west, way before I was born." The seeds again. I hadn't heard of them since our first meeting.

"What was your mother like?" I said. I had wanted to ask her this many times.

"I don't know," Georgia said, lying down across the bottom of my bed, propping her face on her hands, "except that she liked wildflowers. She died of TB when I was about two. I had no other relatives. I don't know about my father. They weren't married. I went to the orphanage when I was three."

"God," I said, not able to imagine what that must have been like.

"I've tried and tried but I can't remember a single thing about her. All I do remember is someone being near me when I was very, very small, someone tall and—well, that's all, just tall and shadowy. I know I felt warm and safe when she was near. It was her, I'm sure of it. But Ida says it was more than likely a saint or the Blessed Virgin, visiting me with her grace, taking care of me and keeping me safe from harm."

"Do you believe that?"

"I don't know if it's possible. But Ida says that many people have been visited by the Blessed Virgin as well as various saints. Even by Jesus himself."

"I like to think it was your mother," I said. Ida was cruel to suggest otherwise.

"So all I have of her is a pretty basket and the pressed flowers and the seeds. The name of each flower is written on a slip of paper placed inside each packet, written in Mother's hand, but the ink has faded. Thank God I memorized them long ago: fireweed and foxglove, columbine and lupine, blue sage and mountain aster, California poppy and camas lily, bunchberry, Indian paintbrush, and, let me see, purple thistle, and one more. I'll think of it in a minute—I know it when I see it. Anyway, the reverend mother at the convent kept them for me all those years, and Sister Mary Magdalene suggested that I keep them until someday when I found a permanent home for myself. Then I could plant them in my garden, and when they came up each year it would be like having my mother with me for a visit, every year, forever."

"What a lovely idea," I said, then looked away, uncomfortable.

"Are you hungry?" Georgia said abruptly.

"No, not really," I said. I was, but I wasn't about to trek off to the Riverview with her in this condition. If I knew Georgia, she probably would do just that with impunity.

"I'm starved," she said. "But I don't guess you'd be all that thrilled to go anywhere with me looking like this."

"We'd never explain it," I said.

"Honest to God!" she said, laughing. "We could always say that Frances's cat went on a mad rampage and crawled up the fire escape and attacked me. It sort of looks like cat scratches, doesn't it?"

"Or like you had a fight with a bamboo rake." She laughed again and hid her face against my bed. "Actually," I said, thinking quickly, "if you want, I could go out and get us a couple of meatball sandwiches. Isn't there a place over by the hospital, right there on Cambridge?" As I left the house, I could let Malcolm in on what had transpired.

"I'm not sure," she said. "Well, maybe there is . . . but no, we won't go there. We must do things as normally as possible. We must not allow this face to get in the way of our fun. What we'll do is wait until dark, then go to the Cellar—the coffeehouse down on Charles Street—it's very dark in there. All these little tables with one small candle on each. We could sit in a corner. I could wear a scarf. And, my dear girl, guess who sometimes plays his guitar down there on Friday nights?" She was now sitting up, her torn face animated, expectant.

"Who?" I said. Hearing her plan our evening as if nothing out of the ordinary had happened made me realize just how sick Georgia was. I had to have help. Somehow I would tell Malcolm.

"You don't seem to be very excited," she said, bouncing the bed a little.

"What?" I said.

"Cesare playing the guitar!" she yelled at me, reaching over and slapping me playfully on the head.

"I'm sorry. I guess I was thinking of something else. That sounds very nice. I'd love that. I love to hear him play."

"I thought so," she said, beaming. "But in the meantime, I have something for you." She sprang from the bed and headed toward the door. I got to my feet and realized that I was afraid again, afraid to let her out of my sight. "It's all right," she said in a placating tone. "I'm just going to get apples. I have a whole bowl of them in my room. They'll help tide us over until it's dark and we can go out to eat. I'll be right back."

I sat down on the bed and waited. When she returned, she carried a wooden bowl full of apples, a pillow, and a quilt. She wanted to sit on the fire escape. She climbed out the window and spread the quilt out to cover the iron grating. I followed her, and we each positioned ourselves against the fire-escape railing, pillows cushioning our backs. She placed the bowl of apples between us and offered me a cigarette, which I gratefully took.

The courtyard was empty except for the two white kitchen chairs under the tree. Someone had swept the spent brown blossoms into a neat pile over in a corner. No one seemed to be at home, either in our building or in the surrounding ones. Now and then I heard the dull swish of traffic rushing past, perhaps on Beacon Street or Charles.

With a sound like a paper fan might make, a small flock of Georgia's pigeons flew overhead. She watched them, smiling.

"Besides," she said mischievously, "Claude may be there. He usually goes on Friday nights. He says the coffeehouse reminds him of home."

"Oh . . ." was all I could muster. What was she thinking of? If Claude was at the coffeehouse, he'd be there with that other woman.

"I can hardly wait," she said. She had become irrational, I thought, as if cutting her face had been a sane thing to do. Once again I realized I had to let someone know. I would prepare myself to tell Malcolm outright if we met him as we left tonight. He would stop us and call someone—Georgia's doctor, maybe. Or I would secretly call him from the Cellar. He would be waiting for us when we returned, with help.

But suppose we did get to the Cellar and suppose Claude *was* there with the French girl, what crazy thing would Georgia do then? I imagined her screaming and wailing. I imagined her charging across the room and flinging herself at them like an angry cat, clawing and biting. Perhaps she'd run out onto the street, into the night, me trying to follow her, trying to stay with her until she ran headlong into traffic or hurled herself into the river. Perhaps she'd grab a knife from a table setting and kill herself on the spot.

"Georgia, I've been thinking," I began. "Maybe I should go out for sandwiches after all. I don't mind going. Really. I didn't want to say anything, but I'm absolutely famished. I don't think I can wait until dark to eat. I had no lunch, you know. Besides, meatball sandwiches are my favorite food on the face of the earth. I adore the way they smell, all wrapped up in paper."

"Just eat your apple like a good girl," she said. "You'll survive. It has all sorts of vitamins and minerals in it. Anyway, I'm not at all that keen about the place across from the hospital. I've known dozens of people who have gotten sick after eating there. Honest to God, they say the health department is down there all the time checking on things." She was lying through her teeth: a minute or so ago she wasn't sure that she knew of the place I suggested; now she knew all about it. She was hell bent on going to the Cellar, and that was all there was to it. "Besides," she said sweetly, "they have such good things to eat at the Cellar. French pastries and sandwiches. They have the best chicken salad on toasted raisin bread. Very nourishing, and out of this world! Honest to God, you'll love it there."

"All right," I said. I stared at the old wrought-iron bars that made up the railing of the fire escape, surrounding me like a small cage. It occurred to me that if I were not so imbued with the necessity for considering every single possible result of every single course of action before embarking upon it, I would simply stand up, walk down the fire escape as far as it went, climb over the blind end of it, and swing like a monkey to the ground. I would remove myself from this dilemma without further ado. But I wasn't like that, and I knew it.

I was afraid for her. I imagined the authorities coming for her with nets and vials of sedatives and a burly squadron of muscle-bound nurses who would carry her off, strapped to a stretcher. I could imagine her eyes staring at me as they took her away, just before the sedative took hold: those wild, white eyes transfixed in terror, her wide lips drawn back over her teeth.

I couldn't stand the thought of her waking up someday in some dark snake-pit of a hospital, cold and afraid, no one to understand her. Suddenly she leaned toward me and passed her half-eaten apple under my nose.

"What does this make you think of?" she said. "The smell of it?"

"Apples?" I said, knowing there must be more to it than that.

"No, silly!" she crooned. "Apple blossoms. There were orchards behind the convent, and I could see them from my bedroom window and smell them in the spring when my window was open— like a little flacon of perfume Ida brought me once from the Hawaiian Islands. And sometimes when we were small we'd go down into the orchard and stand under the trees, and, Annie, our skin looked so white under those blossoms that sometimes I would feel transparent, as if every organ in my body could be seen from outside of me, and . . ."

There was nothing to do but sit back and listen, sit back and let time pass, sit back and wait until nightfall.

TWELVE

The sun had set. Georgia continued talking. I listened sporadically. In the fading light, the abrasions on her face, dark with dried blood, formed a grisly network of crisscrossing lines. If I squinted, it was as if she wore a tattered veil over her face. I wondered how it felt to her, what it was like to look out through battered skin.

I remembered how once, long ago when I was small, I was locked under a barn by prankster cousins. I huddled there in terror, in semidarkness, in dampness, in the smell of old dirt, the smell of rotting wood and in the sharper, sweet-sour scent of something that I knew intuitively was dead. At last I was able to see the open end of this undercroft some distance ahead: a blinding, nearly fluorescent breadth of giddy green grass, ashimmer in sunlight.

I started toward the opening, but cobwebs or spiders' webs snatched at my hair, slithered over my bare arms, and formed a gruesome, gluey cross-hatch veil on my face. One grainy strand tugged at my eyelid and, refusing to free it, lifted it higher than the other; and as if there had been a mirror before me, I suddenly saw my face in its deformity and screamed just as I broke out into the sun and threw myself in a shrieking frenzy onto the clean grass.

My cousins picked the webs from my body, washed me, and

made me promise not to tell. I didn't; but I would never forget the tenacity of those sticky threads across my face, never forget being trapped among the dark and dying, never forget being trapped inside myself with my own dark thoughts.

". . . And one of the girls said, as we were all standing there under this blossoming umbrella"—Georgia was back in the orchard again—"all of us so white beneath it, and one of the girls said, 'Just like a bride.' It *was* just the way a bride would be under her veil—all white and glowing and chaste. You want another cigarette, Annie? Here, let me light it for you." As she did, her hands shook so violently I had to take the match from her and light it myself. But her voice was calm.

"And all that white," she continued breathlessly, "made me feel so fragile, so breakable, I got scared. I felt like paper, Annie, honest to God, as if I was made of paper and could be torn or crumpled or, and this was terrifying, simply blown away. Just blown away. Poof. Gone."

"Hmm," I said, preoccupied. The thought had just come to me that my rent was due tomorrow. Malcolm had asked me to put it in an envelope and slide it under his door. I would pay my rent tonight instead, enclose a note explaining all that had gone on, and slip it under Malcolm's door as Georgia and I left for the Cellar. I would write the note as Georgia changed, later. True, Malcolm might not open the envelope until morning, but at least someone other than me would know what had happened by then.

I certainly could last the night with Georgia, especially if I knew for sure that there was help on the way. I'd have her stay in my room with me and I'd only pretend to sleep.

"Oh my God, I just remembered something!" I said, interrupting her, setting the stage for my actions later. "I just remembered that my rent's due tomorrow. Thank goodness! I might have forgotten it. Remind me to put it into an envelope before we leave tonight, would you?" She nodded. "I got paid today. Finally."

"Oh, good," she said dreamily. She had closed her eyes and didn't speak for some minutes. "You see, I was so sensitive—to be so affected by just standing under an apple tree! Sister Xavier would come down there sometimes with us and she'd stand under those trees and you wouldn't have known it was her. Her face would look all soft and almost pretty, kind of delicate, like she might have looked as a baby. It was hard to be really afraid of her after that."

"She must have been one of the strict ones," I said, breaking in.

"Yes," she said. "She could be cruel."

Just then, peering down into the courtyard, I saw Frances Fellows talking and gesturing to herself, as usual. She was dressed in pink tonight, a blouse and full skirt, the back of which was hiked up by the girth of her hips. Exposed in all their glory were two milky-white, gelatinous thighs gripped about their middles by twin tourniquets, rolled nylons. She looked up and glanced at us, but no sound came from her bright red lips, and I thought of a bowl of blancmange garnished with a runny maraschino cherry.

"Honest to God," Georgia whispered, "she dresses like a kid." Then she looked away from me, her expression so solemn and dark it worried me.

"She seems content enough," I said. Abruptly Georgia stood up, turned, and leaned over the railing.

"Hell-o," she called out to Frances, who had just sat down on the courtyard floor, legs spread wide apart. She neither looked up nor made a sound. "It's hot, isn't it?" Georgia continued, shrugging her shoulders. Frances opened up a paper package and smoothed it out over the bricks to expose a mound of raw meat. "Looking for your cat?" Georgia insisted, pointing. "I saw it climb up into that broken window a while ago. It's a beautiful cat. It'll probably come in a minute." Georgia remained at the railing, a slim figure dressed in pink, while below her Frances sat, motionless and mute, clothed in pink too. To me it was as if they were arranged together purposely, side by side, in a kind of mad tableau that frightened me to death.

"How do people get that way?" I asked, as Georgia sat down beside me again.

"You mean Frances, of course," she said, eyeing me. "Well, kiddo, it helps if you have a positively disgusting childhood surrounded by nasty people. For all we know, Frances might have spent the first fifteen years of her life locked in a closet, brought out only now and then to be tortured, of course. It's amazing how experiences like that can warp you. I knew someone once who went through that." I didn't comment. I wondered if she was telling me the truth. "Of course you'd find that hard to believe," she said, "because nothing like that ever happened to you—ever would— ever could. Why, your ma is rich and your daddy's good-lookin' and they doted on you and loved you to pieces. How could you turn out like Frances?" Her tone was challenging, hard. "Oh, my word, no! You'll just kinda continue following the dots and making pretty pictures for yourself. And life for you will be a piece of cake. A fancy cake." I said nothing.

Below us, Frances's cat serpentined through the jagged opening in the broken window and leapt to the courtyard floor. He jogged to Frances's side and with an extended paw swiped a blob of bloody meat from the paper between her legs, backed away, and began tearing off chunks of it with savage abandon, head tossing.

"But people like Frances and me," Georgia continued, sighing, "get locked up in closets and orphanages and other places where you just thank your lucky stars for every hour that isn't miserable, for even one decent person who doesn't try to torture you."

"Weren't there any nice people at the orphanage at all?"

"Oh, yeah, there were. And then there was Sister Xavier—the old masseuse, as I call her—a horse face of a different color."

"Was she supposed to give massages or something?"

"Or something. Yeah. She'd come up to my room at night and hear my prayers. In the winter she'd come up and just sit there on my bed in the dark, sometimes late at night, and I'd wake up and she'd be talking to me in this low voice of hers, just like a man's, and pretty soon she'd touch me and rub my arms and legs and say all this junk about how I was sent to her by Mary for her to love. Sometimes she wouldn't say a word—she'd just touch me all over and sort of rock back and forth like she was in a trance or something."

"Why didn't you tell her to leave if you didn't like it?"

"Maybe I did like it," she said. "I was lonely. I don't know why I didn't tell. I just didn't. She said she was there to heal me. She said she had healing hands—they were very warm, that's for sure. And she'd say the Holy Spirit was within her and rub me back and forth and make me put my hand on her heart and she'd wrap her crucifix around my fingers and tell me to feel the Holy Spirit coming through her to me and she'd shake all over and breathe funny and say 'Holy Mother of God, Holy Mother of God' over and over again."

"Georgia, I don't know what to say. Was that normal? Do nuns do that?"

"She took care of me when I was sick," she said matter-of-factly. "She made sure I got the good clothes when donations came in."

"Well, that was nice of her."

"Yeah," Georgia replied. "She was just a human being after all. No one's perfect."

"I suppose. I don't know, I think I would have told someone what she did."

"I couldn't."

"But why?"

Georgia smiled and opened her eyes and looked at me through the veil of her abrasions. It was a queer smile, at once halfhearted, embarrassed, and a touch mischievous. Then it vanished.

"Why couldn't you tell anyone?" I repeated.

"I was ashamed."

"Ashamed? Of what?" Georgia threw her head back and laughed; but it wasn't a laugh, it was a dry, gagging sound.

"What?" I said, puzzled.

"She didn't just touch me on my arms or legs, stupid," she said.

"What do you mean? What did she do?"

"Just forget it," she said. She took another cigarette from the pack and stared at it.

"Forget what? You can't just leave me dangling like this."

"I'm thirsty," she said, licking her lips; then she stared at the cigarette she held in her fingers once more and slowly began to tear a thin shred of paper from the length of it. She didn't look up at me but soon began to sway and hum. She gathered the bits of tobacco that had fallen on her quilt into a pile.

"She touched me on my little arms," she began to singsong,

"she touched me quite a lot." She picked up the destroyed cigarette and rubbed its remains between her palms, letting the mess sprinkle down into her lap. "She touched me on my little tush," she sang, "she touched me on the twat."

It was as if a dry gust of wind blew straight at me, forced itself between my lips and filled my lungs with a dull, hard ache. The ugly word she had used hung between us like a tiny, fleshless carcass someone had fashioned into a morbid mobile.

"The bitch," I said.

"I shouldn't have told you."

"It's all right."

"I survived."

"Yes," I said. "I don't know how."

"In the dark, her fingers felt like bloodsuckers on me."

"Oh, God," I said.

"In a way, though, I loved her," Georgia said. That was impossible. "It was almost as if she loved me, you know?"

"No."

"And sometimes when I felt her hands on me, when she would stroke my back and legs, it was as if I was the most loved little girl in the world. I had no one else, and she was like my own sweet mother. I liked what she did to me. It sounds impossible, but I liked the attention almost as much as I despised it. I wanted her with me almost as much as I wanted to kill her. And it was like she and I were the same, each of us ugly and unwanted and lonely and willing to compromise. We were the same."

"But you were just a little child."

"Dr. Sampson says I was not responsible."

"Of course not, how could you—"

"He says I was the victim, that she used me, that she was mentally sick."

"She was," I said.

"But she did so many things for me. He doesn't know how it was. He says a clean break . . ." She stopped talking and bit her lip. "I still remember the good things she did for me. I can't forget them."

"How long did all this go on?" I asked.

"I don't know. Something happened and she left."

"She went to another convent?"

"No. She relinquished her vows."

"Maybe they found out about her."

"No, they didn't—she just left."

"How old were you then?"

"Twelve. But she hadn't, well, done anything to me for a long time. When I got older I think she lost interest anyway. Except that we had this gardener and he got a hold of me one day in the greenhouse—I was about eleven then—and he was trying to pull down my panties, and she came in and rescued me from him, but when she took me up to my room afterward, she started to undress me to put me in clean clothes, and before I knew it she had lifted up her dress and wanted me to touch her between her legs."

"This makes me sick," I said.

"Don't worry—I got away from her. She's never tried anything since then—I mean, she never did, after that. Then she left."

"Thank God," I said. "You've been through so much, Georgia."

"And emerged victorious! Right?"

"Yes! You have! You survived all that and became such a good person."

"Oh, don't be silly," she said. "You don't really know me."

"I do!"

"There are dark places here inside me, places you wouldn't understand."

"Why wouldn't I understand?"

"You don't even understand yourself yet," she said. "You've been so protected for so long. You may never really know yourself."

"How can you say that?" I said.

"You'll only skim the surface," she said gently, suddenly looking up at the dark grey sky as if she were bored with me.

"How can you say *that*?"

"Because, like I said, all you have to do is follow the dots."

In a moment Georgia placed our apple cores in the bowl and stood up, stretching. I looked down into the courtyard; Frances and her cat had gone in. One by one, lights had gone on in the windows of surrounding apartments, and now and then an incandescent figure would appear briefly, framed by light, then vanish.

"Can you help me with my face?" Georgia said, pulling the quilt from under me.

"Of course," I said. "After we dress, though." I climbed into my room after her. She headed toward my door. Good.

"I hope he's there," she said breathlessly.

"Right," I said, knowing she meant Claude, at the Cellar.

The minute my door was closed I went to my writing desk. "Dear Malcolm," I began. "Georgia has cut up her face and I desperately need your help. . . ."

THIRTEEN

By the time we left the house it was ten. I had left my rent money and the enclosed note for Malcolm as planned, with Georgia none the wiser. Malcolm's apartment was dark, but I was almost sure I could hear his television set playing. Whatever the case, my mind was more or less at ease, knowing that very soon I would not be alone in all this.

Georgia, undaunted as always, had decked herself out for our "evening on the town" in a somewhat tattered pale-blue dress with a scooped neckline and a ruffle at the hem. At some point in its life it must have been attractive enough, but in its present state of decline it seemed better suited to be a braided rug than to be the pièce de résistance of a gay old night on the town. Anyone but Georgia would have thrown it out two summers ago, but she thought she looked ravishing in it and spent many minutes before we left the house recinching the self belt at its waist and running her fingers over its frayed neckline.

I had helped her with her face, piling on the Max Factor until the redness and thin tear lines were camouflaged as well as possible. But the swelling around the cuts and scratches was still quite obvious; and, although I said nothing, it would be perfectly clear to anyone that someone or something had torn and hacked her face to pieces.

As for me, I was past the point of upset or fear or shock or sympathy. All I wanted to do was to get the night over with. I wasn't even particularly hungry anymore, nor was I worried any longer that Claude and his lady would be at the Cellar. Whatever would be would be. If Georgia chose to attack Claude and whatever-her-name-was or even destroy the Cellar itself, that could only be to my advantage, as the police department would be called and the whole thing would be out of my hands at last.

The Cellar was just as I had imagined it: one large, very dark room at the bottom of a steep stairwell, filled with small tables, each covered by red-and-white checked cloths and furnished with a single candle stuck in a raffia-wrapped Chianti bottle. At one end of the room a platform served as a stage. It was vacant—no Cesare tonight.

As we walked in, a waitress emerged from behind a counter where the cash register stood, greeted us, and pointed out several empty tables. Luckily, one was in a corner—just the hiding place for Georgia and me. But by this time Georgia was several steps ahead, and before another second passed she had cried out "Claude!"

Every face turned our way. Searching through the semidarkness I caught sight of a limp, disinterested wave and the crouched forms of two dark men.

"It's Claude," she gushed, smiling back at me briefly before setting out toward him. She approached the men in the exaggerated manner of a grand entrance, and I was instantly embarrassed to be with her. I pretended to scan the crowd as she drifted between the tables, her chin raised, her neck as long and curved as a swan's, her arms held delicately behind herself, trailing like an organza stole. She arrived at the corner table, then moved to the back of Claude's chair, draped her arms around his neck, and planted her lips against his ear. A quick whisper, then her cheek lingered, pressed against his. She looked toward me with an expression of exultation.

Somehow I had managed to mince forward, and I finally stood

but a few feet away. The men licked their lips and raised their eyebrows in unison.

Claude was a greasy little man in a gleaming pompadour that rose above a more-than-ample brow and bulbous black eyes. His bristly black moustache was an interesting counterpoint to his full, petulant lips. The lower lip appeared raw and swollen. Georgia sat down beside him.

Claude's friend—Philippe was his name—drew a chair up for me, and as I lowered myself into it, I smelled his body: a smell like winter vegetables boiling in a weak broth. His face, part dumpling, part pig's eyes, was a study in boredom and impotence and total lack of redeeming character, topped with thin, receding hair. He was a little vermin of a man, immaculately attired in a cheap navy-blue suit. Both Philippe and Claude appeared to be in their mid-thirties.

There then ensued the most remarkable four or five minutes' time, during which both men conversed in French and Georgia alternately licked her lips to seductive wetness and batted her nonexistent eyelashes at Claude's every phrase. Although I could understand only a scattered few of the words spoken, I knew they were discussing Georgia's face and the way she had greeted them.

At last the waitress came by, and although Georgia had promised me a variety of delectable sandwiches and desserts from which to choose, before I had a chance to speak Claude had ordered Turkish coffee and pastries all around, and the waitress sped away.

Claude passed a blue box of cigarettes; I now understood Georgia's preference for them. The three of them engaged in small talk and I sat in silence, trying to look friendly, while thinking that if this man was Georgia's idea of heaven, she was sicker than I had ever dreamed. Artist or not, he was disgusting. The only thing I was thankful for was that his "love" of the afternoon had apparently been ditched. Or devoured. Lucky for her. Anything would be a better fate than an evening with this insect of a man, this bright-eyed arachnid poised before me.

But it was Georgia from whom I couldn't take my eyes. She tossed her head every second or two like a mare in heat. She writhed in her chair and moaned from time to time. Her body had undergone a complete change right before my very eyes. Once so spare and angular, once so frankly graceless and unyielding, she was now the epitome of luscious, languid, touchable womanhood in its prime.

How had she accomplished this transformation? I studied her. Her legs were crossed at the knee, and the one foot touching the floor was *en pointe*, which served to elevate her knees to the height of the tabletop. She had somehow gathered the skirt of the blue dress so that it billowed in soft folds around her hips like the dolls old lady Hillyer in Beverly made: dolls made like women from the waist up; from the waist down, just layers of full skirt to spread out across your bed pillow, without pelvis or legs to get in the way. Mother said they were cheap looking. As a child I thought them frightening, these amputated, useless bed-women.

Only Georgia's bruised face was recognizable. The pancake makeup had begun to rub off, and I imagined that at any moment each bruise and abrasion would appear as if by magic and the full extent of what she had done to herself would be plain as day.

Just then the waitress came with our coffee and napoleons, and when she had left, Claude took a bottle of Cointreau from a paper bag on the floor beside him, poured a little into our cups, then squeezed a twist of lemon over each. I took a sip. I loved it and said so. For the first time, Claude turned his attention to me, inordinately pleased with my approval of his concoction.

"Annie, eh?" he said, pronouncing it "Ah-nee."

"*Oui*," I said, "that's my name."

"*Ah!*" he cried with delight. "*En français! Fantastique! Parlez-vous français, mademoiselle?*"

"*Oui, monsieur, un peu*," I said, feeling quite foolish and hoping I was saying what I thought I was.

"*Bien, c'est très bien*," he cried. "*Philippe! Ecoutez!* She speaks French, this leetle Ah-nee." Philippe nodded and smiled, not half as enthusiastic about my linguistic prowess as Claude seemed to be. "*C'est formidable*," Claude said, holding me in his hyperthyroid gaze. I thought his hand moved across the table toward mine, but Georgia slapped her own on top of it before it got to me.

Claude then proceeded to tell me that in France everyone spoke

English and drank Turkish coffee and poured Cointreau down their gullets as if it were water. And speaking of water, no one in France touched it; they all drank wine by the gallon as soon as they were weaned. In France, the food was so much better and fresher than here; each and every Frenchman was a true gastronome. Living accommodations were of course more gracious, service in restaurants so much more careful, highways better, automobiles faster; the gendarmes in Paris always got their man. Frenchmen were the greatest lovers in the galaxy; and women— ah, yes—Frenchwomen were prettier, sexier, cleverer, more artful, less inhibited, and infinitely lustier than their American counterparts. In short, everything was better in France, just everything.

I asked why he had come after all. For schooling, he said, at the Rhode Island School of Design; then he had stayed on to paint and teach. I asked when he was going home, and to my surprise he shrugged and said, "Who knows?" When I told him I admired the bathtub, he shrugged that off too but lunged across the table at me, an intense look in his protruding eyes. He smoothed down the edges of his moustache with his index finger. He looked like a catfish.

"I shall *never* stay here," he said, pronouncing the "here" like "her." "One more year, maybe two, and I shall return to the island of Corsica, my home."

"What is it like?" I asked, sincerely interested. I knew that Corsica was in the Mediterranean. Did it belong to France or to Italy? I noticed that he was smiling at me oddly, as if I had just said something awfully cute or awfully silly. Had I dropped a morsel of pastry on myself? No.

"*Eh, Philippe,*" he said to his friend, who had finished his coffee and was pouring straight Cointreau into his cup, "*regardez. La petite bouche.*" He pursed his lips.

Philippe looked at me, then nodded at Claude and said: "*Oui, oui, oui.*"

"I know what you're saying," I said.

" 'I know what you are saying,' " Claude said, mimicking me through pursed lips in a high voice. Georgia, who had been silent during this whole conversation, suddenly pursed her own lips and blew kisses at Claude. Then she looked at me, grinning, but her eyes were not smiling.

Claude was rummaging in his wallet for something and presently handed me an identification card bearing his photograph at a much younger age. It was a press card and had been issued in his name by a newspaper in Rabat, Morocco. He then proceeded to recount the years his family had spent in Morocco, his father a government agent of some sort and Claude a reporter for a local newspaper. To be honest, I was intrigued and would have liked to have heard more, but Georgia made that impossible.

She was doing all she could to make Claude notice her: outrageous antics, vamping, staring, and writhing. Taking another cigarette out of his blue box, she lit it from his; then she leaned toward him until she was inches from his face and just stared, all the while licking her lips. He covered one of her hands with one of his, placatingly, and gave her a quick smile. But after a moment or two of appeasement, she grasped his hands and pulled them toward her breasts, which now spilled across the tabletop, like gourds from a cornucopia.

Abruptly, Claude freed himself and waved to the waitress to bring more coffee. Georgia burst into peals of semihysterical laughter that stunned us all to silence.

"Come to the ladies' room with me," she finally said, regaining her composure, but I refused to go. I didn't want to be seen walking with her. And I knew when she got me alone she would berate me for usurping Claude's attention. She went without me.

No sooner had she gone than Claude and Philippe turned to me to inquire about her face. I told them as straightforwardly as I could. Claude asked if I had informed Malcolm. I told him of my attempt with the rent envelope.

"But I'm not sure he's home. Even if he is he might not open it until tomorrow."

"Ah," Claude said magnanimously, "allow me to make this simple for you, *s'il vous plaît*. It would be my pleasure. I shall come back to the house with you, and after Georgia is safe in bed I shall go to Malcolm Balch and tell him, if I have to wait all night for him to come in."

"Oh, God, would you?"

"It must be done," he said, gravely. "It has happened before, of course, some trouble like this. And there is a woman, a friend to Georgia, who comes when she is notified; and the last time, a great pity, there was the ambulance and a doctor and this woman, Ida."

"Yes—Ida Printaine," I said.

"Such a great pity," Claude said again.

"*Oui, oui, oui,*" said Philippe, his pasty face drawn down with sadness.

"Such an ugly girl," Claude said. "I feel sorry for her. And she, she try too hard. Is that not what you say? She try to be sexy. It is revolting to me." He made a disgusted face, his upper lip sucked up into his moustache, the lower lip pouting, all wine-red and raw.

"It's very sad," I said, purposely looking down at the tabletop, not wanting to see the cruel look on his face. He was nowhere near caring for her; he never would be.

"She likes to be around me. What can I say to that?" He shrugged his shoulders. "What can I do?" The waitress had brought more coffee and another tiny plate of lemon rind. Claude poured the Cointreau and passed the lemon to me. "Maybe I should take her, eh?" he said, first to me, then to Philippe. "I should take her?" he repeated, his palms up on the table in front of himself in a gesture of helplessness. A slimy little sliver of a smile played at the corners of his lips. It must happen to him every day, I thought. Every day some poor lovesick woman throws herself at him. And who could blame her? And every day he performs the ultimate sacrifice of his manhood and "takes" her. For her own good, of course, he takes her. What a burden the heroes of this world bear, I thought—the handsome devils, the gay blades, the fabulous hunks, the matinee idols, all the devastating men like Claude. I pushed my coffee aside and dropped the unused twist of lemon on the tablecloth.

Georgia came back, apparently cheered, then flopped down beside Claude, tipping Cointreau to her newly reddened lips. Without looking at her, Claude lifted his arm to the back of her chair. After the conversation had resumed, I noticed that his hand had moved to the back of her neck, his fingers at her jugular vein. She let her head fall to one side, as if to increase the pressure of his fingers on her neck, and as she did so, she smiled a little at me, looking out of the corners of her eyes.

He had decided to "take her." I wondered when and for how long. For an hour? a few days? a month or more? Perhaps he meant just once. One night. He would have sex with her and leave, sure in his heart that he had given her what she needed, conscience clear.

She leaned toward him again. The top of her dress gaped open like a wide pocket, and I watched Claude's swollen eyes search it. She had spread her legs open, and the skirt of her dress was looped between her knees. As I watched, she turned in her chair so that her body faced his more directly; and when that seemed insufficient, she stood partially upright and turned her chair so that now her back was all I saw and she had presented all of herself, open and vulnerable and willing, to this horrible little man whom she imagined she loved, who she imagined cared for her. Philippe twitched nervously and fidgeted with the hem of the tablecloth.

"My, but it's getting late," I said, the moment there was a lull in the conversation.

"*Oui, oui, oui,*" Philippe agreed enthusiastically and immediately stood up to leave, bowing formally from the waist, mumbling a few goodbyes all around. Then Claude stood and beckoned to the waitress to bring our check, and in a few minutes Georgia, Claude, and I had climbed the steps to Charles Street and could see Philippe ahead of us at some distance, walking briskly toward the Public Garden and his apartment on the opposite side of town, going "*oui, oui, oui,*" all the way home, no doubt.

Georgia and Claude walked ahead of me, hand in hand. Claude's head appeared to have been created for a man thrice his size; from behind, he reminded me of a poorly designed puppet of incompatible proportions. Again, I wondered how this singularly unattractive man could think that he was desirable to anyone. But I remembered his promise to tell Malcolm about Georgia and tried to be pleasant.

As we walked up the front steps of the house, Georgia hesitated and looked up Walnut Street, staring at a foreign-looking car that was pulled to the curb, its headlights still on. She turned and looked down at me where I stood on the sidewalk, tipped her head to one side, and smiled at me, a wavering, wistful smile, then bit her lip as if in an effort to control herself. She turned the key in the lock and walked on in.

Malcolm and a woman with unusual deep-auburn hair were waiting for us. She wore a black-and-white checked dress. Other than her hair, which was drawn severely back, exaggerating a deep widow's peak and two wide white stripes that swept to the crown of her head as gracefully as horns, the most curious thing about her was the color of her face—stark white, as if dusted with cornstarch. Malcolm had found my note. The woman was Ida Printaine.

"Annie," Georgia moaned inaudibly, her forehead furrowed, wrinkles of skin gathering between her brows. I just looked away, too terrified to speak, trying to absorb the look of agony and betrayal in her eyes. She reached toward me with one limp hand, as if our touching would help to explain what I had done, as if by touching me she would bring me back to my senses and I would tell the others that I had been mistaken, that they could leave us, that we could handle whatever needed to be handled alone.

"You don't know?" she said.

"I don't know what?" I started to say, but Ida Printaine took two steps forward. I looked across the space between us, into her unremarkable hazel eyes. She took two more steps, her mouth set in an obsequious smile. "Georgia, how could you *do* this to me?" Ida said.

Georgia sighed and bowed her head, and in that instant I felt something leave her body, like air slowly expelled from a balloon. And although I didn't look at her, I felt her beside me, slumped, empty, hollow. As Ida moved closer, I fought the urge to jump between the two of them; but Ida held the flat of her hand up in front of me like a traffic cop and instinctively I stepped back.

"Will you answer me?" Ida said, taking Georgia's chin between her stubby fingers and raising it. "Will you say something?" Georgia looked into Ida's eyes and said nothing. "No? No explanation at all?" Georgia continued staring, mute. Claude cleared his throat and quietly started up the stairs. Malcolm moved to the hall table and took a kink out of the telephone cord. "I will ask again," Ida said. "Why did you do this to me?"

I couldn't stand it anymore. I hurried toward the stairs and before I reached the second landing heard Georgia begin to sob.

FOURTEEN

I was awakened the next morning by Malcolm's knock at my door. I had a telephone call. I threw on my robe and went downstairs.

"Male or female, Malcolm?"

"A woman," Malcolm whispered. I picked up the phone. It was Aunt Chloe, calling from the Copley Plaza Hotel.

"I'm in town with Sarah Leach," she said. "I tried to call you late last night. Did Mr. Balch tell you?"

"No, he didn't," I said. "But last night was very rushed and very strange and I suppose he forgot. He wouldn't normally."

"Are you all right?"

"Yes, I am," I said. "But one of my friends here—well, she had a bad night, and . . ."

"Our lecture doesn't start until nine-thirty, and I thought I'd stop by, as Sarah has some business at the Commonwealth Building. She said she'd drop me off. I can only stay for a moment or two, but I want to see that garret of yours. I promised your mother. Are you up?"

"More or less," I said. "I'm dying to see you."

Just as I hung up the phone, Malcolm came out from his apartment and began to apologize for forgetting Aunt Chloe's call the night before. I assured him he was forgiven, then asked him what had happened with Ida and Georgia. Apparently not wanting to discuss things in the hall, he invited me in.

"Well," he said, seating himself in a black-leather wing chair, "first and foremost, I must thank you for alerting me to Georgia's difficulties. I naturally got in touch with Miss Printaine right away." I sat down on his chintz sofa.

"I just couldn't manage it all by myself, and . . ."

Malcolm shook his head soberly. "And who could? It's terribly difficult, a terribly difficult situation. Miss Printaine, of course, has known her for years, they're quite close, and she has access to the hospitals and doctors. None of us has the expertise. All we can do is let Miss Printaine take over."

"I was frightened. I didn't know what to do. There she was in the bathroom when I got home from work, all covered with blood, and for a while I suppose I panicked. I went into my room and shut the door. I'm embarrassed to say so, but that's exactly what I did at first."

"Why, of course you would! The shock of it." He sighed and looked off into space for a moment, an expression of deep concern on his face. What a kind man he was. "But then you got yourself together, didn't you, and that's the important thing." He reached over to the end table beside him and took a sip of his coffee. "Could I offer you some?"

"Oh, no, thank you," I said, jumping up. "I'm afraid I can't. My aunt is coming. She should be here any minute. She can't stay for long. She wants to see where I live. Kind of an inspection, I guess."

"Very well," he said. "To answer your question, I can tell you that after you retired, Miss Printaine and Georgia packed a few things, then left with Tommy, her driver, who was parked outside, by the way. She'll see to it that Georgia is cared for."

"Do you think they'll take her to the hospital? I can't stand the thought of not knowing where she is."

"I'll let you know as soon as I know anything at all," he said.

"You *did* say that she and Ida Printaine were very close, didn't you? I couldn't really tell, I guess. Perhaps I was wrong, but Miss Printaine seemed so angry at what Georgia had done, not sympathetic at all."

"I suppose she's tired. One becomes tired of it, of the constant anxiety, I'm sure."

"I guess I didn't think of that," I said, feeling slightly more naive than usual. "You're right, of course."

"To love one who seems bent on self-destruction . . ." Malcolm said sadly, his eyebrows flat and still.

"Yes," I said, studying the look on his face.

"If you find yourself overly concerned anytime, I'm almost always at home. Just knock. Come in and have a cup of tea with me."

"Thank you, I will," I said, walking to the door. "I'm so glad you're here, Malcolm. I can't thank you enough. I may just do that, drop by to see you, especially if we don't hear in the next few days. . . ."

I had just finished dressing when the front bell rang and I heard Aunt Chloe's voice. In a moment she was at the top of the stairs and I ran to give her a hug, surprising myself with my own fervor.

"Oh, my goodness!" she cried, standing back, holding me at arm's length. "Has it been so long?"

"I've missed you," I said. We both stood on the landing as she surveyed the walls and woodwork.

"Fine old house," she pronounced, as I led her into my room. After a moment of looking, she smiled. "Very serviceable indeed, and certainly attractive and comfortable."

"Come see the courtyard. Look, down there."

"Yes, yes—the bricks and the ivy. Lovely! Did I tell you that all the wrought iron around here was brought over from Spain as ballast in ships? Can you beat that? And look what they did to it. I've always loved the Hill."

I pulled my desk chair out for her, straightened my bed a little, and sat on it. "An artist lives upstairs," I said, not elaborating. She nodded approvingly. "And law students on the second floor, and all around here are all sorts of intriguing people."

"You see now, don't you, why I thought the city was just the place for you. Now tell me about your job."

"Well," I began, "I just love it, I really do. My boss, Ruth

Carmichael, is wonderful. In fact, she reminds me a little of you. She has a niece, Kathleen, who is almost like a daughter to her. Ruth's very kind. I was ill last week and she came over and brought me soup. Imagine!"

"That was lovely of her."

"All I really do there is dust a lot, but I like it."

"We all start at the bottom, don't you know. And who lives in the room across the way?" She sat back down.

"Her name is Georgia. We've become good friends."

"Excellent. She about your age?"

"A little older. She's very interesting, I guess you could say. I've never met anyone quite like her."

"What was the trouble you mentioned on the phone?"

"Oh, nothing really," I said. "Georgia just got all upset about something, that's all."

"I see," Aunt Chloe said, looking at me intently, one eyebrow raised.

"She's not a totally stable person," I said. "In fact, she's even spent some time in the hospital for her—uh—instability."

"Oh, my," Aunt Chloe said.

"She's really wonderful, though, most of the time."

"I'm sure she is."

"She's an orphan and has had some terrible experiences. She doesn't think well of herself at all."

"Poor thing. But it's common enough, poor unfortunates without the benefit of family and love, grow up all twisted and turned, think there's something wrong with them because no one ever cared for them."

"Yes," I said, surprised that she seemed to know. "That's the way she is. She doesn't know she's a good person. I wanted to take her home with me for a weekend before the summer was over, but Mother wouldn't approve, I'm sure."

"I can't imagine that she would, either. It's frightening, don't you know. At least to some. Each one of us has a dark side we do our best to keep hidden. In that case you'll have to bring her out to Marsh Cliff, that's all there is to it."

"You wouldn't mind?"

"I should say not! Seems to me the poor girl needs people who care for her, not people who turn away. Where is she now? I'd like to meet her."

"I'm not sure. A friend of hers came by and took Georgia to her house. I'm sure she'll be back soon, as soon as she feels better."

"It's clear to me that you've become quite fond of her."

"Yes, I suppose I have," I said, wondering why I had been less than absolutely candid with Aunt Chloe about Georgia. "She'll just flip when I tell her she's invited to Marsh Cliff."

"Sounds painful," Aunt Chloe said, a twinkle in her eye.

"She's an unusual person," I said, "somewhat moody. Well, to be honest about it, she's done some awful things to herself in the past. She tried to kill herself. More than once."

"I see," Aunt Chloe said thoughtfully.

"But Aunt Chloe . . ."

"Yes, my dear?"

"Well . . . I don't know. I expected you to be shocked, to start telling me how unsuitable she was. . . ."

She looked down at her gloved hands, folded in her lap. "It can happen to anyone," she said, "anyone at all, particularly those with an artistic bent. Despondency. When everything looks absolutely hopeless, black."

"But I had no warning. . . ."

"She tried it again?"

"No . . ." I said, hesitating. "But she cut her face with the tines of a fork."

"What a pity, Ann. What a great pity. Poor soul. It seems to me that she should be under a doctor's care."

"She is," I said. "In fact, she may be at the hospital right now."

After Aunt Chloe left, I straightened my room and was just going to the utility closet on the landing for the dust mop when I heard the phone ring again. In a moment I heard Malcolm start up the stairs. I ran down to meet him.

"A young man for you," he said.

Oscar! I had almost forgotten about him and our date tonight. Maybe he was calling to cancel. That was fine with me. I would stay at home, read magazines, wash my hair, listen to the radio.

"Hello," I said. For a second there was no sound, then Oscar uttered a breathy "hi" and exhaled loudly into my ear.

"Well, good morning," I said, just the sound of his voice making me hope our date wasn't cancelled after all.

"Hmm," he said sleepily, "yeah. It is now."

"Are you still sick or something?"

"Mmm, I guess you could say that," he said. "Lovesick!" He laughed. "I love your voice—did I ever tell you that?" I loved his too. It was almost as if his mouth were on my ear, not the cold Celluloid of the receiver.

"Oscar, where are you? You sound a little odd."

"Well, let's see," he said. "Where am I? Who am I? Well, I'm standing outside my room in the dorm in my skivvies talking on the pay phone to you. My name is Oscar Benson and I'm all alone in this barn except for two other guys and in a half-hour the painters are going to get here and smell the place up."

"Oh," I said flatly, but in my mind's eye I was imagining him, shirtless, pantless, tall and slender, leaning up against a wall, his eyes closed as he talked to me. His body would still feel warm from bed.

"And where are *you*, Annie?"

"Just where you'd imagine my being," I said brightly. "Down in the front hall talking to you."

"In *our* hallway, Annie? Mmm, I remember it well. What are *you* wearing?"

"Uh, well . . ." I was trying to think of something more alluring than a pair of dungarees and an old blue blouse, but that was the truth.

"Come on," he coaxed, "I told *you*."

"Oh, well, I might as well tell you," I said. "I don't suppose it really matters. . . ."

"What? Tell me."

"My robe," I said nonchalantly. "That's it."

"And pajamas underneath it, right?"

"With nothing underneath it, if you must know," I said, acting as if I had never planned to tell him that.

"Oh, God," he moaned. "Is your hair down?"

"Well, yes, it is." It wasn't. "I was just getting ready to wash it."

"I'd love to see it," he said. "I dreamed about it last night. All night. We spread it out and made love outdoors in the grass like wild animals. You were incredible."

"Was I really?" I said. His words had gotten to me, as well as his tone, and I realized that I was now leaning up against the wall, cradling the phone between my ear and shoulder, my eyes closed. He really was adorable.

"I can't wait to see you tonight," he said.

"I'm looking forward to seeing you also," I said, in as innocent a voice as I could muster. "That new movie sounds wonderful."

"No," he said. "You don't understand what I mean. I mean I *can't*. It would be dangerous to my health." I laughed loudly. "Seriously," he said, "I have to see you earlier."

"How much earlier?"

"I want to pick you up in an hour. I've got my buddy's car. I want to pick you up in one hour."

"What are we going to do all day?" I said, as if I didn't know what he had in mind.

"First we'll have breakfast, then we'll go to the art museum or ride around for a while and go there later, then take a walk in the Fens and people-watch, then we'll have dinner, then the show, then I'll invite you up to see my etchings."

"This is going to cost you a fortune," I said, ignoring the bit about the etchings, recalling that he said he put most of the money he earned at the bookstore away for tuition.

"Don't worry about it," he said. "I got a letter from my uncle in Chicago—my rich uncle. One of his neighbors lives in a house designed by Frank Lloyd Wright and is always bragging about it. I think Uncle George figures that if he plays his cards right some-day he'll be living in a house designed by another famous architect, Oscar Fairfield Benson. They could compare soffits or something."

"Fairfield?" I asked in disbelief.

"Yes," he said, "Fairfield. After the town in Connecticut where my mother was born. It could have been worse, I guess. She lived in Woonsocket, Rhode Island, after that, then in Passaic, New Jersey."

"Actually, I like it," I said. "Very dignified."

"Anyway, he sent me some money just to hack around with. Besides, breakfast will be kind of like a field trip. I'm taking you to Copley Square, to a little place there. Did you know that architecturally speaking Copley Square is one of the most interesting squares in the whole U.S. of A.?"

"No, I didn't," I said.

"Stick with me, baby," he said, à la Humphrey Bogart, "I'll teach you everything I know. No, seriously, you'll be drinking your orange juice right across the street from a prime example of Florentine Renaissance . . . this little short Italian guy selling papers. Just kidding—the library. I'll take you inside. They've got stone lions and paintings and murals and all kinds of stuff. You'll love it. What do you say?"

Putting down the phone, I raced up the stairs, suddenly revived by plans for an entire day with Oscar. I somehow felt as if an enormous weight had been lifted from my shoulders.

Whereas yesterday, at the close of the day, I felt as old as Methuselah, a million light years from innocence and youth and even happiness, today with Oscar I could be myself, Annie, aged eighteen, pretty and romantic and full of fun.

For starters I took a bath in Chanel Number Five–laced water. I began the ancient ritual, my own version, of preparing oneself for a date. I applied lotion to my feet and elbows. I went to my drawer in the closet and chose my best underthings, pale blue with lace, and my best nylons, very sheer. After putting them on, I sprayed myself all over with Chanel.

It occurred to me that although I had gone through this ritual dozens of times, I had never once asked myself why I wanted my body to be scrubbed clean and sweet-smelling and attired in beautiful, lacy lingerie if I had no intention whatever, which I had not, of permitting any boy to touch me or in any way get his nose close enough to, say, my naked abdomen or the backs of my naked knees, to appreciate whether I had perfumed myself or not. One would have thought that I was no more than a harem girl, con-cubine number 201, who had just been told by the chief palace eunuch that the maharajah "wanted" me tonight. I had seen it all in a hundred movies starring Maria Montez.

At least number 201 knew exactly what she was doing and what would happen to her. I was going through the same routine but expected the outcome to be no more than a lot of kisses and heavy breathing and a little judicious feeling up here and there. The harem girl would not be treated to a soda at Howard Johnson's or a movie at the Brattle. Her mission was clear—rampant sex.

If anything did happen between Oscar and me today, I was to feign complete surprise bordering on shock: "How could you think I was that kind of girl?"

Having completed my toilette, as they used to say, having brushed and arranged my hair as Oscar liked it, I went to my closet to choose the most innocent, least alluring dress I owned. It was white eyelet with a full skirt, cap sleeves, and a low, oval neckline. Simple but effective. Innocent but devastating.

The point was that no one who saw me could accuse me of dressing like a harlot, for the express purpose of exciting a man—and yet that was exactly what I had done. Oh, how I would have preferred (sometimes, anyway) to slither down the stairs to meet Oscar, naked except for a satin shift and very high heels and long, silky hair! Standing before him, I would lift his shirt from his pants and with one jerk, buttons flying, open it and pull it from his shoulders. I would press against him again so that he could feel me, all satin. Then I would pull his belt out of his pants and drop it on the floor, then unbutton and unzip them and pull them down for him to step out of, his undershorts with them. I would hold him away from me and look at his penis rising toward me from the hair between his legs, its tip like a ripe, swollen fruit, its white, rippled shaft like a thick, translucent candle with a blue wick through it. I would rise and fall on my heels so that he could feel me, the red satin of me, sliding over it. Then I would lift my dress and stand on tiptoe and feel it between my thighs until I spread my legs for it and he lifted me, my legs grasping his hips so that I could have him there, right then, before I brought him upstairs with me, no matter what Malcolm's rules were. Then I would have him again and again, all afternoon, all night, until this feeling inside had gone.

The doorbell rang and Malcolm answered it. It was Oscar. I heard Malcolm's footsteps on the stairs and I called down to him that I was on my way.

When I reached the final flight, Oscar was at the bottom waiting, looking at me as if I were an angel approaching, or Marilyn Monroe. I felt light-headed when I saw him, either simply from the sight of him or from the fantasy I had just had. I reached the bottom step and would have stepped down, but he was in the way.

"Wow!" was all he said. I couldn't speak. I was still in red satin. I swallowed and prayed for the strength to carry on.

"You MIT men certainly have a way with words," I said shakily. He laughed and glanced down at his shoes. He looked very handsome to me. He was tanned, probably from sunbathing those days when he was sick from the flu. He was dressed in light blue, a button-down shirt open at the neck and seersucker slacks. He gently put his hands at my waist and just barely pulled me toward him. I thought he was going to kiss me on the mouth, but instead he angled his head and his lips met my neck and I felt his hand on my right breast, not squeezing it, just lying there as if we had been married forever and a day, and touching my breast was as natural to him as touching my hand. His mouth was now at my ear and all I heard was his breath and then he whispered, "I love the way you look, Annie." I was overcome with the desire to reach out and hug him to me; he looked so handsome and healthy standing there, so strong and tan and as if he owned the world.

"Come on, let's go," he said cheerfully, and we walked out the door, his arm about my waist.

FIFTEEN

The museum didn't open until one, and after breakfast Oscar and I had time to kill, so we walked around Trinity Church and looked at the statue of Phillips Brooks on the Boylston Street side of it, then toured the Public Library. After a leisurely walk back to the car, Oscar put the keys in the ignition, sat back, closed his eyes, groaned, and said: "It's going to be an awfully long day. Sit closer to me, will you?" I scooched over a few inches.

"I'm looking forward to it," I said. "I haven't been to the museum in so long." Oscar's eyes were still closed.

"Do you want to kiss me as much as I want to kiss you?" he said.

"I . . . I don't know."

"The truth."

"I am telling the truth." He moved closer to me and put his arm around me.

"The truth," he said again. I took a deep breath.

"The truth is that I love your mouth," I said. "I mean, I love the look of it."

"I love the look of yours, too."

His mouth was inches from mine, so close that to see it I looked down the side of my own nose. He didn't move any closer to me, and after a few seconds I became impatient, waiting. It took great concentration to regulate my breathing. I couldn't let him know how I felt, that suddenly I imagined myself lunging for him, hurling myself at him and sucking and biting and absolutely devouring his lips. The smell of him, that odor of blood and marrow, was driving me wild.

Oscar finally kissed me and moaned and drew his legs up as if he were in pain, his knees pressed into the side of my thighs. Then he pulled away from me, looking rather foolish, my lipstick on his mouth.

"I could go on all day like this," he said, his voice rough. "But we can't."

"I know," I said, amazed at his restraint. "Where shall we go? What time is it now?" He looked at his watch.

"Let's go for a ride," he said, straightening up in his seat and checking his mouth in the rearview mirror before we took off up Commonwealth Avenue.

After passing the campus of Boston University, we crossed the Charles River and spent the next half-hour or so driving through the streets of Cambridge, and Oscar from time to time would comment—architecturally speaking, naturally—on the various buildings that impressed him.

"Georgian colonial—over there!" he cried, as we slowed down and passed a long row of houses. I smiled, afraid to tell him that I had no idea to which building he referred.

"Romanesque!" he erupted, waving off to a structure in the distance.

Many of the houses and dignified buildings we passed belonged to Harvard, and Oscar was in ecstasy, pointing out pediments, towers, columns, pilasters, porticoes, façades, friezes, cornices, and dormers here, there, and everywhere.

He had launched into a discussion of things called squinches and pedentives when I noticed we were now driving through a less attractive part of Cambridge, had left Harvard behind us and were, I thought, heading in the direction of MIT, although the route he had chosen was indirect. I wanted to ask him exactly where we were going, afraid that once again he was about to try and lure me to his room to see his etchings; but as I fumbled for just the right words I realized that he was now explaining arch construction through the ages, and I decided to wait for a lull in the conversation, such as it was.

In fact, Oscar was lecturing; but rather than finding him boring or pretentious, I was thrilled at the command he had of his subject. I admired him. There was something sexy about an intelligent man expounding on his area of expertise. "How interesting," I sighed at an opportune moment.

"But it's not an arch in the true sense of the word," he went on, "because it isn't really curved. Nonetheless, that's what they call it."

"I see," I said.

We had turned into a side street. We pulled up in front of a nondescript brownstone. This couldn't possibly be his dorm at MIT—the neighborhood was too shabby. I couldn't see the river, hadn't seen it for some time. We were nowhere near MIT. Oscar took the keys out of the ignition.

It must be almost time for the museum to open, I thought. I was looking forward to the prospect of impressing him with my knowledge of art. Oscar glanced at me furtively. "Where are we?" I finally blurted.

"I promised a friend that I'd feed his cat," he said. He looked at himself in the rearview mirror and ran his comb once through his hair, then looked again at me, eyebrows raised.

"You mean he lives here?"

"Yes, this building right here," he said. "The basement apartment. Barney O'Donnell. That's my buddy's name." Oscar's voice was in a very low register at this moment. He used his hands as he spoke, trying to appear casual. What was wrong with him? He sounded so phony. "He's up at his girl's folks' place for the weekend—I mean, he drives up to Gloucester with them every weekend in the summer. So I kind of promised him that in exchange for using his car, I'd feed the cat. I thought it was the least I could do."

"Oh. I suppose."

"So I won't be long. Just a coupla minutes." He opened his door and put one leg out. "Unless, of course, you want to risk life and limb and come in with me. It'll take just a minute, really, but if you'd feel better staying right here . . ." He looked up and down the street in front of and behind us, as if checking for pickpockets and murderers. "Aw, hell," he said, "let's not be stupid about this. Come on—come in with me. Like I said, it won't take more than a few minutes. Fifteen at the most. What could happen in fifteen minutes?" He was at my side of the car and opened my door. I got out. We walked across the sidewalk, down the steep steps, and stood, as Oscar fiddled with an array of keys in his hand, in front of a peeling, red-painted door. "Just let me find the right key here," he said. "Yeah, this must be the one. . . . There. Open sesame." The door creaked open and Oscar stepped inside. "Hello? Hello? Anybody home?"

"I thought you said no one was here. . . ."

"Just making sure," he said, reaching for my hand and drawing me into the dark room, closing the door behind us. "I'll get the lights." He went across the room and threw the switch on a bulb that hung from the ceiling, with a huge, white paper globe for a shade. The walls of the room were smudged grey; its furnishings, Salvation Army finds.

"Well, this is the living room . . . and back here is the kitchen," Oscar announced optimistically. He led me into the dingy but spacious kitchen.

He switched on a light above a wooden table. On the table was a box of Wheaties, the bowl they had been eaten from, an open half-loaf of bread, and an open, empty jar of peanut butter. A coffee mug filled with old coffee and cigarette butts stood nearby. I saw no cat. Oscar didn't seem to be looking for one, either.

On one wall of the kitchen was a poster from some foreign country, lettered with words that might have been in German— a castle on a hill.

Oscar, by this time, was searching for the cat, looking under things, disappearing into other rooms from which I heard doors open and close.

On the front of a broom closet was tacked a girlie calendar, the

girlie in question having been provided with a pencil-thin moustache and, behind an artfully raised knee, a luxuriant tuft of black
pubic hair, work of the same artist.

Oscar returned from his hunt, saw me looking at the calendar,
said he was sorry, Barney was a pretty cross fellow, and turned
the calendar over against the wall. "Not a bad place for eighty a
month,' he said, surveying the room and nodding his head in
obvious approval. "But I forgot the best part!" He rushed over
to an area on one side of the stove—an odd place for a window,
I thought, staring at the long, dirty white curtain that hung there.
"Just what every good kitchen needs," Oscar said, pulling back
the curtain. "A shower!"

I couldn't help laughing. Oscar then pointed out the stack of
dirty dishes sitting on the floor of the shower. "Or a dishwasher!"
he said. "Or both!"

"This really is rather unbelievable," I said. There were dishes
with egg yolks stuck to them and plates that looked as if spaghetti
had been served on them and an enormous pot encrusted with
something brown.

"Barney makes great chili," Oscar said reverently.

"He also makes a heck of a mess," I said. "Are you serious?
Does he actually do his dishes and shower at the same time?" I
wasn't annoyed or disgusted. I was smiling. There was something
almost cute about this.

"You bet he does," Oscar said with a grin. "He really is a prince
of a guy."

"Yuck," I said. "Sorry I asked."

"Young woman—" Oscar said, purposely using his low voice
this time and walking toward me, peering at me over his horn-
rimmed glasses, "and in that dress you look incredible, by the way;
I could eat you with a spoon—you obviously know nothing at all
about time efficiency." He reached for my hands and stood very
close to me. "Not to mention automation." His hands were now
at my elbows. With the smallest amount of pressure possible, he
pulled me closer to him and rested his chin on my head. "But
Barney has the mind of a true engineer," he said into my hair.

"Don't you know that anytime you can accomplish two tasks with one source of energy you're ahead of the game?"

"You must be right," I said, my lips on his shirt. "This whole place absolutely reeks of efficiency!" I stood back.

"You ain't seen nothin' yet, kid," he said, coming toward me again, taking off his glasses and leaving them on the table next to the peanut-butter jar. "What you see before you is technology at its finest." His arms were around me and his mouth on mine. He had whispered those last few words against my eyelids, and when I felt his lips touch my face, then my mouth, I thought I would die. Technology at its finest, I thought—oh, yes! Yes!

As his magnificent, long, pointed tongue searched my mouth for the tip of mine, every single thought and feeling I had ever had about men of science and mathematics, men with horn-rimmed glasses and slide rules and lab coats, deadly serious men who understood numbers and formulae and periodic tables and the theory of relativity and the speed of light, every single sensuous thought and feeling I had ever had about men like this, like Oscar, flooded every molecule of my body. I became someone I had never known before. My mouth, tongue, and hands became explorers, each with a mission of its own.

But before they set out in earnest on their voyage of discovery, without a single compliant word from me, Oscar moved me along down the hallway to the only room in the apartment I had not seen: the bedroom.

Outside the door we stood gazing into one another's eyes. Oscar stroked my hair. He frowned, looking at me intensely. I looked into his eyes, wanting to see that whatever else he was, he was good. Nothing else seemed as important to me as that. I wanted to be able to remember all this happening to me with someone who was, above all, good. Oscar *was*.

He kissed my hair. He took my hand. We walked into the bedroom together, each of us trembling, each of us breathless, each of us filled with self-doubt.

Oscar touched my hair again, smoothing his palm from my brow to the middle of my back. He kissed me, but I was thinking of my hair and what he had dreamed about it—that we had spread it out and made love on it, like wild animals.

The room was dark. Green, I think. He removed his shirt. He was the color of an antelope—an antelope! Smooth as chamois. Warm against me. Hard against me. Long muscles, long bones, his body sleek and strong as a deer's.

He reached for me and drew closer, as if I were a thicket of brush willow, huckleberry, and alder, and was enfolded and hidden there like branches hold the moon.

I looked into his eyes, then had to look away, to save myself, for his eyes now drew me to him with such force, I imagined my entire being somehow vanishing. I turned my face to the side and shut my eyes.

His ams went around me.

"Oscar," I heard my voice whisper, as if to identify his species, as if to affirm that the smooth skin against my face was his, not some wild animal's, as if to reassure myself that the two hands that stroked and squeezed me, then worked at the back zipper of my dress and pulled it down, belonged to a person whose name I knew well.

The bodice of my dress slid from my shoulders.

I heard his breath catch.

I felt his hands on me, on my neck, my breasts, at my waist. He worked my dress and slip down over my hips, and when they fell to the floor at my feet, I felt him stand back a little, just to look at me in my blue merry widow bra and my blue underpants, my nylons still attached to their garters. I would allow him this, for as long as it pleased and aroused him. I had been born for this, to stand half-naked in front of a man, to present my body to him, to excite him.

"You're beautiful, Annie," he said, at just the right moment. He fumbled with the long row of hooks and eyes that ran up the middle of my bra. "Take it off for me, Annie." His voice was different: serious, restrained.

I glanced up at him, then complied. But as I undid my stockings, slid them down, stepped out of them, then unfastened my bra, all

I thought about was his face, a complex study in adoration and desire tempered, just barely, by self-control.

I looked up at him again as I tossed my bra to the floor, and the thought crossed my mind that Oscar had changed. No longer the lovesick boy whose exaggerated attentions had caused me such chagrin, no more the gawky adolescent whose blatant horniness called for a good hosing down with saltpeter-laced ice water, Oscar was no longer a boy at all.

The thought both terrified and inspired me.

When he pulled my panties down and reached for his belt buckle, I grabbed his hand.

"Let me," I said, though God only knows how I managed to say a word when all I could think of was slamming my body against his and feeling his skin against mine.

Yet, surprisingly, the act of speaking slowed things down. When it occurred to me that he was examining my nipples as I undid his belt buckle, and that in response to his fingering, something in my pelvis swelled, it was a kind of scientific observation.

I reached for his fly.

By now it was abundantly clear to me that every move I made excited Oscar more. Every touch of my fingers elicited gasps. He trembled and moaned. His eyes were cast upward toward the ceiling, his sensuous mouth half-open in pleasure or pain.

The fact was that every move I made excited *me* more as well, and as I slowly unzipped his fly and tried to tell myself that it was just a zipper, an ordinary zipper, I began to lose my composure, my scientific detachment. I imagined that his penis, which until now had masqueraded as the stout pole in the center of a certain voluminous, seersucker teepee at the front of his trousers, leapt out of its enclosure into my hand. I couldn't wait to see it, to touch it.

I slid my fingers tentatively under the elastic of his Jockey shorts, and before another second had passed I had lost all control, and before I knew for sure what had happened, his shorts and pants were gliding down his legs like hot wax on snow.

His penis was a thing of remarkable beauty, perfectly wonderful to look at. I was absolutely amazed. I couldn't take my eyes off it. It was as I had imagined it would be, but much more: all gnarled and sinewy along its rigid trunk, divided by a wide, blue vein; distended, purple and viscous at its head. It was this head that interested me most: soft as velvet, hard as a knuckle, like a rock wrapped in layers of bright silk and displayed like a work of art atop a carved, alabaster pedestal.

Until this time I had not given much credence to the issue of "penis envy," but the sight and heft of Oscar's made me think again. Not that I'd want one in place of what I had; but perhaps one in addition to what nature had provided me wouldn't be too bad a deal. Now was my chance!

I took it in both my hands.

Oscar, meanwhile, had lost his mind. All he did was moan and push himself against me. I had all I could do to keep us from crashing together and falling to the floor in a great heap of sexual frenzy; but I was determined to prolong this moment—not just for the thrill of it but for the educational value as well.

"Look at us," I whispered, letting go of him, placing my hands at his waist. His were on my hips. I eased his lower body toward mine, slowly, quarter-inch by quarter-inch, until his penis rested up against my abdomen. Neither of us dared breathe or move, nor did we want to take our eyes off what we saw there. My own breasts were like pink mountaintops at sunset. The head of his penis was a florid, glistening sun between them.

"Oh, God, Annie . . . you feel so good."

He had led me to the bed. I watched him lie down on his side, then hold out his hand to me. I hesitated and took a long look at him. He reminded me of a sketch by Leonardo da Vinci. I thought of sketching him myself, right now, of painting him just like this, a perfectly proportioned human male animal with skin the color of hide. He took my breath away.

"Please, Annie," he said impatiently. He pulled me toward him. I lay down. His hand slid between my legs and pried them open. His fingers touched me.

He climbed on top of me and lay against me as weightlessly as a reflection lies on water, a perfect fit, his face in my neck, his hips thrusting rhythmically forward, as if by reflex. "Please, Annie," he said again, and in another second he pushed himself up by his arms, his hands rigid on either side of me, and told me to spread my legs. But as I did, and felt my body open to him, all feeling stopped. I was removed. Oscar was the antelope again, stretched out long and tight above me, and as he pushed and I heard a cry erupt from his throat, I said, "No, not yet," and pushed him away.

As if he couldn't believe what I had said or done, as if he hoped to bring me back to my senses, his hand went between my legs once more, and the tip of his finger wiggled at the entrance to my vagina. "No," I said, more forcefully. He fell back, his hand resting on my thigh.

"But you're all wet," he pleaded.

"I just can't yet."

"We'll rest a minute," he said. He leaned over me and began to suck at my breast.

"No, Oscar, don't." He raised his head, then took my hand and placed it on him, on his penis. It was hard and damp.

"Touch me," he said. I stroked him. His penis throbbed against my fingers.

"I can't wait," he said, an urgent tone to his voice. "I can't wait. Oh, God—"

He scrambled on top of me again and tried to open my legs with his knees, then fell down on me and writhed against me hard, then again and again, until he came, with one ecstatic yell after another, and my stomach and chest were splattered with warm semen.

It was over. Oscar's hands, which rested on me, neither excited me nor inspired fear. I was numb, and in my mind's eye the antelope strode silently out of the thicket and disappeared into the landscape, into the chamois color of the summer-dried grass.

The woods grew still.

Neither of us moved.

"Are you all right?" I said, when after a while I couldn't feel him breathing. He lifted his face from the pillow and grinned down at me sleepily.

"Oh yeah," he said as he kissed me on the neck. "Sorry about you—I mean, I'm not supposed to do that. It'll take a few minutes before I can—"

"Oh, no, that's fine," I said.

"You don't feel sick or anything, do you?" Not sick, exactly, just a dull ache low in my abdomen. "You seemed pretty excited."

"Oscar, I . . ."

"Hey, that's the way it's supposed to be," he said, sliding off me. "I mean, I loved it, knowing that you felt that way. I loved touching you there, Annie. He slid one hand between my legs again, then turned onto his side and propped himself up on one elbow. When I glanced at him, he was looking me over as if I were a brand-new car. There was a little smile of approval on his face.

"What are you doing?" I said.

"Just looking," he said.

"Close your eyes!" I commanded, rolling from the bed to the floor, where my dress and underwear had been dropped and lay like half-open buds cast to the earth by a storm. I gathered them to me. I stood and began backing out of the room.

"Where are you going?" He sat up.

"Don't look at me!" I barked. He fell back against the pillow, his eyes tightly shut.

"What's the matter all of a sudden? Stay here, huh?" He opened his eyes and reached out for me with one arm. I continued backing away. "What's the matter?" he repeated.

"Nothing!" I yelled.

"Hey, wait a minute!" he said, jumping off the bed and coming toward me, his arms open.

"I said don't look at me!" I screamed, as I ducked around the corner into the hall and ran toward the open bathroom door. "It wasn't working for me—don't you understand that?" I slammed the door behind me.

For a moment, Oscar was silent as he stood outside the bathroom door. Then, very calmly, he spoke the only possible words he could have chosen that would enrage me: "Baby, calm down, will ya?"

I had all I could do to keep myself from clawing at the door between us.

"Hey, baby, do you think you just might be a little frustrated? Which I don't blame you for in the least. If you'll just come back I'll make it right with you."

"You are insufferable," I hissed. "Why don't you listen to me! Things weren't really working for me, Oscar—I wasn't *with* you, not really."

There was a moment of silence. "Some old boyfriend, huh?"

"And I can't stand being called 'baby.' "

"Some old boyfriend? Is that who you were thinking—?"

"No! Of course not!"

"Who, then?"

"No one. An animal, an antelope . . ." I burst into tears and leaned into the door.

"Huh? I can't hear you. Are you crying?"

"Listen to me!" I sobbed. I sat down on the toilet and let the tears come full force.

"Will you explain to me what happened?" Oscar was against the door, speaking very softly.

"I'm crazy," I whimpered.

He chuckled. "No you're not."

"I think I am." I stood up and looked at myself in the filthy mirror above the sink. I had never seen myself in such pitiful condition. Just looking at my disheveled, disappointed self made me cry harder. How awful this was! What a failure I was! Nothing, absolutely nothing, was happening the way I had once dreamed it would. "It was just that somehow or other, from the moment we came into the bedroom . . ." I began, as I watched the tears stream from my eyes. It was heartbreaking.

"Yeah, go ahead . . ."

"Well, something happened, and I kind of stepped out of reality . . . and . . ."

"You stepped out of reality?"

"I saw you somehow as this really beautiful, sleek, wonderful animal, this antelope. . . ."

"Okay. . . ."

"I can tell you think I'm crazy."

"What were *you*? If I was this antelope, what were you?"

"I don't know. . . ." I couldn't possibly tell him that I had fantasized myself as a thicket.

"I'm really sorry—God, I don't know what to say . . . I mean, the whole . . . uh . . . time was really . . . uh . . . grand for me. I mean, I guess that was obvious. I mean—oh, God, Annie, your body is incredible!"

"Thank you. I'm sorry too."

"Don't cry anymore, okay? It's all right, okay? It's my fault. I guess I rushed things. I mean, it's a really big step to take. I wouldn't think of myself as unique or odd or anything, if I was you."

"I just thought I'd wait until I got married, that's all."

"Yeah, I know."

"I'm not exactly *that* kind of girl."

"Oh, no, Annie—you're not, and I don't ever think of you that way."

"You don't?"

"I swear it," he said.

"Also, I would die if I ever got pregnant. My mother would die. It would just kill her."

"But I wouldn't let you get pregnant, Annie—I already had that planned."

"How?"

"Well, the guy can take it out just before he comes."

"That's pretty risky," I said.

"Open the door and come out, will you? I won't touch you at all if you don't want me to, okay?"

"I want to put some clothes on," I said.

"I'll even put my pants on, if that will make you feel more comfortable," he said.

"If you wouldn't mind . . ."

"Give me a second," he said, and I heard him rush into the bedroom.

I put on my bra and panties and half-slip. I opened the door and stood there, looking down at my feet. "If I put my dress on, it'll get all wrinkled. I mean, it already is. I've hung it up on the hook behind the door here, if that's okay. Until we're ready to leave, that is."

"That's just fine," he said. "Now, where do you want to go? In the living room or back into the bedroom? I promise you I won't do anything you don't want me to."

"Well, in that case, I guess we could go back into the bedroom, now. . . ." Since putting on my underwear and having the talk we had just had, I felt different than I had a few minutes before. He took my hand and led me back to the bed, where he lay down on it on the farther side, then gently pulled me down beside him. I stared at the ceiling. "I'm cold," I said. He turned toward me and carefully put his arms around me.

"I guess I shouldn't be surprised if you didn't really want to see me again."

"Don't be silly," he said.

"I just can't believe this happened like this."

"I know what you mean."

"I mean, I'm beginning to wonder if something's wrong with me or something. I mean, I wanted to be with you—at least I thought I did—I mean, I'm sure I did."

"I think you just got scared."

"Maybe."

"I was a little scared myself."

"You didn't seem so."

"I was, though."

"Of what?"

"Only about a million things."

"Like what? Tell me."

"Oh, I don't know," he began. "That when we made out you wouldn't get excited, or that when I took my clothes off you wouldn't like the looks of me."

"But I did."

"Yeah, I could tell," he said.

"What else?"

"Oh, just the usual stuff—like I hoped I was big enough for you, things guys worry about . . ."

"Really?"

"Yup."

"I wish I could just go and do whatever I want to do, without worrying about what anybody might think, what God might think. Or Mother."

"You really worry about that, huh?"

"Sometimes I think I was born that way," I said. "Still, I think you should be able to do what you want to. Make your own rules depending on what the circumstances are. I was thinking a while back, what do I care if some people think we're bad, or immoral, or—"

Oscar snored. I looked at him. Asleep. I watched him breathe for a while, watched his face twitch now and then. The light in the room was pale and cold-looking. I reached down and pulled a corner of blanket over my legs, then lay back at Oscar's side. I tried to sleep, but an empty, melancholy feeling had come over me, and all I could think about, again, as I had done the day before, was going home to Beverly.

It was some time later that Barney's cat crawled out from under the bed and jumped up onto my pillow, purring loudly. In a few minutes Oscar woke up. After stretching and yawning, he pulled the Indian blanket I had covered my feet with up around us, practically over our heads. We lay there like that, the cat at my shoulder, our arms around one another. Oscar was in a silly mood, humming camp songs, threatening to tell me a ghost story, whispering under the covers. It wasn't long before I was laughing at him, enjoying him.

"You know what I'd like to do?" he said, quasi-seriously, lapping me on the cheek, then wrapping the blanket over my head, gathering it under my chin like a bonnet.

"Hmm—let me think. What *could* it be?"

"You're a hedonist, Annie—don't you ever think of anything but sex?"

I laughed. "I can't go all the way . . ." I warned.

"No, this time it's something else. But you're close," he said.

"Feed the cat?" I offered.

"Yeah," he said.

"Oh, that *is* what we came for, isn't it?"

"Yeah," he said. "First we feed the cat."

"Then what?" I said.

"Then we do the dishes, if you know what I mean." It took me a minute.

"You're going to love it," he growled, springing over me from the bed, then somehow gathering me up into his arms. "Besides, this is a fantasy of mine," he grunted, staggering toward the door with me. "I'll even wash your hair." The cat followed us at the run, meowing loudly.

"I want to tell you something first," I said between giggles as Oscar set me on the floor and ran to get towels. The cat jumped up on the kitchen table and began licking the cereal bowl.

"What?" he said, returning, throwing a pile of towels down on the floor and turning on the shower.

"Wait," I said, restraining him from unzipping his pants. He looked at me quizzically.

"Years from now," I said, "when you talk about this, and you *will*, be kind." It was the last line from *Tea and Sympathy*. I had wanted to use it someday.

SIXTEEN

By midweek, neither Malcolm nor I had heard a single word about Georgia. When Malcolm called Ida Printaine's house on Wednesday evening to see what he could find out, the housekeeper answered, said Miss Printaine was not available, and gave Malcolm the distinct idea that she had been told not to answer any questions from anybody. She wouldn't even say whether Georgia was there or not, which we both found a little odd.

I, for one, let my imagination run wild; and despite Malcolm's assurances that Georgia and Miss Printaine were "very close," I envisioned Georgia imprisoned either in Louisburg Square or in Mattapan State Hospital, with no one the wiser, alone and frightened.

The third floor was a lonely place with Georgia gone. I missed her saccharine poems. I even missed her shoes. It was a letdown to come home from work and find the third-floor landing empty, no one to greet me with bated breath.

I had taken over the chore of feeding her birds. Oscar and Ruth saved bread for me. I liked going into Georgia's room among her things, sitting in the rocker by the window, watching the pigeons eat.

By Thursday morning I was beside myself with worry, and I

spent a few extra minutes before leaving the house talking it over
with Malcolm, who was piqued at Ida's maid and concerned about
Georgia himself.

That morning at work, an enormous libraryful of books, a few
old and rare ones, was delivered to the bookstore on behalf of a
recently deceased owner. I was back in Old and Rare, sorting
through things, trying to organize this windfall, when the telephone rang out front and Oscar called me to the phone. It was
Malcolm.

"I hope I'm not disturbing you at work," he said, "but I wanted
you to know that I heard from Miss Printaine this morning and
Georgia is well."

"Oh, thank God! Where is she? When will she be coming home?"

"Well, not for some time, I expect, as at the moment she is a
patient at Cunningham Hospital."

"Oh, no," I said. "I was afraid of that. I can't bear the thought. . . ."

"Do try not to be upset," Malcolm said comfortingly. "I've heard
good things about Cunningham. If she has to be anywhere, it's a
great blessing she's there. Miss Printaine assures me that she's
doing well, as well as can be expected under the circumstances."

"Really?"

"Apparently so," he said. "As a matter of fact, Miss Printaine
suggests that we might like to visit Georgia this weekend. She
wasn't allowed visitors at first, but beginning Sunday she is."

"Oh, Malcolm, that's wonderful! Would you like to go?"

"Yes. I thought we'd drive out there Sunday afternoon. About
two, I should think."

"Okay, we'll plan on it," I said. "I'm so glad you called me—
I've been letting my imagination run wild. Why didn't she call
sooner?"

"I really couldn't say," Malcolm said. "I suppose some people
are private about such things. Wouldn't necessarily want everyone
to know."

"I guess," I said. "But we already knew the worst, didn't we?"

"Miss Printaine possibly feels it's some reflection on her, Georgia's instability—something she might have done, or not done. It's
terribly upsetting when someone one cares for takes such a turn."

"I've even felt that way myself," I said. "Wondering what I might have done better, that is."

"Yes, one wonders," he said thoughtfully. "It's quite natural, I would think. Heaven knows, I would have been only too happy to do whatever was necessary had I known about her state of mind, and I know you feel the same."

"I guess I'm not very intuitive."

"Now, now, we did what we could," Malcolm said lightly, as if making an effort to be cheerful. "Now that we know a little better what we're dealing with . . ."

"Yes," I said.

"I'll see what I can find in the way of a book she might enjoy, although I can't think of what it might be."

"She loves poetry, Malcolm. As a matter of fact, we have a lovely old leatherbound volume of Elizabeth Barrett Browning right here in the store. Shall I pick it up for you?"

"Yes, do," he said. "Good idea. And you, young lady, take care to calm yourself. She's in professional hands now—all is well."

Malcolm was a great comfort to me.

After hanging up, I realized that Oscar and Ruth had been listening attentively to my end of the conversation. I had told them both all about Georgia.

"She's all right, is she, dear?" Ruth asked, pulling out a chair for me so that I could sit by her.

"She's at Cunningham Hospital," I said.

"Oh my, you didn't tell me that she was wealthy, dear."

"Oh no, she's not," I said.

"Cunningham is a fine private hospital," Ruth said. "It's out near Belmont, I think. Some exhausted movie star or millionaire is always coming east for a rest there. They even have a landing strip so that the stars can come in incognito. It's an elegant place."

"Ida Printaine must be paying her expenses," I said, thinking warmly of the woman for the first time. "She has money, I know."

Oscar was leaning up against the wall, nodding. "It doesn't surprise me, I guess," he said pompously.

"Oscar, you hardly know the girl—don't go pretending you foresaw all of this."

"You have to admit," he said, more gently, "she's a strange person."

"So are you," I mumbled. I looked at Ruth. Oscar stood up straighter and fiddled with his tie. "I'm relieved that she's somewhere nice," I said to Ruth.

"You've become quite attached to her, haven't you, dear?"

"Was it obvious to you that she was—uh—strange, when you met her?"

"I only saw her for a moment," Ruth said. "I hardly noticed her, actually. I was more concerned with you and your flu bug. Your face was green as ivy that day."

"I didn't mean that she wasn't a decent person," Oscar said.

"Well, I *have* become attached to her," I said. "Very attached. She can be quite lovable at times, and she's had a terrible life."

"What a shame," Ruth said, going back to her books. "How kind of you to befriend her. Lord knows, that's probably what she needs most—a good friend like you."

I stood up, ready to go back to work. "Well, I'll be seeing her on Sunday," I said. "Malcolm and I are driving out there."

I started back to Old and Rare without looking at Oscar, but a few minutes later, as I was emptying one of the larger cartons of books onto the floor, he appeared at my side. "I thought you and I were going to do a load of dishes on Sunday," he whispered.

"We'll have to go out on Saturday instead."

"But I have to help Barney paint—I told you that. His girl's parents' cottage, remember?"

"Vaguely," I said.

"I didn't mean to seem unsympathetic to your friend," he said, bowing his head and resting it against mine.

"I'm sorry. I've been awfully worried about her."

"There's really nothing you can do to help her, you must know that," he said.

I handed him a dust cloth, and we began to dust the new books and place them on the oak table. I'd figure out where they all went later.

"I can *care* about her," I said. "Besides, you don't know her—you don't know what she needs. I'm good for her, I really am, and she's good for me."

"You think you can save her," he said.

"Maybe I can."

"You can't," he said. "And she's using you, probably, and you can't see that, either."

"This is a side of you I don't like," I said.

"You don't understand what I'm saying," he said.

"I thought you were a more—well, *loving* person."

"I'm just worried about *you*."

"For what? I'm not at Cunningham—Georgia is!"

"I'm worried about what will happen to you if something happens to her. If the next time it's not just a cut face."

"She's not that crazy anymore. There won't be a next time."

Just then Ruth came around the corner, a key in her hand. "Excuse me," she said, eyeing us. "Oscar dear, they've made new keys for us for that back door, and I can't seem to get this one to work. Could you see to it? You may need a little graphite." Oscar took the key and left. She looked at me. "He's just worried about you, Ann," she said.

"I think he's jealous. He wants me all to himself."

Ruth was pensive for a moment, then nodded her head. "Could be—you may be right. But even that's rather sweet, don't you think?"

"No, not especially," I said, whereupon Ruth patted my arm and started back to the front of the store.

"Oh, I forgot," she said, turning. "Could you come and watch the cash register for a few minutes? I need to talk to Mrs. Emory at Burnell's down the way. She's got a new bookkeeping system she wants me to have a look at. I won't be long." I dropped what I was doing and followed her to the front of the store.

She hadn't been gone long when a young woman with freckles and deep red hair breezed through the doorway and headed toward me.

"I'm Ruth Carmichael's niece," she said, plunking her purse down on the desk. "She's here, isn't she?"

"She stepped out for just a minute to the store down the street. Shall I telephone over there and let her know you're here? She should be back shortly."

"I'll just wait for a few minutes," she said, perching on the side of the desk. "You must be Ann."

"Yes," I said. "And you must be Kathleen." We shook hands. "I've heard lots about you."

"Same here," she said.

"I've heard all about the baby and your trip out west."

She smiled, then laughed good-naturedly. "Poor Aunt Ruth, you'd think I was going to the Antarctic. But my husband's just thrilled to be going to medical school out there, and I must say I'm excited about the trip and living in a new place. It's going to be fun."

"It sounds like it," I said.

"We've found a nanny who'll travel with us, so that I can begin working practically the minute we arrive. And we've already rented a big old house within biking distance of the U and—" She stopped talking as Ruth strolled through the door.

"Well, look who's here!" Ruth said. "I hope you don't have plans for lunch."

"Is that an invitation?" Kathleen asked, a twinkle in her eye.

"Well, I don't know. Ann, what do you think? Shall we ask her to come with us or not?"

"I guess we'd better," I said, "seeing that she's here and all. Of course, if you'd rather not . . ."

Ruth chuckled, then smiled broadly. "Then we'll make it a threesome," she said, taking her compact out of her purse, flipping it open and running her index finger back and forth across her bottom lip.

"I better go and tell Oscar," I said, heading for the storeroom to look for him.

I met Malcolm at his door at two o'clock sharp on Sunday afternoon, filled with excitement at the thought of seeing Georgia again. Malcolm carried the Elizabeth Barrett Browning; I carried a box of Blue Grass dusting powder. I was quite at ease at the thought of going out to Cunningham. The fact that I was going to visit my suicidal friend in a mental hospital seemed as unremarkable to me as a trip to the grocery store—a sophisticated point of view, if I did say so myself.

We headed out of the city in Malcolm's old Renault. Mild-mannered in the extreme, serene, self-possessed, calmness personified in any other situation, Malcolm turned out to be a crazed fiend at the wheel of his little car: in love with speed, an avid brake jammer, a self-appointed commentator on the motoring skills of every other poor driver on the road. This made conversation with him difficult. Either he was concentrating on the road, or mumbling to himself angrily, or gesturing toward other drivers, or simply driving so fast that every bump or turn took the words right out of my mouth.

By the time we had traveled for forty-five minutes and turned into a wooded lane marked CUNNINGHAM HOSPITAL in gold letters on black ground, I was, to say the least, rattled.

The lane climbed and wound its way through woodlots, rolling fields, the greens of a golf course, and a parched meadow with a wind sock mounted off to one side, the air field. Finally the road made a final climb through a birch grove and came out on a sprawling knoll, upon which the dozen or so stately buildings that comprised Cunningham were set, surrounded by shade trees, manicured lawns, and flower gardens.

As we got out of the car in front of the administration building, the sun shone brightly, and the air smelled as clean and sweet as mountain air.

People of every description, dressed in summer clothes, wandered under the trees or sat alone in lawn chairs or congregated in small groups at picnic tables or on the grass. It was as if there were a garden party going on at someone's fashionable country estate.

Three tennis courts could be seen through the trees at a short distance. Farther beyond, on yet another hill, stood a grey barn surrounded by paddocks; in front of it, three horses were being saddled for an afternoon ride. It was difficult to believe that this was a mental hospital and the attractive "guests," in fact, inmates.

I wondered whether being rich and crazy was somehow a cut above being poor and crazy; whether it was possible to be demented yet dignified. It certainly seemed so.

The administration building was a gracious yellow frame colonial with white trim and shutters. At one side was a wide veranda topped with cascading vines, below which a group of old women rocked.

We opened the gate and started up the flagstone walk. After only a few steps we were approached by a woman about my mother's age who had been sitting on a lawn chair reading. Perhaps the administrator herself, I thought, or a secretary who had been notified of our intention to visit today. She pointed her finger at me and smiled.

"You're a Red, you are," she said. "You thought you could walk right by me, didn't you? Well, you don't fool me one bit, and if you came to spy on me, forget it, girlie. I'll have you locked up by sunset." Malcolm took my arm and tried to pull me along with him, but the woman stood squarely in front of me, her face only inches from mine.

"Camille! Camille! Don't bother the visitors!" The voice came from a young nurse about my age, who ran across the lawn toward us.

"I caught this one!" Camille yelled back. She nabbed me by the sleeve of my dress. "Another Red come spying," she said wickedly, glaring at me with a terrifying grimace on her face.

"Go back and sit down and read your book, Camille," the nurse said. "She's not a Red—she's a visitor." Camille did as she was told. "I'm really sorry," the nurse said, smiling. "Your hair has a lot of red in it."

"You're damned right it's the color of her hair," Camille grumbled loudly, sitting down. She shook her finger at me. "You can't fool me, girlie."

"She thinks you're a communist," the nurse said. "Poor Camille thinks that everybody with reddish hair or dressed in red is a communist. Sorry—I was supposed to be watching her. I'm really sorry. She wouldn't have hurt you or anything. She's completely harmless."

"It's perfectly all right," I said, anxious to show that I wasn't shaken, although I was. I looked back as Malcolm and I strode through the front door; Camille was still eyeing me. All I could think of was my poor mother and her Red Menace phobia. I would speak to her about keeping it in check.

"Rather a close one," Malcolm whispered once we were inside. His pretty brows almost joined in the middle, then leapt apart, reminding me once again of dancers. We stood at the half-door of an enclosed area marked ALL VISITORS REGISTER HERE.

"We have come to visit Miss Georgia Mitchell," Malcolm said, sounding like a butler announcing tea. He held his chin high, his eyebrows absolutely still as the woman in charge examined her books.

"Ah, yes. Miss Mitchell was transferred to Dover this morning—doing well, apparently." She wrote our names on a card, then rang a small brass bell. A young man in white appeared from down a corridor to our right. "Hal here will escort you. Present this pass to the head nurse. When you are ready to return, notify the head nurse and someone will be sent for you. Visiting hours end at four."

We thanked her and set off with Hal, out the back door, over a circular terrace furnished with umbrella-topped tables at which a number of patients sat busy at cards, then across a flat shaded area of lawn toward a three-storey frame house painted grey-blue with pale-grey shutters: Victorian, with a wrap-around veranda and an oval stained-glass window beside the front door; there was a turret on the third storey, topped with a peaked roof and a weathervane.

We had just set foot on the veranda steps when I heard Georgia's voice scream out from somewhere behind us.

"Annieeeee, *Annieeee!*" When I turned she was running over the grass, arms waving, the skirt of her sun dress up above her knees. Her hair had been cut—hacked at was more like it. I had heard that sometimes hair had to be shorn before certain brain tests were performed.

I stood at the bottom of the steps waiting for her. Hal had gone inside.

A tall, broad-shouldered black man dressed in white was following Georgia and speaking to her in a calm but loud voice. "Walk, Georgia, walk," he said. "Stop running, Georgia. Your friends will wait."

Reaching us, she hurled herself at me, jarring me painfully as we crashed together, kissing me on the cheek. Then she turned and wrapped herself around Malcolm, jumping up and down. When freed, he was very red but laughing all the same.

"And this—" she announced, whirling and facing the black man at her elbow, gesturing grandly in his direction—"this is my keeper! This magnificent specimen of manhood, this descendent of a feather-covered Masai warrior chieftain and cousin, I might add, to none other than Harry Belafonte, is Rodney Mills! But I call him Umgawa, don't I, Rodney?"

"Calm down now, Georgia—lower your voice," Rodney said cajolingly.

"But I want you to meet my friends, Umgawa—or should I say meet-um my friends. Isn't that African or Swahili or something? Look, Rodney dear, this is my dearest friend in the whole wide world, Annie Merrill, and this"—she reached for Malcolm's hand—"this dearest sweetest man on the face of the earth is your counterpart when I'm at home, my caretaker, Malcolm Balch."

Rodney shook hands with Malcolm and me without smiling. He hardly took his eyes off Georgia. I knew, as a sick, shaky feeling welled up inside me, that Rodney had been assigned to look after her—that he was indeed her keeper, that she probably was not allowed to roam the grounds without him at her side.

And I could see she needed a keeper. Her face was flushed from running, her eyes were wider than I had ever seen them and curiously blank. She shook from head to foot, as if her body were seized by a relentless tremor over which she had no control. Her arms moved constantly, pawing the air as if she were treading water.

The injuries she had done to her face little more than a week ago still marked her. The scabs and red lines had divided her face into quadrants, as if she were the embodiment of some technique in modern art.

"Maybe your friends would like to see your room, Georgia," Rodney said quietly.

"Oh, yes," I said. "What a good idea! I want to see where you live here."

"Exist, darling. That's all that one does here." She had affected a British accent. "One exists until one is set free to live. Or to die. I am reminded of a hotel where I once stayed in Biarritz. I was there for the season. There were so many tourists that year, I stayed put in my room or on my balcony and had the servants bring up all my food, my favorite being the monkfish shipped all the way from the Mediterranean, served in a kind of aspic, as I recall, and . . ."

We had walked up the steps and into the house, into a gracious entrance hall flanked by potted palms. Malcolm struggled along behind us, muttering comments here and there.

". . . later that year," Georgia continued (I didn't have the slightest idea whether any of this was true), "we went to Paris, and the city was so beautiful then, Montmartre and the Seine and falling in love and fucking under all those bridges all night long—incessant French fucking. What a glorious word that is! What do you call a word that sounds like the activity . . . ?"

In Georgia's room at last, Rodney brought straight chairs for Malcolm and me and left us, explaining that he would be at the nurses' station if we should need anything. Georgia sat down on a gaily striped chair by the window. I sat next to her, while Malcolm took the chair across from us on the other side of the bed. I was nervous—alarmed was more like it. I didn't know what to say, how to begin. I placed the box of dusting powder I had brought her in her lap. She held it to her nose and smiled at me and thanked me in a whisper. Malcolm leaned across the bed and placed the book where she could reach it.

"Ann says you love poetry. I hope this will serve." She smiled and looked at the title, then placed the book on the windowsill. It unnerved me that she didn't thank him or comment on his selection, but Malcolm seemed at ease, unbuttoning his suit coat and crossing one knee over the other.

"A lovely room," he said, casting his eyes about at the mahogany furniture, Oriental rug, and ruffled curtains. "Moss roses, I believe those are," he said, pointing at the wallpaper. "How nice, with the rose garden right out the window there. Such peaceful and pleasant surroundings."

"Yes," I said, "isn't it lovely? I wonder how many varieties of roses are in that garden. Quite a few, I imagine."

"Booth *loved* roses," Malcolm said brightly. "I believe I told you that, didn't I, Georgia? I always tried to send roses whenever the show came to Boston or Madison Square Garden, and of course for all his birthdays." Georgia didn't appear to hear him. Who on earth was Booth? An actor? A prizefighter? Oh no, I thought. Booth was the ice skater Georgia had told me about—Malcolm's lover.

"I beg your pardon," Georgia said, realizing that Malcolm was speaking to her, and turning from the window. "What did you say?"

"Booth," Malcolm said. "I was mentioning his love for roses."

"Oh yes, you told me. Yellow ones, wasn't it?"

"Yellow ones were his very favorites," Malcolm said. "But he wasn't particular—oh my, no. He'd take any rose he could get his hands on!" Malcolm laughed. "Once when he was ill and I couldn't get to him—he was on the road, of course—I had them send those adorable little sweetheart roses in a basket, and he was so delighted."

"Of course, of course—what is happening to my memory?" Georgia said, rising from her chair and moving this way and that about the room, one hand at her forehead, a look of pain on her face. "Booth, your lover, loved roses, didn't he? You showed me all the pictures. He's the skater, isn't he? How sweet."

"He passed on several years ago," Malcolm said soberly, looking down at his clasped hands.

"Oh, Malcolm," I said. "I'm so sorry." He nodded quickly and cleared his throat before looking squarely into my eyes and smiling.

"I love a man who loves flowers," Georgia interjected, examining the wallpaper. "It's rare. So rare! I knew a man like that once—he had his own greenhouse and a green thumb and God

knows what else. He loved to poke in the dirt. Honest to God—
things just jumped into bloom when he was around. He had the
magic touch. I always thought how strange it was that a man whose
hands were so rough and dirty could make such beauty grow. He
tried to show me the tricks of his trade, but I was a slow learner."
Georgia looked at me knowingly. "Ha! Yes indeedy. He practically
insisted he show me the tricks of his trade. Do you know—" She
sat down on the edge of her bed, near Malcolm. "Do you know,
he had this really unique technique for cultivating rare blooms.
He felt them up a little, I guess you might say. He felt up their
little petals. Isn't that cute?" She was grinning at me. Malcolm
looked at her, then stared out the window. I had no idea what to
say. I said nothing. I looked at my hands, then at Georgia again.
I got up and walked to the doorway. She sat down on the bed.

"Shall we speak French to one another?" she asked. Her voice
shook. "Do you know French?" She leaned across the bed toward
me. Her voice was pleading. I walked over and sat down beside
her. Malcolm stood, walked to the window, and looked out, his
back to us.

"I'm afraid not," I said. "Not enough to carry on an intelligent
conversation, anyway."

"Liar!"

"I only know a few words," I said, knowing now where this
conversation would lead.

"I recall a certain evening when you spoke French quite well.
It was very impressive. I mean, *very*."

"I took it in school," I muttered.

"There is nothing quite as fetching as schoolgirl French," she
crooned. I looked away. What a mistake coming here had been!

"What happened to your hair?" I asked, deflecting the conversation. Whoever had sawed it off deserved to be shot. Why couldn't
they have done it more carefully? She hadn't answered me. "I've
heard that they sometimes have to do that," I said, "for certain
tests."

She laughed. " 'They' didn't. *I* did. I cut it. Just before I got
here. In fact, that's probably *why* I got here." She laughed again.
"They don't seem to care that you cut your face," she said con-

spiratorially, as if giving advice to would-be inmates. "But you must never, ever, *ever* cut off your hair. They take a dim view of do-it-yourself barbering. If you're a female." She looked at me for a response.

"That's good to know," I said. Malcolm turned, smiled an idiot smile, and nodded.

"A woman cutting off her own hair is as bad as a man lopping off his own balls. That's what Sampson told me. He went to Harvard. He knows all the latest psychological jargon. Brilliant man!"

"Sounds like it," I said.

"And he should know," she said, chuckling. "If anyone should know about hair cutting, it'd be Sampson. Get it?"

"Unfortunately, yes," I said, smiling. Her tone of voice was less challenging. She seemed as if she were beginning to relax.

"We've been terribly worried about you," Malcolm said, apparently sensing the change.

"Thank you," she said.

"The household isn't the same without you there," he said.

"It's lonely here," she said.

"Is it?" I said.

"Yeah. Honest to God, I wish you were here for me to talk to. I get so lonely." Her eyes filled with tears.

"It won't be long before you're home, Georgia," I said, not at all sure if this was true.

"You're not going home right this minute, are you?" she said, bursting into tears and covering her face with her hands.

"No, we'll stay," I said. I looked at Malcolm, who nodded.

"I've lost my job," she said, sobbing. "They—they fired me."

"It's all right," I said. "You'll find another when you feel better."

"I'll never feel better," she said, glancing at me from behind her hands. "I know that now. I'll never feel better. It's the end." I moved across the bed toward her and just sat next to her and listened to her cry. Malcolm placed his hand on her shoulder. The three of us remained that way for some time while Georgia wept, interrupting her sobs with scattered statements about how she felt and what had been happening to her.

If I could have thought of something to say that might have

helped, I would have said it. But whatever she needed was beyond what I knew how to give. And for a few moments, hearing her cry, feeling the bed vibrate under us, seeing her scarred face and shorn hair, I felt hopeless for her.

I heard the rustle of a starched uniform and Rodney appeared through the doorway, went to Georgia's side, and observed her silently, holding her hands in his.

"Let me get you something," he said softly.

"No," she said.

"It's been over three hours," he said, glancing at his watch. "How about it? You'll feel better. That's what the doctor ordered it for—to help you feel better."

She thought for a moment, then nodded, and he left. She asked me to help her lie down. I pulled the spread down to expose her pillow, then brought the neatly folded blanket at the foot of the bed up around her shoulders. She stretched out. I took off her sneakers. She turned her head to one side, closed her eyes, and cried soundlessly, the tears flowing freely, as from an inexhaustible reservoir, as if her whole body were filled with nothing but tears.

Rodney returned with a nurse who carried a hypodermic syringe. We were asked to leave the room. Rodney followed us out, told us that she would feel better soon, that the shot would make her sleepy and that we had better cut our visit short.

Then Malcolm and I just stood there, staring into the grain of the oak door in front of us, looking at the floor. Malcolm sighed. "She's not good," he said solemnly.

"No," I said.

"It was similar with Booth—his dark moods," he said.

"Oh," I said, puzzled. Had Booth been in a mental hospital too?

"Near the end, though, he became almost cheerful. It seemed that he had stopped fighting at last and was finally at peace with himself." Malcolm sighed deeply and stared down the corridor.

Back in Georgia's room after the nurse had left, I positioned myself sitting next to her on the bed and Malcolm took the chair by the window. Georgia looked up at me and smiled weakly and covered one of my hands with hers.

"Soul mates," she whispered.

"Yes," I said. She grinned at me, ropes of saliva strung between her teeth, tears still streaking her face, the hair at her temples damp from crying.

"I love you, Annie," she said, and although I knew she wanted me to tell her I loved her and although at this very moment I felt like I did, that I cared for her as if she were my own sister, all I did was thank her and tell her she was sweet and that I hoped she got better soon. An awkward silence followed. I had not said what she wanted to hear; I had not been able to say what was in my heart. So, instead, I commenced to fill the silence with whatever came to mind. I talked about Oscar. I talked about the bookstore. I mentioned once again the rose garden outside her window, through which several patients strolled from time to time, as if in slow motion, pale figures bleached in the bright sunlight.

In the very center of the garden, surrounded by a low fence of wrought iron, was a sundial, a silver globe on a bronze pedestal. The sun, hitting it at just the right angle, sent a blinding beam of diamond-white light straight at me, as if it had searched me out. It cut into me; and as I sat beside Georgia and talked on about Ruth Carmichael and what I had eaten for dinner during the past week and the last time I had seen Stanley Crosshill, I saw myself for what I was: self-centered, snobbish, afraid to give of myself. Cold. Dead.

Georgia patted my hand. "I'm so glad you came to visit me," she said sleepily. "I was afraid you wouldn't. I was afraid you'd had it up to here with me."

"No," I said, "I've missed you terribly." It was true.

Suddenly I saw Georgia's eyes leave mine and stare at something over my shoulder. I turned.

"Let me get in there, if you please." It was Ida Printaine. She waved me off. I got down from the bed and stood against the wall as she took my place. "Did they give you a shot?"

"Yes," Georgia answered.

"Then rest," Ida said. She touched Georgia's hair with her wide hand. She wore a man's watch and a gold signet ring. She was small-waisted, with narrow hips; but her shoulders, arms, and legs seemed to be made of sturdier stuff. Her limbs were short in proportion to her torso; her wrists and ankles were thick. Until now I had thought of her as being small; but really, had she had longer legs she would have had the physique of an Amazon.

The black silk suit she wore was old but expensive. Her blouse was ecru, tucked and featherstitched by hand, complete with bound buttonholes and beautiful covered buttons. The gloves she had placed in her purse were cream-colored kid trimmed with black. Georgia had said Ida had awful taste. Just the opposite, I thought.

If only she had followed through with her choice of cosmetics. Today, she had added fuchsia rouge to her chalkily powdered face. Her eyebrows, shaved off, then penciled on in thin black lines, vaulted above her small eyes like parentheses. She wore deep maroon lipstick applied with a heavy hand; it feathered into the wrinkles around her mouth, behind which crouched her yellow teeth.

Something about this woman made me despise her.

Georgia's eyes were closed now. Ida stood up, removed her jacket, placed it at the foot of the bed, and rolled up her sleeves. She shot Malcolm and me a glare, but neither of us moved. She reached for her purse and took out a rosary, which at first glance I thought was made of black onyx but on closer examination, as she held the silver crucifix in her fingers, proved to be intricately carved from ebony wood, the surface highly polished from use. She raised her wide chin, closed her eyes and crossed herself. Her lips began to move, and from time to time I could make out a familiar word or phrase.

Soon her fingers moved from the crucifix to the beads above it, and I heard her begin an Our Father. Georgia's eyelids fluttered for an instant; she was awake and listening. Maybe Ida saying the Rosary for her was a comfort.

Malcolm and I stood almost at attention, afraid to move. I tried not to breathe. Georgia's lids fluttered again; one of her legs trembled beneath the blanket, and she rubbed it as if to rub the tremor away.

An older woman in a print dress was in the rose garden with shears and a basket, cutting roses. The house was quiet. If there were patients everywhere—in rooms on either side of us, on the floor above us—they made no sound. No one passed by in the corridor.

"Hail Mary, full of grace, the Lord is with thee. Blessed art thou amongst women, and blessed . . ." Ida fingered the small beads now. Georgia cleared her throat. She was awake, but her eyes remained closed. "Hail Mary, full of grace . . ." The beads moved in Ida's hand; the crucifix lost its footing and slid from her thigh to her side, where it swung easily to and fro, like a metronome beating time.

Outside, the light had changed.

Before long, Ida had gathered her beads and put them back in her purse. She leaned over and touched Georgia's forehead. Her eyes opened. She turned over on her side. Ida rubbed her stout hands together as if to warm them, then arranged them in a wide V-shape and plunged them into Georgia's back between her shoulder blades, between the straps of her sun dress. Georgia groaned, startled, then stared out the window.

Malcolm walked past me into the hallway. I wondered if he wanted me to join him, but he had given me no sign.

"Yup, yup," Ida said. "Just as I thought, tight as a drum here." She kneaded Georgia's back and shoulders. "This is not God's will for you. I've told you that. Our Lord wants you at peace. There, there—that's better, isn't it? You see? You see what I can do if you'll let me?" Ida turned in my direction and smiled her yellow smile. I shouldn't be so judgmental, I thought. The woman was strange, but she obviously cared for Georgia a great deal. She had good intentions. "There, there," Ida crooned, massaging Georgia's upper arm. "God loves you. Can you feel it? You must let it come in. Feel it? Through my hands. Let love come in, Georgia. You must love the Lord thy God with all thy heart, with all thy mind. You must love thy Lord and all his emissaries."

"I do, Ida. You know I do," Georgia said sleepily.

"Then you shall be healed. You shall be healed at the moment when your love and humility are most pure. Then you will get down on your knees before Him and you will be healed—totally healed of all infirmity, all pain. Yup, yup. There, there . . ." She dug into Georgia's shoulders once again, rocking to and fro as she did so, moving Georgia's body forward and backward against her hands. "Can you feel the healing power in these hands?" she asked in a guttural voice, a voice thick with emotion.

"Yes, Ida," Georgia said, as if only semiconscious.

"Can you feel the healing power flowing into you from these hands?" Ida smiled tightly, her wrinkled lips drawn up at their corners, her eyes shut, her head back, her neck extended in an attitude of both concentration and prayer.

Something was wrong. Something about this scene was horribly wrong.

"Yes . . . I feel it," Georgia said, her voice as high as a child's. I heard a blast of air escape from the mouth and body of Ida Printaine.

"Pray with me," Ida groaned, and she and Georgia prayed together, aloud, Georgia's voice a high, faint whisper, Ida's low and pulsating with vibrato.

I stood still. My heart pounded. I had heard all this before sometime, somewhere. My face felt flushed. I forced myself to stare at the two figures before me: Ida was up on her knees, her black body crouched at Georgia's side, her spatulate hands digging rhythmically into Georgia's back. She was now moaning, grunting a throaty sound each time she pushed Georgia forward, then let her fall back. I had heard a horse make that sound as it rubbed its haunches against a fence—the sound of pleasure, the scratching of an itch.

Ida opened her eyes and stared out the window toward the rose garden, still massaging, red-faced. Georgia suddenly grimaced with pain and reached around herself as if to grasp Ida's hand and pull it away, but Ida kept on. I saw her profile clearly, and no expression crossed her face. She was unaware of Georgia's discomfort, unaware of Georgia's hand plucking lightly at hers. My mind raced. This had happened before. It was familiar.

I began to shiver, feeling a cold chill creep along the skin of my upper arms and neck. My head was light. There was nausea at the pit of my stomach. Nausea in waves. My God, I was going to throw up. I put my hand to my mouth.

It couldn't be, I thought, still watching Ida in profile: the fat nose crouched between those wicked, small eyes, the slab of pitted, powdered flesh that spread across her rouged cheek like a flattened dollop of soft cheese, the jutting jawline, the thick neck. The streaks of white in her hair zigzagged up from her temples like bolts of lightning. All I heard was her breath.

And in that moment I was transported in time and place from this house with its garden of roses to a building I had constructed in my mind's eye, a brick building with a statue of the Virgin Mary at its entrance, from whose back windows a little girl might look out in spring to see the apple orchards. St. Theresa's Home, somewhere in Rhode Island.

No. It couldn't be.

I wanted to leave the room, was afraid that any second I might scream something out, heard Georgia's little-girl voice telling Ida to stop, that it hurt her, saw Ida's hands, Sister Xavier's hands, plunge into her flesh again and again.

How could it be?

Yet it was. It was her. I knew it was her. Ida was Sister Xavier. Ida was the monster who had tortured Georgia as a child, Ida who tortured her still. Maybe for Georgia's whole life. Unless someone did something.

I would kill her.

Now.

As she knelt before me on the bed, I planned it, in detail, in my mind. I would creep up behind her. I would lace my fingers together, bend them, form a hard double fist, raise my arms, fix my eyes on the very center of the back of her neck, just above her collar, and let my arms fall with a vengeance, smashing her spinal column with one sharp blow. I would pull her limp body down from the bed by her striped hair, and when I finished kicking her, mercilessly, she would be unrecognizable.

"Better let her rest now, Miss Printaine," Rodney said, bustling into the room, startling me. Malcolm followed him.

"Of course, Rodney. I was just now leaving. All of us were just now leaving." She crawled down from the bed and donned her jacket, turning as she did so and glaring at me as she reached for an armhole. I glared back. She buttoned the tight jacket up to within inches of her chin. She reached to the floor for her purse, retrieved her gloves. And there she was, Sister Xavier, neatly dressed in black and ecru, a pious figure with a homely, hungry face, a pale, powdered face the consistency of cottage cheese. She had eaten her lipstick off.

She smoothed her hair, her fat, stubby fingers lingering for an instant at each temple, a small, hovering gesture as if she were adjusting a veil. Her busy little eyes stared at me unflinchingly, a queer, suspicious look to them. Her left eyebrow raised itself slowly, then remained in that position. "I know who you are," I said silently, and as if she had heard me, she looked away.

"Stay for a minute more, Annie," Georgia said.

"Do what she asks," Ida said with a wave of her hand. "Rodney, I shall have to ask you for a small basin of isopropyl alcohol."

Rodney looked at her, puzzled. "May I ask for what purpose?"

"Why, to disinfect my hands," she said, "of course." She laughed, shrugging her wide shoulders. "I shall be back tomorrow, Georgia. I shall expect improvement." With that, she stood for a moment in the middle of the room and looked around at the walls, the furniture, the carpet. "This place is filthy," she said. "I shall follow you to the utility room, orderly. I don't suppose you have hydrogen peroxide also. . . ." She was gone.

"Are you all right?" I said, sitting down beside her on the bed. Malcolm, sensing that Georgia wanted to speak to me alone, remained outside.

"Yes," she said, covering my hand with hers once more.

"I'm worried about you." I wanted to ask her about Ida but couldn't yet. "Are you sure you're all right?"

"I've been here before."

"Are they nice to you?" My thoughts were running wild. Maybe everyone in this place, the doctors, nurses, everyone, was crazy and out to hurt Georgia, like Ida.

"They're wonderful," she said. "But I get lonely, for you and the Hill and Claude. . . ." She smiled, small and hurt.

"Don't be lonely, Georgia," I said. "You have me, you know. I am with you all the time, at least in my thoughts." I kissed her forehead, placing my hand at the back of her head. Her forehead tasted of salt. I wiped my mouth on my sleeve and hated myself for doing it.

"Soul mates," Georgia said, beaming, and leaned over to kiss my cheek.

"I really have to go now," I said. She nodded and fell back against the pillow. "I'll see if I can get back here sometime during the week to visit. Otherwise, I'll see you next Saturday for sure."

"Call me. I have telephone privileges now. I can receive three phone calls per day."

"Then I'll call you every day, shall I?"

"Yes . . . and tell Claude, will you? You just call the hospital and ask for Dover and then ask for me. Promise you'll tell him?" I promised.

"Georgia, I have to ask you something," I said. It might not be the right time or place, but I had to ask. "I . . . I sort of wonder, you know, about Ida. About whether she really is a friend of yours."

"Believe me, I wonder about her too," she said, rolling her eyes.

"No," I said, "really. I mean, there's something about her. . . ." I watched Georgia carefully for her reaction. "To be honest about it," I continued, "the woman gives me the creeps."

"Ha!" Georgia laughed in one brief burst followed by a quick fluttering sound that ended with a slight gag. "That's because she's a religious fanatic, Annie dear, and she gives everybody the creeps. Ha!" After the final burst of laughter, her mouth went slack, turned down at the corners. "What did you think? What made you feel that way? Poor Ida." She tried to laugh once more, but it simply wouldn't come out.

"I think I know who she is," I said.

"Well," she said, licking her lips, glancing at me with a look of fear in her eyes, "well, of course. Of course you do, silly."

"I just wanted you to know that I knew."

She wrinkled her face up, an exaggerated expression of puzzlement. "I don't really . . . I mean, I don't get what you mean. . . . I

don't think this place agrees with you, Annie. I mean, I have to
laugh at you—just a little, anyway. You'd better get on home
before they find another bed just for you!"

For a moment I didn't move. I stood there quietly, hoping she
would say more.

"You really better go," she whispered. She got down from the
bed and walked unsteadily to the door to say goodbye to Malcolm.

On the way home to Walnut Street, after telling me he had decided
that Georgia didn't look so bad after all, "considering," and re-
marking once again about what a lovely, peaceful place Cunningham was and how generous it was of Miss Printaine to provide
so well for Miss Mitchell, as if she were "her own daughter," I
began, cautiously, to grill Malcolm on the subject of Ida Printaine.

"Almost a Cinderella story, isn't it?" I said. "Someone as wealthy
as Miss Printaine taking an interest in a poor foundling."

"It is, it is," Malcolm said, smiling into the stream of traffic
ahead of us.

"Before actually meeting her, I had assumed Miss Printaine was
an old friend from the orphanage—you know, a classmate of Georgia's. But she's obviously too old for that. Still, they've known one
another forever. Do you happen to know exactly when they met?"

"Quite some time ago," he said. "It's my understanding that
they met quite some time ago. Some years back, I would think.
Traffic seems a bit lighter now, if I'm not mistaken. Of course,
the Printaines have lived on the Hill for years. A fine family, I've
heard. Roman Catholics. Quite active in charity affairs, they were.
My late sister, Louise, was well acquainted with Monica Printaine,
Ida's older sister. Monica has been gone for ten years at least.
Ida's the sole living heir to the family estate, I believe. A substantial
fortune. Shipping and fruit in Cuba—that was their line."

"Fascinating," I said. "I had no idea you knew them so well."

"Not well, really," Malcolm said, "but all of us know *of* one
another—all of the old families do. I imagine it was some sort of
charity work that brought Ida and Georgia together. The family
was active in Catholic charities particularly. Perhaps a sum of money
was donated to the orphanage and Ida went down there to inspect

the place, I don't know, and Georgia came to her attention, and she became fond of the girl."

"So Miss Printaine has lived here, on the Hill, all these years?"

"Hmmm, for the most part, I think . . . although there was a period of some years when she was away—abroad, perhaps; teaching, perhaps. Yes—I believe she had taken a position of some kind, teaching, as did Monica before her. Some girls' school, I believe. And there was a rumor, no more than that, that Ida had taken on a religious vocation. But obviously that wasn't true."

"She became a nun, you mean?"

"Common enough in Catholic homes," he said. "She may have considered it, I suppose, when young."

"But she didn't—you're sure?"

He looked at me, puzzled. "Obviously not," he repeated. "I don't believe they let you out of the convent once you're in. Not usually, anyway. No, it's my understanding that she held a teaching position for some years. Probably a private girls' school, as I said."

"Malcolm," I began, cautiously, "I don't know how to say this, but I'm not at all sure that Ida Printaine is as benevolent a person as everyone thinks. Hasn't it occurred to you that she seems quite harsh with Georgia?"

"I assumed it was her way," Malcolm said. "The Printaines were always an outspoken, rather caustic lot. But she has been more than generous, I think. It is Miss Printaine who pays Georgia's rent. Why, if it was up to her, Georgia would live with her, free of any obligation. But Georgia insists on living apart from her. I'm sure I don't know why. To me, it would make much more sense. . . ."

"That's the point I'm making. Something is wrong there, something we don't necessarily see. Why doesn't Georgia live with her? Georgia doesn't even really *like* her. Ida just seems to have a hold on her, some kind of power over her. . . ."

We were stopped at an intersection. Malcolm looked at me, then smiled solicitously. "It's been a trying time for you. I don't imagine anything like this happens up on the North Shore." He obviously thought I had gone bananas, that I had let my imagination run away with me.

"I *have* led a sheltered life," I said, deciding not to press my point. Maybe he was right.

"Your aunt seemed to be an interesting woman," he said.

"Oh, yes, she is," I said. "She was the one who encouraged me to live in town for the summer."

"How did your parents feel about it?"

"Not as enthusiastic," I said, "although they finally agreed. They thought all sorts of unsavory things would happen to me. I don't think they would understand Georgia at all."

"Or me," Malcolm said enigmatically.

"Oh, I think they'd like you very much," I said, unconvincingly. Malcolm's brows danced a spirited pas de deux across his forehead. He laughed and, like a woman, threw his head back for an instant, then covered his mouth. "Malcolm, they *would*." He laughed again. "Well . . . maybe not—not really," I said, laughing too.

"That's better," he said, controlling himself. He concentrated on the traffic again, a wistful look on his face.

"But it doesn't matter," I said. *"I* do. I like you very much. You're such a kind and good person."

"Thank you," he said. "I try to be."

"Well, you *are*. And that's what matters."

He nodded but said nothing. He reached over and flipped open the glove compartment. "Would you care for a mint?" he said, pulling out a cellophane packet of after-dinner mints. I took one.

We drove in comparative silence for the remainder of the trip, exchanging only occasional comments on the weather, current events. Predictably, Malcolm believed strongly in the proposed plans to desegregate southern schools and spoke highly of the Reverend Martin Luther King, a negro active in the cause. Before long we had turned the corner at Walnut Street.

"That blue sedan has taken my spot two days in a row," Malcolm fumed as we drove past the house and started around the block again. By a miracle, on our next pass the blue sedan was just pulling out. Malcolm naturally honked to speed things up. Then we pulled up, right in front.

SEVENTEEN

Later, after changing my clothes, I sat by Georgia's window and fed the birds. Oscar was still in Gloucester with Barney. After hearing that I would be busy Sunday, he had decided to stay the night there and finish the painting today. I missed him. I remembered the nights during the previous week when we had eaten dinner together, then walked by the river afterwards and lay on the grass, looking up at the stars. I should have told him to come back early from Gloucester so that we could spend the evening together tonight, but I hadn't. I hadn't thought it would matter: I'd see him tomorrow. But it did matter. Now it would be an entire week before we could be alone again at Barney's apartment. I couldn't stand the thought. Of course, there was Oscar's room at MIT, but having heard the details of how he would have to smuggle me in, I never considered that a viable alternative.

I tore the last of the bread into bite-sized pieces and fed it to Eve. As I lowered the window, I heard footsteps on the stairs. In a moment Claude appeared, peering out at me from between two bags of groceries that he juggled, simultaneously grappling with a small suitcase and a blank canvas.

"*Bonjour, mademoiselle.*"

"I was just feeding the birds," I said. "I've just come from seeing Georgia at Cunningham Hospital."

"*Oui?* And how is she?"

"She's all right," I said. "She wants you to call her. I have the number."

"I would be glad to," he said, losing his grip on the suitcase and dropping it to the floor.

"I'll get it for you later," I said. "Can I help?"

"Put it into my hand," he said, nodding at the dropped suitcase. I did.

"I'll bring the number up to you, shall I?"

"Ah, good," he said. "And you will stay and have a glass of wine with me? And a little supper? I have cheese and bread and some music I want you to hear. Edith Piaf—*formidable!*"

"That sounds very nice," I said. Why not?

"*Bon,*" he said, starting up the final flight of stairs. "I have been at the Cape, a Greek market there. In twenty minutes, yes?"

"Yes, that'll be fine." He trudged out of sight.

As I entered my room, I began to think that maybe Claude Belcourt was just what the doctor ordered—for Georgia. He was certainly a cut above Ida Printaine, and he just might be instrumental in helping Georgia make the break from Ida, which I now considered a prime concern. True, I didn't think much of him; but Georgia did, and that was the important thing. How could I get them together?

Love conquers all! That glorious phrase went through my mind. It was true, and had been since time began. Why had I not seen it more clearly before? At the very least it would be a diversion. With a man taking up all Georgia's time, Ida Printaine would be left in the lurch. She could hang around Louisburg Square and rot for all I cared.

Now all I had to do was convince Claude that Georgia was the girl of his dreams. As I started up the stairs to his apartment, I realized that our ever-so-chauvinistic little Frenchman was an easy mark. I would entrap him in a fine web, the obvious foothold of which would be his not-so-diminutive ego.

I had barely set my knuckles against the door when it was flung open, and there in all his glory stood the object of Georgia's affection, the instrument in my plan. He had changed into more comfortable clothes. Bandy-legged in khaki Bermuda shorts two sizes too large for him, gathered about his scrawny waist by an old dark-blue tie, he wore a sleeveless undershirt and heavy brown-leather sandals. Topping it off, the outrageous pompadour rose in crests, like an oil-slicked sea at high tide.

"Ah! Mademoiselle! Entrez! Welcome to my simple home!" He didn't really expect me to rush into those open arms, did he?

"Good evening," I said, walking in past him.

"In a moment we shall have food! And wine! Such as you have nevair tasted!" he shouted festively. "But first, *maintenant,* my work!"

He led me across the living room to a wide area beneath a many-paned skylight window, the kind commonly found in artists' studios. There were easels, two old bureaus that held supplies of various kinds, an old wooden work table, and against the walls and furniture, stacked several deep, stood canvases—finished, unfinished, blank.

There was a bookcase filled with art books, folders full of watercolor paper, brushes for every purpose and medium, cans of varnish, linseed oil, and turpentine. Two open cardboard boxes overflowed with paint-spattered rags. Rolls of unused canvas stood in corners. Partially empty tubes of oil paint littered every surface. Claude, whatever else he was, was a genuine artist.

One by one, Claude lifted each finished canvas for my inspection: landscapes and wharf scenes; still lifes; a portrait of a young woman done with palette knife rather than brush; a snowy day in the woods with the cool winter sun falling through the branches of trees. Gulls. Waves. The obligatory floats with fish net. A box of strawberries. An open market. A portrait of an old man in a shiny black suit.

He then drew me along with him to admire the canvas currently in progress: a nude on a sofa, partially draped with a mauve cloth. I wondered if she was the girl Georgia hated, the girl from Alsace-Lorraine with the glowing complexion. It was hard to tell, for the nude in the portrait had pure white skin outlined in hot pink, her mouth and nipples the same shade. Interesting, I thought. But I felt uncomfortable staring at it with Claude watching for my reaction.

I squinted at it as if to gain perspective, then walked backward to examine it from afar. Finally I moved closer and closer to it until it was only inches from me. Claude's brows knitted.

"Brush strokes," I murmured as if to myself. "I love to see the brush strokes."

"Oui?"

"Oh, yes! You see, for a moment, looking closely at these strokes of the brush, *I* am the artist. I feel the creation of each tiny line. I feel what the artist feels." I leaned forward, closed my eyes, and breathed deeply, my nose nearly against the canvas. Claude didn't move. "I smell the paint. I *am* the paint!" I wondered if I wasn't overplaying this a bit. "The very essence of the moment of creation, and I am there. I am it—it is me. And you, Claude, you have given me this wonderful moment. Thank you." I affected a slight bow and gazed at him intently. I wasn't at all sure of what I had said.

"Oui," he said, his voice hushed and deep. *"Mais oui."* A satisfied smile played at the corner of his lips. He straightened his hunched shoulders, and the cavernous concavity of his thorax seemed less pronounced.

"A friend of yours?" I said nonchalantly, pointing at the nude. The sofa she sat on was his. The same mauve cloth in the painting draped a ratty overstuffed chair to my right.

"Oui," he said, his huge head wobbling back and forth pridefully. *"One* of my dear friends. Very dear." This was going to be a piece of cake.

I raised my arms as if trying to embrace all of his work and whispered, *"C'est formidable."* Then I changed my tone and said brightly, "Did you mention wine?"

"Ah! Mais oui, mais oui. Sit, sit." He raced across the room and dove behind the counter, coming up with a gallon jug of red wine. He partially filled two water glasses. I sat down on the sofa once occupied by the hot-pink nude. Ceremoniously, he presented me with a glass, then stood back and toasted me.

"To Georgia," I offered instead. Claude looked puzzled. He seemed to have forgotten her.

"To Georgia," he agreed lamely. He pronounced her name "Zshaw-zshaw."

"I miss her, don't you?"

"I miss the damage she does when she is here," he said, eyes wide.

"Oh?"

"*Oui. C'est formidable!* What this one woman can do! We are sitting like this . . ." He sat opposite me on the couch. "We are talking together. She is drinking my wine. She becomes excited about some story she tells me. Her arms, they wave—her hands fly in the air—she hits the glass—the wine falls—she screams. She leaps to save it—she knocks the ashtray to the floor. Now she is screaming in a tiny, high voice—'Oh, no, Clode! Oooh. No, I am so sorree, Clode.' And she is running past me to find a rag and she is stepping on my foot and the floor is shaking and a painting falls! This woman is a storm! And feet like two baguettes. This storm I do not understand." He really was quite funny mimicking her. I controlled myself.

"Joie de vivre, Claude," I said. "Enthusiasm. Quite charming, I think. Very American."

"You think so?" he said. "American? Like your amazing hamburger? Too big! Too much! And a steak that falls off the plate—too big. Americans like everything—how do you say?—more big than life. Everything must be big to be good. In France we have just a little of this or the other. One exquisite morsel. Hmm, *c'est formidable.* Your friend is too big a bite for me, and too much bone and gristle. Is too much for me."

"I suppose," I said, angry with myself for forgetting his derision of all things American. "Such a pity," I added, trying to recoup. "It would take quite a man, that's for sure."

"*Oui,* a great pity for a woman to be so ugly. A woman should be dainty. Quiet. For soothing a man. A tiny flower to bring him joy. This woman bring nothing but accidents."

"I meant that it's a pity you have so little regard for her when she admires you so much. I mean, she tells the entire world of your genius."

"A genius? *Moi? Mais non, mais non,*" he said, smiling. He was loving every minute of it.

"She couldn't wait for me to meet you. She told me all about you long before I ever set eyes on you."

"*Oui,*" he said smugly. "Ah! What can I say about her? She is in love with me. She is too *obvious.* The whole world knows what is in her heart. It is written on her face, in her eyes. A woman tells everything with her eyes."

"All I heard about were Claude's eyes and Claude's hair, Claude's *mouth.*" He licked his lips.

"You are making a joke with me, *non?*"

"*Non, Claude—mais non. Ecoutez bien.* She said you reminded her of a statue of a Greek God."

"*Non, c'est impossible!* Ah, Annie, Annie." He leaned his head on the back of the sofa and grinned from ear to ear, his round black eyes squeezed into glowing croissants. Then he glanced at me, helplessly, with a slight shrug of his skinny shoulders, and leaned back again, gloating. I almost laughed. Instead, I asked where the music he promised me was. He jumped up, went to the phonograph, and placed a record on the spindle. "Edith Piaf," he announced. "This woman is singing to you from the heart, from the pain of her life. Listen to her. Not your Doris Day, your—uh—Mantovani! The music of France is the song of passion, of true feeling. It comes from the guts, you would say. Listen!" He poured a tablespoon more of wine for me and filled his own glass to the brim. He then drank down one half of it in one gulp. As Edith Piaf began to bleat, Claude ducked behind the kitchen counter again and returned with a ball of rope cheese, which he began to unwind and eat, passing the ball to me after he had gotten it started. I leaned back and nibbled. Everything was going so well I could hardly believe it.

"Eh?" he said after Edith had finished her first song, "eh?" nodding vigorously in the direction of the phonograph.

"Oh, yes, wonderful," I said. "*Formidable.*"

"You like it!" he exclaimed. "Good for you. Is not pasteurized!" I looked at the cheese, confused.

"The music! Not pasteurized! Raw—from the heart," he said, squinting at me. "Amazing. You might be French, eh? Your mother? Your father?"

"English."

"English? *C'est impossible!* English are serious and sour. Like pickles. You cannot be English. You are like a little French girl, a gamine, a sweet child. You are not English."

"Oh, but I am," I said, "and rather sour and serious as well. It's Georgia who is more like a Frenchwoman," I said, hoping he wouldn't notice I was contradicting an earlier statement about her Americanness. "Like your Edith Piaf. Georgia has *suffered.* She has known love and passion, even hate. She's remarkable. One might say that she truly has experienced life. *Mon dieu,* what that woman has gone through! What unbridled passion for living, for dying, for *everything* she has! Of course, she sometimes goes to extremes. The truly passionate always do, as I'm sure you well know."

"She's crazy," he said, pulling off another rope of cheese, devouring it, and following it with a gulp of wine.

"That's exactly what her former lover told her before he left."

"I am not surprised."

"Nor I," I said. "He was apparently a rather inhibited sort. A bookkeeper. With bland tastes. Do you know what he did? He invited her for the weekend to his family's little summer camp up in New Hampshire, miles from the nearest town, just the two of them together there by a wonderful lake. And when she suddenly became—oh, romantic, I guess one would call it, while they were swimming, and she tried to lead him from the water into the woods, he broke away from her and marched straight back to the cabin and got his things ready to leave instead. He said she was immoral. She told him that she loved him more than life itself and only wanted to be with him, naturally, in the woods. Do you know what he did? He left her there! All alone. Tragic."

"My God," he said, taking another large swallow of wine, sitting upright and glaring at me with a look of great concern on his face.

"She nearly went mad. Her next lover was more satisfying," I said, beginning to realize that I was getting rather carried away. "Passion can make a person quite insatiable," I said. "There have been hundreds since that first time."

"Hundreds?"

"Literally."

"I had no idea," he said.

"Really? She appeals to a wide spectrum, I would say. Certain men obviously consider her a challenge worth taking on. Even though she eventually leaves them—all of them—they seem to think a few weeks with Georgia is worth it. To say the least."

"Yes, yes," Claude said. "At first, I must say, I thought very little of her. But after perhaps our third meeting I could feel something, something between us. Some kind of energy. Something almost like a wild, untamed animal about her, a cat of some kind. The look in the eyes—the look of a cat. Yes. A wild cat."

"Yes," I said, "you're right. You obviously felt it somehow, coming through. . . ."

"How soon will she be back?"

"I'm not sure. She said that we could call her, though. I've written down the number for you and the correct extension." I took it out of my blouse pocket and gave it to him.

"Perhaps if you could just be a little attentive to her. Like calling her at the hospital. Just to say hello. Just to make her feel good." I was obviously chickening out.

"That makes her feel good? To hear my voice? That's it? What? Maybe my voice is magic of some kind?"

"I guess it's you and your French accent," I said.

"My accent, *oui*," he said, as he got up from the sofa and went to the kitchen again. I could hear him rummaging in the refrigerator. "In France we also say that every woman dreams of a French lover. The greatest in the world, each one of us. Because we are not selfish. We know how to please a woman." He returned, carrying a plate of wrinkled, oily black olives and two rounds of flat bread, which he put on the table in front of us along with the rope cheese. He produced a small, greasy package and opened it to reveal two items resembling cabbage rolls. "Dolmathes," he said, taking a bite out of one, showing me the rice inside. "Wrapped in grape leaves. The food of Greece! I have told you, have I not, of the year I spent in Athens? You will not believe this. The Acropolis was shining in the moonlight from my bedroom window each night."

"Oh!" I said, stunned at the thought. I held a dolmathes to my mouth and took a bite. He had provided no napkins. My lap was sprinkled with rice.

"You must go to Europe, you must not stay here. In Europe, everyone sings, everyone dances, everyone makes love all night long—" He broke off in mid-sentence and leered at me for a second, then leapt up and ran to the record player. "We cannot eat Greek food without listening to the music of Greece," he said. He searched through a record cabinet, then put a record on the spindle. Waiting for it to drop, he gulped an enormous swig of wine, then positioned himself in the center of the room. Eyes closed, head thrown back, he raised his arms straight out on either side, spread his legs and bent his knees. As the music began, a rhythmic *oompah,* he bent and straightened his knees in time. I braced myself. The music picked up and Claude began to sidestep in a wide circle, crossing one foot over the other, rising and falling on the balls of his feet. "Come, dance with me," he cried, holding out a hand to me.

"I couldn't possibly," I demurred loudly. He had turned up the volume. The music went faster. Claude was flying, bobbing, dipping, waving his arms in wild abandon.

"Hopa! Hopa!" he yelled. He looked ridiculous. I couldn't keep from laughing. Just then, he squatted, hands on hips, and kicked his scrawny legs out from side to side, like a demented, emaciated Cossack. The look on his face was pure jubilation. Then he stood upright and began a frenzied spin on one foot, but he had had too much wine, and within seconds he came whirling toward me, like a spent top, and threw himself down on the sofa, gasping for breath.

"Wonderful!" I yelled, applauding like an idiot. (Later, I would laugh myself to death.) After a moment he beckoned for me to pour him a glass of wine, then lay back, trying to catch his breath.

"You like it, eh?" he gasped.

"Remarkable," I said.

"*Oui, oui.* We dance like that all night, then make love all morning."

"Oh, I see," I said. Something about the way he was looking at me concerned me. The record ended. The room was quiet. I nibbled at my dolmathes, took a sip of wine.

"In France we say that every woman dreams of a French lover," he repeated. He leaned forward, tore off a crescent of bread, wrapped it around a morsel of cheese. "What about you, Annie— you are dreaming too?" He crammed the food into his mouth.

"Why, Claude . . ."

"Look at me," he said, his mouth full. He swallowed hard. "Tell me you have not dreamed of a French lover."

"I have not dreamed of a French lover."

"I knew it!" he crowed, slapping his thigh, grinning crookedly at me. "I saw it in your eyes! A woman tells everything with her eyes." I looked cross-eyed at him. "I want you to eat some olives," he said magnanimously. "Here—some bread, too. Eat! Food is good for you. Food comes before love. After love you need no other food!"

"Is that right?" I said. I could have been reciting the names in the Social Register; he was hearing what he wanted to hear.

"So little Annie dreams of a French lover, eh?" He was obviously drunk now, and absolutely revolting. He ogled me shamelessly out of the corners of his bloodshot eyes, working his eyebrows. His lips were now deep red and wet from wine. His moustache bore a sprinkling of rice. He was drooling over me.

This had not turned out at all well. My mission had changed. No longer concerned with getting him and Georgia together, thinking I must have been mad even to consider it, I now realized that my immediate goal was to get out of his apartment—alive.

I stood up. "Well," I said, faking a yawn, "I'm afraid I have an early day tomorrow." I had forgotten to give him Georgia's phone number. Never mind.

"*Oui,* in the morning," he said. "I shall paint you then. Early in the morning. I shall take down your hair and take off your clothes and paint you in the morning, naked, the light from this window . . ."

"Sounds very artistic," I said, affecting a breezy tone. I started to the door.

"Wait, wait! You are not going. We have only just begun." He rushed toward me and put his hand on my arm. I was three feet from the door. "Stay with me, little Annie, and let me tell you of the painting I have planned for you." He swayed before me with a queer writhing movement to his body. His eyes were greasy slits.

"I really must be going," I said firmly. "I loved the cheese and the olives and the music. . . ."

"Why do you go when you know so well you want to stay?"

I backed toward the door. His hand held my wrist.

"I have to go."

"You think you can tease me like this and then leave me?"

I reached behind me with my free hand for the doorknob. I began to turn toward it. His hand tightened on my wrist and pulled me back to face him. He pushed me back against the door, pinning my wrist against it, above my head. I tried to knee him and missed. He jumped back just in time. I grappled with the doorknob. His face was against mine. I turned away from him.

"Don't turn away from me like that." His lips were against my ear. "Don't you know I can make your body sing?"

I took a huge breath. "If you don't get away from me, *I'm* gonna start singing, so loud the whole world will hear me. Let go of me!" I yanked my hand from his. He gave no resistance. He stood back.

"As you wish, *mademoiselle.* Whatever you wish." He shrugged his cadaverous shoulders. "I can wait."

I opened the door and walked out.

"One day you will regret this," he said. "When you want to know the ecstasy a real woman can feel. I wait." He turned back toward the sofa.

I closed his door behind me and started down the stairs. I heard him laugh, but I knew he would never try to touch me again. Thank God I had found out what he was really like before I turned him loose on Georgia.

Now my mission, clearly, was to somehow keep the two of them apart.

"My hair is blue," Oscar said. I had just gotten ready for bed when he called. "Federal Blue, I think they call it."

"I love blue hair," I said.

"I can't stand talking to you. I shouldn't have called. I haven't seen you in two days."

"I know. I miss you too."

"Do you really?"

"Yes. I really do."

"I'm gonna take a cab and come over."

"That's silly," I said. "It's late. And anyway, I'll see you tomorrow."

"We'll just go for a walk," he said.

"It's supposed to thunder tonight. We can't go for a walk in the middle of a storm."

"I'll be there in twenty minutes." He hung up. I went upstairs, put on my trench coat over my nightgown, put on my sneakers, combed my hair, and crept downstairs to wait for him. Malcolm heard me, however, and peered out between the curtains on the French doors.

"It's just me," I said.

"Are you all right?" he said. He was wearing a baby-blue dressing gown with an ascot at his throat. He opened the door.

"My boyfriend's coming over. We're going to take a little walk. We haven't seen each other in days." I pulled my coat around me, trying not to be obvious about checking to make sure my nightie wasn't showing.

"A romantic walk on a summer night," Malcolm sighed.

"Yes. I didn't want the bell to disturb you. I thought I'd walk out when I heard him coming."

"Oh, how thoughtful of you," he said, "but we're up late, anyway. They're showing *Green Dolphin Street* on the late show, one of my favorites." I wondered who was there with him and just then saw a shadow move in the light from the TV. "Bryan," Malcolm called. In a moment, the Charles Atlas type I had observed before appeared in the doorway wearing a T-shirt and a pair of plaid shorts. He looked about thirty, much younger than Malcolm. "This is Ann Merrill, the young woman I told you about, Bry," Malcolm said. "This is Bryan Crisp, Ann."

"How do you do," I said. I had never met anyone's lover before.

"Pleased to meecha," Bryan said, smiling his gorgeous smile. He put a hand on Malcolm's shoulder and continued to stand behind him. He had clear aquamarine eyes, the color of my favorite marbles when I was a child.

There was an awkward silence.

"She's waiting for her boyfriend," Malcolm singsonged. I had never heard him talk quite like this. I watched Bryan's hand squeeze Malcolm's shoulder. "Well," Malcolm said, "I guess we'll be getting back to our show."

"Yes, by all means," I said. "He should be here in just a minute. Nice to meet you, Bryan."

"Same here," Bryan said; then, with a twinkle in his eyes: "Don't do nothin' I wouldn't do."

I laughed. "I won't." They went inside.

Watching the late show just like two married people. I wondered how long it would be before Bry's grammar came between them.

Before long, I heard a cab pull up and the door slam closed. I walked out onto the steps. Lightning zigzagged across the sky. Oscar stood on the sidewalk. "One Mississippi, two Mississippi . . ." he said, then leapt up the steps, threw his arms around me, and kissed me just as an enormous clap of thunder rattled and rumbled.

He drew back and looked down at me. "How's that for timing?" he said, hugging me again.

"I'm so glad to see you," I said.

"Yeah," he said. "Let's not do this again, okay? This has been the longest two days of my life."

"I know," I said, taking his hand, starting down into the street. But he stopped when we reached the sidewalk, cocked his head, and looked at me quizzically.

"Did you really miss me?"

I nodded, then looked down, avoiding his eyes.

He was tan from working outside, and with the collar of his raincoat turned up and a lock of dark, blue-frosted hair falling onto his brow, he was irresistibly handsome to me.

He placed his hand at the side of my neck and, as I tipped my head, stroked me gently with his index finger. I reached up to cover his hand with mine.

"I really did," I said, my voice wavering oddly.

He sighed. "I think this is getting serious."

"Maybe so," I said, looking at my shoes.

We started slowly up the street, hand in hand.

"I love walking with you," I said as we turned onto Charles Street. "Just walking. I love the way you hold my hand. It's as if I belong to you, or as if . . ."

"We belong to each other."

"Maybe that's it."

"People look at us," he said. "Have you noticed that?"

"Yes!" I said, laughing. "They do! I thought maybe it was just me, but they *do* look at us, don't they? Especially old people. They look at us and smile."

"Remembering what it was like for them," he said, "falling in love."

I hesitated, then nodded.

"When I'm with you, Annie, I feel like I could *do* anything or *be* anything."

"Do you really?"

We turned from Charles toward the river. A pale flash of lightning lit the street momentarily, but it was some minutes before faint thunder was heard, far away. A breeze blew off the water, and by the time we sat down under a small tree on the Esplanade, I was shivering.

In a few more minutes my teeth began to chatter.

"Are you really that cold?" Oscar said, putting his arm around my shoulder.

"I'm not sure," I said. "Sometimes when I'm excited I shiver."

"I see," he said, putting his other arm around my waist and

lowering both of us to the ground. "I'll make you warm," he said, hugging me to him, hard.

"We must be crazy, Oscar," I said, hugging him back.

"Yup."

"The ground's all wet."

"Kiss me."

On the way back to Walnut Street, Oscar told me he had mentioned me to his mother when he had talked with her by phone several days before.

"What did you tell her?"

"Oh, that I'd met this beautiful girl and I thought I was falling in love with her."

"What did she say?"

"Oh, typical motherly things like 'Be careful' and 'Take your time' and so on."

"Good advice," I said.

"Have you told your parents about me?" he said.

"Not really," I said, "I haven't had that much contact . . ."

"I'd really like to meet them," he said.

"They're very nice people," I said.

"I figure the sooner, the better," he said, matter-of-factly.

"I suppose. Actually, I wanted to pick up some art supplies at home sometime soon."

"Good. I'll take you out there."

Actually, it was a good idea. Mother and Daddy had never approved of my boyfriends, but I knew beyond a shadow of a doubt they'd absolutely love Oscar.

EIGHTEEN

On Wednesday of the next week, I came home directly after work. Oscar had fencing practice, early preparation for the coming year's matches. I had thought I might go along to watch, but Oscar said that after taking part of the summer off, he was too rusty to have me there—as if I would have known the difference.

Nevertheless, I stayed away and planned a quiet evening alone—a fortunate decision, as it turned out. First of all, I needed to put in a call to Aunt Chloe. I wanted to talk with someone about both Georgia and Oscar, and at lunch Ruth had been too depressed over Kathleen's imminent departure to be in the mood.

I had just changed my clothes and gone downstairs to use the telephone. I was about to dial when I noticed a small, cream-colored envelope sitting on the table, addressed to me. It hadn't been there when I came in a short time before. Probably a note from Malcolm.

I opened it. Inside, on a folded note, was engraved the name Ida Marie Printaine. What did that monster want with me?

Dear Miss Merrill,
    I shall be visiting Georgia this evening. I should be happy

to have you accompany me. Georgia seems quite fond of you.

I shall call for you at seven o'clock unless otherwise notified.

Very truly yours,
Ida M. Printaine

A chill ran through my body like the one I had experienced on Sunday at the moment when the truth of Ida Printaine's identity had come to me. What was that woman up to? She must have an ulterior motive. For an instant, I envisioned her conceiving of some madly clever plan to bump me off. Maybe her chauffeur was in on it with her. I'd step into that car with them and disappear without a trace.

I dialed the telephone. Aunt Chloe would tell me what to do.

"I hope I didn't interrupt your dinner," I said when she answered. "But I *had* to talk to you."

"That's quite all right, Ann," she said. "But give me a moment to turn off the hi-fi. You must be in love!" I waited to hear the faint background music stop. "I was listening to *The King and I*," she said, returning. "So tell me, are you in love? You're not pregnant, are you?"

"No, no," I said, laughing. "But as a matter of fact I am interested in someone, and I don't know . . ."

"Well, that's par for the course, don't you know," she said. "Who is this knight in shining armor?"

"His name is Oscar Benson, and he goes to MIT. I met him at the bookstore. He works with me there."

"So far, so good," she said, jovially. "Is he in complete possession of all his faculties? Limbs? He's not Jewish, is he?"

"No," I said.

"Roman Catholic?"

"Methodist."

"Well, your mother should be beside herself with glee. What's the problem, then?"

"I'm not sure there is any, really," I said.

"Is he a good kisser?"

I laughed again. Aunt Chloe always caught me off guard. "He's a very good kisser," I said. "In fact, that may be the problem I'm referring to, or not referring to. . . ."

"Ah, yes," she mused. "Oh, my."

"What is that supposed to mean?"

"I'm just stalling for time," she said, chuckling. *"You* tell me."

"Well, it's nothing. It's just that I've never met anyone quite like him and I'm not sure how I feel about him."

"I think you know precisely how you feel about him," she said. "He's a young, healthy man and you're a young, healthy woman, and I imagine it's pretty obvious how you feel about one another. The question is not how you feel but what do you do about it—am I right?"

"I think you understand," I said tentatively.

"Well, if you think I'm going to tell you what to do, you're sadly mistaken. That's a decision each of us has to make for himself. When it's right, you'll know it, and you won't be coming to me or anyone else for sanction."

"Oh," I said, "I suppose that's true." I felt embarrassed, adolescent.

"Are you in love or in lust?"

"I don't know," I said.

"Well, don't do anything unless you know. I suppose he looks like a Greek god."

"Not really," I said. "I didn't think he was good-looking at all at first."

"He grows on you, then. That's the worst kind. What does he plan to do with his life? Engineers can be bores."

"He plans to be an architect."

"Ah," she said, "a romantic! Does he spend all his time gazing into your limpid pools and reciting obscure poetry?"

"And other things," I said. "I mean, he does a lot of other things."

"Why, Ann, you're making me blush!" she said, chuckling again. "I guess I'm not taking you very seriously, am I? The fact is, my dear, you've come to the wrong person for guidance. Why, at your age, I was on the continent. Need I say more?" There was a pause.

I tried to figure out what to say next. "Don't do anything you'll hate yourself for later. If you can help it."

"Okay," I said lamely.

"Other than that, how are things going?"

"Pretty well, actually," I said, deciding not to say anything to her about Georgia or my suspicions about Ida.

Anyway, I knew what to do about it. I needed to tell Dr. Sampson, the psychiatrist. It was as simple as that. He would know what to do. I would call him tomorrow.

At precisely seven o'clock, the front bell rang. I opened the front door. It was raining. Tommy, Ida Printaine's chauffeur, tipped his cap, then led me down the steps, under the protection of his umbrella. He opened the rear door of the gleaming black Bentley and helped me in.

"I am delighted that you could come," Ida said, offering me her healing hand as well as a yellow smile.

"Thank you so much for inviting me," I said. We pulled into Walnut Street and headed toward Beacon.

"Such a dreary evening," she said, turning toward her window and looking out, her jaw resting on her palm. She wore a deep-purple cotton dress with a purple silk scarf bordered in black paisley wrapped around her head. Her face was white as flour. "Tommy, do be careful—the streets are treacherous," she said, first looking out her window, then turning her gaze to the expanse of seat between us. She absentmindedly began pulling tiny bits of lint or fluff from the surface of the upholstery. *Very* tiny bits they must have been, for it seemed to me that every inch of the Bentley, including the dove-grey seat we sat upon, was spotlessly clean.

"The dreariest summer we've had in years," Ida said mournfully. Although the scarf covered most of her head, her pure white horns were visible at each temple.

"I'll keep a good eye out, Miz Printaine," Tommy said in his cockney accent.

"An excellent driver," Ida said to me, nodding as if to reassure me, her lips as wrinkled as an anus. There was a minute or two of silence, during which Ida leaned forward, touched Tommy on the shoulder, and accepted a clean white cloth that he handed back to her without either of them uttering a word. Chloroform, maybe?

"Have you seen Georgia since Sunday?" I said bravely.

"Yes," she said. "Tommy brought me out there last evening." She turned to her window and mopped at the glass with the cloth.

"How is she?"

Ida sighed. "Well, it is clear to me now that Cunningham was a mistake. I swore I would never send her there again the last time. In a nutshell, she is worse, very much worse." The cloth squeaked as she drew it back and forth against the glass.

"Oh, no," I said. "I'm terribly sorry. She seemed better on the phone. . . ."

"*You* might not sense it. But I've been through this so many times I can read the signs." She regarded me steadily, raising one eyebrow. Then she worked at the window again, running a cloth-covered finger around its edges. "I would like to take her out of there," she said.

"And transfer her to another place?"

"And take her out of the country," Ida said. "For a rest." She handed the cloth forward to Tommy.

"Oh," I said.

"She has been under such pressure. The position I arranged for her just didn't work out. It was extremely hard on her knowing that she wasn't capable of handling it, wanting so much to please me by doing well. It completely destroyed her equilibrium." She picked at the upholstery again.

"I see. I had no idea about this."

"She wouldn't have told you," Ida said, looking directly into my eyes, then smiling at me sympathetically. "You are not the first to be misled by Georgia Mitchell." There you go, Ida, I thought, discrediting the witness. She turned to her window again. "So grey," she whispered, accompanying her words with a helpless wave of her right hand. "More like March than the middle of summer."

"It certainly is," I said. We sped across the bridge to the Cambridge side, our car like a shiny water bug skating on a pond.

"Sometimes," Ida said, removing a purple crystal atomizer from her purse, "sometimes, the old remedies work best. One spends a few thousand dollars on up-to-the-minute care only to find out that the malady could have been cured by a patent medicine." She sprayed the atomizer's contents around the interior of the automobile. An acrid, antiseptic smell filled the air.

"Isn't it so," I said, trying to carry on this little conversation as politely as I could, when in reality what I really wanted to know was where Ida planned to take Georgia and when. "My mother has always sworn by mustard plasters."

"Really," she said, drawing her lips back drily from her yellow teeth and flashing a halfhearted smile at me. "Then you know what I mean. I suppose Georgia has undergone the best treatment money can buy. Her doctor is the finest, very well recommended, on the staff of the Massachusetts General." I nodded. "But I was talking with one of the nurses the other day. She's been there for years. Mrs. Patterson. I've always had great faith in her, and she said that in cases like Georgia's, sometimes the very best thing for them is rest, just rest, in a pleasant locale. She says she has seen them turn around just like that."

"Where were you thinking of taking her?" I asked.

"Tahiti, perhaps," she said.

"Oh. I had no idea you meant anyplace like that." To my complete amazement, Ida then removed a comb in a silver case from her purse, sprayed it with the atomizer, wiped it with a clean tissue, and replaced it in her purse.

"Yes," Ida said, "Tahiti." She now sprayed one of her palms. "Georgia tells me that you have always wanted to travel." She wiped her hand with tissue and sprayed the other.

"Well, yes," I said. "It has always been a dream of mine. Someday, anyway."

"My family has owned property in Tahiti for years. I cabled my cousin in Paris to ask if the house there was available. It is in the hills outside of Papeete—on the slopes of Mount Orohena, to be exact. Except for a few servants, the villa is empty." She handed the soiled tissues up to Tommy and put the atomizer back in her purse.

"It must be beautiful there," I said. My mind raced. Tahiti! I couldn't believe it. An island in the South Seas with a villa in the hills. Ida had said "Tahiti" as nonchalantly as I might have said "Vermont."

"What do you think of it, this idea of mine?"

"Well, it might be very nice," I said, choosing my words carefully.

"I thought you might like to go with us. As a companion for Georgia. There would be no expense involved, of course."

"Me? Oh, I don't think I could do that," I said, stunned at her boldness. I could just see the three of us on some luxury liner cruising to Tahiti, then setting up housekeeping in her villa, miles from civilization. "I start college in the fall."

Her upper lip twitched. "What a pity," she said, the look in her eyes threatening. "Invitations come so infrequently. And Georgia insisted I ask you, said that all you ever talked about was travel."

"I'm very grateful for the invitation," I said. "It's very kind of you, really. . . ."

"Perhaps your schooling could be postponed for a year."

"Well, I don't know. . . ."

"I was afraid you wouldn't. Georgia asked me to ask you, but she herself did not have high hopes. . . ." Her voice trailed off, and she smiled sweetly at me, her lids humbly lowered.

"Georgia really wants to go, then."

"She has great difficulty knowing what is best for her," Ida said. "She is so self-destructive, you know."

"Yes, I do know," I said.

"Ah, well," Ida said, brushing off her lap and straightening up in her seat. "Just an idea. Have you ever been on a sea voyage?"

"Oh, no," I said. "But an aunt of mine had a friend who sailed down the west coast of South America—"

"The villa," she broke in, "is quite charming, in the Tahitian manner, with areas open to the tradewinds and everything in bright colors. There's a waterfall and pool on the premises, and a view of the sea." She looked at me expectantly. She drove a hard bargain.

"I can't begin to imagine it," I said. I couldn't.

She laughed. I had never heard her laugh before. It was a warm, melodious laugh. "If you could see your eyes," she said. "As big as saucers. You *must* consider coming. I may insist on it." She reached over and patted my hand, continuing to smile.

"What about Dr. Sampson? Does he think it is a good idea?"

"He is hesitant," she said, fidgeting a little with her head scarf. "I can't say that I blame him. I pay him well to care for Georgia. Yup, yup, they don't like to lose good patients, you know."

I said nothing. She was getting desperate: first discrediting Georgia, now attacking Dr. Sampson. A clever woman.

"It's the Garden of Eden," she said, staring out the window once more, her voice low, "a Garden of Eden. And Mount Orohena is the dwelling place of the old gods."

"Hmm," I said. Maybe she was a witch doctor in her spare time.

"A place for healing," she said.

"Sounds like it," I said unenthusiastically.

We drove along in silence for some time before we turned into the driveway and proceeded up the hill to Cunningham.

"Native peoples have always known how to generate the power to heal," she said suddenly. "Georgia will be healed in Tahiti. I shall heal her myself with their aid. Gauguin went there because he was dying, you know."

"I didn't know that," I said.

"Most people don't, but he *was*. Dying. He went to be healed. He suffered from the same disease I do." She paused and looked at me, waiting for me to question her about whatever illness she had.

"I didn't know that about Gauguin," I said.

"Oh, yes. Yes," she said. "Came all the way from France. They couldn't do a thing for him there. Conventional medicine never works in cases like ours." She waited.

"Just exactly what sort of malady did he suffer from?"

She smiled, appeased. "An extreme sensitivity to what for normal people are known as 'normal flora.'" She laughed heartily. "For those who are normal they are harmless. Microbes. Bacteria. Invisible to the naked eye. In the air, all about us, everywhere. On every conceivable surface. Even on your hands." I covered one of my hands with the other. "No, it's quite all right," she said.

"I have sanitized the car already. One must be very careful, bathe frequently, sleep in clean sheets every night. They multiply with a fury in the dark, under blankets. They seem to grow best on glass surfaces—mirrors, windows, large trays, bric-a-brac. One must be constantly on guard."

"Really," I said, nodding my head, looking out the window at the parking lot ahead of us. She was bananas. Out of her ever-loving mind. I had taken an honors course in microbiology in high school; I knew exactly what "normal flora" were. Whatever Ida had was in her mind. Gauguin, my foot.

"But the extreme heat of the tropics kills them in most cases," she raved on, "provided the sufferer adheres to certain healing requirements. Gauguin, for example, *was* healed, then he went and spoiled it all by refusing to live in purity and chastity afterwards, as he had been taught. Although microscopic, they are very much the same as rats. They are drawn to unclean spirits as rodents are drawn to garbage. Death under these circumstances is quite painful." She sighed. "There are some who will not take the miracle of healing when it is offered them, you know. . . ."

I nodded. We had arrived.

Tommy pulled the Bentley up in front of the administration building and helped Ida and me out. He raised the umbrella over us and escorted us to the front door.

"I shall be counting on you to convince Georgia to come to Tahiti, my dear," Ida said, as we followed the corridor to the office. She put her arm through mine. "And I think you must reconsider your plans for fall. Travel can be every bit as educational as school."

"Yes, I've heard that," I said, cringing at her touch, at the thought of traveling with her any farther than I already had.

"We are here to visit Miss Georgia Mitchell," Ida stated to the bespectacled woman in the office.

The woman opened one of her notebooks, leafed through a page or two, and said, "Doctor has provided us with a new visitors' list for Miss Mitchell. May I have your names, please?"

"Ann Merrill," I said, as Ida pushed me forward a step.

"Ida Printaine. I've been here many times before. Miss Mitchell is my ward." Really?

"One moment, please," the woman said, then looked up from her book. "I regret that only Miss Merrill is on the approved list. Miss Printaine, I'm terribly sorry. There is a notation here that Dr. Sampson tried to contact you today about this."

"I was out. What do you mean, contact me?"

"It just says that he tried to contact you about this—to save you a trip, I guess. I'm—"

"What has happened?" Ida said. "You mean to tell me I can't see her?"

"I'm terribly sorry, but—"

"Let me see this list," Ida barked, lunging over the half-door toward the desk top on the other side. She couldn't reach the book.

"The list has only three names on it," the woman said, purposely using a calming voice. Ida's eyes were wide and glaring. "Ann Merrill, Malcolm Balch, and Claude Belcourt. If you have questions about this, you will have to discuss it with Dr. Sampson, I'm afraid."

"This is obviously a ridiculous error on your part. I pay Miss Mitchell's bills. She is my ward. I fully intend to see her regardless of what you say." Ida looked down the hall in the direction of the room Hal had come out of on Sunday.

"I'm afraid you can't do that," the woman said. "If you got past me here, they would stop you at Dover anyway. I would call ahead. The building would be locked until you were escorted off the grounds. This kind of thing is done for the patients' welfare. It doesn't necessarily mean anything personal at all. Not at all." She smiled graciously at Ida, whose lips were pulled into a tight, wrinkled line. "Just for the patient's welfare and comfort—nothing personal."

"I see," Ida said. "And when did this go into effect?"

"Today at noon."

"And when will it be lifted?"

"I really can't say. You'll have to—"

"In that case, I will ask you to get Dr. Sampson on the telephone for me. Now."

"I'm afraid he has left the hospital for the day."

"I would like you to try to reach him. Now. At home, if you must."

"I'm so sorry, but Dr. Sampson is off call until Friday morning."

"Is there no one covering for him?"

"I believe there is a house officer on call for him. Shall I try him for you?"

"If you would be so kind," Ida said between clenched teeth.

The woman at the desk picked up the phone and asked that a Dr. Martin be paged. In a second or two the hospital intercom came on and a nasal voice said, "Dr. Martin, Dr. Martin, Dr. Allen Martin," over and over again. Ida's face relaxed; a small smile of satisfaction crept across her lips. Finally the phone on the desk rang and was answered. "Dr. Martin, this is Emily Whiting at visitor check-in. A Miss Ida Printaine is here to see Georgia Mitchell, a patient of Dr. Sampson's. Her name is not on the approved visitors' list, doctor, and she's—uh—a little upset. She would like to speak with you." There was a pause. Ida was handed the telephone.

"Dr. Martin," Ida said loudly. "Thank you so much for speaking with me. There has been an oversight here. I am Georgia Mitchell's guardian. She has no family but me. My name has been left off the approved visitors' list in error. Will you please take care of this matter? Miss Whiting here simply will not let me pass without word from you." There was a pause as Ida listened to whatever Dr. Martin said. I dared not look at her face.

"That is not true!" Ida suddenly shouted. She listened once more. "That is absurd!" she said, then listened for another moment. "Then, if I understand you correctly, you will not approve my visiting her?" Ida's nostrils were flared, her voice shook with rage. I glanced at Miss Whiting, who sat perfectly still, a nervous smile frozen on her lips. "Very well, then," Ida hissed, and slammed the receiver down on the desk. She turned in my direction. "I shall go home now. Tommy will call for you when visiting hours are over. Meet him in front." Her eyes were wedged wide open in an unflinching glare. She strode away from me without anything more in the way of explanation.

Miss Whiting summoned an orderly with a black umbrella to accompany me to Dover. I set out with him through the back door of the building, over the flagstone terrace I had crossed on Sunday. I was unnerved. Ida's anger had radiated from her like a powerful, electric current. It had shaken me. Her attempt at manipulating me for her own purposes had shaken me, too. I wondered if one's proximity to someone evil could always be *felt*, internally, as I felt now: threatened, fearful, yet ready to defend myself or run for my life.

At least I was no longer alone. Dr. Sampson knew, too. Georgia must have told him all about Ida, or at least enough for him to find cause for keeping Ida away from Georgia. I was relieved.

Inside Dover, I hurried past the potted palms and down the corridor toward Georgia's room. I found her sitting by the window in the striped chair. Hearing my footsteps, she turned and stood up. "Annie!" I walked toward her. Her face was pale and drawn; her hair was unkempt. We hugged one another. "Where's Ida?" she said. I told her what had happened. Her appearance worried me. Her face was so ashen, so fragile-looking. "I wasn't sure that the order Dr. Sampson left would go into effect in time," she said. Her voice was tired and thin.

"Yes, it did." I sat down beside her on the bed.

"And she didn't take it well, huh?"

"Not well," I said. "She was furious. She's gone. She said she would send Tommy after me as soon as he got her back to Boston. It could have been much worse, I guess."

"But she was mad, huh?"

"She didn't look too thrilled," I said. Georgia laughed.

"Ha! Serves her right."

"I know," I said. "Justice at last. What happened? I mean, anything new?"

"Not really—I mean, not recently. Well, it just wasn't appropriate that she come here anymore. It always upsets me when she visits me."

"I could see that the other day, when she was massaging you and praying and—"

"Tell me all about what you've been doing!" Georgia interrupted, changing the subject.

I began to tell her the news of the past three days, since I had seen her last; but my heart wasn't in it, and after a moment or two I noticed that she was looking out the window, not really listening to me at all. "And then I had the good fortune to see Claude the other—" I said, but she interrupted me.

"Did Ida tell you about Tahiti?"

"Yes," I said. "I didn't know what to say to her."

"She wants another chance at me."

"She said you would be healed there. Something about some mountain and the old gods."

"She's so full of crap," Georgia said.

"Why can't she visit you anymore?"

"Because I told Dr. Sampson—I told him certain things, and he said it was no longer appropriate that she visit here. I have to get away from her. I have to make the break."

"I'm so glad to hear you say that," I said. "Then I was right, wasn't I—that she . . ." Georgia turned her face toward me and stared at me expressionlessly. "I mean, when I saw her praying over you and massaging you, it reminded me of something you had told me. . . ."

She jumped from her chair and walked past me to the door, closing it. "No, no, no," she singsonged, her eyes bulging, a wavering smile crossing her mouth. She put her index finger in front of her lips. "There are some things we never, never say out loud. We keep our little mouths tightly shut, and that's the way it has to be." She stood in front of me, her hands on my shoulders. "Sometimes *I* can say the words. Sometimes *I* can. With someone. With Dr. Sampson."

"I'm sorry."

"No, it's all right." She sat back in her chair. "When you have kept secrets for so long, letting them out—I can't describe what it's like. It's scary. You see, when you keep secrets from people, you're also keeping them from yourself. You must have kept them secret for a good reason. When you blurt out the truth, you change your own world. Things will never be quite the same. Maybe they'll be worse. Telling someone a secret is like setting a fire or dropping a bomb or throwing a grenade. You never know quite what the result will be."

"You've gone through some terrible things."

"I know," she said. "And I thought for so long they hadn't had any effect on my life at all, that somehow I had escaped scot-free. Honest to God, I thought that. I saw myself as this brave survivor. But they had, in such surprising ways. Ways you'd never think of."

"The things that happened to you had to have affected you," I offered.

"You know," Georgia said, shaking her head back and forth, "I've always thought that I had a kind of magic power over men, over everybody, as a matter of fact. I knew I didn't look the part, but I thought I had some really unique quality that kind of drew people to me. Then old Sampson tells me that all girls who've gone through what I've gone through feel that way. We only *hope* we have some power. It keeps us from being terrified."

"Interesting," I said.

"And, you know, I hate to admit it, but I've always had problems with sex. Honest to God, I don't *feel* much, not when it comes right down to it. I'm frigid."

"Are you sure?" I wasn't sure what being frigid meant. I wondered if I could be frigid and that was the real reason I couldn't go all the way with Oscar.

"Yeah. I have, as it is known in the trade, a 'paralyzed cunt.' "

"That's not what they call it, is it?"

"That's what *I* call it." She laughed.

"Ida said you weren't doing well," I said. "But it doesn't seem that way to me."

"She only wishes," Georgia said. "The point is, if I get well, I walk."

"You mean away from her?"

"Yes. I've never been able to."

"Why?"

Georgia smiled, then bit her lip. "I just figured that out, really, the other day, with Sampson." She stared out the window, into the semidarkness of the yard and rose garden.

"Why?"

"Love," she said, sighing. "I was hanging on for love."

"From her, you mean?" I couldn't conceal my contempt.

"Can you believe it? It's pitiful, isn't it? I used to imagine that someday I'd marry and Ida would come and live with me in my house, in a guest room that I'd made just for her. When she was old, I'd take care of her. I would take her out for lunch and to the opera—she loves the opera. I used to dream we'd have such fun together and she'd be just like a real grandmother to my kids and all. Honest to God, hope springs eternal! Can you believe it? That I thought that? I even dreamed of her deathbed. I would hold her hand, and as she drew her final breath she would tell me that she had always loved me like a daughter and that I had grown up in a way that had made her proud of me. That scene used to make me cry just thinking of it."

"It's not very realistic, I guess."

"No kidding! But for years I dreamed—" Her voice broke. "Sorry, it still hurts. Part of me still hopes . . ." She covered her face with her hands and wept.

After a moment more, Georgia dried her tears and asked me to take a walk with her through the corridors. It helped to calm her, she said, this little bit of exercise. Along the way she stopped from time to time, to peek into another patient's room and say hello. She showed me the room that the patients used during the day for painting or making pottery or other handicrafts, and introduced me to the nurses as we strolled by the front desk.

No sooner had we returned to her room than the telephone rang and she went to answer it.

"Hello," she said, then listened intently for several minutes. She cleared her throat. "Well, Dr. Sampson was supposed to call you, and . . ." She turned to the wall and wrapped her forearm over the top of her head, as if shielding herself from a possible blow. "I had to, I don't expect you to . . ." Her voice shook. "No, Ida, please don't do that—Dr. Sampson says . . ." She was close to tears again. She leaned against the wall, forehead first. "You're not even supposed to call me. How did you get through?" She pounded the wall softly. I took a step or two toward her, then jumped back, startled, as Georgia roared, "I hate you!" She pounded the wall once, hard. "Leave me alone!" she cried, her voice a wailing scream. "Bitch! Bitch! Bi—" She broke into sobs. The phone crashed down, missing its cradle. Georgia collapsed against the wall, both palms pressed against it, fingers spread wide, like a prisoner in a cell. "Let me go," she wailed.

I approached her and hung up the phone. I couldn't touch her but stood nearby. In a moment, she turned around, wiping her eyes. "She says I have humiliated her. *I* have humiliated *her*. Ugly bitch." I shook my head, unable to think of anything to say. "She says she won't pay for me to stay here anymore, under the circumstances."

"She wouldn't really do that . . . ?" I said, but as soon as the words were out of my mouth I knew they were foolish.

"I was just beginning to get somewhere," Georgia said mournfully. Then, without a word of explanation, she walked out of the room and disappeared down the corridor toward the nurses' station.

I waited for her, thinking over what had happened. Soon she appeared again, a nurse following her with a hypodermic syringe. "I need to go to sleep, Annie," she said coldly. "Do you mind?"

"Oh . . . no, of course not," I said, coming slowly to the realization that she was dismissing me. I hurriedly picked up my things and left the room. Starting down the corridor, I heard the nurse shut her door.

NINETEEN

"I don't know if I should knock or not," I said, peering through the screen door into the entrance hall of my parents' house.

"You don't have to, do you?" Oscar asked.

"Well, I *have* been living elsewhere. And they don't know we're coming."

"We should have called," Oscar said nervously. "Wow, this is a huge house."

"Oh, it'll be all right," I said. "My parents really don't stand on ceremony that much. They're actually quite nice people. You'll see. It looks bigger than it really is."

"Beautiful old brick," he said. "Oh, I'm really looking forward to meeting them." He was trying to sound offhand, but his voice was unusually deep.

"Mother? Daddy? Are you in there?"

"Ann? Is that you, darling? Come in, come in!" Mother flew down the hall from the kitchen in back, flung open the screen door, and offered me her cheek.

"Mother, I'd like you to meet—" I began, after kissing her and turning to Oscar.

"The phone rang a while ago," she said, interrupting me. "That must have been you calling."

"No, Mother, I didn't—"

"Come right in," she said. "Have you had dinner? What a shame you didn't let me know! Your father and I had dinner hours ago. But you know that—we always eat earlier in summer. You go and sit down in the living room and I'll see what I have in the refrigerator."

I towed Oscar into the living room with me and sat him down in a chair by the fireplace. "Mother, come in and sit—"

"Charles?" she called up the stairs. "Charles? Guess who came to call. It's Ann." She appeared in the doorway from the front hall.

"Mother, I'd like you to meet—" Oscar jumped up to greet her.

"He'll be right down, right down. What a surprise! You look marvelous! I told you we were going to Chebeague. . . ." My father came down the stairs and into the room, beaming.

"Well, look what the cat dragged in. How are you, lovey? Your Aunt Chloe said you were doing fine."

"Daddy," I began again, "and Mother, I'd like you to meet Oscar Benson." At last. They shook hands.

"Mrs. Merrill," Oscar said, "grand to meet you—and sir, a pleasure."

"Charles, Oscar is the boy who works as a janitor at Ann's store," Mother said. She then turned to Oscar, glowing with pride. "I suppose she's told you that *she* will be entering Wellesley College practically any day now. She was an honor student, you know. National Honor Society!"

"Wellesley is a fine school," Oscar said, patting me on the shoulder. "She should do very well there."

"Oscar is a junior at MIT," I announced.

Daddy sat down on his chair, opposite Oscar.

"Magnificent old house you—" Oscar began.

"Lovely surprise, just lovely," Mother said, smiling wetly at me.

"Oscar is a junior at —"

"I *heard* you, darling," she said. "Would you care for tea?"

"Do you have something cold?" I said.

"Engineering, huh?" Daddy said.

"I hope to become an architect, sir."

"I have a carton of Pepsi-Cola," Mother said. "Lemonade, Charles?"

"I've got to get back to work," Daddy said.

"Now, you stay for a minute and entertain Ozzie—uh . . ."

"Oscar, Mother."

"You stay with *him,* Charles, while Ann helps me with the Pepsi-Cola."

"Mother, aren't you acting a little odd?" I said, as she was rifling through a low kitchen cabinet. "Is everything all—?"

"Me? Oddly? Well, I think anyone would be a little less relaxed than normal when there are unexpected guests. Just give me a few moments to get myself together."

"You haven't been exactly gracious with Oscar."

"What a peculiar thing to say, Ann," she said, glaring at me. "Why, we just shook hands. I've never heard anything so ridiculous in all my life." She placed tall glasses on the counter top. "Had you called, I could have welcomed you with a chiffon pie."

"No, that's not what I meant," I said. "You just don't seem all that interested in him."

"Should I be?" She paused, about to open the first bottle. "Should I be interested in the janitor at your store?"

"In the first place, it's not *my* store."

"Is something going on between you two?"

"Not really," I said, hating myself for being such a chicken. "But we have been going out together."

"He has a very limp grip," she said, sotto voce. "And I must tell you that I am concerned that his eyes are so close together."

I was speechless for a moment. She opened the second bottle of Pepsi, and it foamed all over the counter top. "His eyes are close together?"

"You hadn't noticed?" she said, a victorious smile playing at her lips. "One of the first things I look for," she said, mopping. "A sign of duplicity." I rolled my eyes and sighed. "That and head size. I never trust a man with a small head."

"Where do you get these ideas?"

"You'd better watch your tone of voice, young lady. I'm still your mother. Now take this tray and serve your friend his drink. I shall be the epitome of the gracious hostess. As usual." She followed me into the living room.

"Well, Mr. Benson, you shall have to tell us all about MIT," she said, in a high, very elegant tone of voice.

"I was just telling him that most of the Merrill men went to Brown or Dartmouth," Daddy said, taking the glass of Pepsi that was meant for me.

"I had a cousin who went to Brown," Oscar said brightly. "Dan Monihan. He was a tackle on the football squad. Perhaps you remember him, sir."

"Monihan . . . Monihan," Daddy said thoughtfully.

"Oh, Monihan," Mother said. "A fine Irish name if ever there was one. May I take it, then, Mr. Benson, that you are a Roman Catholic?" She sounded like Sherlock Holmes.

"Oscar will be fine, Mrs. Merrill. No, as a matter of fact, I'm a—"

"He's a Buddhist, Mother. His father is a Tibetan monk." Mother's face twitched. Then, seeing my expression, she burst into peals of laughter.

Oscar laughed, too. "I'm Methodist," he said.

"Oh, how lovely!" Mother said. "They're almost like Episcopalians, aren't they? An offshoot, I think."

My father was rifling through some books in a book case by the fireplace. "Monihan, hey?" he said in a suspicious tone, one eyebrow raised. "You sure it was Brown he went to?"

"Absolutely, sir," Oscar said. "Daniel Monihan, the class of '52. Second-string halfback, I believe."

"Well, I'll look it up some other time," Daddy said, settling back into his chair. "Do you have any lemonade, Betsy? Pepsi-Cola doesn't agree with me."

"Why, that was Ann's glass, you silly thing." She forced a gay stage laugh, then flitted to my father's side and picked up his drink. "I asked you if you wanted lemonade—you said you had to go back to work."

"I do," he said, rising. "Bring it up to me, will you?"

"Of course, dear, I'd be glad to. Ann, why don't you show your friend the garden and the gazebo?"

"Sure," I said unenthusiastically. My parents had changed. What had happened to them? I was embarrassed. I had always thought them so refined and genteel.

I took Oscar by the hand, and we went out the doors to the backyard and the old gazebo I had played in as a child. "I'm really sorry," I said as soon as we were alone.

"For what?" Oscar said.

"Them!"

Oscar laughed. "They're not so bad," he said, grabbing my hand and squeezing it. I glanced quickly toward the house to see if Mother or Daddy was watching. They would have a perfect view of us from practically every room in the house. I could feel Mother's eyes.

"So this is where you used to play when you were a kid," Oscar mused.

"Yes," I said. "It was wonderful fun, really."

"Was it?" Oscar said, drawing me into a corner of the gazebo where an enormous honeysuckle was amassed. "They'll never see us here," he added, pulling me toward him behind the bush.

"They will, Oscar—please." I moved away.

"What did you play here?" he leered.

"You know you couldn't care less," I said. "Come on, let's go in." He reached for me again.

"I really want to know," he said, sitting down on the bench that circled the interior of the gazebo. He yanked me toward him again and pressed his face between my breasts, his hands at my waist.

"We played house," I moaned. "Oscar, my mother is getting old, her heart . . ."

"She must have been young once," he said huskily, nuzzling me.

"I don't think so."

"Let's lie down for a minute," he said, letting me go and stretching out on the bench. "Come on," he said. "Right on top of me—no one will see." He was laughing.

"Oscar, you are purposely trying to embarrass me in front of my parents. Get up!"

He continued to laugh. "Gee, I thought I already *was!*"

"Was *what?*"

"Come here and kiss me and I'll show you," he said, stretching out longer, placing his hands beneath his head.

"Oh, no," I whimpered, glancing at his erection. "Oscar, somehow you're going to have to stop—uh . . . *that.* We have to go back into the house, and you can't go in like *that.*"

"Ann, would you and Oscar like some ice cream? I just found some in the freezer I didn't know I had. Maple walnut." My mother was standing outside the door to the breakfast nook. Her voice didn't sound at all natural. She knew what we were up to.

"We'll be right in, Mother," I called, waving at her from around the girth of the honeysuckle bush.

"Sounds grand, Mrs. Merrill! Scoop some up, will ya?" At last Oscar jumped to his feet. "Just give me a minute," he whispered to me, adjusting his trousers.

"How could you?" I hissed. "My parents do not approve of this sort of thing."

He burst into laughter again. "They had you, didn't they?"

"That was different—they were married. They were in love."

"So are we."

"Ann? Dear? I'm afraid it's melting."

"Coming, Mother," I called. "Do you think we are?" I asked Oscar. "In love?"

"Yup."

"I'm not sure yet," I said.

"Would it make a difference if you were?" he said.

"How do you mean? . . . We have to go in . . . ."

"Wait. Would you do it if you thought you loved me?"

"Probably. Come on." I took his hand.

"You would?"

"Yes," I said.

"You really would?"

"*Yes!* Now . . ."

"Even before we got married?"

252

"If I was sure I loved you, I would."

Oscar kissed me on the mouth. "Thank you," he said, following me into the house.

As we finished our ice cream, sitting side by side on the couch, Mother carrying on an inane little monologue concerning my childhood, my father descended the stairs again and strode into the room, a little more majestically than usual. He fixed Oscar in a thoroughly suspicious glare.

". . . And you should have seen her," Mother continued. "Like a little doll she was, no bigger than a minute, skipping in from the backyard to tell me that she had seen a 'busserfly on a fla-la.' " Oscar nodded and smiled approvingly, then watched my father approach his bookshelf again and begin haphazardly searching its contents. "She was always advanced for her age—wasn't she, Charles?"

Father grunted, then settled back into his chair again, skimming through a certain volume that I identified as a Brown University yearbook. After no more than seconds of flipping the pages, he slapped the book closed. Obviously, he had not found any proof that a Dan Monihan had gone to Brown and, refusing to admit that he needed to look harder, had come to the conclusion that Oscar was a liar.

"I'm sure if you can just find that '52 issue, you'll see him there, sir," Oscar insisted bravely. My heart went out to him.

"You think so, eh?" Daddy said, squinting dubiously. "Oh, I'm sure, I'm sure." There was an awkward silence. I moved over closer to Oscar and boldly took his hand in mine.

"What sort of work does your father do?" Mother inquired innocently.

"He's a foreman in a machine shop."

"Well, there's nothing wrong with that," she replied, her mouth suddenly going all slack.

"Nothing wrong with that at all," my father mumbled.

"I should say not," Mother said.

"I'm very proud of my dad," Oscar said softly. I wanted to put my arms around him.

"You know," my father began amiably, "my brother Andrew—
he's chief engineer for United Gear Manufacturing Corporation—
claims that a good foreman means everything. The man who's not
afraid to get his hands dirty. Andrew goes in there himself sometimes, into the shop. He's got these young fellas right out of MIT,
and he says they're not worth a damn. They won't get their hands
dirty. They have all the theory and all the brains, all right, and he
says they're just about useless to him. He has his foreman show
them the ropes. They don't like it much. They want to start at the
top, damned fools."

"Well," I said to Oscar, taking a deep breath and rising from
the sofa, "I'll get my stuff and we'll go."

"Oh, no, you can't leave yet, dear—can she, Charles? I wanted
to ask you something, Oscar. Something I've heard about that
absolutely intrigues me. About MIT."

"I'll do my best," Oscar said, smiling like the dear person he
was. He was taking all of this so well, so confidently and good-
naturedly, so nobly.

"Well . . ." Mother began, as I started up the stairs to my bedroom to get my art supplies, the reason for our coming to Beverly
in the first place, "is it true that MIT scientists share all their secret
information with communist scientists?" I covered my ears with
my hands, hurried into my room, and closed the door behind me.

After a moment I heard Oscar laugh. He could deal with them
better than I could.

"They're snobs!" I said, as we cruised down route 128 toward
Boston.

"It's okay," Oscar said.

"It's not okay. I swear to you that I never knew what snobs
they were until today."

"I believe you," he said.

"Mother said your eyes were too close together."

He burst out laughing.

"That's what she said."

"It's okay, Annie. I don't know why you're so upset. I thought
they were kinda funny."

"Funny? I should never have taken you there. They treated you like a second-class citizen. I'm so sorry, Oscar." I moved closer to him.

"It doesn't matter," he said patiently. "I know who I am. I don't care what they think."

"They saw us holding hands outdoors, I guess. They panicked."

"Thank God they didn't see any more than that," Oscar said, putting his arm around me.

"I never realized they were so narrow-minded and prejudiced and rude. Oscar, I don't know what to think about them anymore. I don't think I even like them." This was a perfectly horrible revelation to me, and it would take time for me to absorb it. "Daddy didn't believe you, didn't think your cousin had gone to Brown at all. He thought you were lying!"

"It's all right—it doesn't matter," he said, patting my shoulder.

"And you were so good about it all," I said, looking up at him, seeing him differently than I ever had before.

"Let's face it," he said, "I'm a prince of a guy. Didn't you realize that until now?"

"I guess I really didn't," I said. "I guess I didn't appreciate you until now."

"Does that mean that tonight's the night?" he said. "Please. . . ."

I didn't answer right away. Amazingly, I was thinking it over. "Not tonight," I finally said. "But soon."

"The summer'll be over soon," he said sadly.

"Then before the summer's over."

The afternoon had been so traumatic that after grabbing a bite of supper at Schrafft's, I asked Oscar to take me home instead of going to the movie as we had planned. I was still angry and upset by my parents' behavior. The most confusing part of it was that I wasn't sure whether they had always been like this or not. How could they have been? Why had I not seen it all so clearly before?

As we approached Walnut Street, I remembered that it was entirely possible that Georgia had arrived home from the hospital. It had been over two weeks since Ida Printaine had threatened to withdraw her financial support; and the last time I had spoken with Georgia, she wasn't sure how much longer she had at Cunningham. She had heard a rumor that she was about to be discharged. That had been two days ago. I was not surprised, then, as Oscar and I drove up in front of the house, to see a light burning in her window.

I sat out in the car necking with Oscar for a while, then went in. As soon as I closed the front door behind me, Malcolm opened his. "She's home," he whispered.

"I saw her light," I said. "How does she look?"

"Not bad," he said, but his eyebrows wiggled nervously.

"How *are* things?"

"We've had a *busy* afternoon."

"Oh?"

There was a peculiar, timid look on Malcolm's face. "You'll see," he said, then ducked inside his apartment. Thank heavens he had a smile on his face. Things couldn't be too bad.

I took a deep breath and started up the stairs.

Georgia met me at the third-floor landing and spread her arms wide—not to hug me, as I thought she would, but to block my way. "What are you doing?" I said, hugging her anyway. "I'm glad to see you. They threw you out, huh?" Might as well act as cheerful about this as I could.

"Yeah . . . tell you later," she said. She looked a lot better than at our last meeting. "I want you to close your eyes," she said.

"Oh, all right. What are you up to, anyway?"

"You'll see, you'll see," she said, leading me along in the direction of her room. "Okay, you can look," she said, followed by a blaring "Ta-da!"

It took a few seconds for me to see what she had done. Her room was changed around. My bed was across the floor from hers, move in here during my absence. My dresser was near her bright-blue chest. Her floor was bare except for my scatter rugs.

Without saying a word, I walked across the hall to my room and hardly recognized it. An old love seat that had once graced the second-floor landing was against the wall where my bed had been. My desk had been moved to a corner. My little red lacquered table was next to the love seat, like an end table. The teapot and cup had been removed from it, and instead Georgia's basket, the one that had stood under her crucifix, was on its top. Thank God the rosary beads were nowhere in sight. I was stunned. She just watched me, giggling.

My closet door was open. Inside, my desk chair was pulled up to what had been a low storage shelf. Georgia's paper and notebooks were arranged on top of it, books stacked at each end. "My office!" she exclaimed. "The shelf is my desk. Don't you just love it? This way I can write in here when I need to concentrate or you need quiet. Honest to God, you won't even know I'm here. I left your sketchbooks near the window."

"Thank you," I said. Her hooked rug was now on my floor.

"Malcolm said we could have the love seat. No charge. He said we could do all this, rearrange our rooms, and at no extra charge. It's like our own apartment now. This is our living room—or we could call it the salon, just like Gertrude Stein and Alice B. Toklas."

"They were queers."

"Well, then, whatever you want, I don't care—but like artists, living together. Tell me you love it."

"Where are my clothes?" I said, horrified at what she had done, noticing that my shoes no longer occupied their usual shelf and that the bar on which clothes were normally hung was empty except for one dangling monkey on a stick.

"In our bedroom closet," she said. "And don't worry—I put all your things away just as you would have done. I always watch the way you do things, you know."

"But I didn't do this, any of it."

"Oh, Annie, don't be mad! Look—look at this." She pulled open the bottom drawer of my desk, the drawer that normally held my journal. She took out the hot plate which had been returned to Malcolm weeks ago. "Malcolm says we can make tea on it in the winter."

"I won't be here then." Had she lost her memory?

"I forgot." She looked at me solemnly.

"You should have asked me before you did this."

"You don't like it at all, do you?"

"You should have asked me," I repeated. "I mean, it looks very nice and all that, but I liked my room the way it was. I loved it . . . the way it was."

"Oh, but the summer's almost—"

"I can't stand anyone touching my things!" I screamed. Georgia winced.

"I just thought that things were going so well, and we seemed so close now and all. . . ."

"What, exactly, has been going so well? You haven't even been here!"

"Shit," she said, turning away.

"Yes, shit! That's what I think of this, you know?"

"I am really . . . very, very . . . sorry," she said, her voice shaking with emotion.

"I don't care how sorry you might be. I can't be concerned with that. All I am sure of is that I want things back where they belong." Every now and then Mother would rearrange my things and I'd want to kill her.

"You can be a real bitch, you know?" She faced me. "No, I mean it. A bitch! I bet old Oscar knows that about you. I'll just bet he does. You kind of lead people on to thinking they mean something to you, then when they try to show it, like I did today with all this rearranging . . . well, then you push them away, back where they belong. You don't want anyone close to you. You're too pure and refined and—"

"Georgia, what are you talking about? Don't say any more. Let's just get the beds back where they belong, and the clothes, and we'll work everything else out later, or tomorrow. Just so I have somewhere to sleep tonight." I headed for her room and closet. I was so angry I could hardly contain myself.

I pulled the bedding off my bed and carried it in an uncontrolled pile into my room. I dropped it on the floor off to one side, out of the way. Georgia was at the window. I knew she was crying. This was the time for it—the perfect, on-cue moment. I ignored her. Let her cry. I went back to her room and wrestled the mattress off the bed and tried to hold it on end as I pushed it across the hall into my room. I let it flop over on itself and lean against the wall.

"There is absolutely no need to cry over this. It is not the end of the world."

"That'll come soon enough," she said sulkily.

"What is that supposed to mean?" I said impatiently. "You made a mistake about how I'd feel about all this, that's all. There's no reason to be so dramatic. I'm not the maddest I've ever been, and I'll be fine when everything is back to normal. I'm glad you're at home. I hope you're okay. I've been worried about you."

"I'm fine," she said, sniffling.

"Good. She really stopped the money, did she?"

She nodded. "Fall will be here soon," she said. "The light is already changing."

"It always does." She was trying to sound pitiful and make me feel sorry for her.

"Spring's green leaves have grown old. They're still green, but old green, dull green, like shutters on a window. . . ."

"Write it down before it slips your mind. Where did you put my things—my underwear and shorts and tops and stuff?"

"In the blue chest," she said.

"I'm so hot I can't stand it. If this is fall, then . . ." I went into the bathroom to change in private.

"It's coming sooner than you think," she called to me, a thin tone to her voice. She really could be a drag. Yes, fall was coming, and not a minute too soon for me.

I heard Georgia taking my bed apart. As I walked back into the hall again, she was toting the iron headboard back into my room. I picked up the piece that went at the foot and followed her; then, without speaking, we each went back to her room and carried the springs with attached side rails into my room. It took the two of us to reassemble the bed and hoist the mattress into place. This done, she looked at me with an indulgent smile.

"Happy now, Your Majesty?"

"There is no need to be snide," I said.

"You really are a strange person," she said.

"*I'm* a strange person? I beg your pardon. It wasn't me who tried to take over someone else's very life. It was you. If anyone is strange, it's you." By her expression I could tell that I had hurt her, but right then it didn't matter. She deserved it. "You don't like it when someone tries to take over *your* life—why did you expect me to?" I added, tucking my sheets in and spreading my blanket.

"Are you trying to tell me I'm just like Ida?" she asked. I hadn't thought of that, but it was true. "How very perceptive of you," she said, too sweetly.

"Not in all ways, certainly," I said. "But . . ."

"Oh, no," she said, "you are quite right. I am. In *all* ways." She held her hands out to me and wiggled her fingers as if she were about to "feel" me. I glared at her and pushed her hands away. "It shouldn't startle you to hear that," she continued. "We all become like that which we most despise. I'm like Ida—you're an exact replica of your mother."

"You have never set eyes on my mother and besides, I don't despise her at all. She is a wonderful, fine woman who—"

"You are very critical of her, and I don't need to meet her, having met you. She is just like you, I know."

"She is *nothing* like me," I hollered.

"She is cold, opinionated, bigoted, straightlaced, and terrified of her own feelings. So are you."

I walked into my closet, threw Georgia's writing supplies into an empty carton on the floor, and plunked it into her hands. I followed her out the door and went to her closet for my clothes. If I said another word, I would cry. It wasn't true. It couldn't be.

"One morning you'll wake up," she teased, "and as if you've been thinking all night long, you will suddenly know beyond a shadow of a doubt that you are just like her. As much as you didn't want to be."

I went to my room to hang things up.

"And after the shock wears off, do you know what your reaction will be?"

I said nothing.

"You will feel a deep love for her for the first time. You will understand her completely. You will want to rush and throw your arms about her and comfort her, realizing for the first time that she needs your comforting. You will love her and forgive her. For everything."

"Is that what you've done with Ida?" I snapped, moving my desk back to its original spot.

Georgia laughed, briefly. "It must be done. The alternative is to die. Did you know that truth can kill?"

"No," I said, leaving for her room again for another batch of clothes.

"Well, it *can*," she said. "It can kill you. But I don't suppose you've given great thought to dying."

"No," I said, sitting on my desk chair to take a breather.

"I think of it all the time," she said.

"I know," I said, feigning a bored attitude. Here we go again.

"I can image *this* dying," she said. "This body, this flesh and bones and hair. But I can't imagine this in here dying"—she pointed first to her head, then to her chest—"this consciousness of mine, this spirit."

"You've mentioned death several times now. Are you thinking about dying sometime soon?"

"No-oo," she said, elongating the word to point out to me just how quickly I had jumped to asinine conclusions. "After we see the truth and absorb it, we must go bravely on, undaunted." Oscar had said something like that to me once. "I've *told* you," she said, "I'm a writer and I must examine all these things, even morbid things. I have a new poem—about what we've been discussing, in a way. May I read it to you?"

"No," I said. I couldn't stand one of her sappy poems, especially right now.

"It's about Ida and me."

"Have you seen her lately?"

"No," she said. "She called once."

"What did she say?"

"She talked in this high, fragile little voice."

"She was trying to make you feel guilty, maybe."

"Well," she said, "that was a lost cause, trying to make me *feel* anything. Sometimes all I feel is empty. You know, they take you apart and sometimes can't put you together again. They lose some of the parts." Georgia wasn't speaking to me. She was talking to herself, aloud. "They just keep taking things out of you until you're empty, a vacuum. And inside you're nothing but all this dark, quiet space." She shrugged her shoulders.

"I don't think you should see her," I said, "even after I've gone and you may be lonely for a while."

"I haven't told you yet, have I?" She jumped down from my bed, then jumped in place a few times like an excited child.

"What?"

"Starting September seventh, I have a job."

"Where?"

"At the clinic, the Cambridge Mental Health Unit. It's only three afternoons a week, but I get to answer the phone and file records and maybe a little typing."

"Georgia, that's wonderful!"

"Yes—and I get to see Sampson there, at clinic rates I can almost afford."

"That's perfect," I said. It had never crossed my mind that things could have been resolved so easily. "I'm really happy for you. Everything's working out, isn't it?"

"It looks that way, doesn't it?" She smiled wistfully. "I'm sorry, Annie," she whispered, gesturing around the room.

"It's all right," I said. "I went out to Beverly this afternoon, with Oscar, and it was upsetting. I shouldn't have gotten so mad at you. But I was already angry with my parents. They've changed or I've changed or something."

"Hmm," she murmured. "I always hoped I'd meet them sometime," she said.

"No. I'd never put you through that." When I looked at her again, she was staring off into nowhere, a sad look on her face. "But you know what?" I said cheerfully, feeling almost normal again. "My Aunt Chloe would like very much to meet you. She said we could come out to Windsor Marsh some weekend."

"For the whole weekend?" I had only meant a day trip.

"Why not?" I said. "She lives near the beach."

Georgia turned toward me all of a sudden and leaned forward, greatly interested in what I had proposed, it seemed. "Near the beach—are you kidding?"

"Really," I said. "Right down the road from Palace Dunes Beach. Have you been there?"

"Never," she said quietly. "We could have one last fling there, couldn't we? Before you leave me for school?"

"Yes, if you like," I said.

"We have so little time left, Annie."

"Don't say it like that, Georgia. It makes it sound like I'll be dropping off the end of the earth or something. We'll see one another in the fall and winter. Often."

She smiled her watery smile and mumbled something about getting a calendar so that we could plan our weekend better.

When she came back across the hall, we agreed on a date for our getaway. She was about to return the calendar to her room when I noticed her basket still on my table and got up and handed it to her.

"Don't forget this," I said.

"Oh, no," she said. "I want you to keep that for me."

"Why?"

"It's my seed packets," she said.

"Why should I keep them for you?"

"My closet is so small and damp, I'm afraid they'll be ruined in there. Your closet is dry because of all the sun you get, and I don't like to keep them out in the open all the time—somebody could knock them over. Do you mind?"

"I'll just put them here, then, on the top shelf, if you should want them." She had funny ideas sometimes.

Oscar called before I went to bed, and when I went down to answer the call, Malcolm left his door open a crack and told me to come in when I was finished.

"Well, what did you think of what she did?" he asked as I walked into his living room. I could hear Bryan milling about in the kitchen.

"To be honest, I hated it, Malcolm," I said.

"I heard you moving things back," he said.

"We'll need help with the love seat." He nodded. I told him about her new job and her plans for therapy. "And she doesn't see Ida anymore. There really was something wrong there, Malcolm." His eyebrows arched.

"Was there? Really?"

"I'd rather not go into it," I said.

"I understand completely."

"I never did trust that broad," Bryan said, appearing from the kitchen carrying a tray of cold drinks. He was bare-chested, wearing only a pair of shorts. "There was somethin' about the way she looked. Mean broad." He put the tray down. "Malcolm and me always have a nightcap. Can I get you somethin'? You drink?"

"No, I don't," I said, "but thank you. I'm fine." He passed me a bowl of peanuts. He sat down beside Malcolm on the sofa and each of them took a swallow from their drinks.

"I just always had this feelin', ya know?"

"Bry's awfully intuitive," Malcolm said, gazing at Bryan adoringly. "You can't learn that, you're born with it."

"Yeah," Bryan said, smiling back at him, then at me, "he says I know what he's gonna say before he says it." He threw his head back and laughed. I was a little embarrassed seeing them behave so affectionately with one another.

"I admire that in you, I really do, Bry, I have none of it, myself."

"I just knew, ya know. The minute I laid eyes on her, I says to myself that's one mean broad."

"Well, she was," I said. "However, I think Georgia has broken with her . . ."

"She's not a"—he shot a glance at Malcolm—"a dyke, is she?"

"No, I don't think so," I said. "If you want the truth," I began hesitantly, "she was the kind of person who does, well, 'things' to little children. She knew Georgia when Georgia was a child." Malcolm looked dumbfounded.

"You kiddin' me?" The look on Bryan's face was one of absolute horror.

"I'm afraid not," I said.

"Oh, I find that difficult . . ." Malcolm started to say.

"Well, that explains it," Bryan said. "I can usually spot that kind a mile away. Yeah, that was what I picked up, all right." Bryan's voice shook.

"Now, Bry," Malcolm said, covering Bry's hand with his own.

"Every time I meet one of those sick creeps I wish I'd have nothin' to lose by breakin' their necks. So help me." Malcolm patted his hand.

"Bry had an unfortunate childhood experience as well. . . ." Malcolm's voice trailed off.

"You can say that again," Bryan said, standing up and moving toward the kitchen, his empty drink in his hand. "You ready for another?"

"I've still got a few drops left," Malcolm said, following Bryan with his eyes.

"Well," I said, starting to go, "the main thing is that Georgia really doesn't seem any the worse for wear since she came home. . . ."

"Watch her, Ann," Malcolm said, walking me to the door.

"Don't worry—I will."

TWENTY

It was late Friday afternoon. "Once again, I must say how sorry I am for this change in plans," Aunt Chloe said, bidding all of us goodbye at the gate after Oscar had brought her Chrysler around from the garage. "When you get to be my age, these little missions of mercy are all too frequent, don't you know. Lydia Lancaster and I have been friends for fifty years, and we've always stood by one another. I can't leave her alone up there when she's ill, and she's never been a hardy soul. . . ."

"Say hello to her for me," I said, "and I hope she feels better soon."

"And don't forget," she added to Georgia, "we'll have our apple-harvesting spree in October, and I'll be counting on you to climb those trees for me."

"I wouldn't miss it for the world," Georgia said, holding the car door open for her.

"Those Winesaps make the best darned hard cider you've ever tasted, young fellow," Aunt Chloe said, shaking Oscar's hand.

"I'll *be* here," Oscar said. "You can count on it."

"Yes," Aunt Chloe said, giving him a long look, then glancing at me. She liked him—that had been obvious right from the start. "And you, young lady—make sure your friend here leaves at a reasonable hour. It's bad enough that I'm leaving you and Georgia to fend for yourselves for the weekend. If your mother gets wind of the fact that I left a young man here as well, she'll have me tarred and feathered."

"Oh, no problem at all, Mrs. Langley," Oscar said, looking a little embarrassed. "I'll probably hit the road, oh, any time now."

"It would be best," she said softly, reaching toward him and patting his arm. "Well," she added, getting into the car, "I want to get to Nashua well before dark. You know where Lydia's number is—don't hesitate to call, Ann. I gave you the keys to the De Soto, didn't I?"

I produced them from the pocket of my skirt and showed her. "See you late Sunday," I called as she pulled the Chrysler into Palace Dunes Road and was on her way.

"I can't believe it!" I exclaimed, turning to Georgia. "We have Marsh Cliff all to ourselves for the whole weekend."

"Yeah," Georgia said. "Sorry not to get to know your aunt better, but this is unbelievable."

"I guess I'll take off," Oscar mumbled.

"No, not yet," I said, taking his hand and strolling toward the backyard. "Would you like to take a walk?" I wanted to be alone with him.

"Yeah, let's," Georgia said, as I gave her a look that would kill, "and then I'll do you guys a favor and retire to my bath for about four hours. See? I'm more sensitive than you think."

"You're incredible, Georgia," Oscar said, patting her on the shoulder.

"Gee, thanks," she said. Then, for no apparent reason, she broke into a run and headed out toward the field in back.

Oscar shook his head. "How old is she?"

"Twenty-four."

He shook his head again. "You could have fooled me." He put his arm around my waist and kissed me on the cheek. I sighed. "What's the matter?"

"Her," I said. "I want to *be* with you. Alone."

He stared down at me, a serious look on his face. "Yeah," he said, "let's get this over with. Hey, Georgia, wait up for us, will ya?"

It was dusk. After what had seemed like an endless walk through the fields and down into the marshes, Georgia was finally upstairs drawing her tub. Oscar and I sat on the porch swing.

"I knew it was going to be like this," he whispered. "I don't want to leave you now."

"I know," I said, leaning my head on his shoulder.

"I want to stay with you tonight," he sighed, nuzzling my neck.

"Mmm . . . I wish you could."

"Georgia wouldn't mind," he said. "You have the softest neck in the world."

"*I* would, though. If we were here alone, completely alone . . ." He kissed me, long and hard. "Oh, Oscar," I said, "sometimes I wish there was someplace where we could be all alone, just the two of us—a place of our own, not Barney's, not here with Georgia, not someplace we'd have to sneak into. . . ."

"When we get married, after I finish graduate school and you graduate from Wellesley and we're ready to settle down someplace permanent, I'm going to design a house for us, with a studio for you to paint in and one wing for the children and then, off to one side, a wing just for us, private and quiet."

"That sounds wonderful."

"With a fireplace and an enormous built-in bed and mirrors . . ."

"You give me goosebumps when you talk like that," I said, putting my arm around his waist. "You really think we'll get married someday?"

"I love you," he said, kissing my eyelids. "And—"

"And I love you," I said steadily. I pulled away from him slightly. "I really do. It feels so good saying it. I love you, I *love* you." I threw my arms around his neck and kissed him.

"Say it again."

I looked up at him. "I love you, Oscar. So much I can hardly stand it. I think you're the most wonderful person I've ever known. I love the way you look and the way you talk and all the crazy things you say . . . and there are other things too—like your mouth.

I could eat it." I licked his lips, then kissed him, then sat back.

"Are you done?" he asked, disappointed. "Don't stop on my account."

"I love your mind," I said, "and the way you smell and feel, and—oh, Oscar, I have the wildest fantasies about you, things I didn't think I was capable of thinking."

"Ha!" He convulsed with laughter.

"I realized the other day that kissing you would never be enough. . . ."

"What do you want, then?" he whispered, his lips against mine. "You can have anything you want."

"Oh, Oscar, don't say that. I want it all. Soon. It can't be today, but soon."

He pried my arms from around his neck, took my hands in his, and stood up. "Come here," he said.

"Oscar, what—?" He put his index finger on my mouth.

"Shh," he said. "Just listen. We're going back out to the field."

"But Georgia . . ."

"This has gone on long enough," he said. "Too long. We're going to make love tonight, Annie, out there in the grass, and that's all there is to it."

He swept me up into his arms and started down the porch steps with me.

"Georgia will wonder—"

"Will you shut up?" he whispered into my ear. "Any other woman in the world would just put her head on my shoulder and enjoy this."

I did.

When we reached the open field, he put me down. He looked around, at the grass, off into the distance, into the sky. "Now," he said solemnly, looking deep into my eyes, "it's just you and me. No one can see us or hear us. He drew me near to him, his chin on my head. "It's the perfect place, isn't it?"

I nodded, a little nervously.

He saw the look in my eyes. "It's okay," he whispered, pulling his shirt out of his pants, unbuttoning his cuffs. "We'll make a bed of our clothes. You'll see." He spread his shirt out, flattening the tall grass beneath it. He kicked off his shoes. I followed suit.

"Now your blouse," he said gently, reaching for the top button.

"How about your glasses first."

"Sorry," he said, removing them and hanging them from a nearby bush.

"I'll do it myself," I said, unbuttoning my blouse. He watched me. I pulled it out of my skirt.

"Let me," he said, peeling my blouse back and placing it on the grass next to his shirt. He came toward me again, looking me over, his eyes dark and serious. "You have perfect breasts," he said, a slight breathlessness to his voice. When I saw him reach for me I thought he was going to touch me there, but instead he began pulling the pins from my hair. I felt it fall. I tossed my head to shake it out. He took a length of it in each hand and combed it through with his fingers. I closed my eyes, feeling the brush of his fingers on my neck.

"You're perfect," he said, in a voice I'd never heard before, his mouth on my forehead, my eyelids, barely touching my lips.

"I'm not," I said, moving closer to him, touching his chest with trembling hands, loving the feel of his smooth, warm skin.

He undid my bra and pulled it gently off me. I looked up at him. His eyes were closed. His hands hovered for an instant, then found my waist. He drew me toward him until my breasts just grazed his chest. His breath caught. "Oh, God, Annie, Annie . . ."

Our arms went around one another. I felt his teeth on my shoulder. We held each other as tightly as we could, lost in one another, swaying slightly, as if to music.

"What do you feel right now?" he asked. "Tell me. Do I feel as good to you as you—"

"Oh, yes!" I said.

"Just let go, Annie, do anything you want to. I want to know what you're like, everything. . . ."

I just held on to him, my eyes tightly shut, wondering if I could do what he asked. Just then his hands slid down from my waist to my buttocks. He held me there, pushing his lower body into mine. I felt his penis, long and hard, against my stomach, through his pants and my skirt.

I moaned a little, pushing back. I wanted to feel it more. Oscar's breath was ragged. I stood on tiptoe so I could feel his penis lower on me. I spread my legs a little, rubbing against it.

"Annie," Oscar groaned, his body trembling.

I reached down and undid my skirt. It fell to the grass. I wore only my panties. He jerked me against him again.

"Oscar, please," I whispered, "now." I wedged my hands between us and felt for his belt buckle.

But abruptly he dropped to his knees and peeled my panties down. He wrapped his arms around my thighs, his face between my legs, nuzzling me, licking me.

"I love you," he said, over and over again, in a voice I'd never heard before.

"Oscar, stop," I whined, not wanting him to, wanting more. I couldn't think. I couldn't see or hear.

Suddenly, I lost complete control. I pulled his head away from me, by his hair. For an instant I saw his face contorted with passion, the mouth I loved open and wet.

I knelt on the ground in front of him and kissed him, my tongue in his mouth. He tasted like me.

Frantically, I grabbed his penis through his clothes. He undid his pants. I reached inside and pulled it out as if it belonged to me. I fell forward and took it into my mouth.

"Oh, God!" he shouted. "More!"

"Oh, Oscar—now, please!"

We fell onto the ground. He was on top of me, thrusting wildly against me. I spread my legs. I felt the head nudge my opening, hard. He pushed. I pushed.

"Harder," I said, lifting my hips.

Oscar came down on me full force, plunged into me. He shuddered and growled, thrilling me.

I wrapped my legs around his and took him in deeper.

I couldn't get enough.

He began moving in and out of me with long, smooth strokes.

"Faster," I said, tightening my legs around him.

He straightened his arms on each side of me and raised himself up over me, picking up speed, watching me for my reaction, trying to please me.

"Yes . . ." I moaned, as both of us watched him slide in and out of me in quick, short jabs.

"Look at us!" he gasped. But I was beyond him. My eyes fell closed. All I wanted to do was feel.

"Go ahead," I heard him say. "Come."

And the minute I heard that word, it began. It was as if something within me opened wide again, then wider and wider, and I convulsed with wave after wave of excruciating pleasure. Just as it reached its greatest intensity I felt Oscar lift my hips from the ground, felt his body pound against me. For a fraction of a second he was completely still. Then he moved in me violently, his face in the grass, his breath coming out of him in great growling sobs until he was done.

We lay like that for a long time, getting our breath, our spent bodies wet with perspiration. Now and then I felt his mouth move against my neck. Now and then I would taste his skin. We didn't speak.

It was like floating, lying there.

At some point Oscar raised himself up on one elbow and looked down at me. "Hi," he whispered sleepily.

"Hi," I said, hiding my face in his shoulder.

"How was it?" he said, smiling at me.

"Tolerable," I said, giggling like an idiot.

"We'll have to try it again sometime. . . . Was it good for you?"

"It was wonderful. I loved it."

"Was I—uh . . . okay? You know what I mean. . . ."

I started to laugh, rolling him off me. I got on top of him and kissed him on the mouth. "Oscar, you were incredible."

"Really?"

"You feel so good inside me. Your penis is just perfect—so enormous and hard. Any woman in the world would give her eye teeth to screw you."

He raised his eyebrows for a second, amazed at my language, then grinned from ear to ear. "Yeah. That's what I figured."

It was over an hour before Oscar and I came back to the house. Miraculously, Georgia was still upstairs. We were sitting on the porch swing when we heard her start down. "Get decent, you guys—here I come."

"I love you," Oscar whispered, jumping up and brushing himself off for the hundredth time.

"I know," I said, doing the same, then flopping back down, affecting a casual pose.

"You *are* a hedonist, Annie—I always knew it." He sat back down and threw his arm around me. "We can do that every day for the rest of our lives—think about it. It was wonderful, Annie. You were so beautiful."

"No, it was you."

"Where are you two? I can't see my hand in front of my face." Georgia came out through the screen door.

"Here on the porch swing."

"Once, honest to God, I could have sworn that there was a rocking chair somewhere here." She fumbled for it in the darkness. "Well, what do you know—here it is." She sat down. "I've made my decision." She removed the white towel she had wrapped around her head and began to rub her hair dry.

"What decision?"

"Sleeping arrangements." Oscar squeezed my hand. "I'm going to tuck myself away in that little hole in the wall. Literally. The one with the ladder. Did you know about that, Oscar?"

"Yup," Oscar said sleepily.

"I'll just climb that little ladder and jump right in under the stars. A Dutch bed, is that what you call it? Of course, somnambulism is contraindicated under these conditions, if you get my drift."

"Gotcha," Oscar said. "That first step can be a real killer." We all laughed.

"Honest to God," Georgia said. She fumbled around for a minute, then lit one of her French cigarettes. Oscar squeezed my hand and stood up.

"I guess I better hit the road," he said. "You walking me to the car?"

"Of course," I said, taking his hand.

"And you'll pick us up on Sunday night?" Georgia said.

"About five, right?" he said.

"Yes," I said. "Around five. We should be back from the beach by then."

Oscar and Georgia said goodbye to one another, then he and I strolled out to the car.

"You see? This isn't right," he said. "We should be spending the night together."

"I know," I said. "Someday."

"I can't stand the thought of the entire weekend without you," Oscar moaned. "Especially now." He kissed me.

"I know," I said. "I'll miss you too. But I had to do this for her, you know that."

"Yes. Little Florence Nightingale, ministering to the sick and needy."

"She doesn't have anyone but me. You *could* call me tomorrow night."

"I will. Or I'll come out. If I can't stand it anymore, I'll come out. Otherwise, I'll call." He put his arms around me. "You better get back to your patient."

"She's a lot better than she was," I said.

"That's true," Oscar said, touching my hair, then opening the car door.

"Oscar, wait," I said. "Kiss me."

"Of course," he said, sliding his arms about my waist.

What began as a rather straightforward kiss became something more within seconds. "I'm thinking about this evening," I said. "I can't help it. You were so wonderful."

"I'm not that wonderful," he said, his forehead against mine. "But I love you, and I'd do anything I ever could to make you happy. I'll never want anyone but you."

As I went back to the porch, it dawned on me that I really didn't want to talk to Georgia right then; I wanted to be by myself for a while. All I could think about was Oscar and what we had done and how I felt with him. I sat down on the edge of the porch swing.

"Do you mind if I leave you again," I said, "for a shower? I'll only take a minute. I've been in these clothes all day."

"Somehow I doubt that," she said, giggling. "Sure—go ahead. I'm fine. My hair's almost dry." I stood. "He doesn't like me, does he?" she said.

"Oscar? Don't be silly."

"He wants you all to himself," she said. She took another drag on her cigarette, and for an instant her face glowed ghoulishly. "Do you love him, Annie?"

"Yes," I said.

"You really do?"

"Sometimes I think I love him so much I can't stand it. The way he looks at certain times, or something he says." I didn't elaborate.

"Have you gone all the way with him?"

"We're getting a little personal, aren't we?"

"What are you waiting for?"

"All of this is none of your concern, Georgia."

"What's he like to be with?" she said.

"What do you mean, 'what's he like'? You've met him."

"I mean in private. I think I know. But tell me anyway." Her chuckle, in the dark, sounded almost sinister.

"What do you mean? What do you think you already know?"

"You know," she singsonged. "You can tell certain things about a guy, about what he's really like, the minute you meet him."

I had no intention of telling her anything. "Well," I said, good-naturedly, "as long as you know everything anyway, there's no point in my saying a thing—except that he's very nice and sweet and . . . oh, there's something rather noble about him."

"That is hardly what I was thinking, my dear Annie—that he was nice and sweet, etcetera. What I was thinking was that—well, you see, right after I meet a guy I can tell just how big he is, you know? Usually within a fraction of an inch, I might add. I can tell how high he comes up when he's hard. Really, I can! And I can tell whether he takes his time or shoots off the second he gets near you."

"You really can be disgusting, you know," I said.

"I know," she said. "It's part of my charm. I say what others only think. Anyway, getting back to Oscar, I can tell that he is—well, how shall I say this delicately? Well endowed. Huge, basically. Enormous, basically."

"Fascinating. Absolutely fascinating," I said.

"I can tell by the shape of their mouths and a certain way they carry themselves when they walk. I would bet money he's a glorious specimen!"

"I'll tell him you said that if you like. Would you care to make a formal guess as to his exact measurements? Someday I might verify them for you. We could put the whole thing in writing and have the document notarized—with photographs, of course. We could have Oscar notarized as well—stamped on the appropriate spot. Signed. Witnessed. Recorded with the Library of Congress." We both laughed.

Georgia threw her blue box of cigarettes at me. "Don't say a word to him!" she screamed. "They must never know how we think about them. That's for women only. Anyway—am I right? Tell me I'm absolutely right, and don't tell me you don't know because I know that you do."

"I refuse to answer on the grounds that I might incriminate myself."

"You bet you would, Miss Innocence. I *am* right. I know I am. I have X-ray eyes. I can just see it. I can spot a hefty prick at a hundred yards, honest to God. What can I say? Some people play the bass violin, some people sing Wagner—I am a prick spotter."

"And I am leaving!" I said, leaping up from the swing. "Back in a few minutes."

As I ran upstairs to shower, she was ranting on about things phallic, screaming something about cucumbers and rocket ships that was lost on me as I went into the bathroom and closed the door.

As I undressed, I heard music coming from the record player downstairs—music from *The King and I,* which I normally enjoyed. But right now I wanted quiet. Something important had happened to me tonight, and I wanted only to think about it, to remember it, everything about it, without interruption. I turned on the shower and stepped in.

Coming out onto the landing from the high bedroom, I looked down to see Georgia twirling through the living room, dancing to the music, which she had turned up loud. She had taken off her robe and was wearing only her nightgown. Seeing me, she ran to turn the hi-fi down. "Come out to the porch," she yelled, grinning from ear to ear. "I've got a surprise for you, a little something I brought with me to celebrate!" I hurried to join her in the dark again outside. Sitting down, I heard her take a drink of something.

"Well," I said, "I'm here."

"Have a snort of this," she said. "Hold out your hand." She handed me a bottle.

"What is it?"

"Booze. Canadian Club. Ever have it?" She sat beside me on the swing.

"No," I said. "Am I supposed to drink it out of the bottle? Straight?" I envisioned a hundred movies I had seen in which somebody took a swig of liquor, then swallowed it, gasped, and clutched his throat.

"If you know what's good for you, you will. It's already open. Pass it to me when you're done."

"Here goes nothing," I said and tentatively took a small sip. It tasted awful. I passed the bottle to Georgia and felt my small sip travel down my throat, trickle down the entire length of my esophagus like a flaming ribbon, and pass in a neat lump of hot coals into my stomach.

"Yum . . . good," Georgia said as she passed the bottle back to me. As I took another pull, for no good reason whatever, I decided to get drunk. I had never done it before, but it was probably about time. As long as Georgia passed me the bottle, I would drink from it. "Let the celebration begin," Georgia said cheerily. "Where were we, anyway?"

"I have no idea," I said. "I just took a shower, remember?" How much had she already drunk?

"Right, right," she said, kicking the swing into motion.

"How can you stand the taste of this stuff?" I said after taking another gulp.

"You are such a baby! There's Coke in the fridge—you want one? I suppose you want a glass for it too. I'll go get it for you." She got up and went into the kitchen. I heard cupboards open and close. "You want some cheese?" she called back in a holler. I was glad that the nearest neighbors were a mile away.

"Yes," I yelled back. "You want me to help you?" She didn't answer.

It was a beautiful night. I could smell the salt marshes. The moon had risen; the porch was no longer in total darkness. In fact, the entire backyard and orchard were now bathed in pale moonlight. The tops of the apple trees glowed.

On her way back to the porch, Georgia stopped off at the baby grand long enough to play a chorus of "Chopsticks," then came through the screen door, rattling drink tray in hand. She put the tray on a nearby wicker table, then poured my drink, turning to hand it to me.

"Are you aware that you are serving drinks in china cups instead of highball glasses?" I said, carefully balancing the cup on the saucer. She was obviously feeling the punch of her Canadian Club.

"Open your mouth," she said as she reached toward me with a piece of cheese. "It's a tea party, you goose. For you. 'Cause you're such a damned little lady and everything has to be just so for you and if I gave it to you in a highball glass I'd feel so damned guilty and anyway, this is a party for girls. Your cup has bunches of violets on it and mine has tulips. So there. And if you don't behave yourself, I won't let you stay." We grinned at each other in the silvery light. I dutifully drank an elegant sip from my china cup, my pinky finger extended. It tasted very good to me, this Coca-Cola concoction. Harmless as Kool-Aid.

"God, we have to be careful with these cups," I said. "They're English bone china." My mouth did something sort of uncontrolled with the *sh* in "English."

"And this is very good booze," Georgia said. "You like it better with the Coke in it?"

"I love it," I said, draining my cup, reaching for the bottle.

"Good cheese, too," Georgia said. "Good crackers. Ritz. The best in the world. There was a Ritz factory right down the street from the convent, about a mile away. I used to think that was so remarkable. I thought they made all the crackers in the world there. It made me feel sort of famous myself. I guess 'Nabisco' was one of the first words I could read." There was no doubt about it now: Georgia was getting tipsy.

"Battle Creek, Michigan," I announced, somewhat too loudly.

Georgia burst out laughing. "What does that have to do with anything?"

"You said 'Nabisco' and it reminded me of Kellogg's and then Battle Creek," I said.

"Oh, excuse me. Of course," she said. "You ever been drunk?"

"Of course not," I said. "Tonight may be the night, though. I feel wonderful—all relaxed and even a little sleepy."

"Honest to God, Annie—if you're that kind of drinker, the kind that falls asleep just as the party gets rolling, I'll kill you. Here, have some more. There's only one way to find out. There you go. Drink up, girl, drink up."

"I am, I am," I said, holding the cup to my mouth. I started laughing at that point and couldn't stop. Georgia watched, her mouth agape.

"Honest to God, that's more like it. A happy drunk. That's the spirit, the spirit of Alakazoo!"

"Isn't that about a mile from Battle Creek?"

"I thought that was Kalamazoo! Maybe not," Georgia said, beginning to giggle at me. "Nope, that's Alakazoo! 'Kalamazoo' is some friggin' African word. . . ."

"Like 'Umgawa,' " I said.

"Honest to God, Annie old friend, wasn't he a hunk? If I hadn't been so out of it . . ." She stopped talking and gave a low moan. "He used to have to take me for walks to calm me down and we'd go all over the place and when I think of the opportunities I missed with him . . ."

"Did he like you? I mean, in that way?"

"How do I know? But I could have liked *him* in that way. He looked exactly like Nat King Cole, only taller. . . . Oh, my God, I just remembered something! Did I ever tell you about the time I saw Yul Brynner?"

"In person?"

"Right in the middle of the street."

"You're kidding," I said.

"No. Really. It was him. I was in Cambridge and I'd spent a couple of hours in Harvard Yard feeding the squirrels and looking at guys and I decided to go over to the Co-op and I was crossing the street and there he was coming right toward me from the other side in a pale-grey suit. Bald as a badger."

"And you knew right away who he was?"

"He couldn't have been anyone else. He looked just like he does in the movies. Just exactly."

"I think he's gorgeous," I said. "In an intense, almost exotic kind of way. Something about his eyes."

"He's short," she said. "Extremely short."

"Oh," I said. "I imagined him as being tall."

"With him it wouldn't matter—you know?"

"I love *The King and I,*" I said, and then we sat without speaking for a few minutes, just listening to the music.

"She shoulda stayed there with him," Georgia said sadly.

"You mean Anna?"

"She shoulda stayed."

"But he died in the end, didn't he?"

"He wouldn't have if she had let him know how she felt."

"I'm not sure she really felt anything for him—are you?" I said. "They were whole civilizations apart." Georgia rubbed her eyes. She sniffed. "Georgia, are you all right?"

"She shoulda stayed," she groaned. "And all those children . . ." Georgia burst into tears. I couldn't keep myself from giggling. "They coulda all been happy, every lashed one of them," Georgia sobbed. I laughed out loud, and after a minute Georgia was laughing and crying simultaneously. "*I* woulda stayed."

"I know you would have," I said, comforting her between giggles. I took another swig from the bottle and stood up, testing my sobriety. The lamps in the living room were all haloed with fuzzy yellow light, but I felt steady on my feet.

"You goin' somewhere?"

"To the john," I said, walking gracefully through the door. I felt almost weightless.

"You gonna be sick?"

"I'm going to pee," I said regally, curtsying, then floating up the stairs.

In the bathroom, I stood and looked at myself in the mirror. My face seemed sunburned. A blotchy red rash decorated my neck and shoulders. I was toasty warm from head to foot, although I wore only a summer nightie.

So this was what booze did to you. It felt good. I liked it. It felt wonderful. "I wish you were here, Oscar," I said into the mirror. I licked my lips, lowered my lids, and said it again in a low, sexy voice. "Because I am a man," I added, lifting one brow, "and you are a woman. I mean . . ." I burst out laughing at myself, then at Georgia for crying over Anna leaving the king of Siam, a few minutes before. She was something else. It suddenly occurred to me that I had never had a friend I loved as much as Georgia, and never would again. Nothing like this summer would ever happen again.

I didn't care what the rest of the world thought of her—my mother, Oscar, various assemblages of student nurses. No matter what became of us, we would always be in touch, somehow—by letter, by telephone. Someone had once told me that all the best friends you have in grade school and high school are nothing compared with the friends you meet when you grow older. They become your friends for life.

Maybe Georgia could find an apartment or a room close to Wellesley, and I could spend weekends with her or an occasional night during the week. It was the perfect solution. I would talk to her about it tomorrow, when we both had clearer heads.

As I walked back downstairs, Georgia was in the living room, singing and swaying along with the music. She gave me a wave. I went back onto the porch and took another drink of whiskey, straight. I sat down and watched the trees in the orchard begin to shimmer in the faint breeze. It looked almost as if their leaves were wet. It was the whiskey, changing everything.

Georgia came out to the porch, a wrap of some kind over her shoulders. She plopped down on the rocker. Something about the wrap she wore was familiar. Horrified, I recognized it as the piano shawl that usually graced the top of the baby grand. She must have lifted up the Ming vase, Aunt Chloe's most prized possession, to get at it. Even under the best of conditions Georgia was not the steadiest person on two feet.

Just then the orchestra struck up with "Shall We Dance," and Georgia leapt up and stomped wildly across the porch floor in time to the music, the shawl flying from her shoulders. "Don't you just love this song?" she yelled, sidestepping in my direction. Frantically, she grabbed the bottle from me and tipped it to her lips, sending it spilling down the front of her nightgown. The shawl dropped to her feet. She grabbed my arms and pulled me up and danced this way and that with me. Then she broke away and stumbled down the steps into the yard under the trees, with me after her. She took me in her arms and waltzed around in huge steps until we both fell down breathless onto the lawn.

I looked straight up at the sky, at the whirling stars. The grass was damp, but it felt good and cool. Georgia breathed hard and sighed, humming bits of the song over and over again. Then she stood and raised her arms and slowly pulled her nightgown up over her head. She let it drop to the grass beside me.

"What are you doing?" I asked, the effort needed to speak those few words astonishing me. I was over the hill now, drunk out of my mind.

"Ah have always wanted to dance naked in the moonlight, y'all," she said in a tipsy southern drawl. She picked up her nightgown again and held it out dangling from one hand like a scarf and began a slow, would-be interpretive dance across the lawn, stumbling as she went, singing "Shall We Dance" in slow cadence. I turned on my side and watched her, her pale body moving through the semi-darkness like a luminous moth. She pirouetted and waltzed and bent from the waist to scoop nonexistent blossoms into her hands, then flung them to the sky. "It's so free, darlin' . . . it's so impossibly free, dancin' in the moonlight . . . the night air caressin' my body. . . . Ah have lived for this moment. . . . Shall we dance? Come on, Annie."

"I can't, I'm too—"

"Take your clothes off. Be as our dear Lord intended you to be." And she looked so free falling through the soft night air, like a moth's wing dipped in phosphorescence, that I stood up and eagerly undid my nightdress and let it fall smoothly from my body to the damp grass as if it were an outer membrane; it felt like that as it fell and grazed the skin on my thighs and calves—meant to be shed on a night like this. I hesitated, my hands covering myself; then, beginning slowly, I danced or flew or floated toward her. She took my hand, and we danced into the orchard, beneath the trees.

The full moon, bright and white, cast mottled shadows of leaves and limbs, shadows upon shadows; and in the silvery green glow our bodies were as green as trees, covered with trembling leaves, our arms and legs like branches swaying in the wind. I could dance then, garbed in the shadows of trees; I could dance through the liquid light as if it had been condensed to shining water, for I could feel no firm ground beneath my feet at all, and every movement of my body was fluid, effortless, graceful.

How long we danced like this I can't recall. How much time passed before I found myself reclining on the grass again, falling in and out of soft, light sleep, I do not know. I remember clearly only that the moon still shone above me and that the night air was balmy, that music played and that Georgia danced on as I smiled, at peace and full of love for her, the night, and the pure young heart I heard beating within me.

Sometime later Georgia lay beside me again. I sensed her there, saw her out of the corner of my eye. I marveled at the sight of her: a shape both long and curved, stark white, drenched in moonlight, like bleached, polished, weathered wood adrift beside me. I heard her drink from the bottle and pushed it away when she handed it to me. She laughed—or I laughed. The stars were moving. Where had the moon gone? I watched it race across the sky chased by arrow-shaped clouds.

My eyes fell shut. The moon still shone, captured on my inner eyelids.

Georgia took my hand. Just like Mary Armitage and me so long ago. All I saw was a sea of retreating stars.

"Where do the stars and moon go when they cross the sky?" I said.

Georgia laughed. "You sound like a little girl," she said. She sounded funny, not at all like herself.

"I was so beautiful when I was a little girl," I said.

She laughed again. "Have you been drinking or something?"

"I mean it," I said. "I was. You should've seen me. I wish I was little again." My lips trembled. It seemed so sad. I couldn't help it. I began to cry. Georgia laughed and laughed and laughed. Then she was quiet. Tears fell out of my eyes and streamed back through my hair and into the grass. I was so sleepy.

"I love you, Annie." Georgia's voice, deep and husky from drink, scratched my consciousness.

"Do you?" I said. "Do you really?"

"An-nie?"

"What?"

"You are the most beautiful, most wonderful friend I have ever, ever, ever had."

"I know," I said, fighting to keep from sleeping. "It's been absolutely wonderful, hasn't it?" I heard her drink from the bottle once more. I reached for it and placed it to my lips and tried to pour some of it into my mouth. Most of it ran into the grass. I wiped my face with the back of my free hand; Georgia still held my other one. I closed my eyes again. Something touched my stomach.

Georgia's hand moved from mine. She made a little sound, a tiny sound, an all-but-inaudible moan. Something touched my breast, lightly. A moth. I brushed whatever it was away.

The night was so beautiful: the smell of the grass, the moon gliding through the trees, leaves cast with shimmering light, the velvet air. On a night like this there would be moths about—lunar moths, the color of the moon, or huge beige moths with rose-colored splotches on their wings, like eyes.

A hand stroked my breast, or a moth lit, or my own hand touched me, or a light breeze blew in from the west, or wings, or fingers, or . . .

I heard Georgia breathing, as if she were close to me.

I opened my eyes. I saw her face where the moon had been, over me: an open mouth, loose lips, shut eyes. I felt her hand on me, squeezing. One of her legs attempted to wrap itself around me. I watched her face lower toward the place where her hand felt me, toward my breast. No, I thought, then felt her mouth on me, sucking, heard her breath, felt her leg slide over my thighs, felt her fingers at my other breast. *No.*

"No!" I shouted.

I pushed her. She grunted and fell away from me. Off-balance, I struggled to sit up. Her hands reached for me. I flung them away. She fell back again. Her mouth moved silently. I sat up. Her hand grabbed my thigh. I rolled away from her, then crawled, then backed away on hands and knees, trying to see her as she lay there, crumpled, senseless, trying to make out an expression on her face, a gesture, anything at all that would indicate a mistake had been made, that all the while she had thought I was someone else.

But I couldn't see well. I couldn't focus. I couldn't hear what she said to me—just my name, "Annie," accompanied by an ex-piration of breath that rattled from her chest and spewed out between her motionless lips.

Half crawling, half walking, I backed away from her toward the porch steps. I dragged myself into the house and up into my bedroom. I locked my door, fell onto the bed, and passed out.

At some point during the night I found myself sitting on the edge of the bed, my feet dangling over the side. I had the distinct feeling that something out of the ordinary, something more than a surge of nausea, had awakened me. I had heard something, like a queer cacophony of bells or the rush of wind chimes or a sudden shat-tering of glass. I had dreamed it, perhaps.

Then, this time unmistakably, I heard something scraped against something else, like some article of metal being drawn across stone. The sound came from below me, either from downstairs or from outside in the yard.

But it was too early for Georgia to be up and about. Then I heard shuffling, more scraping, and, finally, footsteps—or, specifically, the thudding of bare feet, the merest trembling the house made when someone walked through it. Georgia *was* up. What could she be doing at this hour? I lay back down. I didn't care. I felt too miserable to care about much. And anyway, what more could she do to ruin everything? The last thing I wanted was another confrontation with her.

She had probably just come in from the backyard. The strange sound that had awakened me was probably the sound of the porch door slamming shut. She was coming back in. In a second she would climb the ladder to the Dutch bed and fall back to sleep. I closed my eyes.

The house was silent.

Or almost silent: if I listened very hard I could still hear faint rustles, whispers, rapid breaths, muttering, a voice, a humming.

I sat upright once more, straining to hear. I lowered myself soundlessly to the floor and padded toward my door. I carefully unlocked it. I reached for my robe on a hook near the door and put it on.

I edged the door open and slipped out onto the narrow balcony above the living room and looked down.

There she was, crouched before the fireplace, coaxing a fire to catch within it. She crawled on her hands and knees for more kindling in a nearby wood box, then crawled back to the center of the hearth, where she arranged sticks of kindling over flaming wads of crumpled newspaper. She was dressed in her nightgown, but Aunt Chloe's piano shawl was tied around her neck, falling around her shoulders like a flowing cape.

I looked on silently as she sat back to watch the flames rise, then bent forward again to add more sticks. The light from the small fire shone up at her face, through her beige hair, giving it the character of torn steel wool. As the flickering light illuminated her kneeling body, Aunt Chloe's Calder mobile twirled over her head. I thought of witches and vague satanic rituals, demons and curses.

I was becoming frightened when I saw what at first appeared to be an enormous pile of spent petals from a late-summer flower strewn across the stone floor of the living room near the piano. The room was by and large still in darkness. I trained my eyes on the spot where the petals lay and tried to define their shape, and as I did they appeared to rise from the floor and glow as white as porcelain held to the light. Suddenly I knew that they were not glowing petals at all but fragments of the Ming vase.

I covered my mouth so she would not hear my cry. "No!" I whispered, falling to my knees, leaning against the railing.

For the next few minutes it was as if time had ceased, as if everything fragile and warm were turned to metal, rock, and ice, as if the world had been struck with utter silence. Georgia remained crouched motionlessly, soundlessly before her little fire, a bronze silhouette. The baby grand was cold blue steel. Even the windowpanes glimmered darkly, like thin slivers of transparent ice formed over the surface of a winter pond.

My breath caught in my throat. It couldn't be. I ran down the stairs and across the living room toward the piano and the vase fragments beneath it.

"I hadda li'l accident," Georgia croaked, still very drunk. She had stood and faced me, a flaming branch of kindling wood held in her hand like a torch. "I was gonna put this thing, this doily I'm wearing, back on the . . . the piano . . . tryin' to make everything all better, all better. . . ." She whirled around and bent over to retrieve a small liquor bottle I had not seen before from the floor beside the hearth. "Want some? Brandy. I brought it for after dinner . . . anyway, that was the plan . . . like real civilized people we'd be, with brandy for after dinner. . . ."

"Give that to me, Georgia—you've had enough." I walked across the room toward her.

"Don't come near me or I might have to hurt you," she sing-songed. She raised her flaming torch higher, and the look in her bulging eyes almost stopped me.

"God damn you, Georgia—put that thing down and give me

the bottle. You're going to set the place on fire. You don't know what you're doing. . . ." I walked forward again, one hand outstretched, ready to receive either the bottle or the torch.

"Stay back!" she bellowed.

I continued walking slowly toward her. I watched her as she planted her feet firmly on the floor, far apart, and tossed her head back so that her eyes were trained on the apex of the roof. She opened her mouth. I saw the arch of her upper teeth. I watched her long neck expand and throb in readiness. I heard the sound that emanated from some hollow place within her, more like a wail than a scream, a loud howling sound that poured out of her smoothly until at the end it was compressed and fragmented into gurgles by her half-closed throat.

When her eyes met mine again, I didn't flinch. "You don't frighten me," I said.

"Stay back!" she repeated softly.

"Just put that thing back into the fireplace," I said, amazed at the calmness in my voice.

"If you come any closer you'll be sorry. I swear to God. I won't be responsible for what happens."

"Yes you will," I said. "You don't frighten me anymore, anyway. All I want you to do is put the torch back in the fireplace."

"I'm not going to do any such thing. What do you think this is, anyway—some stupid movie or some dramatic play or something? What do you think? That this . . . this Marsh Field or Swamp Hill or whatever the name of this place is, is some counterfeit Tara and I'm gonna turn the place to cind-ahs, honeychile, to signal the end of an ear-ah? Hmm?" She had walked forward a few paces and now stood before me, swaying. "Or maybe you think you're some sweet little Jane Eyre type and I'm the lunatic from upstairs and the only way that good can win out over evil is for me to set the whole goddamned place, including me, on fire? You're pitiful—that's what you are! Not to mention common. With all your fancy ways you've got a lot to learn." She turned and walked away from me, back toward the fireplace, where she took another swig of brandy and, bending to the fire once more, returned her torch to its place in the blaze. She strolled over to the wood box, rummaged in it, and withdrew a long, club-shaped piece of wood and held the bulbous end of it in the flames. When it caught, she laid the handle end on the hearth. She turned to me again.

"What you don't unnerstand is, this is gonna be more like a religious play, a morality play—a pageant, that's what you call 'em." She looked down at herself and picked at the folds in her nightgown as if arranging it. She adjusted her cape. "Yeah, a pageant, 'cause I'm more Catholic than the pope." She raised her left hand to her ear, its fingers spread wide. She listened, then smiled to herself. "Let's just see now if you can guess what it's gonna be about. Honest to God, when we first met I thought you were so friggin' smart. Now watch me and guess. I can't say anything, like charades." She managed a bow, seemed about to pantomime something in my direction, then cleared her throat dramatically, apparently opting for a talkie.

"Ladies and gentlemen," she began, "I have been hearing voices! Mean voices! And they have said to me, 'Joan, you are a very, very bad little girl and you have broken everything, including your word and certain important beautiful vases, and . . .'" She began to giggle uncontrollably, wrapping her arms about herself as if to steady herself. The angry look was gone from her eyes, and I began to relax. I would listen to her and in a minute or two put her to bed. I would think of all the wreckage surrounding me tomorrow. As I watched her take another pull from the brandy bottle, it occurred to me that she would probably pass out before long anyway.

"Yes, nasty Joan, you have broken promises and vases and, upon occasion, you little pig you, wind. And for that, dear saintly Joan, you shall burn in Hell and every other place." She turned toward the fire again, bent, and picked up the flaming, club-shaped torch and held it close to her face; then, with the other hand, held the shawl away from her body and touched the torch to its fringe. One by one several strands of it caught, burst into flame briefly, then went out in miniature tornadoes of smoke.

I didn't move or speak, but I stared into her eyes, willing her to stop. She ignited a few more strands, then more, until one long end of the shawl had been lit and was either burning in minuscule magenta flames or smoldering like spent wicks.

I was furious. It was perfectly clear to me that this exhibition was meant to frighten me. She had no intention of harming herself. Even in her advanced state of drunkenness she was extremely careful not to set the entire shawl or any part of her nightgown on fire. This dramatic scene was a sadistic ploy meant to draw attention away from both what she had done to me earlier in the yard and what she had done to Aunt Chloe's Ming vase. I wasn't buying it.

"Put your torch back into the fireplace like a good little saint," I said in a bored tone. "Besides, there isn't a decent stake to be had anywhere this far north of Salem." I walked over to the piano again and crouched beside the broken pieces of the vase.

Daylight, cool silver, glassy grey, fell through the living-room windows. I knelt on the cold stone floor and began to gather the fragments of glass in rough piles, the larger pieces off to one side, the smaller ones separate. Later in the day, I would find individual containers to hold the various sizes; perhaps some expert from a museum might put the vase together again. In broad daylight I would use the dustpan and brush to scoop up even the tiniest fragments, the pieces no larger than grains of sand.

Suddenly, I heard Georgia poke the fire and whisper to herself. I heard her walk around behind me. I smelled the smoke from the burning fringe again.

"What I was trying to tell you," she said, "what I was trying to tell you was that I have looked inside myself. I have seen what is good and what is bad. The bad is much worse than I expected. The bad outweighs the good by so very much. There is so little good in me, so very little, such a tiny, weenie—"

"You're no worse than anyone else and much better than some," I said impatiently.

"And all the bad stuff is like a never-ending song, running through my head day and night, even in dreams. Ugly song. Never stops. You know what I mean?"

I didn't turn and look at her. I crawled over to the window and took a magazine from the window seat, tore the cover off plus a few sheets of print, and made a flat shovel for the splinters of glass I could not pick up with my fingers without cutting myself.

"You get it? . . . Annie, talk to me."

"You're one giant smoke screen," I said. "Lots of melodrama, no substance. You just know that if you go crazy you'll be forgiven for breaking this vase. So you set fire to the shawl hoping that it will make everything look authentically insane. Honest to God, I'll tell Aunt Chloe, she was so out of her mind that she tried to set herself on fire. Never mind the vase. Think of it—self-immolation. Not to mention the house—it could have gone up in flames. When a mind snaps like that, you never know what they'll do. We're lucky, that's what we are!" I turned to her. Her eyes were angry slits. I went back to sorting broken glass.

Soon she walked toward me. With my peripheral vision I saw her replace the fringed shawl on the piano. Thank God, I thought. At least most of it was intact. Perhaps now she would climb the ladder to the Dutch bed and go to sleep.

I heard her retreat toward the fireplace. Yes, she was going to bed. I stayed where I was. I would let her fall asleep before I went back upstairs.

I waited to hear her mount the ladder. I waited, pretending to examine some of the glass fragments on the magazine page in front of me.

"Annie?" Her voice was unsteady.

"What now?"

"Annie?"

It wasn't over yet.

"Annie?"

I turned.

"I'm Saint Joan," she wailed, as she touched the torch to her nightgown hem, which immediately smoldered, then burst into a V-shaped gore of yellow fire.

She dropped the torch. Her hands stretched high over her head and waved in a frenzy of motion. Her face grimaced in horror.

I flew across the room. I dove at her. I tore at the front of the nightgown. It separated in flaming halves from her body, buttons popping. I snatched at it and, running behind her, stripped it from her shoulders, and let it drop to the floor, where it immediately smothered itself out. I picked it up and threw it into the fireplace. I looked at her, examining her body for burns, then let her turn away from me and walk toward the ladder, to bed. She began to cry. I didn't care.

Back in my room, I lay facing the window. All was quiet downstairs. I tried to sleep, tried to put off making a decision about what to do until morning, but I couldn't.

The one thing I was sure of was that I was finished with Georgia. I had rescued her for the last time. As soon as she was up, I would pack her things and take her back to Boston in Aunt Chloe's old De Soto, deposit her at Walnut Street, pack up my own things, and head back to Windsor Marsh. I would never set foot in Malcolm Balch's house again. With only a couple more weeks to work at the bookstore, I could easily commute every day instead.

As for the broken vase and the burned shawl, all I could do was to explain the horrifying events of this night and hope and pray Aunt Chloe could somehow forgive me. What more could I do? All of them had been right about Georgia—Mother, Oscar, everyone.

It was hours later when Georgia tiptoed up the stairs, crawled into bed beside me, and curled up, wrapped in the blanket she had brought with her. I pretended to be asleep. As we lay together for the next hour or so, an intermittent shudder accompanied by a wavering inspiration of breath reminded me that she had been crying earlier.

When I finally got up and left her sleeping, looking back at the slender figure with unkempt hair curled up in an old rose blanket, one long, emaciated arm draped over the bedside, I saw her wrist scars for the thousandth time and something within me gave in again, gave up again.

TWENTY-ONE

It was ten A.M. I had showered and dressed before I literally forced myself to go downstairs and face the carnage of the night before. If anything, the living room looked better than I had expected, almost as inviting as it did on any other summer morning, with the bright sun streaming in from the small stained-glass window high on its east wall.

If one could ignore the debris from the wood and the fire, the singed piano shawl, the drained brandy bottle, and the neat piles of shattered porcelain beneath the piano, the big room looked as colorful and welcoming as always.

I walked out onto the veranda, and the air was heavenly: soft and warm against my body, fragrant with grass, flowers, and salt. Air like this always stirred me. Whatever had happened last night belonged to yesterday.

I neatly rearranged the porch furniture, gathered the cups and saucers, the half-eaten plate of cheese and crackers, and carried them into the kitchen.

After putting the coffee on to perk, I took the broom, went back to the living room, and swept the bits of charred wood into the fireplace. I tidied up the wood box, returned records to their folders, and carried both the empty whiskey bottle (which I found tucked away under the pillow in the Dutch bed) and the brandy bottle to the kitchen, where I wrapped them carefully in Georgia's burned nightgown and deposited them in the trash can.

I made orange juice, drank two huge glasses of it with three aspirin, and sat down in the dining room for my first cup of coffee. I didn't feel as bad as I'd thought I would—just a little nausea coming in waves now and then, a queer, jumpy feeling inside, and an incredible, insatiable thirst.

I poured myself some more orange juice and went to a storage cupboard, where I found several coffee tins, perfect containers for the broken vase. I lined the cans with napkins. I had no idea how I would tell Aunt Chloe that her prized possession had been destroyed. I couldn't imagine her response. I went to the living room and carefully transferred the sorted piles of glass to the appropriate cans.

Although my memory of the previous night was not entirely clear, I had not experienced a complete blackout, like the ones I had heard friends describe, a complete loss of memory. Fragments of the scene in the yard—the mad, naked dancing in the moonlight, Georgia's hand on my breast, her mouth on me, her legs sliding over mine—came through in merciless detail. And every time they played themselves back to me, a shiver of both revulsion and disbelief overtook me. Had she known it was me? My breast? Had she become so disoriented that she thought I was Claude or some long lost lover? The whole thing could have been an accident—or a dream. Or it happened just as I remembered it, and she knew only too well who I was, and I was a complete fool to hope otherwise.

In that case Georgia was a lesbian. I had suspected that, in the back of my mind, right from the start. Her avid interest in men must have been a foil. I had fallen for that "paralyzed cunt" routine lock, stock, and barrel. Paralyzed as she may have been around men, she was disgustingly horny around women.

I took a deep breath and poured myself another cup of coffee. It was after eleven now; the house was still. Outdoors, it was a perfect day for the beach. If only Georgia hadn't ruined the whole thing. I considered my options again: of taking her back to Boston and moving out of Walnut Street myself, or of going ahead with the plans we had already made and just making sure she stayed away from me instead.

I then had a horrifying thought. I had no idea what Georgia would be like when she finally got up and came down here. Obviously, I could make no plans until then. All I could do was to wait for her—a familiar enough situation.

By the time ten or fifteen minutes had passed, I realized that I could not spend another night in the house alone with Georgia. I might go to the beach with her, depending on her mood, then put her on a train back to Boston tonight. I wouldn't sleep a wink with her in the house. I would simply tell her the truth: that I was not interested in her sexual advances and was afraid of what she might do to me.

I was having a cigarette when I heard Georgia running water in the bathroom sink upstairs. In a moment I heard her start down the stairs. I rose quickly and went into the kitchen and began to rinse off a plate under the faucet.

Presently, she appeared in the doorway, both hands holding her head. "I must have had a great time last night," she said, grimacing. "Well, did I?" She got herself a cup and reached for the coffee pot.

"You must remember *something*," I said. I went back into the dining room and sat down. She followed and plopped down across from me at the table. I couldn't look at her.

"The last thing I almost remember is dancing around in my birthday suit. Honest to God, I must have been out of it." She took a tentative sip of coffee, one hand still at her brow.

"I don't feel so good either," I said.

"Yeah, you seem kinda . . . subdued, I guess you'd call it."

"That's not exactly the word I had in mind," I said.

"So tell me," she said, "did I do anything really stupid? One time when I got drunk I tried to call Milton Berle in New York." I couldn't stop myself from smiling. I got up and topped off my cup. "You might as well tell me now, instead of later," she said. "I hate it when I black out like that. Kinda like *The Lost Weekend* or something. I mean, it makes me paranoid and nervous, not knowing what I did or—"

"No, you didn't call anyone."

"Thank God," she said. "I mean, the poor man would have just died if I'd gotten ahold of him, which thank God I didn't. I wanted to tell him I thought he was my father. I mean, I believed it at that moment. I just had this feeling that I was related to a famous person, and all of a sudden it dawned on me that it was him. Uncle Milty was my daddy. I was looped."

"You must have been," I said. She was in fine fettle, as if nothing had happened, nothing at all.

When I looked up from my cup, she was staring at me. She leaned across the table. "Your face is telling me I did *something* crazy."

"Several things, I guess you could say." She looked down at the tablecloth and for a few seconds traced one of the flowers printed on it with her fingernail.

"But nothing bad, huh?" she said hesitantly. She didn't remember. Well, I would tell her.

"Except for breaking the Ming vase."

"What?" She jumped up from the table and charged toward the grand piano. "I didn't," she shouted, pulling at her hair. "I couldn't have. I couldn't have, Annie! I didn't, did I?" She rushed back toward me, a look of absolute horror in her wide eyes. She bent over me, plucking at my hands with hers in an odd, impatient gesture. "Tell me I didn't," she pleaded. "Where is it? Where did you put it?"

"I've saved the pieces for Aunt Chloe. I've put them away." It was then that it really hit me, as I heard myself speak those calm words. I began to tremble with anger. "How could you have done it?" I said, my voice shaking. "Stupid!" I yelled. "You are stupid! And self-centered! You don't give a *shit* about anyone but yourself!"

Georgia flinched. Her hands covered her mouth. Her eyes bulged. "I could die," she murmured.

"Sometimes I wish you *would*," I said, not caring if I hurt her.

"I didn't mean to do it."

"I know," I said, sighing. "You never mean to do anything that you do—never mean any harm, never mean to upset anyone. . . ."

"I feel horrible about it. I feel horrible, period. I shouldn't have brought the booze along. I can't drink. I've known that for years." She sat down again, then sipped her coffee and stared at the tablecloth for a few minutes in silence. "That was it, then, that was it? I didn't do anything else . . . ?" I couldn't answer her right away. Suddenly she stood up. "You want some eggs or something?"

"You acted like some damned lesbian, that's what you did!"

"What do you mean?" She gazed at me wide-eyed.

"Just what I said."

"Oh, shit," she said, covering her face with her hands.

"It was all pretty obvious."

"Just *how* obvious?" She turned her back to me. "Tell me!" she shouted.

"You got a little free with your hands!"

"Oh, shit!" She walked away, into the kitchen. "What did I do?"

"For starters, you held my hand, which I really didn't mind—by then I was drunk myself, thanks to you and your thoughtful hostess gift. Then you kind of leaned over me and put your hand on me. On my *breast!*"

"Oh, Jesus," she moaned.

I got up and followed her into the kitchen. I went to the refrigerator and gave her the eggs. I opened the cupboard where the pots and pans were and pulled out a cast-iron frying pan. The thought of eating made me sick, but I had to move around, do something. "The butter's under that covered dish there," I snapped, walking back into the dining room and sitting down.

"Are you sure I did that? I mean, if you were drunk yourself . . ."

"Yes," I said. "You did it."

"I must have thought you were somebody else—a man . . ."

"You said my name."

"I didn't mean it, Annie." She stood in the doorway, looking at me, an intense, pained look on her face. "Not like that."

"There was more," I said.

"Don't tell me any more," she said. "Whatever I did, I didn't mean it like that. I'm not a lesbian, Annie, I'm not!" I shook my head. She leaned against the door jamb and picked at her fingers.

"Then there was the business of your trying to set yourself on fire," I said.

"Oh, God!" she said. "I mean it—don't tell me any more."

"That's about it, actually."

She went into the kitchen. I heard the gas jet turn on, then the sound of a spatula against the iron pan and, after a few minutes, the sound and smell of melting butter. She cracked two eggs. The smell of the butter nauseated me.

"What can I do to make all this up to you?" she said, coming toward me, one arm extended.

"You must be kidding," I said, turning away from her. "What's done is done."

"Could we just kind of go on anyway, almost like it didn't happen?"

I gazed up at her, not attempting to hide the look of contempt on my face. I shrugged my shoulders. "Maybe we should just go back to Boston," I said.

She hesitated for a moment before going back into the kitchen. What did she expect of me? That I would just conveniently forget everything and carry on as if nothing had happened. No; it would be better if we just canned this whole weekend before it got worse. I'd rather be with Oscar, anyway. I could drop Georgia off at Walnut Street, then pick up Oscar and bring him back to Windsor Marsh with me. I didn't really care what anyone thought anymore—Mother, Aunt Chloe, Queen Elizabeth herself.

I didn't want to sit with her while she ate. I got up and walked out to the porch. As I sat on the swing and looked down into the yard, all I could think of was Georgia dancing through it as I lay on the grass and looked at the moon.

I stood up, about to go upstairs and begin packing. Georgia was at the screen door, a plate of toast in her hand.

"I made you something to eat," she said meekly. "Shall I bring it out?"

"I don't think I can . . ."

"You'll feel better," she said, pushing the door open for me.

"You never think it'll help, but a hangover is easier to take with something in your stomach."

I followed her in to the table. She had also scrambled an egg for me. I couldn't refuse it. The look on her face was one I had never seen before: she was genuinely sorry.

"I don't blame you for wanting to go back," she finally said.

"I don't know what else to do," I said.

"I had looked forward to this so much—we were going to have such fun. I really messed up this time."

"I guess it was everything you had to drink," I offered, calmer now.

She looked past me, through the living room. "It's a beautiful day. What a shame to waste it like this."

"I know," I said. "I haven't gone to the beach all summer."

"I don't have any more bottles, anywhere, Annie. I couldn't drink if I wanted to, and you don't have to worry that I'd *do* anything."

I just looked at her.

"And if it doesn't work out, we could go back later," she said.

"I don't know . . ."

"Annie," she said gently, "I'm sorry. I can't tell you how awful I feel. My God, poor Aunt Chloe! How could I have done that—dropped it?"

"I don't know," I said, my voice thin.

"I'll tell her about what happened. I'll tell her I got drunk. Somehow I'll make it up to her."

"How?"

"And . . . about what I did to you . . . I can't say why, because I was out of it, so drunk I can't remember anything. I'm not a lesbian or anything. So help me, I'm not."

I wanted to believe her.

"I love you, Annie, like a sister, like a dear sister. That's all."

"I hope it's true," I said.

I looked across the table at her. She had covered her face with her hands and slumped forward. Soon, she put them down and reached for her coffee, her eyes averted from mine. I could still see a few faint lines on her face from the fork tines. I could see the scars on her wrists. What would she do if I took her home and left her there?

"We could probably go to the beach, anyway. For a while."

"If you want," she said sadly.

"I'm not sure about tonight . . . uh, about staying here."

"I guess I don't blame you," she said, smiling at me wetly.

"We'll see about that later on."

"All right, whatever you say. . . ."

"Georgia, it's just—"

"Really, whatever feels the most comfortable to you."

"Okay," I said, standing up, picking up my plate and cup and going to the kitchen with them.

"Maybe I could ask Ida for the money to replace the vase," she said, following me.

"That doesn't seem very likely," I said, shocked that she would even think of such a thing. "You don't see her anymore, do you?"

"Oh, no! No!" She grinned sheepishly. "I guess that *was* a bit stupid."

"Well," I said, "if we're going to go, we better get ready."

"Thank you, Annie," she said.

"You *do* know how to swim, don't you?" I said, smiling at her for the first time this morning.

"Like a *fish*," she said. I looked at her dubiously. "Honest to God! Seriously! I'm a pretty fair swimmer, if I do say so myself."

"I don't relish the thought of having to rescue you from the waves."

"Naw, don't worry," she said. "Are we going to take a lunch?"

"Why not?" I said, beginning to feel some genuine enthusiasm. "I think I saw some tuna fish here in the cupboard."

Late-morning mist hung over the marshes like a faint, smoky mirage as Georgia and I drove out Palace Dunes Road, over the South Slough one-lane bridge, toward the beach. Though it was early in the day, traffic had begun to pick up; and as we came in sight of the broad, flat place that served as the beach parking lot, we moved at a snail's pace, bumper to bumper.

Other than our lunch, which we carried in a picnic basket, we had brought along a jug of Kool-Aid and tossed all our other beach paraphernalia into two beach bags. We each carried an old blanket over one arm. Georgia wore, one on top of the other, two dissimilar straw hats with wide brims, which she had convinced herself we would need and which I refused to wear.

Thus burdened, we started off across the parking lot to the boardwalk that led over the dunes and down the beach on the other side, toward the sea. There was a point, halfway along, where the dunes crested and where one could look down and see the water for the first time as it careened into the beach, great wide tiers of blue waves. We stood for a moment there, just looking, then waded into the deep, hot sand and headed down the beach away from the crowd.

After what I thought was a lengthy trudge (I could feel the heat from the sand burning through my sneakers), I dropped my blanket in a likely spot, but Georgia insisted that we go farther. I followed her.

"This is it," she finally said, waving her arm toward a swale between two sparsely grassed dunes. "Right up in here'll be perfect. Look, all those other dummies are crowded together like sardines down at the other end. We have this spot all to ourselves." She walked a few more paces, then dropped everything she carried at her feet. I spread my blanket neatly, but Georgia was already stripping off her blouse and shorts.

"You're going in right now?"

"Yeah. Aren't you?" She wore a Gertrude Ederle special, a navy-blue knit tank suit with a moth hole perched jauntily at one bony hip. Only serious swimmers would ever be caught dead in a suit like it. Channel swimmers. Or maybe old people. "Aren't you coming?" she repeated.

"Well, I guess so. I just thought I'd get our things arranged."

"That can wait," she said, pulling her sneakers off her feet without untying them.

"Then I'll be right there," I said. I yanked my shirt off and unbuttoned my shorts.

I hoped to hell she really could swim. The surf was high and the lifeguard a mile away. I didn't want to have to validate my Junior Life Saving badge today.

But as I watched anxiously, expecting a frenzied dog-paddle, face upturned, body sinking, she leapt in wide, high strides, first over one and then over another breaking wave. She dove beautifully into a third one just below its crest and disappeared. Finally getting my sneakers untied, I loped down the beach toward the water's edge, my eyes fixed on a stretch of sea ahead of where she had gone in. But when she finally came up, it was much farther out. She had swum an enormous distance underwater. Tossing her head to flip her hair out of her face, smoothing it back from her brow with one hand, she then proceeded to swim out beyond the waves, where easy swells rose and fell.

I watched her with a combination of pleasure, admiration, and pure, unadulterated envy. I, who had grown up within walking distance of numerous beaches and was known, I thought, far and wide as an accomplished water sprite, was outclassed for the first time, by Georgia Mitchell and her precisely executed, powerful Australian crawl.

How stupid I felt. The last place in the world where I needed to worry about Georgia's safety was in the water.

I was pretty in the water. Georgia was magnificent. I couldn't believe it. I stood there feeling my feet begin to ache from the melting ice lapping against them. I walked in a few steps more. Georgia, by now, was halfway to London. My calves throbbed. Palace Dunes had the coldest water in the world. I took a deep breath and moved timorously forward, trying like a fool to keep the breaking waves at bay with my two outstretched hands. Georgia yelled to me. I could have sworn she said something about the White Cliffs of Dover. It was now or never. I dunked myself.

I came up gasping and swam out toward her. Usually supremely confident at swimming, I moved awkwardly at what seemed to be a sea turtle's pace. A cramp in the toes on my left foot forced me to abandon the flutter kick. She was still miles ahead of me.

Water gave Georgia a grace and power and supremacy she could never achieve on dry land. I looked ahead and saw her bobbing, treading water, and it dawned on me that her pale, often green eyes were the eyes of a marine creature, a fish or a dolphin.

She lay floating on her back as I drew near, opting for the so-sophisticated, frankly geriatric breast stroke for my final, exhausting lap. I joined her, sky gazing. "Why didn't you tell me you were the world's greatest swimmer?" I said, still breathless.

"I thought I did."

"You said you were fair."

"Don't tell anyone, okay?"

"Why on earth not? You're a beautiful swimmer."

"Just promise me you'll never tell anyone that. I mean it—I don't want anyone to know." She rolled over and treaded water beside me.

"It's probably not going to come up every hour on the hour for the rest of our lives, you know."

"I know," she said, spurting water at me like a spouting whale. "Just humor me and say you won't tell. I like to be humble about my achievements, unlike certain people I know."

"Then I swear by all that is holy that I shall never divulge that Georgia Mitchell, who can't walk across the smallest room without tripping over herself at least once, is the world's greatest, most powerful swimmer. I swear," I said. Still floating, I raised my hand solemnly.

"In the absence of a Bible, perhaps you'd swear on this little guy," she said, scooping up a half-dollar-sized jellyfish and placing it on my chest.

"Georgia! Those damned things are poison!" I screamed, swatting it off me and churning through the water away from her. "I hate those things, Georgia—they scare the you-know-what out of me!" She threw her head back, laughing, then chased after me as I swam as fast as I could for shore. By now the water was covered with jellyfish, a thick soup of them all around me—tiny ones, big ones, the largest the size of dinner plates.

I shut my eyes and swam. I would not take a breath until my feet touched bottom. Georgia, giggling and swimming, followed me at a considerate distance.

A stiff westerly breeze blew the tops from the dunes, sending a thin cloud of sand skittering low across the length and breadth of the beach. Standing up to rearrange my blanket, I felt the blowing sand sting my ankles. It was late afternoon. We had decided not to go back to Boston after all, to stay at the beach until dark. Georgia's behavior had been absolutely normal all day. The night before had begun to seem like a bad dream.

The crowd once camped cheek to jowl in the area of the lifeguard's perch had dissipated. A steady column of homeward-bound sunbathers marched in the direction of the boardwalk.

Ahead of me, closer to the water, Georgia sat in the sand armed with Dixie Cups for molds and her comb and brush for sculpting tools. She had constructed a sand castle complete with moat, surrounded by rolling hills. She had dug down deep below the dry surface to find the damp, firm sand best for sculpting. The castle bore two turrets, one at each end.

I had finished *Silver Screen,* with its photographs of Natalie Wood and Robert Wagner, its stories of the elegant lives of Elizabeth Taylor and Janet Leigh. I put the magazine with the others in my beach bag and watched Georgia.

Her lips moved. She talked to herself or sang. She gathered fistfuls of dry sand and sifted it through her fingers over the rooftop of her castle. I waved to her. She gave a lazy wave back, then stood and walked toward me, shielding her eyes against the sun, which was now behind us. Whether she had tanned or not I could not say. Perhaps it was just the light, but her usual pallor was gone, and in its place her skin was the color of raw honey. Her usually colorless hair was streaked with gold. She stood on one corner of my blanket, stretching and yawning, her arms raised to the sky.

"The beach agrees with you," I said.

"Peace, peace at last," she said, looking up and down the beach, then collapsing onto her blanket beside me, face down. She turned her head in my direction and closed her eyes. "What's the latest on Natalie and—"

"I didn't really read it," I said, "just looked at the pictures."

"Mmm," she said sleepily. "It's not real, anyway—none of that stuff is. All that star stuff—everyone trying to get famous and make their mark on the world. What a waste of time, hoping for immortality."

"I suppose," I said. "Do you want another sandwich?"

"I'll take a half," she said. I reached for the picnic basket and took out a waxed-paper-wrapped tuna-salad sandwich. I handed her her half. "God, I love these things," she said, "all soggy like this and the lettuce all limp. The smell of them is something you never forget. Now that's what I call immortality."

I noticed the sky was changing color.

"Immortality," she repeated. "What a laugh. Most people don't know what the hell to do with the lives they've got, but they want to take on eternity. Funny, you know? Ironic. That's a good word for it." She propped herself on one elbow to eat. A few minutes later, when I finished my sandwich and lay back to look at the sky, I noticed she was smiling.

"What are you thinking about?" I asked.

"Nothing really—just people and life and how you can go on and on batting your head against walls and wondering what to do and suddenly, *pow!*—you've got the answer and it's so damned simple. And easy! And foolproof! Jeez."

"I have no idea what you're talking about," I said. "But maybe it doesn't matter."

"I'm being philosophical," she said.

"Apparently," I said.

"If you don't cover yourself up," she said, "you're going to need medical attention. Here." She threw a towel over my chest and shoulders. I watched high clouds inch westward.

A long moment passed before she spoke again. "There is only one way to ensure oneself of immortality," she said.

"And what would that be?" I said, but I wasn't really listening; I was listening to the blowing, whirring sand instead, the gulls and the breaking waves. The sun was still warm on me. I closed my eyes.

I awoke, shivering. Georgia sat beside me, facing away from the water, wrapped up Indian-style in her blanket, only her face and head visible. She was watching the sun begin to set to the west, over the dunes. Our end of the beach was completely deserted now, and at the other end only an occasional beach umbrella, bright as a pinwheel, marked the location of other dawdlers. The lifeguard's long-legged chair, empty now, stood like some species of giant heron. I got up, brushed the sand off, took a clean sweatshirt and dungarees out of my beach bag and put them on. "The sun must be almost down," I said. "I'm cold." She sat stoically watching the sky.

It would be a beautiful sunset. The clouds I had seen gathering earlier were now stacked in a low band at the horizon. When the sun met them, they would blaze with color: at first yellow, then gold, then orange fire burning down to the deep rose red of dying embers. The first star would shine then, a pinprick of white flame.

"I suppose we should think about going," I said.

"No, not yet. Let's stay until sunset." Georgia smiled up at me. She seemed peaceful and happy. I sat down beside her and wrapped myself in my blanket. Sunset was just minutes away. The sun would slide down the sky so slowly, so slowly, until a certain moment when, as if accepting its fate completely, it gave up and plunged precipitously from sight.

"I want just one more dip," Georgia said. "Then we'll go."

Even the sky straight overhead was turning color now, white clouds changing to pink, pink ones to mauve and palest orange. "If I went in again, I think you'd have to carry me out," I said. "I'm freezing." The blue firmament turned pink.

Georgia laughed, two small puffs of air rushing from her lungs. Her face in this light was bronze, polished. Her eyes gleamed as if each contained within it a bright, ignited ember.

The sun dipped behind the strand of clouds at the horizon, and within seconds they were lit with gold, their edges like smoldering paper. The sky turned coral. The sun continued down, until only an oval grey cloud with frayed edges, shaped like the head of a bird, was untouched by color. But soon the sun shone through an elliptical gap in the bird's head, like a burning eye.

Georgia grinned, delighted. Then she stood and let her blanket fall to the sand. She remained posed for an instant before the setting sun, her body shimmering, her bathing suit no longer blue but black and matte as charcoal.

"One last swim," she said, "then, home." I turned and watched her run down into the waves.

I folded our blankets. I put on my shoes. I placed her towel where she could find it easily when she came out. I walked down to the sand castle, retrieved her comb and brush and picked up the Dixie Cups. She had written something in the sand—her name, I supposed—then rubbed it out.

In the water, Georgia stroked powerfully toward the British Isles again.

The first star had appeared. I walked back up the beach to wait for her. She'd be coming in any minute now.

At the other end of the beach, the lifeguard carried his white boat up the boardwalk, carried it above his head balanced by strong arms.

I had lost Georgia momentarily in the waves. There she was, still out very far. I lost her again. I scanned the water. She was underwater. I would see her come up for air and whip her hair from her eyes. Yes—there she was, there was the dark oval of her head, there the two white arcs, her arms, cutting through the water.

In a second she was gone again. I couldn't find her. Maybe I had misjudged the distance. She must be out farther now, farther than I had thought, or in toward shore, coming in. I couldn't find her. She was there; I knew she was. I had just lost sight of her. The dark oval. The splash.

Just one oval of head was all I needed. Just one small splash of white. One thin white arc of arm. I heard my voice whimper like an infant. I heard myself whimpering.

Where was she?

Somewhere in the waves and swells and shadows and fragments like mirrors under the blood-red sky. The water was filled with blood.

I ran.

I stumbled.

"Georgia!" The scream erupted from the depths of me. "Georgia!" I ran down the beach to the sea. "Georgia!" I was crying, pulling my shoes off, running out of my dungarees, ripping my shirt off, whimpering hysterically. I fell into the water, not daring to let my head go under lest I miss catching a glimpse of her.

That was what you did, what I had been taught, a shallow dive if a dive at all, head up, eyes straight ahead, searching. I swam, my eyes trained on the water ahead of me. She was there. She would be out there, cramped, stomach cramps, and I would save her.

She was stronger than me and perhaps panicked. I went over in my mind the things to do. She'd be strong with panic, much stronger than me. It didn't matter. I would swim up close to her, in plain sight of her; then at the last minute I would suddenly dive under her and swim around her and come up behind her so she couldn't see me, couldn't grab me in panic and pull me under with her. I would reach over her shoulder and grasp her chin in my cupped hand. I would yell at her to be still, to relax, as I had been taught. I would turn her and begin sidestroking to shore with her, her head raised against my shoulder, cradled against me. If she struggled, I'd dunk her quickly and swim on.

"Georgia!" I screamed. I treaded water, moved in a circle, looked around me in every direction. I searched the length of the beach, too. I would see her there, laughing at me. She would stand there toweling her hair dry as I swam in, angry but relieved. "I came in way down the beach, silly," she would say.

But I saw nothing, no one. "No," I said out loud. "No!" I screamed to the sky, to the red sea around me. "No!" I cried, willing it not to be so. I shut my eyes tight and ground my teeth together.

I was alone in the water, alone at the beach, alone with the waves and the swells and the darkening sky.

Suddenly I was weak, incapable of swimming or floating, of breathing or calling out again. Water covered my face, filled my mouth, then receded, then covered me again; the sky was water, the water, sky. I grew cold and still, numb, filled with an unearthly calm. My heartbeat slowed. I was cold inside, as cold and still as

ice, slipping down through the water, into an eerie, silent darkness
that seemed to hold me there, suspended.

My body convulsed. My arms moved. I could not, would not
die. I broke through the surface and saw the moon. I was weightless, buoyant, like some dark hull of a phantom ship. I would float
on this endless sea forever, like a forgotten memory drifts in the
unconscious mind.

Somewhere beneath me, Georgia lay still in her chosen grave,
her face as white as limestone, her hair blowing in the current like
seaweed, her eyes like grey Tahitian pearls.

I dragged myself up onto the beach and scrambled across the sand
like a crab, scratching and clawing at it, then touching it with my
flattened palms, feeling the sand for what she had written there,
some clue. The sounds emanating from me were not sounds I had
heard before. A high whine, the thinnest possible stream of sound,
came from my throat as I searched the sand, interspersed with a
savage, guttural gag as I tore the sand from the beach.

All I found was the castle. I sat beside it and looked out to sea,
still thinking I would see her, something pale on the dark water,
Georgia swimming in at last. I saw only the running lights of a
fishing boat far out on the horizon.

Suddenly I got up and ran for the boardwalk through the deep
sand, screaming at the top of my lungs. Halfway there, I saw a
figure approaching, a man running toward me. "Help me," I cried,
falling to my knees in despair. "Help . . ."

"Annie!"

It was Oscar. He had come back after all. I tried to get up but
fell forward onto the sand again.

"Annie, what happened?" he said, reaching me, crouching beside me. I couldn't speak. I clutched his shirt, stared up into his
face. "Georgia," he said, shaking me. "Where's Georgia?"

TWENTY-TWO

Aunt Chloe came home early Sunday morning, and the three of us spent the day by the telephone waiting for news from the police. In midafternoon, however, we learned that the search both in the water and along the coast had been called off, that no trace of her had been found. It might be months, if ever, before there was real proof that Georgia had drowned; until then she was listed as missing, presumed dead.

Aunt Chloe wanted me to stay with her for a few days; but by evening, after talking with Malcolm by telephone, I was anxious to get back to Boston. Intuitively, I knew that I would more easily come to grips with what had happened at Walnut Street, with people who knew Georgia, in my room across from hers. A part of me still questioned whether Georgia was dead at all. Perhaps she was alive, her drowning a ruse. She could have swum to shore under the cover of darkness and begun a new life, with a new identity somewhere. I had heard of people doing that. Or maybe she had swum out so far, she couldn't come back to shore and had spent the night hanging onto a drifting log and was now far out at sea waiting to be rescued.

I had gone through all the things she had brought with her to Marsh Cliff and found nothing—no clue, no note, as to whether

she'd meant to die. I could not believe that she would leave me
in limbo like this; and although Malcolm had assured me he had
searched her room with a fine-toothed comb, I would not be
satisfied until I looked myself. After a light supper which Aunt
Chloe insisted I try to eat, Oscar and I left for Boston.

Malcolm must have seen us pull up in front, for he was at the
door, holding it open, as we got out of the car. The minute I saw
him, I began to cry uncontrollably. Once I was inside the hallway,
he put his arms around me and held me while I wept.

"I have to go upstairs," I sobbed, pulling away from him. I had
to see her room. And as I climbed the three flights, Oscar and
Malcolm following, I halfheartedly imagined her *being* there, sitting by the window. I still thought it possible.

But when I reached the landing, her door was open, her room
dark inside. I just stood there looking into the darkness. I couldn't
go in. She wasn't there. That was what I had come back to Walnut
Street for. To know.

Malcolm opened the door to my room. I went in and sat on
my bed. Malcolm pulled up my desk chair and sat facing me, staring
at the floor, his hands clasped between his knees. Oscar busied
himself hanging up the dress I had carried back.

"Thank you," I said, as he came back out into the room and
smiled at me comfortingly. Then he went to the window and
opened it, letting in the cool night air.

"I keep going over it again and again in my mind," I said.

"I know," Malcolm said. Oscar sat down beside me on the bed
and held my hand.

"I keep going over everything she said, and I said or didn't say."
Malcolm nodded. "Of course."

"I keep thinking that I should have known, especially after the
vase and the fire. If I'd only had my wits about me, I could have
done something."

"But you couldn't have," he said, looking up at me, his eyebrows
raised. "You must know that. There is nothing any of us could
have done."

"But we—"

"Listen to him," Oscar said. "He's right."

Malcolm shook his head. "There was *nothing* any of us could have done," he said. "There never is. Once a person makes the decision to take his own life, there is nothing . . ." He glanced toward the window, his voice drifting off.

"I wish I could believe—"

Malcolm held up his index finger, stopping me. "Booth . . ." he began, clearing his throat, his eyebrows twitching nervously. "It was much the same with him."

"Booth? When he passed away, you mean?"

"He shot himself," Malcolm said.

For a moment I couldn't speak. "No," I said, shocked. "You didn't tell me. I thought he was ill, that he died of—"

"It was a suicide. In Chicago. He'd just been home here with me for several weeks. The show was packed up for the summer. Booth's family never—well, they never accepted him . . ." Malcolm's brows arched and remained so for several seconds. "High society, they were—New Yorkers," he continued, "with a cottage in Newport. Well, he got it into his head that he would visit his mother—an awful woman, just awful—and I couldn't dissuade him. It never ended well when he went down there. But he called them all the same, and said he was coming, and even when his mother told him not to, that he wouldn't be welcome, he went anyway and that was, I suppose, the beginning of the end. I didn't know then, of course."

"What happened?" I asked gently.

"Well, he pulled into the long drive that led up to the house and thought he saw smoke, something burning, near the entrance, but assumed it was the gardeners burning brush or workers repairing pavement. It wasn't." Malcolm hesitated, looking into my eyes, his mouth trembling. I waited.

"They'd taken all his things, old things from the room he had used as a boy, even the drapes and the bed linens, old toys he'd saved, musical instruments, a guitar, a violin, clothing, and set it all ablaze on the front lawn."

"Oh, Malcolm . . ."

Oscar swore under his breath.

"There was no one there. They'd all left. The house was empty."

Malcolm stood unsteadily and went to the window.

"Three weeks later he was dead. Shot himself in the mouth. In Chicago on some business, something to do with costuming for the following year—he'd gotten into that. I spoke with him only hours before he did it. He seemed fine. We were leaving together on a trip to Nova Scotia the following week, and he told me of an inn he'd heard about." Malcolm sniffed, then took out a handkerchief and blew his nose. He returned to the chair in front of me, his eyes red. He shrugged his shoulders.

"I can't tell you how sorry I am," I said, looking to Oscar for help.

"Can I get you a drink of water or anything?" Oscar said, getting up and patting Malcolm on the shoulder. Malcolm shook his head and swallowed hard.

After a moment he said, "He left no note, no explanation. But a week or so before he left for Chicago, he gave me a signet ring he'd had made, said he'd gained some weight and it didn't fit him anymore." He held out his hand for us to see it, on his ring finger.

"It's beautiful," I said.

"I think he'd been planning it all that time. I'm sure of it. Later, a doctor told me they do that sometimes, give their valuables away."

"I guess Georgia didn't have many valuables, if any," I said, thinking about it, about whether she had given me anything at all in the past months.

"Perhaps Ida received something," he said vaguely. "Perhaps not."

I shook my head. "I hope not. I shouldn't say that, but . . ."

"Well . . ." Malcolm said, clearing his throat, "now, about that drink, young man—but I plan to make it a little stiffer. Why don't you two join me for a nightcap, or a cup of tea if you wish?"

"Let me get my sweater," I said, looking toward the open window. "I'm cold."

I went to the closet. I took down my red cardigan from the shelf and slipped one arm through. No matter what Georgia thought about my closet being dry, the sweater smelled musty. I started back into the room but stopped.

I turned around. I looked up into the top shelf of my closet. The basket. Georgia gave it to me to keep for her. I reached for it, but, oddly, it was farther back on the shelf than I could have placed it. "Oscar!" My voice broke. I began crying. "Get it for me," I sobbed, pointing to it.

"That?" he asked.

"Hurry!"

He put it into my hands. "Annie, what's . . . ?"

I lifted the lid off it. The folded note lay on top of the seed packets, my name scrawled across it.

"Jesus . . ." Oscar whispered.

I unfolded the paper and read silently.

Dear Annie,

I want you to have this, my most prized possession. Sorry it's not a diamond ring. I hope you keep the basket forever and plant the seeds someday, in a place where you're going to live for a long time. Tell Malcolm goodbye for me and thanks for everything. I don't know what to say, except that some things are meant to be. I'm just tired. I just want to be somewhere quiet.

Love ya,
G.

I handed the note to Malcolm and waited for him to read it.

"If *we* couldn't save her, Malcolm, why didn't God?"

He carefully folded the note up the way it had been and placed it back on top of the seed packets. His eyes met mine. "I like to think He did," he said.

During the remainder of my stay in Boston, living at Walnut Street and working in the bookstore were difficult. But I chose to work, even after Ruth offered to let me go early to spend a little time at home in Beverly before I left for Wellesley. My mother and father were supportive and sympathetic, wanted me to come; but after thinking it over, I knew it would be best for me if I stayed in Boston with Oscar and others who had known Georgia.

Malcolm, particularly, was indispensable. He above all others understood what I was going through and always had time to listen. I needed to talk about Georgia—all about her, from the moment we met until the last time I saw her—and if Malcolm tired of my constant reminiscing, he never let me know.

Something else was on my mind, too. I was having second thoughts about starting school. Too much had happened. The idea of donning knee socks, a blazer, and a freshman beanie and marching off to Wellesley right now seemed almost ludicrous. Had I ever really wanted to be a teacher? Or had I just gone along with what my parents had planned for me, without giving much thought to what *I* wanted?

I had told Oscar about my misgivings, and his answer was for us to marry immediately, with the idea that I could go to school later, when he finished. But that didn't seem quite right, either.

I was about to ask Ruth if I could stay on at the bookstore indefinitely when an event no one could have predicted solved my problem.

Four days before she was to leave for the Pacific Northwest, Ruth's niece Kathleen called the bookstore, distraught. The nanny she had ordered from England had taken sick and was in the hospital about to undergo major surgery. It would be weeks before she was able to travel. On such short notice, it was unlikely that the agency would be able to replace her. Kathleen was to begin her new job as soon as she arrived in Seattle. Naturally, she was disturbed at the thought of having to hire a nanny quickly, in a strange place. That had been the whole point of taking one with her.

Immediately it occurred to me that I might go myself—if she would have me, that is.

I told Ruth, who was both stunned and pleased. "Well, of course that would be lovely for Kathleen," she said, her bright blue eyes as big as saucers. "But Ann, my dear, I can't imagine you passing up Wellesley. And Oscar—oh, my. He'll be beside himself. I don't think he could stand it with you gone."

I wouldn't tell Oscar until later, when we were alone. I waited for him to get busy in the storeroom before I called Kathleen's number.

Kathleen answered. I could hear the baby crying in the background.

"This is Ann Merrill," I said. "From the bookstore."

"Oh, hi," she said. "Aunt Ruth's okay, isn't she?"

"Yes, just fine," I said. "I heard about your nanny problem."

"Oh, God, isn't it a mess? We've had it all arranged for so long, I just can't believe it. Hiring someone out there, where I don't know a soul, will be like buying a pig in a poke. It terrifies me."

"Well, that's why I'm calling," I said. She was silent. "If the job is still open, I'd like to have it."

"Are you kidding?"

"No, of course not. I know you don't know me very well, but I can assure you I've had a lot of experience babysitting, and I can furnish references."

"Oh, don't be silly. Aunt Ruth says you're wonderful! Ann, this is an answer to our prayers. I'm so excited!"

"Then you want me?"

"Of course! Of course! I don't believe it." She covered the phone and said something I couldn't make out. Then she was back. "I had to tell Richard," she said. "He can't believe it, either." She laughed. "But wait a minute—how about school? Aren't you supposed to start at Wellesley?"

"So many things have happened this summer, I'm not sure anymore about what I want. I need time to think about things, I guess."

"Oh, yes," she said. "Aunt Ruth told me about your friend. I'm so sorry, Ann—it must have been terrible. Maybe some time away . . ."

"I think so," I said. "I feel quite confused about everything."

"When can we get together, Ann? I've got so much to tell you. Why don't you come home with Aunt Ruth after work? I'll pick you up there and bring you to our house."

"That sounds fine," I said. I'd have to tell Oscar a little white lie. And I'd have to wait until the next night to tell him what I was going to do.

It was Friday. We were at Barney's apartment after work. We had just made love, and Oscar was talking about our choices for dinner. He was in the mood for Italian, he said, and had suggested a place called the Edelweiss, which didn't sound especially Italian to me.

"Come on," he said, getting up from the bed. "I'm starving. After what you put me through, woman, I have to eat to keep my strength up. As well as other things." He leaned over me and kissed me on the mouth, then bit me playfully on the neck.

"I have to tell you something," I said. "Lie down."

"You're insatiable," he said, kissing me on the nose. "You have a perfect nose. It's absolutely perfect."

"This is serious."

He propped himself on one elbow, his brows knitted. "I don't like the sound of this."

"I love you," I said, "more than ever . . . it's not that."

He sighed. "Good. What is it?"

"I'm not going to go to school this year. . . ."

"That's fine."

"I'm going to Seattle with Kathleen."

He just stared at me, his mouth open a little. "Shit!" he said, burying his face in my neck.

"It'll be for a year, till next summer."

"Oh, Annie . . ."

"If you really don't want me to go, well . . ."

"Oh, Annie," he moaned into my shoulder, "you know I would never keep you from doing something you wanted to do."

"I want to do this. I can't go to school right now. But I don't think I'm ready for marriage, either."

"You're not sure about me, are you?" He was up on one elbow again, looking at me intently.

"You're the only thing I *am* sure of. I love you so much. If I thought anything was going to happen to you and me, I think I'd die."

He put his arms around me and pulled me close to him. "You can't go, Annie—I mean, I'm not going to stand in your way, but please don't go. . . ."

"I don't want to leave you," I said. "But I need to do this."

"God, I can't stand it," he said, "the thought that I won't be able to touch you or hold you or make love with you. . . ."

"I know, I know."

"You might meet someone else."

"Never."

"Are you sure, Annie?"

"Never," I said again, but it suddenly occurred to me that no one could be totally sure of anything.

"The thought of anyone else having you . . ."

"*You* could meet someone else, Oscar."

"No," he said. "Even if something happened, I mean something terrible, I could never love anyone but you. I'd never be able to forget you."

"I'd never be able to forget you, either. Even when I turned eighty, I'd still remember everything about you."

"We can call one another," he said, brightening slightly.

"We'll write back and forth."

"Maybe I could rob a bank and come out there for spring break."

"Yes! You see? We can do it."

"I guess," he said.

"I'll write to you every day," I said.

"Wildly sensuous letters?" he asked.

"Insane, ravenous, turgid letters," I said, giggling.

"With drawings?" he asked, grinning at me wickedly.

"Oscar!" I said, hiding my face against his chest.

"You *are* an artist," he whispered in my ear. "Are you good at collages? Things with moving parts?"

"Oscar! I thought we were beyond all this!"

"We are, Annie," he said seriously.

"Then let's get you something to eat and talk about how we're going to spend the next two days before I go."

"That'll be a very short discussion," he said, his mouth on mine.

Later that night (Oscar was in the shower) I called Aunt Chloe to tell her my plans, then called Mother. Aunt Chloe, predictably, thought the trip and the year away were a marvelous idea. She suggested I tell Mother as gently as possible, then stand back, so to speak. I did not relish the thought of Mother's reaction, but I had no other choice. I obviously couldn't just disappear and send her a postcard.

"Mother," I began bravely, as soon as she had answered the phone, "I have some news for you."

"I'm so glad you called, darling. Your father has been so worried about you. I was just thinking of you. I got all your cleaning back today, all your sweaters and skirts. . . ."

"Is Daddy there?"

"Well, of course he is."

"Put him on the extension, Mother."

"Oh. All right." I heard her calling my father and directing him to the upstairs phone.

"Hi, lovey," he said. "How're you doing?"

"Well, Daddy, I have some news. I hope you're not going to be too upset."

"Charles, she's getting married to that Oscar," Mother said.

"No she's not," Daddy said.

"I can tell by the tone of her voice."

"That'll happen next year," I said.

"Oh, my God," Mother said, bursting into tears.

"I'm not going to go to school this year."

There was silence, just Mother sniffling. "What did you say?" she managed.

"I'm not going to go to Wellesley. At least not this year—maybe never, I don't know."

"She's just upset, dear," my father said.

"I'm going out west to Seattle with Ruth Carmichael's niece, her husband, who's a medical student, and their baby. I'll be there for one year working as their live-in sitter."

"Where?" Daddy asked.

"Seattle!"

"There is no need to raise your voice," Mother said.

"I'm sorry. Seattle, Washington, Daddy, in the Pacific Northwest."

"Oh, I've heard of it," he said.

"Well, it is my understanding that the place *is* populated, Daddy."

"Probably," he said.

"We're leaving on Monday, by train, ten a.m., from South Station. We go to Chicago, then take the Empire Builder west from there. I'll be able to see the Rockies, Mother, and Glacier National Park and all the northwestern states."

"You will do no such thing, young lady."

"I'm going, Mother."

"Your Aunt Chloe is behind all this."

"It's my own decision."

"We won't see you until Christmas," she moaned, her voice breaking.

"You won't see me until the end of the summer, next year, Mother. I won't be able to get enough time off to come home for the holidays." She burst into tears again, and I heard the receiver drop to the table.

"Going by train, huh?" my father said.

"Daddy, I need a few clothes. Ask Mother to pack my big suitcase, the one I got for school. I need everything from the cleaners plus the wool slacks in my closet and my winter nightgowns and bathrobe. Aunt Chloe is coming in to see me off. Have Evan take the suitcase over to her on Sunday night. If I need anything else, I'll write."

"Call collect," he said, "for your Mother's sake."

"All right, I'll call. Please try to explain to Mother. . . ."

"Why don't we come in to see you off ourselves. I could take the day off from the office."

"I wasn't sure you'd want to."

"You want us to stop by at Walnut Street and pick you up?"

"Oscar's taking me to the station," I said.

There was silence again.

"You say you're going to marry that chap next year?"

"Yes, that's the plan at this point."

"Isn't he a little flashy for you?"

"Daddy, I can't think of anyone less flashy than Oscar."

"He was wearing a pretty loud tie."

"Perhaps he was, Daddy, I don't remember." There was a long pause. For some reason there were tears in my eyes.

"I'm going to miss you, lovey."

"Oh, Daddy," I said, my voice unsteady, "I'm going to miss you, too."

"As long as you're happy, lovey."

"Thank you, Daddy. Talk to Mother, will you?"

"You know the sun sets on the wrong side of you out there?"

"What?"

"And the water's on the wrong side."

"Yes, of course," I said, smiling.

"It's pretty uncivilized out there," he said, chuckling.

"Indians in the streets, Daddy."

"A cultured person is a real rarity out there—you should make quite a hit!"

"They'll probably hail me as some great white goddess, come to save the heathen!"

"I hear you can buy almost anything if you have a few pairs of shoes to trade."

"I'm sure."

"Should be quite a treat to come home to New England after roughing it out there for a year."

"I'm sure it will be, Daddy. I'll see you Monday."

By eight-thirty Monday morning I was dressed, packed, and ready to go. Oscar would come for me in fifteen minutes. I stood by the window and looked down into the courtyard one last time. In this surprising year of rainy summer days, there had been an early frost. The leaves on the courtyard tree had begun to turn and fall. I watched several of them fly like golden birds from the tree's branches, then tumble along the brick courtyard floor.

I raised the sash. The air was crisp. Somewhere nearby, someone had kindled a morning fire; and above the neighboring rooftops, streaks of smoke, more pungent than incense, smudged the bright autumn sky.

A gust of wind and the tree shivered, dropping more leaves. Before long, this tree will be naked, I thought, black and dormant, its spring blossoms and autumn color the stuff of winter dreams, of silent memories, a mortal monument to the transience of all living things. Only memories live forever.

I lowered the window and closed the curtains.

I checked my suitcase one last time. Georgia's basket was there, with her old seeds safe in their packets: foxglove, fireweed, purple thistle, and more, her legacy to me. I snapped the case closed and took it out into the hallway with my other bags, ready for Oscar to pick up when he came.

I looked across the hall at Georgia's door. I walked over and opened it, stepping into her room. The morning sun poured through her window in one golden shaft. I stood silently in its warmth, waiting—for what, I wasn't sure. A sign, perhaps, even at this late date—some little happening, some small feeling within me, some smell, some sound, a shadow across the wall, something to put my mind at ease at last. But nothing came, just the sun streaming in, the sounds from the street, not even a bird streaking past the window like an arrow. Nothing. Georgia was gone.

As I walked back onto the landing, the front bell rang. Oscar. It was time for me to go, too.